Charles Cowden Clarke

# Shakespeare-Characters

SALZWASSER VERLAG

**Charles Cowden Clarke**

# Shakespeare-Characters

Reprint of the original, first published in 1863.

1st Edition 2022 | ISBN: 978-3-37500-187-2

Verlag (Publisher): Salzwasser Verlag GmbH, Zeilweg 44, 60439 Frankfurt, Deutschland
Vertretungsberechtigt (Authorized to represent): E. Roepke, Zeilweg 44, 60439 Frankfurt, Deutschland
Druck (Print): Books on Demand GmbH, In de Tarpen 42, 22848 Norderstedt, Deutschland

# SHAKESPEARE-CHARACTERS.

# SHAKESPEARE-CHARACTERS;

## CHIEFLY THOSE SUBORDINATE.

BY

CHARLES COWDEN CLARKE,

AUTHOR OF THE "RICHES OF CHAUCER," ETC.

"Alas!
There are no more such masters: I may wander
From east to occident, cry out for service,
Try many, all good, serve truly, never
Find such another master."

1863.

Drawn by J. Thurston

Engraved by W. Finden.

WILLIAM SHAKSPEARE.

*From the Monumental Effigy in the Church at Stratford upon Avon.*

Edinburgh. James Nichol.

# PREFACE.

UPON various occasions, after I had quitted the profession of public lecturer upon dramatic and general poetic literature, applications came to me, from both friends and strangers, to print the courses I had formerly delivered upon "The Subordinate Characters in the Plays of Shakespeare."

I heeded, and not heeded, one after another, those gentle admonitions, until, some time since, an accomplished friend made me the same recommendation; and having had full experience of his judgment, also firmly believing in the sincerity of his appeal, I have revised and remodelled my manuscripts, for the purpose of presenting them to the reading public. It became evident, in the course of a careful scrutiny, that the form in which I had addressed my observations to a popular audience would be advantageously exchanged for one more suited to perusal; and also, that while in my lectures it was not necessary to treat of more than the subordinate characters in each play, far greater completeness and interest would be secured by including an examination of the more prominent characters.

I have therefore prepared the following Essays, with the hope that they will aid in directing attention to the ethical scope and design of the several dramas, and to the sustained harmony with which the Poet has delineated his characters throughout: accordingly, I may express my trust that the Essays will prove acceptable to all who are interested in the due appreciation of our great Moral Teacher.

It is a pleasure to me thus to give permanence to my hold upon the regard of my former hearers, and to believe that in another form will be recalled the disquisitions we formerly enjoyed together upon the greatest and most lovable genius that was ever vouchsafed to humanity,—a genius so lovable as well as so great, that, in pondering and repondering his productions for the chief portion of my life, I can sincerely say my admiration has ever increased in proportion with my study.

An addition to my pleasure—and I think it will likewise be one to my old hearers and new readers—is in the occasion afforded me of mentioning, that my affectionate study of Shakespeare has always been shared by one whom it were scant praise to pronounce the "better part" of me, and that to her feminine discrimination are owing many of the subtlenesses in character-development which we traced together, and which form part of this volume.

In conclusion, I shake hands in spirit with all brother Shakespeare-lovers who do my book the courtesy of perusal, commending it to their kindliest reception.

CHARLES COWDEN CLARKE.

GENOA, *July* 1863.

# CONTENTS.

*Contents.*

# SHAKESPEARE-CHARACTERS.

## I.

## Macbeth.

# I.

# MACBETH.

WHEN I first proposed to myself the undertaking of a Course of Lectures upon the Genius of Shakespeare, my first feeling was, that I could scarcely hope to originate any new theory upon the *principal* characters in his dramas; for they have been subjected to and have passed the ordeal of the most acute critical intellects of the most civilised nations of the world during more than a century past; and therefore for a while I suspended my intention. But then it occurred to me that the *secondary* movements, the "*subordinate characters*" in his plots, have, to a considerable extent, been neglected,—the satellites of the several systems have been merged in the rays of their presiding and controlling suns. Of these "subordinate characters" it became my "hint to speak," according to my homely wit; and I hoped to show passages of beauty that have been either too superficially, even thoughtlessly read, mayhap altogether overlooked, and some delicate points of character that have been undeservedly neglected. I did not, therefore, take up this subject *because* the principal points in the plays have been treated to repletion, but to make manifest that the secondary ones are rich in nature and dramatic effect; and, in consequence, upon addressing myself to my task, I was constantly impressed with one feature in Shakespeare's intellectual organisation, and that is the pervading harmony of his inferior characters with the great and single end he had in view towards the developing and maturing of his plan. I do not mean, in using the word "harmony," that his subordinate characters are as consistent *with themselves* as are the heroes and heroines of his plots;—that would indeed be a gratuitous remark, of which it would require no ghost to come and inform us; although, in many of the inferior dramatists, this discrepancy in characteristic development might be quoted to a considerable extent;—but what I mean by the pervading harmony in his secondary characters is, that they are both consistent in themselves, and consistent in fulfilling the designs of the poet or creator:—in short, that, like contrary movements in a grand musical composition, their intention and action combine in imparting unity and continuity to its design and progression. Shakespeare had doubtless an instinctive perception of propriety in "keeping," (as the painters term it,) and his range of mind would simultaneously grasp the combinations of qualities requisite to conceive and perfect two such beings as Othello and Iago; but it comes not within the range of human accomplishment that all those profound, heart-shaking bursts of passion and indefinable subtleties of character, like the minute threads in our nervous system, all combining to produce the one grand result of sensation,—that all that Creator-like harmony of design (I speak not irreverently; for, with his divine faith in "goodness in things evil," and his toleration of the infirmities of his species, Shakespeare was an emanation of the Author of all Good,)—that all his wonderful harmony of design, I say, should have cost him no more brain-effort than to write the poems of the Venus and Adonis, and Tarquin and Lucrece, exquisite as those compositions are, it were childish for an instant to conclude.

I do not say that there is manifestation of *effort* in anything that Shakespeare wrote, but there is prodigious contrivance, and a felicitous consummation of cause and effect; and all this harmonious arrangement, I assume, did not come to him with the facility of hooting to an owl.

In this very play of Macbeth, for instance, not a scene, not a character in the *dramatis personæ* occurs, which does not tend, with undeviating current, to carry us on towards the catastrophe, and magnify its qualities; while the inferior agents are individualised with a minuteness of surpassing truth to nature.

And before entering upon a discussion on these minor characters, I will commence by as brief a summary as I am able of the ruling qualities in the two master-springs in the structure—Macbeth and his wife.

Macbeth, from *circumstance,* has become wholly engrossed and swayed by ambition; but it is to be noted, that his is essentially the ambition of *opportunity.* The *accident of his birth,* which places him within as approximate a claim to the crown of Scotland as the reigning monarch, first excites it. Then the predictions of the weird sisters—or, in other words, the suggestions of his own imagination tampering with possible chances—are the next incitement. Then comes the tempting occasion of the king's housing with him at his own castle. And to crown all, his wife's representation of the ease with which the deed of the murder may be perpetrated. In perusing his character, we become conscious that Macbeth is an irresolute being; he perpetually seeks support and confirmation from his accomplices. In almost every point he is the very antipodes of Richard III., with whom he has been compared, (the single motive of ambition being excepted;) and how finely has the poet individualised and made historical the royal murderers! So far from "seeking support," (like Macbeth,) Richard relies solely on himself, using others merely as his agents—his tools. He has an unmisgiving confidence in his own powers, and an insolent scorn for those who stand as obstacles in the way of accomplishing his purposes. Macbeth admits the excellences of Duncan even while meditating his assassination, and almost allows the circumstances of their mutual position to sway him from his intent. Richard treats his implements of crime with business-like order and despatch. The scene wherein he sends the two murderers to kill his brother Clarence is almost gay, in its bold, blunt, resolved tone.

How different from Macbeth's conference with the men he employs to waylay Banquo! In every point it is suggestive of the man who feels his way to the matter in hand, and who tries the dispositions of the men he would make the instruments of his deed. There is positively a strong infusion of the *national* quality of *caution* imparted to his nature and course of action. He begins by an indication of his own distrust in them. He bids his attendant "go to the door" during their stay, and "wait there till called." He next shows that he has previously had an interview with these men, in which he has sought to stir their resentment against Banquo by representations of ill offices on his part towards them. He urges this again, and goads them. He goes on enlisting *their* interest of hatred to strengthen them into fit instruments of serving his own. While Richard commands and commends the diligence of his ruffians, Macbeth lures and almost courts these fellows into being villains enough for the secure execution of his purpose. It is the wary dealing of the self-misgiving man, who seeks to confirm his own resolution at the same time that he desires to make sure of theirs.

A singular touch occurs in the next scene, confirmatory of this uncertainty and mistrust that pervades Macbeth's actions. It is at the place appointed for the men to lie in wait for Banquo and Fleance; and it begins thus:—

"*Enter* THREE MURDERERS.

"*1st Murd.* But who did bid thee join with us?
"*3d Murd.* Macbeth.
"*2d Murd.* He needs not our mistrust, since he delivers
Our offices, and what we have to do,
To the direction thus."

It is precisely this feature of indecision—the indecision of a soul unhardened in guilt—which accompanies Macbeth throughout in his pursuit of the objects of his ambition, (so accurately in tune with the character given of him by his wife,) which individualises that ambition, and renders it a quite different passion from that which actuates Richard. Richard's ambition renders him inflexible, reckless, insolent; Macbeth's allows him to be full of hesitation and compunction. Macbeth's ambition is scarce sufficiently potent to hold him to his purpose. He himself feels it to be thus inadequate; he owns, by one little sentence in soliloquy, that it requires urging and stimulating. He says:—

"I have no spur
To prick the sides of my intent, but only
Vaulting ambition."

"*Only* vaulting ambition!" In that moment he confesses it to be insufficient to furnish him with arguments against those he had just admitted to be of force in withholding him from the act which should secure him the object of his ambition. It is this very betrayal of something imperfect in Macbeth's ambition, something which permits it to be touched and swayed by the workings of his feelings, that causes the character of Macbeth to take that strong hold upon our sympathies. It is because we behold in him a mirror of human frailty that it possesses so powerful an interest with us, and that we cannot find it in our hearts utterly to cast him out and condemn him. We cannot, unmoved, hear of the agitated betrayals of countenance which reveal Macbeth's inward struggles. What an awful picture is twice conveyed to us by the comments of his wife upon his appearance! One, the well-known passage:—

> "Your face, my Thane, is as a book where men
> May read strange matters."

And the other is her remonstrance:—

> "Come on!
> Gentle my lord, sleek o'er your rugged looks;
> Be bright and jovial 'mong your guests to-night!"

How horribly and palpably is thus presented to us the convulsed features and gloom of expression which paint the desperate tumult of the soul within!

As an instance of Macbeth's proneness to throw himself upon others for encouragement in his ambitious struggles, and of his want of complete self-reliance, may be noted his resorting to the witches in the 4th Act; seeking from their predictions fresh instigations to fresh deeds of cruelty and bloodshed. With all this minute detail in mental portraiture, Dr Johnson pronounces Macbeth to exhibit "no nice discriminations of character!"

Entirely different is the quality of Lady Macbeth's ambition and mind altogether. It requires neither encouragement nor "spur," as Macbeth's does. It is, with her, an ever-present, a paramount consideration. It suffices to absorb and obliterate all other feelings. It enables her to control her imagination, and to keep it ever fixed upon the one aim she has in view. It inspires her with courage to face and despise all contingent obstacles, and with firmness to supply that which she instinctively knows is deficient in her husband's nature. It has no hesitation, no vacillation, like his;

it yields to no compunctious visitings of conscience. "Conscience" is to her an unknown tongue,—it is a sixth sense: she admits no nice casuistry of right and wrong. The object of her ambition must be obtained—come it how it may. Means are nothing to her;—the end is everything. The means are merged in the end. It becomes to her a necessity, to which all other circumstances must give way. She neither sees nor will hear of any let or hindrance to the accomplishment of her purpose. She neither listens to the promptings of her own mind, nor to those of her husband. She has neither scruples, doubts of success, nor fears of consequence. She is in one blaze and sunlight of hope and exultation, when once the golden promise of her ambition shines fully before her. She unflinchingly fixes her gaze upon it—eagle-like; and never after suffers her imagination to be for one instant diverted or withdrawn. She no sooner beholds it as a possibility, than that very moment it becomes to her a certainty. Her first exclamation is:—

> "Glamis thou art, and Cawdor;
> And *shalt be what thou art promised.*"

The only thing wanting, she feels, is steadfastness in her husband; and this she knows she can supply. What energy, what grandeur in her invocation to him:—

> "Hie thee hither,
> That I may pour my spirits in thine ear!"

She sets herself the task of controlling and effectually stifling all weak misgivings that might have lingered within her, and is at once prepared to meet her lord with that resolute bearing which shall infuse its spirit into his:—

> "Great Glamis! worthy Cawdor!
> Greater than both,—by the all hail hereafter!"

The words she uses in speaking of her guest and victim, King Duncan, are wonderfully characteristic, and carry with them a slight womanly redemption, which Shakespeare so well knew to convey. She says to her husband :—

> "HE *that's coming*
> *Must be provided for:* and you shall put
> This night's great business into my despatch."

In the next scene, we note how closely she keeps her purpose in sight, and adheres to her plan of carrying it forward. Her eye has been fixed upon her husband—has noted the vacillations in him which she dreaded, and the conflict of mind which causes him to leave the supper-chamber. She follows him, expostulates with him; rises into remonstrance and reproach,—even into the bitterness of taunt :—

> "What beast was 't then,
> That made you break this enterprise to me?"

And when he falters out—

> "If we should fail?"

she rejoins—

> "We fail!—
> But screw your courage to the sticking-place,
> And we 'll not fail."

Lady Macbeth neglects nothing which shall assure the accomplishment of her purpose. When the deed of murder is to be enacted, we find that she has not omitted to partake of the sleeping-cup—the posset—upon retiring to rest. Having then drugged the possets of the grooms, she enters upon the scene with these tremendous words :—

> "That which hath made them drunk hath made me bold;
> What hath quench'd them hath given me fire."

This was a grand dramatic circumstance to introduce, illustrating the manners of the time; and singularly illustrative of the character of the woman, who disdains no means that may help to nerve and confirm her. Wonderfully in keeping, too, is her obtuse reply to her husband's agony of remorse, and affecting apostrophe to sleep:—

"Still it cried, 'Sleep no more,'" &c.
"*Lady M. What do you mean?*"

Impressive indeed is the lesson the poet reads upon the fruits of a bad ambition reaped by unhallowed means in the after-career of Lady Macbeth. Not only has he presented us that terrible vision of her haunted and restless sleep; but even in the very first glimpse we have of her *alone*,—after she is crowned queen,—is there any triumph? any satisfaction?—Oh no!—sadness, discontent, despondency. This is her tone of musing:—

"Naught 's had, all 's spent,
Where our desire is got without content:
'Tis safer to be that which we destroy,
Than, by destruction, dwell in doubtful joy."

Inexpressibly affecting, and profound in its admonition, is the half envy of the murderous survivors for their victim. Macbeth, too, says:—

"Better be with the dead,
Whom we, to gain our place, have sent to peace,
Than on the torture of the mind to lie
In restless agony."

With all her energy, however, to screen and sustain her husband, where is her own spirit?—Cast down—prostrate. She is capable of immense exertion while the pressure of necessity lasts; during that excessive demand upon her, during the banquet scene, she appears omnipotent: but when the guests are gone, we behold the sudden reaction: —she sinks down into the utterly dispirited being, and utters but a few languid sentences in reply to her husband's words.

It is, indeed, a striking lesson to behold Lady Macbeth as she is now, and to recall what she was. Her vigour, her animation, her fiery eloquence, when the object of her ambition was in view, and as yet unattained; her broken spirit, her depression, alternated with spasmodic efforts in her husband's behalf, her saddened days, her awful nights, her premature death, as we find them when her ambitious desires are crowned. When we desire to realise the intense bliss of rectitude and innocence, we have but to analyse the motives, the actions, and the consequences of a blood-guilty ambition, as thus depicted by Shakespeare. In scrutinising the career of such people as Macbeth and his wife,—and especially of Macbeth, who was an impressible and imaginative man,—who does not sympathise with—who does not pity him? and, in the comparison of suffering, who does not even envy the victim of his ambition?

And now, to proceed to the minor agents in this illustrious drama, and to notice their no less individuality and truth to nature, with their uniform current of action, carrying us on to its grand catastrophe.

Thus we have the first victim of Macbeth's ambition, "the good king Duncan," described as a man formed in the very mould of unoffending gentleness; even his murderer is constrained to testify that he

> "Hath borne his faculties so meek, hath been
> So clear in his great office, that his virtues
> Will plead like angels, trumpet-tongued, against
> The deep damnation of his taking off."

And so beautifully do these qualities in his nature shine

forth, that they have nearly pushed the traitor from his purpose. And when the deed has been perpetrated, with what appropriate and poetical licence has the poet heightened its circumstances, calling in the elements to

> "blow the horrid deed in every eye,
> That tears shall drown the wind."

With what a simple and, consequently, forcible effect has he introduced that conversation between the Earl of Rosse and an "old man," without the walls of the castle, the morning after the murder, the circumstance of their wonder and amazement harmonising so finely with the romantic and preternatural character of the whole story!

> "*Old M.* Threescore years and ten I can remember well;
> Within the volume of which time I have seen
> Hours dreadful, and things strange; but this sore night
> Hath trifled former knowings.
> "*Rosse.* Ah! good father!
> Thou seest the heavens, as troubled with man's act,
> Threaten his bloody stage. By the clock, 'tis day,
> And yet dark night strangles the travelling lamp.
> Is 't night's predominance, or the day's shame,
> That darkness does the face of earth entomb,
> When living light should kiss it?
> "*Old M.* 'Tis unnatural,
> Even like the deed that 's done. On Tuesday last,
> A falcon, towering in her pride of place,
> Was by a mousing owl hawk'd at and kill'd."

[Note the felicity of that image,—the courtly falcon, the familiar of the royal fist, struck to death by a night-bird of prey—a "mousing owl." How apt, too, the epithet!]

> "*Rosse.* And Duncan's horses, (a thing most strange and certain,)
> Beauteous and swift, the minions of their race,

Turn'd wild in nature, broke their stalls, flung out,
Contending 'gainst obedience, as they would
Make war with mankind.
"*Old M.* 'Tis said they ate each other.
"*Rosse.* They did so, to the amazement of mine eyes,
That look'd upon it."

The next victim to the ambition of the usurper is Banquo, whose offence, in the eyes of his murderer, is traceable to the prime movers of the whole tragedy—the weird sisters. They prophesied that he should be "lesser than Macbeth, and greater;" that he should "beget kings, though *he* be none." It is interesting to notice, in the career of Banquo, how skilfully the poet has avoided a dramatic tautology (if I may so use the term) in bringing about the death of two worthy men immediately upon the heels of each other. Banquo was endowed with those qualities which Lady Macbeth attributes to her husband. Banquo, also, is too "full of the milk of human kindness to catch the nearest way to advancement." He too "would be great; is not without ambition, but without the illness which should attend it. What he would highly, that would he holily." And these qualities stand all apparent in the course of his brief career. For instance, the prophecy of the witches having been verified in the point of Macbeth's being created "Thane of Cawdor," the recollection that "the greatest was yet behind," and to be fulfilled, acted like a spark upon the dormant tinder of Banquo's ambition; but the singleness of his nature restrained him even from an unjust aspiration. Thus, at the close of the banquet with King Duncan in Macbeth's castle, when he is retiring to rest, and is evidently brooding over his destiny, he says, in soliloquy—

"A heavy summons lies like lead upon me,
And yet I would not sleep. Merciful powers!

*Restrain in me the cursed thoughts* that nature
Gives way to in repose."

And immediately after, in conversation with Macbeth, still ruminating upon their scene with the witches, he says :—

"I dreamt last night of the three weird sisters ;
To you they have show'd some truth."

Macbeth, knowing that he is at that moment preparing to murder the king, indifferently replies—

"I think not of them ;
Yet when we can entreat an hour to serve,
We would spend it in some words upon that business,
If you would grant the time.
"*Banq.* At your kindest leisure."

Then upon Macbeth's sounding the disposition of his brother soldier, and saying—

"If you shall cleave to my consent when 'tis,
It shall *make honour for you*"—

Banquo's answer to the insinuation strictly harmonises with his straightforward disposition. He says—

"So I lose none—[that is, no 'honour']—
In seeking to augment it, but still keep
My bosom franchis'd and allegiance clear ;
I shall be counsell'd."

The next time we meet with Banquo is in the courtyard, when the household are summoned upon the discovery of Duncan's assassination, an hour or so after the conference just quoted ; and still the transparent frankness of his nature reveals itself. In a spasm of horror at the deed, he exclaims—

"When we have our naked frailties hid,
That suffer in exposure, let us meet,
And question this most bloody piece of work,
To know it farther. Fears and scruples shake us.
*In the great hand of God I stand;* and thence
Against the undivulged pretence I fight
Of treasonous malice."

Again—the poet brings him to brood over his future fortune, as connected with the fulfilment of the witches' prophecy in that of Macbeth. He has just witnessed his coronation at Scone.

"Thou hast it now, King, Cawdor, Glamis, all
As the weird women promised;—and, I fear,
Thou play'dst most foully for it:—yet it was said,
It should not stand in thy posterity:
But that myself should be the root and father
Of many kings. If there come truth from them,
(As upon thee, Macbeth, their speeches shine,)
Why, by the verities in thee made good,
May they not be my oracles as well,
And set me up in hope?—But, hush;—no more."

This is one out of multitudes of examples, showing the undeviating watchfulness of Shakespeare in preserving the proportion and harmony of his characters:—this last speech of Banquo is strictly in keeping with his first: he closes his mind against every prompting of a sinister ambition. His whole course of action is a running comment upon his first ejaculation:—

"Merciful powers!
Restrain in me the cursed thoughts that nature
Gives way to in repose."

He really is, as the witches said,—

"Not so great as Macbeth, yet much greater:"—

he has the power to resist temptation, and the courage to fear an unjust act.

It is worthy of notice, too, that Shakespeare impresses us with the one prevailing quality in his characters, quite as much by casual actions or insignificant remarks, as by the most formal display or announcement of them. For instance; true gentleness of heart is rarely unaccompanied by an appreciation of the beauties of nature, animate and inanimate. To Banquo, therefore, with delicate taste and propriety, is given that lovely reflection upon the characteristics of the house-swallow, confirming Duncan's commendation of the pleasant position of Macbeth's castle. He says:—

"This guest of summer,
The temple-haunting martlet, does approve,
By his lov'd mansionry, that the heaven's breath
Smells wooingly here. No jutty, frieze, buttress,
Nor coign of vantage, but this bird hath made
His pendent bed, and procreant cradle: where they
Most breed and haunt, I have observ'd, the air
Is delicate."

Banquo has himself noticed this fact in natural history, and the exquisite polish of his diction displays the man of quality and attainment. Macbeth testifies to the superiority of his nature:—

"Our fears in Banquo
Stick deep; and in his royalty of nature
Reigns that which should be fear'd: 'tis much he dares;
And to that dauntless temper of his mind,
He hath a wisdom that doth guide his valour
To act in safety. There is none but he
Whose being I do fear; and under him
My genius is rebuk'd, as, it is said,
Mark Antony's was by Cæsar."

It has been objected, as a violation of propriety, the introduction of one of the murderers during the banquet. But, in the first place, we must bear in mind the different ordination of ceremony, or rather the absence of all ceremony, in that early and rude stage of society, when royalty, in its rough-hewn simplicity, sat, as it were, "at the receipt of custom," and was accessible to all comers. Besides, the ruffians in this play were gentlemen of broken fortunes; they had been fellow-soldiers of Macbeth and Banquo,—men "whom the vile blows and buffets of the world had so incensed, that they were reckless what they did to spite the world." It is with such instruments that such deeds are commonly achieved.

I will dismiss these remarks upon the character of Banquo with one more observation, and that upon the disposition of one of the incidents in this wonderful drama. Of all the appalling situations, (and it is brimful of them,) no one makes so powerful an appeal to my own individual feelings as the unprepared introduction of Banquo's spirit at the supper-table. The idea of such a visitation, at such a point of time, is sufficiently ghastly in itself; but the effect is enhanced by the consummate skill and simple power of the poet in causing the murderer to recognise his victim. The Earl of Rosse says to Macbeth—

"Please it your highness
To grace us with your royal company?
"*Macb.* The table's full.
"*Lennox.* Here's a place reserv'd, sir.
"*Macb.* Where?
"*Lennox.* Here, my lord. What is't that moves
Your highness?
"*Macb.* Which of you have done this?"

The abrupt and startling force of this incident has, I should suppose, never been surpassed; and it is one which an ordinary writer of plays would have diluted, and spread over pages of talky-talk, and, in consequence, he would have missed his point. Whereas, Shakespeare has simply denoted the action, and left the result to the imagination of the reader. The first impulse of Macbeth's mind in saying, "Which of you have done this?" is, that his treachery has been discovered, and that the real body of Banquo, with its twenty gashes, has been placed in his presence in order to confront and confound him;—a course of proceeding perfectly reconcileable with the primitive and savage era of the history.—The next impression is, after his wife has sneeringly told him that, "when all's done, he is but looking on a stool!" that the spirit of his victim has come to taunt him; and he makes that tremendous appeal to the apparition, "Take any shape but that, and my firm nerves shall never tremble:" &c. And lastly, upon her upbraiding him with his unmanliness, he gives her the most convincing excuse for it: "If I stand here, I saw him!" How artful, too, is the using of that relative pronoun, "*him*," upon the occasion, not naming the object of his thoughts—she knowing it. After all that may be said in the way of comment and eulogy, it is such minute points as this that confirm the true poetic genius.

The purlieus of a court have never been famed for breathing the pure air of homely and sincere speech—scarcely, mayhap, of sincere thought; but in the region of a usurper, and who is also tainted with violence and crime, men had need bear "charmed lives," if they are afflicted with incontinence of speech. Then the feeble-minded and the self-seeking become strengthened in duplicity; and the bolder resort to the equivocation of irony,—the only freedom triumphant, and which cannot be quenched under a tyranny. Even this subtlety has not escaped Shakespeare in drawing the characters subordinate to the hero in this tragedy. It is to be remarked, that whatever conversation arises among them relative to the murder of the king, he has contrived to impress the reader with the feeling that they all suspect the same man of the crime, and no one breathes a suspicion to his fellow.

Their dialogues are short, and conducted in dry sentences. The Earl of Rosse says to Macduff: "How goes the world, sir, now?" "Why, see you not?" is his brief reply. "Is't known," he resumes, "who did this more than bloody deed?"

"*Macd.* Those that Macbeth hath slain."

The man who makes the nearest approach to a plain attainder is Lennox; and his speech is ironical throughout. In conversation with another lord, he says:—

"My former speeches have but hit your thoughts,
Which can interpret farther: only, I say,
Things have been strangely borne; the gracious Duncan
Was pitied of Macbeth: marry, he was dead:
And the right valiant Banquo walk'd too late;
Whom you may say, if't please you, Fleance kill'd,
For Fleance fled. Men must not walk too late.
Who cannot want the thought, how monstrous
It was for Malcolm and for Donalbain
To kill their gracious father?—damned fact!
How it did grieve Macbeth!—did he not straight,
In pious rage, the two delinquents tear,
That were the slaves of drink, and thralls of sleep?
Was not that nobly done?—Ay, and wisely too?
For 'twould have anger'd any heart alive
To hear the men deny it. So that, I say,
He hath borne all things well: and I do think,
That had he Duncan's sons under his key,
(As, an't please Heaven, he shall not,) they should find
What 'twere to kill a father; so should Fleance.
But peace!"

Again, towards the close of the play, in the dialogue between the physician and Lady Macbeth's waiting-woman, an ordinary play-writer would have followed the usual recipe for concocting a lady's maid, by making her clack like a mill-wheel. Shakespeare knew that courtly serving-women hear, see, and say nothing; and in such a court as that of Macbeth, an attendant would scarcely be over-confidential. The whole of this scene is a masterpiece of natural effect; the first two or three sentences of which will be sufficient to confirm my previous remark. The curiosity of the Doctor,—who is, moreover, a court-doctor, and characteristically inquisitive,—and the cool reserve of the waiting-woman, are, in their respective vocations and habits, both edifying. The Doctor says:—

"I have watched two nights with you, but can perceive no truth in your report.

"*Gent.* Since his majesty went into the field, I have seen her rise from her bed, throw her night-gown upon her, unlock her closet, take forth paper, fold it, write upon it, read it, afterwards seal it, and again return to bed; yet all this while in a most fast sleep.

"*Doct.* A great perturbation in nature! to receive at once the benefit of sleep and do the effects of watching. In this slumbery agitation, besides her walking and other actual performances, what at any time *have you heard her say?*

"*Gent.* That, sir, which *I will not report after her.*"

"*Doct.* You may to *me,* and 'tis most meet you should.

"*Gent.* Neither to you, nor to any one, *having no witness to confirm my speech.*"

Such points as these, interwoven with the tissue of the plots of his plays, produce that harmonious proportion mentioned in my introduction; and which we may vainly seek, in equal proportion, from any other dramatic writer.

Again,—and still referring to his consistency in maintaining the propriety as well as the harmony in his characters,—I may bring to recollection the grand manner in which he has made Macbeth and his wife severally to descant upon the indelible testimony of their crime—their bloody hands. He, the masculine and more robust being, uses the stronger and more magnificent image:—

> "Will all great Neptune's ocean wash this blood
> Clean from my hand? No, this my hand will rather
> The multitudinous seas incarnardine,
> Making the green, one red."

She, upon the same dreadful theme, with womanly feeling, personal feeling, and association, says, "Here's the smell of the blood still: all the perfumes of Arabia will not sweeten this little hand." The whole of the sleep-walking scene, with the doctor's ejaculation, "God! God! forgive us all;" and the simple beauty of the waiting-woman's protestation, "I would not have such a heart in my bosom for the dignity of the whole body," is one of the most solemnly affecting appeals ever penned.

I have spoken of the duplicity to which all are compelled, who by the force of circumstances draw their resources from the dispensations of a usurper and tyrant. The feeble-minded and the pliable-conscienced sink their scruples fathoms below their interests. Such only remain about him; and such only we find to be the retainers of Macbeth. Macduff, his early friend, has retired from the court. In his character it is interesting to notice how the poet has preserved its consistency, and placed it in high relief with the other persons of the drama. Macduff is an honest, but impetuous man, and, therefore, no tactician. He acts from impulse; and when he does give utterance to his thoughts, he delivers himself in concise and blunt sentences. That he is a man of sudden movement, and no method, appears in his flight into England, leaving his family unprotected, and ignorant of his course. By no other apparent contrivance than the one adopted could the poet have judiciously disposed of Lady Macduff and her children; moreover, the barbarous massacre of the whole brood,—"all the pretty chickens and their dam,"—from its enormity and wantonness, lashes the husband into revolt against, and extermination of the murderer.

The other feature in Macduff's character that has been noticed,—his honesty of speech,—shines conspicuously in the conference between himself and Malcolm, to whom he has fled in England, for the purpose of assisting him in his design to regain the crown of his inheritance. The whole management of this dialogue is eminent for the subtlety with which the dispositions of the two men are sustained. Malcolm is wary, and suspicious of his new adherent; and, in the sequel, gives good reason for being so. He says:—

> "What you have spoke, it may be so perchance;
> This tyrant, whose sole name blisters our tongues,
> Was once thought honest; you have lov'd him well;
> He hath not touch'd you yet. I am young; but something
> You may discern of him through me; and wisdom
> To offer up a weak, poor, innocent lamb
> To appease an angry god."

Macduff bluffly answers:—

> "I am not treacherous.
> "*Mal.* But Macbeth is.
> A good and virtuous nature may recoil
> In an imperial charge. But, crave your pardon,
> That which you are, my thoughts cannot transpose:
> Angels are bright still, though the brightest fell;
> Though all things foul would wear the brows of grace,
> Yet grace must still look so."

Not only is Shakespeare the closest of all reasoners, but the web of his argument is always of a golden tissue.

The Prince next upbraids him with deserting his wife and child—"those precious motives, those strong knots of love"—without leave-taking; and he adds—

"I pray you, let not my jealousies be your dishonours,
But mine own safeties; you may be rightly just
Whatever I shall think."

Macduff can bring no antidote to these surmises against himself; in accordance, therefore, with his impetuous nature he attempts no excuse, but cuts short the conference with—

"Fare thee well, lord;
I would not be the villain that thou think'st
For the whole space that's in the tyrant's grasp,
And the rich East to boot."

Malcolm, still unsatisfied, and reasonably so, notwithstanding the other's asseveration, (for the greatest defaulters make the loudest protests,) adopts a third course to try the integrity of Macduff's nature, by taxing himself with vicious propensities. He describes himself as being lustful, avaricious, covetous of the wealth of others, quarrelsome, and treacherous. His object is to discover whether Macduff be a spy from the usurper, or, at best, a mere worldling, who had come over to the old legitimacy, knowing the instability of the new dynasty, and which he had hitherto served. With an excess of candour, therefore—and yet consistent with youth—after the detail of his own vices, he puts it to the new partisan whether it were patriotic and just to substitute one tyrant for another. "If such a one be fit to govern," he concludes, "speak: I am as I have spoken." Now the indignant honesty of Macduft bursts forth, and stands revealed.

"Fit to govern! No! not to live!
O Scotland, Scotland! O nation miserable!
With an untitled tyrant, bloody sceptred,
When shalt thou see thy wholesome days again?
Since that the truest issue of thy throne
By his own interdiction stands accus'd,
And does blaspheme his breed.

> Fare thee well:
> These evils thou repeat'st upon thyself
> Have banish'd me from Scotland. Oh, my breast,
> Thy hope ends here."

This hearty and unequivocal declaration has blown from the firmament of the Prince's mind all clouds of doubt and suspicion. It is pleasant to contemplate the smile at heart with which he must recognise the success of his scheme; and his good fortune, too, in securing at least one true friend to his cause, in which that of his native land is involved. Malcolm's last speech comes upon us like the morning sun into one's room, after darkness and perplexing dreams. It is precisely the effusion which would afford relief to a young and generous nature, rendered prematurely distrustful by snare and stratagem. I scarcely could name a more cheering contrast than is presented to us in this scene, coming, as it does, against the previous reiterated stunnings of treachery, cruelty, and blood-guiltiness. The young Prince joyously exclaims:—

> "Macduff! this noble passion, child of integrity," &c.
> —*Act* iv., *sc.* 3.

Malcolm's diction is marked throughout by princely eloquence, and a beautiful moral rectitude. It is he who in the fourth scene of the play makes that fine speech, relating the death of the rebel chieftain, the thane of Cawdor. It concludes:—

> "Nothing in his life
> Became him like the leaving it: he died
> As one that had been studied in his death;
> To throw away the dearest thing he ow'd,
> As 'twere a careless trifle."

Of the porter-scene in Macbeth's castle, writers have been at variance; some denouncing it utterly, and Coleridge going even so far as to assert that "unquestionably" it is not

Shakespeare's. With the full deferential feeling upon me in such a presence, I cannot but think that it is accurately the poet's manner. And not the less is it his, from its being so closely conjoined with the late scene of the assassination and terror; because such associations are constantly recognised in real life. The American editor, (Hudson,) in a masterly comment on this tragedy, gives full justification to the speech of the porter. He says: "This strain of droll broad humour oozing out, so to speak, amid a congregation of terrors, has always in our case deepened their effect; the strange, but momentary diversion causing them to return with the greater force."

It may be thought that I ought to include among the "subordinate characters" in this consummate romantic tragedy those awful anomalies, the Witches—agencies employed in this our Gothic Drama, as the Fates and the Furies were in the ancient Greek Drama; each impersonation being strictly in harmony with the faith, the spirit, and the design of both ages of the world—their history, poetry, and architecture. The witches of this drama, however, can scarcely be said to be (in the strict sense) "subordinate" members of the *dramatis personæ*, seeing that, by their power and control, and by their influence, the poison of diabolism was infused into the mind of the hero. They are the prime movers of his whole future course of action, and by their will he is urged on with blind impulse and delusion to his eternal ruin. It may be well, however, upon this point to note again the consistency of moral action in the poet. Although he has made the witches to assume a supremacy over the mind of Macbeth, yet a careful reader of the play will, I think, perceive that they have only done this when they found that mind prepared to commit the crime of murder. He was an instrument of mischief ready made to their hands, and they turned it to full account, and with a double purpose. They stimulated him;

they "pricked the sides of his intent;" they prompted and confirmed him in his design upon the life of King Duncan; then they wound him in their devil's web, and finally sacrificed him. By this arrangement in the plot, the grandeur of the moral is enhanced. Had Macbeth been made the mere passive instrument of this principle of evil, without *any* power of self-control, he would have claimed no other feeling than that of sympathy and commiseration; and this was by no means the intention, or indeed the moral code of Shakespeare. The witches were supernatural and master-agents in the plot; but they were never intended to be the partners, still less the rivals of Omnipotence. We are to bear in mind that they addressed the two men at the same time—both ambitious men—and cast upon each the seeds of temptation. That one only was ensnared is a proof, I think, that Shakespeare meant to give due sway to the freedom of the will; and that the soil of Macbeth's mind was apt for maturing that seed. Also, that his after course of action was but the result of a *foregone conclusion* should appear from his sudden self-betrayal, (as at an abrupt presentation of his own preconceived idea, when the witches first hailed him as king,) noted by Banquo's words:—

> "Good sir, why do you *start;* and seem to fear
> Things that do sound so fair?"

And again, afterwards, by the rejoinder of his wife, when his mind for the moment misgives him, and he repents of his purpose:—

> "We will proceed no farther in this business.
> He hath honour'd me of late; and I have bought
> Golden opinions of men;"

and she retorts upon him,—

> "What beast was't, then,
> That made you *break this enterprise to me?*"

. . . . . " Nor *time nor place*
*Did then adhere, and yet you would make both.*"

The conduct of Lady Macbeth, by the way, throughout their joint career, may, I think, be cited as a corroboration of my argument. Be it remembered, she has never seen the witches, she has only heard of them; and yet she plunges into the scheme with more vehemence, more unmitigated cruelty, than her partner—the tempted and the swayed being: the simple account of the prophecy at once overbears and consolidates her determination in their unmatured project. Lady Macbeth has not a single misgiving from the moment the plot is entertained. With unparalleled sublimity of language she ejaculates:—

"Come, you spirits
That tend on mortal thoughts, unsex me here,
And fill me, from the crown to the toe, top-full
Of direst cruelty! make thick my blood,
Stop up th' access and passage to remorse;
That no compunctious visitings of nature
Shake my fell purpose, nor keep peace between
Th' effect and it! Come to my woman's breasts,
And take my milk for gall, you murdering ministers,
Wherever in your sightless substances
You wait on nature's mischief! Come, thick night,
And pall thee in the dunnest smoke of hell,
That my keen knife see not the wound it makes,
Nor Heaven peep through the blanket of the dark,
To cry, 'Hold, hold!'"

No such language as this is put into the mouth of the man. She goes beyond him in purpose, having no other spur than her own cruel nature, and tremendous impulse of WILL. I think I may conclude, therefore, that Shakespeare, having availed himself of the weird machinery, made it wholly subservient to dramatic effect; the double use to which he has put it, resembling the *Two Times* of the *Action* which occur in some of his dramas; and which the author of the "Noctes" (Professor Wilson) so ingeniously detailed in *Blackwood's Magazine*, in his series of papers entitled "Dies Boreales." Had Shakespeare intended to insist upon the uncontrolled potency of those beings, he would have brought it to bear upon Lady Macbeth also; and, moreover, he would not have wholly rescued Banquo, who was equally tempted with his fellow-soldier. There could then have been no misapprehension as to his design. Of the personal character of Lady Macbeth, in the teeth of all her unmitigated cruelty, amounting almost to a violation of nature, Shakespeare redeems himself, (as he does in every charge,) by giving us one solitary touch of human sympathy, even in her conduct. I need hardly note the well-known instance, where she says, (speaking of the old king, Duncan,) "Had he not so much resembled my father, as he slept, *I* had done it!" And, like all violent natures, she is the first to give way; the mental energy has worn out the physical one, and both become diseased. If this be not Nature, and at once an awful lesson, I should be glad to have one more home-striking pointed out to me.

The employment of the fearful agency of the witches in swaying the destinies of those whom they fascinated, and after destroyed, has been resorted to by Shakespeare but once in the course of his numerous productions; and with that sublime effort he (as usual) preoccupied and exhausted his subject. The statement respecting Middleton's drama of the "Witch," asserted, and for some time believed to be the precursor of "Macbeth," has been proved to be a chronological error. Had it been otherwise, however, the merit of originality must still have been awarded to Shakespeare, for his treatment of the weird creations, who are totally distinct beings from the squalid, ribald hags of the other poets.

One of the grandest images out of the thousand that are to be quoted from this play is the exclamation made by Banquo to Macbeth, upon the vanishing of those beings at their first interview with them on the heath. In astonishment, he exclaims :—

> "The earth hath bubbles as the water has,
> And these are of them : whither are they vanish'd ?
> "*Macb.* Into the air ; and what seem'd corporal melted
> As breath into the wind."

Nothing can surpass this for vividness and intensity of description. Had the poet himself witnessed the scene, he could have made no more of the event ; and this is the prerogative of imagination, to "give to airy nothing a local habitation"— an absolute identity.

It has been objected to the incantation scenes in Macbeth, that the subjects and language in them are revolting. They are so ; nothing, however, can be more irrational than to take exception against them on that score. The witches are an impersonation of those qualities which are antagonist to all that is gentle, and lovely, and peaceful, and good. They are loathsome abstractions of the "evil principle," and are the precursors, as well as providers of all the stormy passions that shake this poor citadel of man. They represent the repulsive as well as the cruel propensities of our nature ; every one, therefore, who is a slave to his lower passions, is spell-bound by the "weird sisters ;" and this, I have little doubt, was the moral that Shakespeare intended to read to his brother mortals : for, we should bear in mind that Macbeth was, by nature, an honourable and even generous man ; but as he was unable to withstand the impulse of an unworthy ambition, and could not resist the sneers of his uncompromising partner, he rushed into that bottomless hell of torment —a guilty and an upbraiding conscience. What can be more affecting than his self-reproaches after he has made his first step in the blood of a fellow-creature ? That dreadful voice ringing in his ears—"Still it cried, *Sleep no more!* to all the house." His piteous anguish to his help-meet in crime—"Oh, full of scorpions is my mind, dear wife!" Then his envy of his victims:

> "Duncan is in his grave;
> After life's fitful fever he sleeps well."

And next, his bitter regret for his lost good name, and its attendant peace of mind:—

> "I have liv'd long enough: my way of life
> Is fall'n into the sear, the yellow leaf:
> And that which should accompany old age,
> As honour, love, obedience, troops of friends,
> I must not look to have; but in their stead
> Curses, not loud, but deep, mouth-honour, breath,
> Which the poor heart would fain deny, and dare not."

And lastly, as the climax of horror, when he has become stupefied with the pressure of remorse, calamity, and despair, he enquires "What is that cry?" and adds:—

> "I have almost forgot the taste of fears:
> The time has been, my senses would have cool'd
> To hear a night-shriek; and my fell of hair
> Would at a dismal treatise rouse and stir
> As life were in't. *I have supp'd full with horrors:*
> Direness familiar to my slaughterous thoughts
> Cannot once start me."

A more terrific picture of a mind recoiling on itself, and effecting its own retribution, who shall quote? Oh, let the over-zealous purist, when he proceeds to question the morality of Shakespeare, turn to and reflect upon the homily he has preached against cupidity, injustice, and cruelty, in the most unhappy career of Macbeth.

II.

# As You Like It.

## II.

# AS YOU LIKE IT.

AND now from the pitchy smoke of Acheron, and from the hot and stifling atmosphere of injustice and cruelty, midnight murders and haunting spirits, bloody wrongs and fierce resentments, we emerge into the blue and sunshine of God's own heaven, and feel the "unchartered winds" from the mountain in our faces, blowing away towards the deep ocean of oblivion all clouds of mistrust and despair at man's unkindness and folly. We are in the forest of Arden; and under the green shaws will we crack nuts and jokes with that pretty squirrel, the pranksome Rosalind, or descant upon her blithe wisdom with that sedate and most loving of all cousins, the devoted, the cordial, the confiding Celia. To make the world one "perfect chrysolite" of happiness, let every man respect the predilections of his fellow: nothing is worth quarrelling about, not even unkindness; for that is a mistake which always brings its own retribution, silent or revealed. So we will talk of the gallant and gentle bearing and stalwart proportions of her lover with the crystal-hearted Rosalind; and repeat within hearing of the exiled Duke (for elderly gentlemen—especially aristocratic ones—love to hear themselves quoted) his own moral reflections upon the "sweet uses of adversity;"—worthy, by the way, to be quoted at all seasons, for it is perfect in itself, and is an amulet to hang round the necks of the desponding. No one can know anything of Shakespeare and be ignorant of his first speech,

> "Now, my co-mates and brothers in exile," &c.
>
> —*Opening of Act* ii.

The exiled Duke is a perfect exemplar of what should comprise a Christian's course—a cheerful gratitude for the benefits that have been showered upon him; a calm, yet firm endurance of adversity; a tolerance of unkindness; and a promptitude to forgive injuries. How sweet, and yet how strong is his moral nature! It seems as though no trial, social or physical, could change the current of his gracious wisdom. In a scene subsequent to that containing his celestial confession of moral faith, we have the proof that his philosophy is no cold profession merely,—no lip-deep ostentation,—no barren theory without practice. His conduct shows that his cheerful morality nestles in his heart, and inspires his actions. It is the seventh Scene of the second Act, where he and his followers are about to sit down to their woodland meal, when Orlando rushes in with his drawn sword, and demands food. There is in every point of the Duke's behaviour on this occasion, the forbearance, the gentleness, the charity, and the cordial courtesy which grow out of such philosophy as his—that of unaffected contentment. "Sweet are the uses of adversity," indeed, when they teach such lessons as these! We cannot fancy that this true-hearted gentleman could have so perfected his native character had he never known the reverse of fortune, which exiled him from his court, and sent him among the forest-trees to learn wisdom from all-bounteous Nature; to know the worth of his true friends, who forsook land and station to share his seclusion; and to secure a peace of soul seldom known to those who live perpetually in the turmoil of public life. We find how dear his sylvan haunts have become to him; how happy have been the hours spent among them with his friends; how entirely their calm has penetrated his soul, and made part of his existence, by the unwillingness with which he prepares to quit these scenes at the end of the play, when his dukedom is restored to him. He receives the news with his own philosophic composure; and, by a word or two that he lets fall, it may be shrewdly suspected that he only intends returning to repossess himself of his birthright, in order to secure it for his daughter Rosalind, and her future husband, Orlando; and then that he will quietly leave the young people at court, and steal back with a few of his faithful friends to close their days in retirement on the spot where they have been so contentedly happy. Mayhap, as the years creep on, and age-aches warn him not to disregard the "seasons' difference," he will exchange the table under the greenwood tree for one beneath the oaken roof. But be sure that his house will be close upon the forest glades, and on his table will smoke a haunch of the red deer for old lang syne.

When we design to change our course of the moralising in this most perfect of Arcadian plays, we will accompany the "melancholy Jaques"—albeit not an especial favourite with us, for he is somewhat tinged with the *affectation* of melancholy and philosophy. Besides, we recognise no more affinity with "melancholy" than did Shakespeare himself, who never misses an opportunity of girding at your pompous and affectedly pensive character, and of proclaiming the superior qualifications of cheerfulness and good-humour. Instances of this might be multiplied; while I know of none that encourage melancholy, or even gravity, as being in itself, and for itself, a test of wisdom. "Laugh if you are *wise*," says one of his characters. "Frame your mind," says Kit Sly's page, "to mirth and merriment; which bars a thousand harms, and lengthens life." "Let me play the fool," says Gratiano; "with mirth and laughter let old wrinkles come." That chirping rogue, Autolycus, sings:

> "A merry heart goes all the day;
> Your sad tires in a mile-a."

And, in the mouth of Falstaff, he urges it as a *vice* in the cold blooded-nature of Prince John of Lancaster, that "a man cannot make him laugh."

Jaques, nevertheless, is a great character in his way, and good too; as, indeed, says the Duke, "there is good" (more or less) "in everything." His chuckling account of the court fool, whom he stumbles upon in one of his rambles through the forest, is choicely good, and is as famous; both as giving a capital sketch of the man described, and as affording a characteristic picture of the mind of him who is describing. Jaques finds the fool-jester's conventional affectations irresistibly comic, while he betrays his own individual affectations even in the act of laughing at the other's.

Jaques is the model of a man addicted to self-contemplation; he always appears to be before his own mental looking-glass. He has inherited or acquired the tact to discern the worthlessness of artificial society, but he has not carried that tact into the wisdom of turning his philosophy the sunny side outwards. He, forsooth, would undertake to reform the world, having seen no more of the world than is comprised within the precincts of a court. Jaques says some of the finest things in the play; but, lest he should become an authority with the world, (and here again we note Shakespeare's watchfulness in inculcating a bland and *cheerful* philosophy,) by one stroke we are let into the secret of his character,—that it is, or at least has heretofore been not altogether the exemplar to place before a reforming society.

Strong conclusions are to be drawn as to the amplitude and benignity of Shakespeare's moral code, from the slightest and most casual hints and incidents. His most home-striking injunctions are conveyed by actions, rather than by saws and theories. When Jaques, in his sudden admiration of the fool, after he had met him in the forest, and, with the fantasticalness of a self-worshipper, will undertake the office of reformer-general, he proposes that the Duke invest him with the insignia of the order. He says :—

"Invest me in my motley ; give me leave
To speak my mind, and I will through and through
Cleanse the foul body of the infected world,
If they will patiently receive my medicine.
"Fie on thee (answers the Duke), I can tell what thou would'st do.
"*Jaq.* What, for a counter, would I do but good?
"*Duke.* Most mischievous foul sin, in chiding sin ;
For thou thyself hast been a libertine,
As sensual as the brutish sting itself;
And all th' embossed sores, and headed evils,
Which thou with licence of free foot hast caught,
Would'st thou disgorge into the general world."

From this rebuke, it appears clear that Shakespeare had in view the overweening mouth-moralist ; for, with all the reflections and sarcasms he has put into the mouth of this self-asserting philosopher, and which have the air of being gleanings from the harvests of other men rather than the result of his own growth, it is to be remarked that he never brings him point to point in contest of wit with any of the other characters of the play, but he is foiled ; they, being natural people, outwit the artificial one. He first tries his hand with Orlando, and upon a tender point—his mistress and his love-making; and the bout between them is as good as a match at single-stick :—

"*Jaq.* I thank you for your company; but, good faith, I had as lief have been myself alone.

"*Orl.* And so had I; but yet, for fashion's sake, I thank you too for your society.

"*Jaq.* God be with you, let us meet as little as we can.

"*Orl.* I do desire we may be better strangers.

"*Jaq.* I pray you, mar no more trees with writing love-verses in their barks.

"*Orl.* I pray you, mar no more of my verses with reading them ill-favouredly.

"*Jaq.* Rosalind is your love's name?

"*Orl.* Yes—just.

"*Jaq.* I do not like her name.

"*Orl.* There was no thought of pleasing you when she was christened.

"*Jaq.* What stature is she of?

"*Orl.* Just as high as my heart.

"*Jaq.* You are full of pretty answers: have you not been acquainted with goldsmiths' wives, and conned them out of rings?

"*Orl.* Not so; but I answer you right painted cloth, from whence you have studied your questions."

[This answer of Orlando's refers to grave points of morality, which it was the custom to impersonate, by painting them on cloth.]

"*Jaq.* You have a nimble wit: I think it was made of Atalanta's heels. Will you sit down with me? and we two will rail against our mistress the world, and all our misery."

Now, note the answer of the man who had just reason to "rail at misery," having been fortune's foot-ball from his infancy. How beautifully the moral of a cheerful endurance comes out against the affectation and petulance of a querulous selfishness! Orlando's reply is the very offspring of a modest self-knowledge and experience. How few can trace their ill fortunes to any other source than ignorance or indiscretion. With a beautiful candour he replies :—

"I will chide no breather in the world but myself; against whom I know most faults.

"*Jaq.* The worst fault you have is to be in love.

"*Orl.* 'Tis a fault I will not change for your best virtue. I am weary of you.

"*Jaq.* By my troth, I was seeking for a fool when I found you.

"*Orl.* He is drowned in the brook; look but in, and you shall see him.

"*Jaq.* There shall I see mine own figure.

"*Orl.* Which I take to be either a fool or a cipher.

"*Jaq.* I'll tarry no longer with you; farewell, good Signior 'Love!'

"*Orl.* I am glad of your departure: adieu, good Monsieur 'Melancholy!'"

The fact is they all smoke him for being a solemn pretender to a quality not natural to him. When he desires to make the acquaintance of Rosalind, her objecting reply is, "They say you are a melancholy fellow." And he takes but little by his answer when he says, "Why, 'tis good to be sad, and say nothing;" for she retorts, "Why, then, 'tis good to be a post."

Another instance (to my mind at least) that Shakespeare intended Jaques for a grave coxcomb, appears with some strength in that short parley between him and Amiens, after the sprightly song, "Under the greenwood tree." Observe the pomposity and patronising air with which the philosopher condescends to encourage the ballad-singer :—

"More, more, I prithee, more.

"*Am.* It will make you *melancholy*, Monsieur Jaques."

Amiens is hoaxing him. What is there in a merry roundelay to make a man melancholy? Jaques, however, is so engrossed with himself that he takes the songster gravely and literally.

"I thank it," he says—that is, for its melancholy. "More, I prithee, more. I can suck melancholy out of a song, as a weasel sucks eggs. More, I prithee, more.

"*Am.* My voice is ragged. I know I cannot please you.

"*Jaq.* I do not desire you to please me—I do desire you to sing. Come, more; another stanza. Call you them stanzas?

"*Am.* What you will, Monsieur Jaques.

"*Jaq.* Nay, I care not for their names; they owe me nothing. Will you sing?

"*Am.* More at your request than to please myself.

"*Jaq.* Well, then, if ever I thank any man, I will thank you."

What a prig! Why not thank him? Is it requisite, when a man sets up for a philosopher, that he should begin by being a hog? So he continues:—

"When a man thanks me heartily, methinks I have given him a penny, and he renders me the beggarly thanks. Come, sing; and you that will not, hold your tongues.

"*Am.* Well, I'll end the song. Sirs, cover the while. The Duke will drink under this tree. He hath been all this day to look for *you.*

"*Jaq.* And I have been all this day to avoid *him.* He is too disputable for my company. *I think of as many matters as he; but I give Heaven thanks, and make no boast of them.*—Come, warble—come."

Shakespeare certainly intended the character of Jaques to be a satire upon your pretenders to wisdom; and I have the rather enlarged and insisted on this reading of it, because the world (both literary and theatrical) appear to have misunderstood the poet's intention. One more reason for my opinion, and which reason, be it observed, is one of the numerous instances displaying Shakespeare's habit of drawing conclusions as to his characters from *acts,* and not from *descriptions*:—Jaques, the ostensibly melancholy man, and who is always talking about himself, has no trials to perplex him, and is unstricken by adversity. The Duke, who has most cause to complain of all the characters in the play, is not only the least querulous, but he is uniformly the most hopeful and cheerful. With all his moral professions, Jaques is either not a sincere man to himself, (and consequently is not true to others,) or he is really a man without affection or attachment. It may be retorted that he follows the fortunes of the banished Duke. He does so; but it is evident that he takes that course to please his own humour, and from an affectation of singularity—also, to carry out the character he has assumed, of a cynic philosopher; and, at all events, he prefers that course to a steadiness of friendship, since he deserts the Duke when he is restored to his patrimony. But, after all, let us part upon pleasant terms with "Monsieur Melancholy," if it be only for his gentle reflections upon the wounded deer; and for his perfect portraiture of the "Seven Ages of Man," (*Act* ii., *sc.* 7.)

In the character of Orlando, Shakespeare has depicted the very perfection of gentleness in manliness—modesty in manhood. He is an exemplar of the power of gentleness, and the gentleness of power. His inadequate training and breeding—the result of his despotic brother's tyrannous restraint and miserly allowance—induces a withdrawing, a self-mistrust, that is only counterbalanced by his inherent nobleness and high spirit. Orlando is by nature generous, warm, eager, without one spark of conceit or presumption. He is by conformation robust, athletic—a model of manly vigour—and yet, as old Chaucer hath it, "Meek of his port as is a maid." The dramatist has markedly and vividly kept before us this point of Orlando's personal strength as a counterbalance to the extreme mildness of his disposition. He perpetually reminds us of his might of frame, his might and command of limb, and his bodily force, in order that his tenderness of heart and modesty of deportment may in no wise show like effeminacy, or an undue softness, but in their full advantage and truth of manly gentleness.

His consciousness of a too homely and unworthy nature is well set off by his spirited remonstrance to his ungenerous and unjust elder brother; his signal encounter with Charles, the wrestler, and complete overthrow of the "strong man," enhance the pathos of his self-resigned speech, uttered immediately before he enters upon his athletic trial; and his firm yet courteous reply to Duke Frederick, and his self-possessed bearing to the courtier, Le Beau, heighten by contrast the diffidence and touching emotion of his address to the two princesses—or rather of his *reception* of the words which they address to *him*.

Afterwards, too, when we find him comforting, sustaining, and cheering the good old Adam, with words well-nigh womanly in their affectionate kindness, the poet takes distinct care all the time to maintain in us the recollection of the young fellow's massive proportions, by making him bear the aged serving-man in his arms, and carry him to where he may have food and shelter.

The most manifest display of Orlando's combined qualities of personal force and courage with moral suavity is in the scene where he rushes with drawn sword to the greenwood table of the banished Duke, to demand food for his faithful old servitor; and where, upon being received with that mild inquiry—

"What would you have? Your gentleness shall force
More than your force move us to gentleness;"

he at once resumes the bearing natural to him; and after explaining his urgent need, concludes with,

"Let gentleness my strong enforcement be:
In the which hope, *I blush*, and hide my sword;"

a perfect illustration of manly diffidence. But the triumph of Orlando's generous nature—at once capable of revenging itself by force of arms, yet incapable of revenge by force of gentle-heartedness—shines forth in his slaying the lioness that would have killed his sleeping brother: that brother who had dealt so unjustly by his orphaned youth; and, indeed, who had treacherously sought his life. Orlando uses his strength of body, instructed by his strength of bland spirit, to protect, not to injure his enemies. He destroys their enmity instead of themselves; converting it into gratitude and love by the high tone of his magnanimity. He disarms by dint of forbearance, in lieu of by dint of blows and opposition; and such forbearance comes with double effect from a man whose thews and sinews insure victory. The conquest is irresistible and complete which is achieved by gentleness, when power might have enforced submission.

Rosalind is one of the most enchanting among jocund-spirited heroines. Her first scene shows the womanly sentiment, as well as the womanly vivacity of her character. We see her natural cheerfulness clouded by sympathy for her banished father; revived at the instance of her cousin, the crystal-hearted Celia, who cannot endure to see her cast down. Their opening dialogue well displays the affectionate nature and playful wit of both women; for Celia is hardly inferior to Rosalind in witty accomplishment, though rarely displaying it, in order, with a generous prodigality, that her cousin's may shine forth uninterruptedly. But, perhaps, the two most gifted of Shakespeare's women, with that peculiar power of fancy and instinct called "wit," are Rosalind and Beatrice. But how individually and distinctively has he characterised the wit of the respective heroines! That of Beatrice is sarcastic—that of Rosalind, playful. The one is biting, pointed, keen; the other is sprightly, sportive, sympathetic. The one is like the lightning, sudden, dazzling, startling, and sometimes scathing; the other is like the sunshine, cheerful, beaming full of life, and glow, and warmth, and animation. We are apt to shrink from the wit of Beatrice; we *bask* in that of Rosalind. The one is fulminated in brilliant coruscations, occasionally heedless whom they wound; the other shines with gentle, genial radiance. It may be that one secret of this difference in character lies in the fact that Beatrice's wit is apt to verge upon the *personal* and *home-thrusting* in its rapier-like play; whereas Rosalind's is more general, and deals with subjects rather than with people. It is difficult to make choice of a scene, where all are of almost level perfection, in which this enchanting creature shines; but, perhaps, the most sportive is that one where, in her disguise of a forest youth, she pretends to play the part of her lover's mistress, and has been acting the marriage ceremony through with him, before her cousin Celia, (*Act* iv., *sc.* I.)

Of that cousin, I must take leave to descant *at will;* for she is of inestimable worth. Celia is one of those characters that pass through society in almost unrecognised perfection. They are beloved for their tempers, and respected for their understandings and attainments. They make no display of their qualities; and yet they are an unfailing resource when a friend needs assistance or advice—domestic or mental. It is difficult, upon demand, to indicate any prominent example of their intellectual or social excellences—the impression in their favour is general and unequivocal. And so with the career of Celia in this play: it leaves a bland and gratified impression upon the mind of the reader; with a sense of uncertainty as to what scene we should quote as a specimen of more than quiet excellence. Indeed, it would be difficult to point out a more perfect example of the spirit of loving-kindness than the character of the cousin to Rosalind. She is generous, warm-hearted, unselfish; so enthusiastic in her attachments, that she can see no fault in those she loves; and almost loses sight of herself in the contemplation of their excellences. By deed, as well as by word, she is ever ready to prove the strength of her affection; and when the time comes for making active demonstration in the shape of sacrifice, so unhesitatingly, so unostentatiously is it made—so much is it taken for granted, and so completely as a matter of course, by her—that she absolutely strips it of all appearance of sacrifice, letting it seem a fulfilment of her own pleasure no less than theirs. And *it is* her own pleasure; it is her pleasure to please her friend—to minister to her comfort; it is her happiness to secure the happiness of her cousin. So entirely does she love that cousin, so perfectly has she made her well-being part and parcel of her own, that she can only dwell contented herself so long as she knows Rosalind to enjoy content. If "Rose" will not be "merry," why, then, no more will she; if "Rose" be sad at her father's absence, why, then, she will be sad for company. Or rather, as sadness is not for such loving hearts as hers, or for such blithe natures as Rosalind's, she will e'en teach her to look upon her own father as a parent, vowing that Rose shall be his heiress instead of herself.

By banter, part made up of cheerful images, part of the profoundest tokens of her answering affection couched beneath light-seeming words, she constantly contrives, with her own gentle witchery of loving-kindness, to maintain Rosalind's spirits in their native element of buoyancy and airy mirth. She has such fond and implicit admiration for her cousin's powers of fancy, of eloquence, of playfulness, of imaginative wit and humour, that she would fain have them never dulled, or silenced by anxiety or uneasiness; and she whets her sharpest ingenuity to divert her from pondering on existing vexations, as well as to ward off ills that may threaten. On the first intimation of her father's harshness, she consoles her cousin beneath his sentence of banishment by no less a measure than instantly proposing to share it; and she not only proposes this, but actually does accompany her into exile. Throughout the play, wherever Rosalind appears, there too is Celia. When one approaches, the other is not far distant. They enter together; and they make their exit in company. In one scene we have, "*Enter Rosalind, reading a paper;*" and a moment after, "*Enter Celia, reading a paper.*"

Celia is a worshipper of her cousin; and yet so pure in her loving idolatry, that neither the idol appears conscious of superiority, nor does the idolater become inferior. Celia accompanies and attends her friend implicitly, but so genuine and spontaneous is her personal attachment that she scarcely seems to *follow* Rosalind. She is, in fact, her double, her very shadow; yet so clear and lustrous is her own affectionate nature that it is never thrown into shadow, even by the effulgence of Rosalind's wit. The very generosity with which she constantly, and as if involuntarily, cedes the precedence to Rosalind's keener intellect, only serves to heighten the effect of her own fine understanding and just perception. Indeed, Celia would be a wit and heroine of the first water in any other play, and as a character by herself. But seen by the side of Rosalind—to whom her own modesty (the modesty of loving-kindness) chooses to yield the palm, in standing silently by, while her cousin keeps up the ball of wit-raillery with others—she does not display to the same brilliant advantage. What she does say, however, amply testifies that, if she chose, she could shine to the full as brightly as the gifted Rosalind: by which means the poet has ingeniously conveyed to us the impression that hers is a *voluntary non-speech*,—a silence arising from preference to hear her cousin, and from no deficiency on her own part.

He has another artistic subtlety, in the resemblance with which he has invested Celia's wit in its congenial quality with that of her cousin. It is the resemblance—totally apart from the servility of imitation or plagiarism—which unconsciously colours the thoughts and mode of speech of one who lovingly admires another.

Rosalind is Celia's ideal of excellence—morally, intellectually, and personally—and she unwittingly allows her heart, mind, and frame to become as much *one* as possible with those of this cherished being. Her spirit assimilates by intensity of appreciation, as her exterior conforms, in matters of gesture, conduct, and habit, by daily and affectionate companionship. This is no copying; it is just the similarity, the accordance, that naturally grows out of a strong and enduring attachment.

As an example of what I mean, with regard to this resemblance in the tone of the two cousins' imaginative wit, I would point to the circumstance of their both dealing in classical and poetical allusions, which seems to tell of their having read together, thought together, and discussed together the beauties of the old mythology. This is remarkable; for the instances might be multiplied to a curious extent.

It is a singular thing,—as a corroboration of the loving terms on which Celia feels herself with her cousin, of the perfect ease of heart which reigns between them, and which characterises the regard that Celia bears towards Rosalind,—that the flow of wit, which betokens Celia to be no less accomplished in intellectual sprightliness than her cousin, always pours forth most freely when she is *alone* with Rosalind. When they are both in the company of others, she stands tranquilly by, letting her brilliant cousin take the lead in conversation and bandy repartee with the rest. She seems not only content, but best pleased, to listen while Rosalind gives free scope to her gay-souled sallies. When they are by themselves, she rejoins, retorts, and tosses jests to and fro, with as playful animation as her friend,—bantering her, teasing her, sporting with her curiosity, plaguing and joking her about her love and her lover, with as hearty a spirit, as much roguery and mischief, as much pretended mercilessness of wit, as need be. But, true to her kindly nature, her humour is always affectionate, her sportiveness ever gentle; and both have the genuine soul of kindness—*they know when to cease.* Celia, loving Celia, always checks the career of her wit, when it curvets beyond the comfort of her interlocutor. She regards the feelings of her friend, even beyond the prosperity of her jest,—a rare virtue in a *wit,* more especially in a *woman-wit.*

But Celia is pre-eminently *womanly.* She has the best qualities of womanly nature. She is devoted, constant, femininely gentle, yet frank and firm in opinion. She has touches of warmth, both of liking and disliking—of out-and-out eager partizanship, and at times of vehement indignation; and these qualities are essentially womanly. For instance, how like a woman in its acknowledgment of the want of personal strength her taking refuge in a crafty device—and that *an unfair one* —is that exclamation of hers when Orlando is about to try his match with Charles, the wrestler. She says:—"I would I were invisible, to *catch the strong fellow by the leg.*" One would swear that none but a woman would have thought of that speech. Then observe her womanly delicacy, and discretion too, on behalf of her cousin Rosalind, who betrays her incipient love for Orlando by returning towards him, affecting to think that she hears him address them, and saying:

> "He calls us back: *my pride fell with my fortunes:*
> I'll ask him what he would. Did you call, sir?
> Sir, you have wrestled well, and *overthrown*
> *More than your enemies.*"

This palpable hint is enough for Celia; and Orlando, not able to respond to it, being overpowered with his own new-born passion for Rosalind, Celia smilingly recalls her friend with the words, "Will you go, coz?"

Again, afterwards, what nice consideration and complete womanly tact she betrays, when Rosalind, recovering from her swoon, well-nigh reveals the secret of her disguise by answering Oliver's, "Well, then, take a good heart, and counterfeit to be a man," with "So I do; but i' faith, I should have been a woman by right;" Celia interposes, and says, "Come, you look paler and paler; pray you draw homewards. Good sir, go with us." Even those simple words, "Good sir, go with us," are in perfect keeping with the feminine beauty of the character. They secure support for her fainting cousin, and secure the prolonged stay of the man with whom she has just begun to feel herself falling fast and deeply in love.

The whole of this "love at first sight" on her part, is managed with Shakespeare's masterly skill. I have always felt those three little speeches to be profoundly true to individual nature, where the ladies are questioning Oliver respecting the incident of the lioness and the snake in the forest, and of Orlando's timely succour. Celia exclaims, in amazement, "Are you his brother?" Rosalind says, "Was it you he *rescued?*" And Celia rejoins, "Was't *you* that did so oft contrive to kill him?" Celia's first exclamation is surprised concern to find that this stranger, who interests her, is that unnatural brother of whom she has heard. Rosalind's thought is of her lover,—Orlando's *generosity* in rescuing one who has hitherto behaved so unnaturally towards himself; while Celia recurs to the difficulty she has in reconciling the image of one who has acted basely and cruelly, with him she sees before her—who is speedily becoming to her the impersonation of all that is attractive, estimable, and loveable in man.

Her affectionate nature cannot persuade itself to believe this villany of him; she therefore incredulously reiterates, "Was't YOU that did so oft contrive to kill him?" And his reply is a beautiful evidence of the sweetness which beams transparent in her; since it already influences him, by effecting a confirmation of the virtuous resolves to which his brother's generosity has previously given rise, and by causing him to fall as suddenly in love with her, as she with him. He says:

> "'Twas I; but 'tis not I;—I do not shame
> To tell you what I was, since my conversion
> So sweetly tastes, being the thing I am."

It is one of the refined beauties that distinguish Shakespeare's metaphysical philosophy, to show us how a fine nature acting upon an inferior one, through the subtle agency of love, operates beneficially to elevate and purify. At one process it proclaims its own excellence, and works amelioration in another. Celia's charm of goodness wins the unkind brother of Orlando (Oliver) to a passionate admiration of herself, at the same time that it excites *his* emulation to become worthy of her. It begins by teaching him the bravery of a candid avowal of his crime—the first step towards reformation. Celia's loving-kindness, like all true loving-kindness, hath this twofold virtue and grace; it no less benefits her friends than adorns herself. In enumerating the touches that go to make up the exquisite character of Celia—a character often too lowly rated, from the circumstance of its being seen in juxtaposition with the more brilliant Rosalind, (for, in fact, its own mild radiance of loving-kindness is no less *intense;* it is only less *striking* than the vivid intellectual sunshine of her cousin;)—in alluding, I say, to the lovely touches that characterise her, I would not omit to note that interesting and natural one, where, on Rosalind's swooning,

Celia's first impulse is to call upon her by the old familiar name of "Cousin!" The hurry of anxiety for her she so loves causes the old fond word to spring to her lips: the next moment, however, the womanly instinct, the feminine presence of mind, come to her aid, and she redeems the inadvertency by exclaiming "Ganymede!"

It is a glowing instance of Shakespeare's prodigality of loving resources, and his potency, as well as plenitude of means to inspire infinity of liking, that he makes us admire and love Rosalind the more for her vicinity to the sweet-hearted Celia, and Celia the more for hers to the bewitching Rosalind. We love and esteem each the better for the other's sake. Shakespeare has this in common with Nature—and how many qualities does he *not* possess in common with her? The love he causes us to feel for his several characters—individually distinct and dissimilar as they may be, or sympathetic and analogous one with the other as they may be—never interferes with your love for them all. In teaching us to see the enchanting qualities that embellish a Rosalind, he never lets us lose sight of the tender devotion and unselfish beauty that distinguish a Celia. In making us feel the full value of a gentle, affectionate being like Celia, he never suffers us to overlook the grace and fascination of her cousin. Like the love which Nature puts into our heart—with its own bounteous magic, it fills our soul for one selected object, while it still affords room for loving regard and estimation towards all existing human merit. Nay, the exclusive preference for the *one* beloved, but expands our capacity for perceiving excellence elsewhere, and for yielding it our admiration and our loving-kindness.

We have another proof of the estimation in which Shakespeare held a cheerful philosophy, in the personal qualities he has given to Touchstone, the clown. Touchstone—the universal favourite—the man of mirth and good-humour; but who, nevertheless, can tang out a sarcasm with any professor of cynicism. Touchstone is a fellow possessing genuine qualities of attachment and affection. When Rosalind is expelled the court by the usurping Duke, and Celia, in that gentle speech, resolves to share her fortunes, the question is started, whether it were not good to have the Fool for their safeguard; and she says, "He 'll go along o'er the wide world with me: leave me alone to woo him." And in this act Touchstone makes a generous sacrifice; for he has been born and bred in the luxury of what the Neapolitans call the "dolce fa niente"—the "delicious do naught:"—he had all his days run about the court and amused himself: he is an over-fed lap-dog, with all the snappishness, and none of the ill-temper. The court-life was to him a second nature; nevertheless, it becomes a second object in his choice when his young mistress is to leave it. And although it may be said that he was ignorant of what he had to encounter in following a woodland life, subject to the shrewd caprice of the elements; yet, when he does encounter them, he bears the change from that he prefers, with all the playfulness and sweet temper of the wiseliest ordered mind. "I care not for my spirits," he says, "if my legs were not weary." And to Celia, who can walk no farther, and begs them to "bear with her:" "For my part, I had rather bear with you than bear you; yet I should bear no cross if I did bear you, [the cross was a coin;] for I think you have no money in your purse. Now I am in Arden; the more fool I: when I was at home I was in a better place; but travellers must be content."

Touchstone has good and gentlemanly feeling: witness his rebuke to the courtier Le Beau, who gives a description of the hurts and wounds of the three young fellows who have been overthrown by Charles the wrestler, and the moan made over them by their poor old father; and which encounter he details with a cruel relish and enjoyment as "sport," and expressing regret that the ladies have missed seeing it. Touchstone asks: "But what is the 'sport,' Monsieur, that the ladies have lost?"

"*Le Beau.* Why, that that I speak of.

"*Touch.* Thus men may grow wiser every day! It is the first time that ever I heard breaking of ribs was sport for ladies."

Touchstone has also *right* feeling; for, although his worldly-reaped terrors of matrimony give him a qualm or two, and a momentary thought of availing himself of the hedge-parson's services to wed him, that so slip-knot a marriage might give him a chance of retreating, in case of repenting at leisure; yet his good faith and "right feeling" hold good, and he determines to act honourably by the trusting and doating Audrey.

He has a keen eye for pretension; for he sees through Professor Jaques's pretended immaculacy, and his assumption in moral philosophy. He treats him with a kind of old-glove easiness of familiarity,—a negligent, dressing-gown air of equality, as amusing in effect as it is warranted in fact:—

"Good even, good Master What-d'ye call 't:—How do you, sir?—You are very well met. I am very glad to see you.—Nay; pray be cover'd."

He has the delightful quality (quite that of a sweet-natured person,—one who is at once good-hearted, good-humoured, and good-minded,) of being able to make himself happy and contented wherever fortune chances to cast him. He is gay and easy at court;—he is good-tempered and at ease in the forest. He makes himself at home anywhere and everywhere; for he carries his own sunshine about with him. Touchstone is not a mere jester—a mere extracter of *fun* from what occurs around him; and he is not in the least a buffoon:—there is nothing low or common in his composition. He has excellent sense, and the good feeling to draw truth and beauty, as well as fine humour, out of passing life. How charmingly he and his lady-mistress interchange gay philosophy! She tells him he'll be whipped one of these days for his saucy speeches; and he replies:—

"The more pity, that fools may not speak wisely what wise men do foolishly.

"*Celia.* By my troth, thou say'st true: for since the little wit that fools have was silenced, the little foolery that wise men have, makes a great show."

As a specimen of his good sense,—how fine his answer as to the various degrees of the "lie!"—his celebrated speech:—

"O, sir, we quarrel in print, by the book; as you have books for good manners. I will name you the degrees. The first, the Retort courteous; the second, the Quip modest; the third, the Reply churlish; the fourth, the Reproof valiant; the fifth, the Countercheck quarrelsome; the sixth, the Lie with circumstance; the seventh, the *Lie direct.*—All these you may avoid, but the lie direct; and you may avoid that too, with an '*If.*' I knew when seven justices could not take up a quarrel: but when the parties were met themselves, one of them thought but of an '*If;*' as, '*If* you said so, then I said so:' and they shook hands, and swore brothers. Your *if* is the only peace-maker; much virtue in *if.*"

How many portentous quarrels in certain grand assemblies have been polished off with this same oily monosyllable!

It was a happy thought to introduce the court-jester among the shepherds and shepherdesses of a pastoral drama. His pert railleries and waggishness come with the best possible relief to the honey-dew sentimentalities of the writers of love-verses. His quizzing of Rosalind is in the best style of light o' love, and mock romance. "I remember when I was in love," he says, "I broke my sword upon a stone, and bid him take that for coming a-nigh to Jane Smile. We that are true lovers run into strange capers; but, as all is mortal in nature, so is all nature in love mortal in folly." Rosalind tells him that he has "spoken more wisdom than he was aware of;" and he answers with amusing conceit and mock humility: "Nay, I shall never be aware of my own wit, till I break my shins against it." It *was* a happy thought to bring the court-fool into this scene; for, although he always has the best of it when he is bandying speeches with the philosopher and the sentimentalists, yet Shakespeare has paid the highest compliment to a life of rural simplicity in the dialogue between him and the shepherd Corin. It is an amusing specimen of cock-a-whoop insolence to bear down the poor rustic with the notion that he will be damned, because he has never been at court!—and what a reason to give for his being in a state of perdition!—what a deduction!—what a "sequitur!"—"Why, if thou hast never been at court, thou never saw'st good manners; and if thou never saw'st good manners, then thy manners must be wicked; and wickedness is sin, and sin is damnation:—thou 'rt in a parlous state, shepherd!"

Poor Corin's reply to his hoaxing clatter is nevertheless much to the purpose:—"Sir, I am a true labourer; I earn that I eat; get that I wear; owe no man hate, envy no man's happiness; glad of other men's good, content with my harm:—and the greatest of my pride is, to see my ewes graze, and my lambs suck." Many a wordy preachment upon the merits of content are less to the purpose than this simple summary of honest Corin's.

It was good, also, to pay that compliment to rural simplicity, that the court-bred clown should become honestly attracted by a primitive clod of mother-earth; and most true to nature that the country-wench should have her head turned by the wooing of a gentleman, who had been the companion of princes. Audrey is the most perfect specimen of a wondering she-gawky. She thanks the gods she is foul; and if to be poetical is not to be honest, she thanks the gods also that she is not poetical. When Touchstone inquires of her whether he is to be the favoured individual—the man of her choice, how thoroughly rustic is her reply: he might just as well talk Greek to her,—

> "Come apace, good Audrey: I will fetch up your goats, Audrey.—And how, Audrey?—Am I the man yet?—Doth my simple feature content you!
>
> "*Aud.* Your *features!* Lord warrant us! *what features!*"

She would be anything that her new lover might require of her. She casts off William, as if he were a broken patten, and gallops away with his rival, as she would to a harvest-home, or a wake at a fair. She has no idea of marriage beyond a merry-making,—a new gown and ribands, cakes and ale, and a rousing country-dance. Audrey is a homely type of human nature—a rough clod turned off the great lathe, untrimmed, unglazed. Happy for her that she made choice of one who did not make a goddess of her at first, and a broken-spirited drudge afterwards. Touchstone is a kind-hearted fellow, and who has no idea of being laughed out of his wife, since he chose her himself:—"An ill-favour'd thing, sir, but *my own.* A poor humour of mine, sir, to take that, that no one else will. Rich honesty dwells like a miser, sir, in a poor house; as your pearl in your foul oyster." Blessed is the woman, conscious of a plain face, with a loving heart, that owns a Touchstone for her mate.

Jaques, it is true, when he takes his leave of the company —leaving at the same time his sting behind for each of them— says of Touchstone and Audrey, that their "loving voyage is but for two months victualled." But Jaques is a cur, and I think better of Touchstone than to fancy he could be unkind to any one who had received his preference and favour; and as for Audrey, she evidently looks upon him as a prodigy of accomplishment,—and that, in itself, is a certain holdfast upon a woman's affection.

We must not pass over unregarded that beautiful little sketch of a character in old Adam, with his heart of fourteen, and his body of fourscore years. He must have honourable mention, if it be only for the lovely homily put into his simple and confiding mouth, when he shares with his young master, Orlando, his little "all" of savings, trusting for the hereafter to Him, that "doth the ravens feed, yea, providently caters for the sparrow." And how sincerely characteristic is his honest self-commendation :—

"Here is the gold ;
All this I give you :—Let me be your servant ;
Though I look old, yet I am strong and lusty ;
For in my youth I never did apply
Hot and rebellious liquors to my blood ;
And did not with unbashful forehead woo
The means of weakness and debility :
Therefore my age is as a lusty winter,
Frosty, but kindly."

There is no point in which Shakespeare displays the trustingness and sweet humility of his nature more heart-homely, than when he inculcates an implicit and cheerful reliance upon that benevolent principle, which, indeed, is the only cement and bond of humanity. A similar instance to the above (and an affecting one it is) occurs towards the close of Hamlet's career :—"Thou knowest not, Horatio, how ill all is here about my heart :—'but' we defy augury. There is a special Providence, even in the fall of a sparrow."

A word has heretofore been spoken of the "cheerful philosophy" in this most exquisite play of "As You Like It ;"—but, indeed the whole composition is one varied homily upon the many-featured moral and social philosophy. There is Touchstone's philosophy ; the Duke's philosophy ; the old shepherd Corin's philosophy; the old serving-man Adam's philosophy, all here brought into subtle contrast. There is the Duke's—a serene wisdom of contentment, born of adversity in a placid nature:—there is the ostentatious moralising and sententious dictatorialism of Jaques,—engendered by disgust of the world, when the world's pleasures have been revelled in to satiety:—there is the simple common sense, plain sense, good sense, best sense of old Corin,—the fruit of a pure life of daily toil in the eye of Nature, and her clear, self-evident lessons:—there is the reliant philosophy of old Adam,—produced by duty, fidelity, and honest worth:—and there is Touchstone's philosophy,—a choice and rich amalgam of sweet temper and untiring humour.

"As You Like It" has been denominated a "Pastoral Drama." I have no objection to the term, and have no inclination to discuss the principles of the pastoral:—in this instance, suffice to me to arrive at the conclusion, that no composition of the same class will bear comparison with it, for the combination of exquisite poetry,—both descriptive and moral, fanciful, playful, and passionate; for variety and amiability of character; for gravity, wit, and broad humour. It is altogether so perfect a piece of homage to the happy state of a rural, unartificial life, that every scene in it, untainted with bad passions, occurs amid the pomp and garniture of God's creation—the green fields and the forest glades. Well is it said by Coleridge, "In Nature there is nothing melancholy:" so also in this great composition, the only evil of man's contrivance is perpetrated under his own artificial roof:—the usurping Duke and the unnatural brother vent their evil machinations within their own walls. And, (to echo the poet Campbell's cordial remark upon the play,) "even these culpable, but at last repentant beings, we easily forgive, by reason of our hearts being so stricken with the other benevolent beings in the comedy."

# III.

# Hamlet.

# III.

# HAMLET.

---

HAMLET is the prince of *poetical* philosophers. To philosophise is the habit of his mind. To reflect and reason upon every thing and every person that comes within his sphere,—to ponder upon every event that occurs,—to consider and reconsider each circumstance that arises,—is with him a part of his nature. He can no more help philosophising than he can help breathing; it is his mental atmosphere, as the air is his vital one. He philosophises upon his mother; upon his mistress; upon his friend; upon the king; upon the old courtier, Polonius; upon the water-fly, Osric; upon "the sponge," Rosencrantz; and upon the spy, Guildenstern. He even philosophises upon himself, and upon himself most of all. Yet, with all this, as the poet has managed it, there is nothing dictatorial or dogmatical in Hamlet; for Hamlet is a gentleman—a more accomplished, a more courteous gentleman than he, is not to be found in all Shakespeare, (and, I was going to say,) or anywhere else. Hamlet is not either dry or prolix. He is not didactic; for his reflections are rather for his own behoof than delivered as precepts for others. He is not sententious; for his words flow on in the shape of reverie and musing rather than in that of terse, brief phrases, uttered for effect. His moral philosophy is not studied; it has no rule, no set or specific rule, but is a rich emanation of his own spiritual being—flowing from his profound heart, his noble mind, his fertile imagination, his great and lofty soul. He moralises almost unconsciously; so naturally, so spontaneously do his ideas take that form.

How artistically has Shakespeare made Hamlet fall into that habitual mode of parlance, even in the very hour of awaiting the dread apparition on the platform at midnight. On his first coming in,—when we may imagine that they have all dropped into silence, as they approach the haunted spot,—Hamlet complains of the chill night breeze:—

"The air bites shrewdly; it is very cold."

But no sooner has the cannon sounded which announces the royal carousal, and the voice of his friend Horatio is heard, asking whether this be a custom, than the Prince answers in the philosophic strain natural to him:—

"Ay, marry is it:
But to my mind,—though I am native here,
And to the manner born,—it is a 'custom'
More honour'd in the breach than the observance.
This heavy-headed revel, east and west,
Makes us traduced, and tax'd of other nations:
They clepe us drunkards, and with swinish phrase
Soil our addition; and indeed it takes
From our achievements, though perform'd at height,
The pith and marrow of our attribute.
So, oft it chances in particular men,
That for some vicious mole of nature in them,
As in their birth, (wherein they are not guilty,
Since nature cannot choose his origin,)
By the overgrowth of some complexion,
Oft breaking down the pales and forts of reason;
Or by some habit, that too much o'er-leavens
The form of plausive manners;—that these men,—

Carrying, I say, the stamp of one defect,
Being nature's livery, or fortune's star,—
Their virtues else (be they as pure as grace,
As infinite as man may undergo,)
Shall in the general censure take corruption
From that particular fault:—The dram of base
Doth all the noble sustance often d'out,
To his own scandal. [*Enter Ghost.*]
"*Hor.* Look, my lord,—it comes!
"*Ham.* Angels and ministers of grace defend us!"

This is wonderfully striking; and as characteristic as it is striking. No one like Shakespeare for consistency in character, and for making that consistency a heightener of his dramatic and poetical effects, as well as of his portraiture-effects. Monsieur Guizot, in his clever book upon our great English poet,—"Shakespeare and his Times,"—declares "unity of impression" to be the great law of Shakespeare's dramatic art; and the marvellous harmony and consistency in his characters forms one portion of this "unity of impression."

Hamlet's proneness to soliloquy bespeaks the reflective man; and it not only serves to denote his philosophic mood, but it paints the perturbed condition of his spirit under the onerous task of revenge, imposed upon him by fate. Inexpressibly affecting is that eagerness he betrays to get by himself,—to feel free and unwatched,—that he may revolve the thoughts of his burthened heart at liberty. We feel the load taken from him in those words of his, "*Now I am alone,*" when Polonius, the players, and the two sycophant lords, Rosencrantz and Guildenstern, leave him. And also, afterwards, on the journey, when he bids the two latter prying personages "Go on before," that he may indulge his reverie upon meeting with the captain of Fortinbras's forces. The vast responsibility laid by the Ghost upon him constantly rises upon his tide of thought, haunting, and urging him to his settled course of action. When all the company have gone on,—soldiers and courtiers,—he breaks forth :—

> " How all occasions do inform against me,
> And spur my dull revenge! What is a man,
> If his chief good, and market of his time,
> Be but to sleep, and feed? a beast, no more.
> Sure, HE that made us with such large discourse,
> Looking before and after, gave us not
> That capability and god-like reason
> To fust in us unus'd. Now, whether it be
> Bestial oblivion, or some craven scruple
> Of thinking too precisely on th' event,—
> A thought, which, quarter'd, hath but one part wisdom,
> And ever three parts coward,—I do not know
> Why yet I live to say, '*This thing's to do;*'
> Sith I have cause, and will, and strength, and means,
> To do it." * * * * *

And he concludes his twentieth vacillation with this resolve :—

> " Oh! from this time forth,
> My thoughts be bloody, or be nothing worth!"

Hamlet's philosophy not unfrequently takes the form of bitter jests, while foiling the eaves-dropping treachery of those two hireling courtiers. He contemptuously dallies with their curiosity, and plays with their puzzled perceptions. He even strikes off into a wild levity and startling humour at times; and this eccentricity of demeanour, it is unnecessary to observe, was prepared and adopted by him to carry out his plan of subterfuge-action in assuming the character of insanity. For instance, where he replies to the King's inquiries after the dead body of Polonius, with those scoffing answers :—

" *King.* Where is Polonius?

" *Ham.* In heaven: send thither to see. If your messenger find him not there, seek him in th' other place yourself. But, indeed, if you find him not within this month, you shall nose him as you go up stairs into the lobby.

"*King.* [*To some attendants.*] Go, seek him there.

"*Ham.* [*Calling after them.*] He will stay till you come."

This dash of the grotesque, in his occasional words, enhances the effect of the profound and settled sadness dwelling within Hamlet's soul; just as the circumstance of the skull, which the grave-digger throws up at Hamlet's feet, being that of a jester, augments the solemnity of the event. Its being the skeleton head of that soul of whim and mad waggery, upon whose shoulder the boy Hamlet had ridden a thousand times, gives additional awe to the sympathetic shudder with which we behold him handle and moralise upon it. In the same manner, the boorish jokes of the two grave-digging clowns increase the grim melancholy of the church-yard scene.

I will say a few words upon the feigned madness of Hamlet, and, as succinctly as I am able, justify my argument by authorities from his own speech and action.

The readers of this most mysterious of all the characters in Shakespeare are divided into those who believe in his real insanity, occasioned by that awful accumulation of circumstances,—the revealing of his father's spirit; the promulgation of his murder; and the tremendous responsibility arising out of it, to avenge his violent and unnatural death:—while the other party hold the opinion that the poet intended to convey nothing more than the assumed madness of the prince, for the purpose of shrouding his course of retribution.

That this latter is the true reading of the character, the following passages appear to be confirmatory.

In the 1st Act, after the scene with the Ghost, he prepares Horatio and Marcellus for the part he is about to act:—

> "As I perchance hereafter shall *think meet*
> *To put an antic disposition on.*"

Afterwards, in the scene with his mother, (*Act* iii., *sc.* 4,) when he has again seen his father's ghost, she calling his behaviour upon the occasion, "ecstacy, the coinage of his brain," he replies:—

> "Ecstacy!
> My pulse, as yours, doth temperately keep time,
> And makes as healthful music: it is not madness
> That I have utter'd: bring me to the test,
> And I the matter will re-word; which madness
> Would gambol from."

And at the close of the same scene, he counsels his mother not to allow the king to worm from her his secret:—

> "Let him not
> Make you to ravel all this matter out,
> That I essentially am not in madness,
> But mad in craft."

But the strongest proof of all that his insanity is assumed is, that in his *soliloquies* he never utters an incoherent phrase. When he is alone, he reasons clearly and consistently;—it may be inconclusively, because he seeks in sophism an excuse for deferring the task of revenge imposed upon him;—but it is always coherently. At the close of the celebrated soliloquy,—"To be, or not to be,"—than which nothing more grandly reflective and heart-absorbing was ever penned by poet, he is surprised at finding that he has been overheard in his rationality by Ophelia, who is at the back of the scene; and he then immediately begins to wander, in order that he may maintain his scheme of delusion; his language to her being the naturally conceived expression of an over-heated and excited brain, and not the disjointed incoherency of the incurable maniac.

Especially fine, too, is he in that soliloquy of the 4th scene, Act iv., after meeting with the forces of Fortinbras; and which speech Schlegel justly describes as being the key to the character of the prince. Hamlet says, sedately reflecting:—

> "Rightly to be great,
> Is *not* to stir without great argument,
> But greatly to find quarrel in a straw,
> When honour's at the stake. How stand I then,
> That have a father kill'd, a mother stain'd,
> Excitements of my reason and my blood,
> And let all sleep? While, to my shame, I see
> The imminent death of twenty thousand men,
> That for a fantasy and trick of fame,
> Go to their graves like beds."

This greatly reasoning scene is never represented on the stage;—and, by the way, it has not unfrequently been the practice to argue on a question in Shakespeare's plays, from what is known of them through the actors; yet the theatrical copies are so notoriously abridged, that it is impossible to judge fairly of the poet's delineation of character, who never wrote a line that did not harmonise with, and tend to define the portrait he was limning.

In the scenes, too, with his heart-friend, Horatio, Hamlet is uniformly rational:—with one exception only; and that is immediately after the play-scene, and the discovery of the king's appalled conscience, when the wild words he utters may be fairly imputed to the result of his excitement, consequent upon the confirmation of the Ghost's murder-tale.

With the players, too, and the grave-digger, where it is unnecessary to maintain the consistency of the part he had assumed, he is perfectly collected, and even utters sound criticism and profound philosophy. His apology to Laertes, wherein he decidedly imputes his former misconduct to mental aberration, is the nearest approach to a confirmation of the idea that he has been really insane: but this scene takes place in the presence of the whole court, whom he has all along intended to deceive,—his revenge, moreover, being still left unaccomplished. I therefore conclude, and I think reasonably, that they have read the whole play with very little reflection who conceive that Shakespeare intended to portray real, and not feigned madness in the conduct of Hamlet.

I should suppose that there never was a more artistical piece of dramatic event achieved (at all events, my own reading cannot quote its rival) than the arrangement of the machinery in the first scene of this play, for the introduction of the Ghost. How gradual, how solemn, and withal how serene, are its approaches;—the opening eyelids of the dawn not more impressive. We first behold the soldier, Francisco, on his watch. The stillness of the scene is broken by the password of his comrade, Bernardo, who comes to relieve guard, and take Francisco's post. His natural question to his predecessor,—"Have you had quiet guard?" for Bernardo knows of the spirit's appearance, and wishes to discover whether Francisco have seen it also. To him, however, "not a mouse has been stirring." And here I would draw attention to one of the most signal examples of the far-sightedness and comprehension of his subject on the part of the poet, which occurs in the first two sentences of this play; the purport of which is so subtle, that it must escape the casual and light reader. Francisco is the guard on duty; and Bernardo, coming in to relieve him, calls out, "Who's there?"—which challenge the other naturally retorts, with, "*Nay, answer me;* stand, and unfold yourself." Bernardo being full of the apparition that he and Marcellus had witnessed the night before, in his perturbation questions everything he encounters in the night gloom. And when he is about to be *left alone* on the platform,—midnight close at hand,—the awful point of time for the visitation, he anxiously commissions Francisco, "If you do meet Horatio and Marcellus, the rivals of my watch, *bid them make haste.*"* Immediately upon this, the two in question enter: Horatio having come to prove the truth of what had been reported to him by the other two,—he doubting the fact. Marcellus, who had been a witness of the apparition, calls it, "This dreaded sight twice seen of us." Now, all this appears to me the perfection of forethought, with contrivance. Horatio, still doubtful, says: "Tush, tush, 'twill not appear." Then Bernardo adds circumstance to the testimony of his companion:—

"Last night of all,
When yond' same star that's westward from the pole,
Had made his course t' illume that part of heav'n
Where now it burns; Marcellus and myself,
The bell then beating one,—
"Peace! break thee off," exclaims Marcellus, "look where it comes again."

How thrillingly grand is all this! and how natural! Still, the dignity of the event is to be sustained; and Horatio being the "scholar," also the bosom-friend of Hamlet, is urged to address the spirit:—and here again, it is noticeable, that though all three are officers and gentlemen, yet the language of Horatio is cast in a more classical mould than that of the others, and this unvaryingly so throughout. How solemn and how deprecatory is his abjuration!—

"What art thou, that usurp'st this time of night,
Together with that fair and warlike form,
In which the majesty of buried Denmark
Did sometimes march?—By heaven I charge thee, speak!"

The spirit stalks away, deigning no reply; the consummation of its errand is yet to be fulfilled: it is yet to speak; and

* This lecture was written some years before a zealous and clever article appeared in the *Quarterly Review*, upon "Hamlet,"—in which this prevision of his plan by the poet was noticed.

to no ears but those of Hamlet. Marcellus now exclaims to his doubting comrade :—

"How now, Horatio! you tremble, and look pale.
Is not this something more than fantasy?
What think you on't?
"*Hor.* Before my God, I might not this believe,
Without the sensible and true avouch
Of mine own eyes."

In the midst of a conversation of conjecture and surmise that ensues upon this event, Horatio again brings forward his classical accomplishments; and, what is remarkable, Shakespeare has put into his mouth a complete anticipation of the Newtonian theory of the tides. All this bye-play is to add dignity to Horatio, the friend and companion of the hero. After speaking of the prodigies that are said to have appeared in Rome previously to the assassination of the "mightiest Julius;"—

"The graves stood tenantless, and the sheeted dead
Did squeak and gibber in the Roman streets;"—

he concludes :—

"And the moist star [the moon]
Upon whose *influence* Neptune's empire stands,
Was sick almost to dooms-day with eclipse."

Then follows that sweetly solemn winding up of the scene, after the second vanishing, at the crowing of the cock, with the remembrance of that pious superstition as recorded by Marcellus;—and what an exquisitely poetical term to use!

"It *faded* at the crowing of the cock."

Let any one try to find a more apt phrase than that to describe the dissolving of a shade into the elements, and he will be lucky if he succeed. Macbeth presents an even more vivid picture to the imagination upon the vanishing of the witches:—"What seem'd corporal," he says, "melted as breath into the wind."

Marcellus then concludes:—

> "Some say, that ever 'gainst that season comes
> Wherein our Saviour's birth is celebrated,
> This bird of dawning singeth all night long:
> And then, they say, no spirit can walk abroad;
> The nights are wholesome; then no planets strike,
> No fairy takes, nor witch hath power to charm;
> So hallow'd and so gracious is the time."

Horatio, the scholar and the philosopher, consistently answers:—

> "So have I heard, and do *in part* believe it."

It will be recollected that he was sceptical as to the appearance of the ghost. Wonderfully artistical is that discrimination between the minds of Horatio and Marcellus. And then, lastly, what poetry in the breaking up of their conference!

> "But, look, the morn in russet mantle clad,
> Walks o'er the dew of yon high eastern hill.
> Break we our watch up."

In this introductory scene we are presented with all the chief characteristics of the sublime; and of which, not the least prevailing feature is the effect produced by the gigantic power of stillness. The quiet midnight; the cold and misty moon; the wondering under-breath discourse of those who had assembled to witness that tremendous vision. The awful and unsubstantial form itself, in silent and majestic sorrow passing among, and about them, and yet not with them; present, and yet absent; cognisable, identical, and yet intangible. This all-absorbing, this mighty abstraction, congealed, as it were, into a stern reality, in dumb eloquence and thrilling stillness announces to us the coming events of a heart-shaking tragedy. Great is the majesty of "Silence," says Thomas Carlyle; and I know of nothing comparable in grandeur with the still and silent course of the first introduction of the Ghost in Hamlet.

At the subsequent appearance of that awful form, which occurs in the closet scene between the Prince and his mother, Shakespeare, so far from having committed an anti-climax, (which must have happened to an ordinary dramatist,) has even more deeply rooted our interest in the sorrows of the "perturbed spirit;" for, on his first coming, the motive for appearing to his son being to stir him to revenge, he would tardily and scantily have carried our sympathies with him; but his second appearance is blended with an emotion of tenderness towards her who had lain in his bosom in her days of innocence and happiness; in those days when—

> "She would hang on him,
> As if increase of appetite had grown
> By what it fed on:"

and who now was stricken to the heart with blood-guiltiness and remorse.

> "But look, amazement on thy mother sits:
> Oh! step between her and her fighting soul."

In the first scene with his son, when charging him to revenge the "foul and unnatural murder," he enjoins exception in behalf of his guilty queen:—

> "But, howsoever thou pursu'st this act,
> Taint not thy mind, *nor let thy soul contrive*
> *Against thy mother aught; leave her to Heaven,*
> And to those thorns that in her bosom lodge,
> To prick and sting her."

It was just like the divine humanity in our poet to foster

the idea of love in that life beyond life, still hovering with angelic tenderness and pardon over his weak and repentant partner in the flesh. And how beautifully this little touch of yearning emotion on the part of the spirit harmonises with the previous character given of him by his son :—

> "So loving to my mother,
> That he might not beteem the winds of heaven
> Visit her face too roughly."

It is the verifying these points of harmony and consistency in the creations of this wonderful genius, that makes the study of his productions a constant source of astonishment as well as delight.

Horatio is not merely the gentleman and scholar, as has been observed, and therefore worthy to be the companion of Hamlet; but the higher attractions of his honourable nature, his bland and trusting disposition, his prudent mind, and steadfastly affectionate heart, have raised him to the highest social rank that man can attain in this world—he is his prince's confidant and bosom-friend. The character of Horatio is the only spot of sun-light in the play; and he is a cheering, though not a joyous gleam coming across the dark hemisphere of treachery, mistrust, and unkindness. The cheerfulness of the grave-digger arises from an intimacy with, and a callous indifference to his occupation, which, as Horatio says,

> "Custom hath made in him a property of easiness."

It is the result, too, of a healthy old age; or, in some sort, it is not a sentiment, but a physical consequence; even a negation.

But in the deportment of Horatio we have the constant recognition of a placid and pensive man; making no protestations, yet constantly prepared for gentle service. Modest, and abiding his time to be appreciated, his friendship for Hamlet is a purely disinterested principle, and the Prince bears high testimony to it,—an illustrious and eloquent tribute to the qualities of his head and heart:—

> "Horatio, thou art e'en as just a man
> As e'er my conversation cop'd withal.
> "*Hor.* O! my dear lord!
> "*Ham.* Nay, do not think I flatter:
> For what advancement may I hope from thee,
> That no revénue hast, but thy good spirits,
> To feed and clothe thee? Why should the poor be flatter'd?
> No, let the candied tongue lick absurd pomp;
> And crook the pregnant hinges of the knee,
> Where thrift may follow fawning. Dost thou hear?
> Since my dear soul was mistress of her choice,
> And could of men distinguish, her election
> Hath seal'd thee for herself: for thou hast been
> As one, in suffering all, that suffers nothing;
> A man, that fortune's buffets and rewards
> Hast ta'en with equal thanks: and bless'd are those
> Whose blood and judgment are so well co-mingled,
> That they are not a pipe for fortune's finger
> To sound what stop she please. Give me that man
> That is not passion's slave, and I will wear him
> In my heart's core, ay, in my heart of heart,
> As I do thee."

And all this is no lip-deep attestation. Horatio has it, and has earned it. As he adhered to his friend through life, so would he have followed him in death; and only consented to survive him that he might redeem his character with the world. It is worthy of notice, that Horatio's speeches, after the first scene, consist almost entirely of simple assents to the observations of Hamlet; but when the final catastrophe has ensued, he comes forward, and assumes the prerogative of his position; and, as the companion and confidant of his Prince, he takes his station by Fortinbras, and the ambassadors, and at once assumes the office of moral executor and apologist for his friend. Was there no forethought,—no contrivance in all this subtle consecution of action? To me there is an indescribable charm in this Doric order of friendship and attachment, which Shakespeare has so frequently repeated in his plays:—simple, and unornate in exterior pretension; but massive and steadfast in design and structure.

With scarcely an exception, no one character in this tragedy has, I think, been worked out with more pains and accurate consistency, than that of the Lord Chamberlain, old Polonius. In his conduct and demeanour the critical task has been achieved of blending the highest useful wisdom (the knowledge of mankind) with the garrulity of an imbecile old age. Although Polonius, however, prates away at all times, and never omits an occasion to proffer his opinion, yet he does not babble; for no one dispenses sounder advice, or speaks more practical axioms. These, it is true, from his courtly education and gold-stick employment, he frequently converts into the "crooked wisdom" of cunning and manœuvre; for, so carefully is his conduct laid out by the poet, that every one of his plans has in it a double-move, as it were, (like a game of chess,) before he makes his hit. Polonius is a thorough-paced diplomatist, and seems to have (like the bulk of his tribe) a positive horror of simple and sincere action: as if stratagem and circumvention were the genius and staple of political commerce. His well-known advice to his son, Laertes, upon the young man's leave-taking for France, is as fine as an essay in Bacon:—it consists of a string of axioms that would make a perfect gentleman and man of business, whether civil or commercial:—

"Yet here, Laertes! aboard, aboard, for shame!
The wind sits in the shoulder of your sail,
And you are stay'd for. There,—my blessing with you!

And these few precepts in thy memory.
Look thou charácter. Give thy thoughts no tongue,
Nor any unproportion'd thought his act.
Be thou familiar, but by no means vulgar.
The friends thou hast, and their adoption tried,
Grapple them to thy soul with hooks of steel;
But do not dull thy palm with entertainment
Of each new-hatch'd, unfledg'd comrade. Beware
Of entrance to a quarrel; but, being in,
Bear 't, that th' opposéd may beware of thee.
Give every man thine ear, but few thy voice:
Take each man's measure, but reserve thy judgment.
Costly thy habit as thy purse can buy,
But not express'd in fancy; rich, not gaudy:
For the apparel oft proclaims the man;
And they in France, of the best rank and station,
Are most select and generous, chief in that.
Neither a borrower, nor a lender be:
For loan oft loses both itself and friend;
And borrowing dulls the edge of husbandry.
This above all,—to thine own self be true;
And it must follow, as the night the day,
Thou canst not then be false to any man.
Farewell: my blessing season this in thee."

Here we see the instinct and native disposition of the man; but when his object is to obtain an account of the mode of life his son is leading in Paris, he descends to subterfuge and manœuvre; even with their servant Rinaldo, who is about to join his young master; giving him licence to lie, and traduce the conduct of Laertes at home, in order that he may induce his French associates to betray any irregularities that he may have committed in their company. This scene is the first of the 2d Act; and a masterpiece of writing it is;—at that point of it especially where the old man hurries himself out of breath with explanation, and suddenly forgetting the thread of his instruction, exclaims:—"Where was I? Where was I?" It is like a dialogue taken in shorthand.

Again, in the scene with his daughter, (the conclusion of the one just quoted,) when she comes running in to inform him of Hamlet's altered behaviour, how characteristic is the self-rebuke of the practised courtier, in having desired her to decline the prince's advances, and refuse his letters; and with what close and practical experience he concludes his observation upon her report:—

"*That* hath made him mad.
I am sorry that with better heed and judgment
I had not quoted him; I fear'd he did but trifle,
And meant to wreck thee; but, beshrew my jealousy!
It seems as proper to our age
To cast beyond ourselves in our opinions,
As it is common for the younger sort
To lack discretion."

Here, we see, he regrets his over-caution; for, that he would have promoted (and rationally) a safe alliance for his daughter with the heir to the throne: yet afterwards, in conversation with the king and queen, he makes a merit of having confronted her, and solely on the ground of the disparity of their conditions:—

"Lord Hamlet is a prince, out of thy star;
This must not be: and then I precepts gave her,
That she should lock herself from his resort,
Admit no messengers, receive no tokens."

How accurately does all this shuffling and moral imbecility square with the temporising courtier! Yet again; his tendency to manœuvre and insincerity are noticeable in his making Ophelia act a part in the scene he had contrived for discovering whether the madness of Hamlet were confirmed or not:—

"Ophelia, walk you here, . . . .
. . . . . . . . . Read on this book;
That show of such an exercise may colour
Your loneliness."

And then the genuine nature of the honourable man stares out of the artificial man of society. He says to himself:—

> "We are oft to blame in this,—
> 'Tis too much prov'd,—that with devotion's visage,
> And pious action, we do sugar o'er
> The devil himself."

So thorough, so pliant, and hard-working a courtier is he, that he even offered to act the eaves-dropper to the king, that he may report to him the result of the interview between Hamlet and his mother—an act which brings upon him so terrible a retribution; but which, at the same time, preaches a caustic moral to all disreputable, uncompromising time-servers: the moral being the more stringent in his case, because, by nature, Polonius possessed an instinct of honour and self-respect, which a course of unworthy pliancy and intrigue (perhaps almost inseparable from his office) had soiled and tainted.

In introducing the character of the ill-starred and forlorn Ophelia, I will, previously, take occasion to offer a remark or two upon that part of the celebrated dissertation on Hamlet, by Goethe, in his "Wilhelm Meister," which bears upon one phase in her conduct.

The eminent German critic starts with the position that Ophelia possessed a temperament which would lead her to become an easy prey wherever her fancy had been attracted; and, having taken that point, he draws his conclusions from the warnings given to her by both father and brother, to be upon her guard in admitting the addresses of the Lord Hamlet; and he crowns his inferences by quoting the snatches of songs she sings during her madness, as the foregone conclusions of a mind (to use the mildest term) not tempered with the chariest discretion, or habituated to the most delicate associations.

Now, all this appears to me the question-begging of one who would merge all love into the *sensual*, at the expense of the *ideal*—a conclusion totally unwarrantable in the case of Ophelia; for the only confession we have of her love for Hamlet is wholly comprised in the absorbing adoration of his intellectual endowments—a higher order of love than Goethe seems to think her capable of even discovering. With a passionately chaste lament, she says:—

"Oh! what a noble mind is here o'erthrown!
The courtier's, soldier's, scholar's eye, tongue, sword;
The expectancy and rose of the fair state,
The glass of fashion, and the mould of form,
The observ'd of all observers, quite, quite down!
And I, of ladies most deject and wretched,
That suck'd the honey of his music vows,
Now see that noble and most sov'reign reason,
Like sweet bells jangled, out of tune and harsh."

This is not the language of a gross or even a light-minded female, which Goethe, with all his wariness, and ingenuity of expression, would have his readers think Ophelia to be. Nor would Shakespeare have given to her a complaint of such character and tone, had she been deceived, and then deserted by Hamlet. Moreover, we may be sure that she was not—in any form—a victim to her wantonness, or his infidelity; for, after her death, in an ecstacy of genuine passion, he says:—"I loved her above forty thousand brothers!" And he would not have used that language had his intercourse with her been a merely *illicit* one.

As to that branch of the critic's argument, drawn from the warning of Ophelia's father and brother, it is unnecessary to remind any adult that such a precaution is perfectly consistent with the most spotless purity of heart, where that heart is wholly occupied and absorbed by the one sentiment and passion of love and admiration: the father and brother both recognising the irresponsible position of the prince ; and this, joined with their fears and jealousy lest she bewray the family honour ; while that is a natural precaution on their part, (both being men of the world, and the artificial world of a court—and such a court as that of Claudius the murderer and adulterer ;) whatever the precaution (I say) on their part, it by no means involves, or even implies, a laxity on hers.

With regard to the critic's inuendo (and this is the least reputable of his insinuations) respecting her real character, drawn from the songs she sings during her insanity ; Goethe, as a psychologist, ought to have known that no such conclusion can be drawn from the actions of a person under that suspension :—on the contrary, it is an argument of her native *innocence* of *character;* and Shakespeare knew this two hundred years before Goethe lived ; experience constantly reminding us that insane people are wont to be, for the time, the total opposites of their real natures—your madmen plotting to kill those whom they most loved when in a state of sanity ; your profligates breaking forth into piety ; your pious into blasphemies ; and your most reserved and chaste indulging in a laxity of expression astonishing to those who knew their former course of life and principles. And, after all, these same snatches of songs, alluded to by Goethe, and which, by the way, consist of two, and not much in those, they display the constant thought and contrivance of the poet to carry on *within* as well as *without* the scene a continuity and consistency of thought, as well as of action in the character. Upon referring again to the passage for my present purpose, I can come to no other conclusion than that he intended to convey in those wanderings of Ophelia the reflected lights of *past* reflections in her sane moments, resulting from the warning and advice that had been given to her in admitting the advances and protestations of her royal lover ; but that they were intended to be the foregone conclusions of an unstable virtue, could only proceed, I think, from a prurient mind, apt for catching at such a suggestion.

I regret, though I confess I am not surprised at the tone of this commentary in the eminent critic, since I have never been able entirely to shake off the idea that Goethe himself was not wholly untainted with the leaven of grossness; and therefore was the more apt at imputation. The celebrated Bettina, in one of her letters to him, makes the remark, that she wonders from what class in society he chose his heroines, they are such questionable people. I am sure that in the self-absorption of the homage toll-fee Goethe's appetite was grossness itself.

In how much finer a spirit has Doctor Bucknill, in his admirable work on the "Psychology of Shakespeare," appreciated the character of Ophelia. Doctor Bucknill is the superintendent of a lunatic asylum, and therefore speaks with authority. He says, "The not very delicate warning of Ophelia's disagreeable brother, that she is likely to lose her honour to Hamlet's unmastered importunity, is evidently distasteful to the poor girl, and gives occasion to the only sparkle of displeasure which the gentle creature ever shows, in that quick-witted retaliation of advice:—

'But, my good brother,  
Do not, as some ungracious pastors do,  
Show me the steep and thorny way to heaven;  
Whilst, like a puff'd and reckless libertine,  
Himself the primrose path of dalliance treads,  
And recks not his own read.'"

Ophelia's reference to the primrose path of dalliance which her libertine brother was likely to tread, *shows, from the first, that her purity of mind is not the result of ignorance.* Her belief in the honour and truth of her lover, Bucknill adds, is the "*credulity of innocence*, but not of *stupidity*." Old Dan Chaucer says of the Duchess Blanche of Lancaster,

"I say not she knew no *evil,*
Then had she known no *good,*
So seemeth me."

Rosencrantz and Guildenstern are favourable samples of the thorough-paced, time-serving court knave—servants of all-work, ticketed, and to be hired for any hard or dirty job. Shakespeare has at once, and unequivocally, signified his opinion of the race, by making Rosencrantz, the time-server, the schoolfellow of Hamlet, and, under the colour of their early associations, professing a personal friendship—even an affection for him, at the very time that he had accepted the office of spy upon his actions, and traitor to his confidence. "Good, my lord, what is your cause of distemper? You do surely but bar the door upon your own liberty, if you deny your griefs to your friend." Immediately upon the heel of this protestation he accepts the king's commission to convey his "friend" to England, where measures had been taken for his assassination. Rosencrantz and his fellow would designate themselves as thoroughly "*loyal* men;" they make no compromise of their calling; the "broad R" is burnt into them; they are for the king's service exclusively; and with the scavenger's calling, they would scoop all into that reservoir. The poet has sketched them in few and bold outlines; their subtleties of character stare out like the bones of a starved beast. They are time-servers by profession, and upon hire; and "verily they have their reward." The great Hebrew legislator has said, "Thou shalt not muzzle the ox that treadeth out the corn;" but the corn that such oxen tread out no noble beast would consider worthy of "protective duty" at all. No one works so hard as a time-server; and, under the fairest auspices, his labour is well worthy of his pay. The machinery he constructs to accomplish his little ends, is always complicated and eccentric in movement—like the Laputan's invention for cutting a cabbage, requiring a horse-power to put it in action; or like the painstaking of Bardolph, who stole the lute-case, carried it seven leagues, and sold it for three-halfpence. The same great master-spirit —Shakespeare—has made another time-server say, "How wretched is that poor man that hangs on princes' favours!" but how much more wretched is that poor prince who needs such hangers-on as Guildenstern and Rosencrantz! What a hell on earth has the man who is the suborner of meanness and villany!—the constant sense of subjection—the instinctive sense of insincerity and sham respect—the rising of the gorge at the fawning and the mouth-honour, the self-inspection, (which will come,) the surmises, the fears, the trepidations, the heartaches: "Verily, both parties have their reward," even here, "on this bank and shoal of time." I know of no bitterer satire upon the compact between state hire and state service than is put into the mouth of this Rosencrantz, addressed to such a king as Hamlet's uncle!—

"The single and peculiar life is bound,
With all the strength and armour of the mind,
To keep itself from 'noyance; but much more
That spirit, upon whose weal depend and rest
The lives of many. The cease of majesty
Dies not alone; but like a gulph doth draw
What's near it with it; it is a massy wheel,
Fix'd on the summit of the highest mount,
To whose huge spokes ten thousand lesser things
Are mortis'd and adjoin'd, which when it falls,
Each small annexment, petty consequence,
Attends the boist'rous ruin. Never alone
Did the king sigh, but with a general groan."

This is a specimen of time-server logic for an act of state-policy: it is the argument of a hireling to sugar over the king's act to murder Hamlet, in order that the peace and safety of the suborner may be secured. Assuredly, no one has been less of a flatterer, with stronger inducements to be one, than Shakespeare. In the spirit of just retribution, these two worthies fall into the trap they had set for their old friend and schoolfellow.

On another occasion I have spoken of Shakespeare's large discourse upon the "Philosophy of War," and its utter worthlessness. In the short scene between Hamlet and the captain of Fortinbras,—and which, as already observed, is never acted,—we have the poet again upon the same theme, but in a calm and lofty vein of satire, exposing the contemptible grounds upon which these vicegerents on earth will play their bloody gambols at the expense of the life and treasure of those uninterested in the game. Shakespeare was our first poet who saw and exposed its absurdity; and Cowper was the last, who followed it out with a dash of radicalism in the sentiment:—"But war is a game, which, were their subjects wise, kings would not play at."

The dialogue I have alluded to is an edifying commentary upon the light causes and grave effects of strife and contention. Hamlet says to the captain:—

"Good sir, whose powers are these?
"*Capt.* They are of Norway, sir.
"*Ham.* How purposed, sir, I pray you?
"*Capt.* Against some part of Poland.
"*Ham.* Goes it against the main of Poland, sir, or for some frontier?
"*Capt.* Truly to speak, and with no addition,
We go to gain a little patch of ground,
That hath in it no profit but the name.
To pay five ducats, five, I would not farm it;
Nor will it yield to Norway, or the Pole,
A ranker rate, should it be sold in fee.
"*Ham.* Why, then, the Polack never will defend it.
"*Capt.* Yes, 'tis already garrison'd.
"*Ham.* Two thousand souls, and twenty thousand ducats,
Will not debate the question of this straw;

This is th' imposthume of much wealth and peace,
That inward breaks, and shows no cause without
Why the man dies."

How searching that philosophy! and what truth and felicity in the metaphor, with its application! Hamlet, afterwards, when ruminating upon this circumstance in connexion with his own irresolute action, says, (as already quoted,)—

"To my shame, I see
The imminent death of twenty thousand men,
That for a fantasy and trick of fame,
Go to their graves like beds; fight for a plot
Whereon the numbers cannot try the cause,
Which is not tomb enough, and continent,
To hide the slain."

I have always been struck with the dialogue between Hamlet and Osric, the "gilded water-fly," as he terms him, who comes to announce to the Prince the wager at fence with Laertes. Who that has ever observed the action of that peculiar insect,—skimming to and fro, and round and round upon the water's face, with no apparent purpose but mere inconsequence,—can fail to recognise the aptitude of that assimilation?—the "*gilded* water-fly" too!

The choice language and peculiar idiom of the dandy lord, with the superior bearing and regal dignity of the Prince, not carrying with it the slightest tinge of insolence or "pride of place"—(I repeat, there is no perfecter gentleman drawn than Hamlet)—his fooling Osric to the "top of his bent," is in the pure spirit of the highest-bred gentility:—

"Your bonnet, sir, to his right use; 'tis for the head.
"*Osr.* I thank your lordship; 'tis very hot.
"*Ham.* No, believe me, 'tis very cold; the wind is northerly.
"*Osr.* It is indifferent cold, my lord, indeed.
"*Ham.* But yet, methinks, it is very sultry and hot; or my complexion—

"*Osr.* Exceedingly, my lord; it is very sultry,—as 'twere, —I cannot tell how."

With all his vapid pliancy, however, when Osric comes to speak upon the accomplishments which alone, in those days, betokened the gentleman, Shakespeare knew that he must no longer make him contemptible: in descanting, therefore, upon Laertes' pretensions, he is made to use the choicest terms, describing him as an "absolute gentleman, full of most excellent differences, of very soft society, and great showing." And he dilates upon the weapons that are to be used with an accurate and professor-like technicality, and in language as polished as their blades: "Six French rapiers and poniards, with their assigns, hangers, and so. Three of the carriages, in faith, are very dear to fancy, very responsive to the hilts, most delicate carriages, and of very liberal conceit." Upon referring to this scene, it will be observed, I think, that Shakespeare, in Hamlet's mouth, intended to ridicule the dandy nomenclature of the day; for, with an amusing air of simplicity, he takes the tone of a stranger to the mysteries of the profession of arms, requiring an explanation of the terms so fluently used by Osric. It may appear affected to attach importance to a scene like this—trifling, indeed, as compared with the solemn and gigantic events that have transpired in the course of the drama; yet this simple and very natural prelude to the quenching of the noble spirit of the hero, produces, in my mind, a sense of reality and of pathos that are more easily suggested than explained, and suffers no detraction; if, indeed, it be not heightened by the gentle and modest tone in which the Prince dismisses the messenger:—

"Sir, I will walk here in the hall: if it please his majesty, it is the breathing time of day with me: let the foils be brought, the gentleman willing, and the king hold his purpose, I will win for him if I can; if not, I will gain nothing but my shame, and the odd hits."

Amid the glittering firmament of beauties with which this amazing drama is studded, it is no questionable homage to turn aside and examine with interest so insignificant a character as that of Osric; and, moreover, for the mind to come to the satisfactory conclusion that even the great master-movers in the scene are not more ably conceived, or produced with greater force or truth to nature.

It is immediately after his accepting the challenge that the "coming event" of his death, "casting its shadow" across the mind of Hamlet, draws from him that affecting confession to his bosom friend, Horatio; and which, as associated with all the circumstances of his unhappy mission, together with the deep and solemn piety of his comment, I confess, I never even recur to without an indescribable emotion of awe and reverence. He says:—

"Thou wouldst not think how ill all's here about my heart;—but 'tis no matter.

"*Hor.* Nay, my good lord,—

"*Ham.* It is but foolery; but it is such a kind of gain-giving as would, perhaps, trouble a woman.

"*Hor.* If your mind dislike anything, obey it:—I will forestall their repair hither, and say you are not fit.

"*Ham.* Not a whit;—we defy augury: there is a special providence in the fall of a sparrow. If it be now, 'tis not to come; if it be not to come, it will be now; if it be not now, yet it will come:—*the readiness is all.*"

Ah! when the ignorant or the thoughtless, or, the worse than both, the hypocritical, talk of Shakespeare's immorality, refer them to this simple and beautiful little homily upon resignation and reliance.

Laertes is one of that large class in humanity of the level standard in morals,—loud, turbulent, and boisterous in profession; yet so weak in judgment, and unjust in act, (and injustice must always involve a perversion of intellect,) that, for the purposes of revenge, he will become the principal in a plot to commit treachery and murder :—at the same time, in strict accordance with such a disposition and temperament, he is remorse-stricken at the issue of his villany. This is human nature in fac-simile. It was a touch of fine art in the poet to place the character and deportment of Laertes in contrast with that of his victim, at the immediate point of time when he was about to put his plot in action.

The apology Hamlet makes for his previous excitement towards the brother of Ophelia, at her grave, is conceived in the very highest sense of magnanimity and gentle bearing ;—"gentle" in every sense ;—a perfect gentleman. In concluding his speech, he says :—

> "Sir, in this audience,
> Let my disclaiming from a purpos'd evil
> Free me so far in your most generous thoughts,
> That I have shot mine arrow o'er the house,
> And hurt my brother."

While we are upon the subject of "contrasts," how fruitful a theme for reflection is the whole of the grave-digging scene: how full of character; full of unexpected thought; and how free from effort and display of every kind,—in short—for the thousandth time—"*how natural!*" The thoughtless gaiety of the sexton, singing over his work; "Custom having made it in him a property of easiness," as Horatio says; and, as Hamlet beautifully follows up the explanation, "The hand of little employment hath the daintier sense:"—a philosophical apology for those unimaginative classes in society whose sole occupation is connected with the *last* offices of life, and the *first* of death. Indeed, our beloved Shakespeare had a considerate and a gentle heart.

Again,—"in contrast,"—the recognition of Yorick's skull, and the two men's characteristic associations with the same individual;—the clown remembering him for a "pestilent mad rogue, who had poured a flagon of Rhenish on his head;"—the practical jokes only of the jester remained in the sexton's memory. Hamlet recalls his social and intellectual qualities; an epitaph to his fame, and a lecture upon vanity that will be coeval with poetry itself:—

"Alas, poor Yorick! I knew him, Horatio: a fellow of infinite jest, of most excellent fancy: he hath borne me on his back a thousand times; and now, how abhorred in my imagination it is!—my gorge rises at it. Here hung those lips that I have kissed I know not how oft. Where be your gibes now? your gambols? your songs? your flashes of merriment, that were wont to set the table in a roar?—Not one now to mock at your grinning? quite chapfallen?—Now get you to my lady's chamber; and tell her, let her paint an inch thick, to this favour she *must* come:—make her laugh at that."

The rise, progress, and consummation of the whole plot of the tragedy of Hamlet is a consistent theme upon the conflict between determination and irresolution, arising from over-reflection; and in nothing throughout the whole scheme of the play is the art of the poet more grandly developed than in making the vaccillation of the hero to turn solely upon that over-reflectiveness of his nature; and indeed, under the circumstances, it was Shakespeare's only resource. Had Hamlet wavered from any other cause, we must have dismissed him with disrespect; as it is, we make the handsomest excuse for him; and, in short, elevate him in our esteem by the acknowledgment that he was the most unfit instrument for the mission imposed upon him, simply because he had a mind superior to the carrying of it out in detail.

And, to conclude so pigmy a comment, as the one now presented upon this giant of philosophical dramas; rise from it when we may, and as often as we may, our hearts are warmed by wiser and holier thoughts; and our sole comment upon the creative mind that was permitted to give such a work to his fellow-mortals may well be summed up in the words of his own hero:—

"How noble in reason! how infinite in faculties! in action how like an angel! in apprehension how like a God!"

IV.

# Midsummer Night's Dream.

# IV.

# MIDSUMMER NIGHT'S DREAM.

---

THE play of a Midsummer Night's Dream is plausibly conjectured to have been composed when Shakespeare was in his thirtieth year; that lusty season of life when the luscious honey-dew of youth has not yet dried up or evaporated, and when the sinews of genius have consolidated into the firm maturity of luxuriantly developed manhood.

This, and the play of the "Tempest," are the only ones in which the poet has availed himself of, and rendered important for the purpose of his plot, the agency of the fairy world; and although in no one of his dramas are there to be found more exquisite flights of fancy than in the "Midsummer Night's Dream," yet, as a compounded whole, the most ordinary judge would be able to recognise in it less of the developed experience and tact in dramatic arrangement than in that superb composition and uninterruptedly perfect plot of the "Tempest." There, the several classes of character keep their appointed state, and become more or less prominent according to their several grades. The important beings—I mean those on whom the onward march of the story depends—never decline into secondary consequence in the reader's imagination. From the storm and shipwreck, in the first scene, raised by Prospero, to the dissolving of the mighty pageant by the same magician-power, when his plans are fulfilled, in the last scene, the consummation of events is in undeviating progress. A less complicated, and more interesting story, with more varied forms of fanciful creation, has rarely, if ever, been combined than in the "Tempest."

In the play now under consideration, the "subordinate" agents pre-occupy the mind, by reason of their great potency and surpassingly beautiful creation; or by the engrossing demand that others make on our attention, on account of their fine dramatic nature and verisimilitude, with side-shaking broad humour. Really and truly, Demetrius and Lysander, Hermia and Helena, with their love-crosses and perplexities, constitute the chief agents in the drama. Their way of life is the "plot"—disturbed, it is true, by the madcap sprite Puck, whose mischievous agency is so admirably employed to distort the course of their true love; and, with a two-handed scheme to befool poor little Titania, becomes not only the important movement in the machinery, but, in fact, we scarcely think of any other in conjunction with him; he and his fellow-minims of the moon's watery beams are the great (though little) people of the drama. Bottom and his companions are the cap and bells; and the classic stateliness of Theseus and Hypolita, with their sedate and lofty nuptialities, form—as Schlegel happily observes—"a splendid frame to the picture." These take no part in the action, but appear with stately pomp, and dwell apart in royal exclusiveness. Their discourse upon the pleasures of the chase, with his descriptions of his hounds, is the best, and, indeed, almost the only passage that presents itself to the memory when we think of the characters themselves. The whole of that scene is redolent of rural life; like Esau's garment, "it smelleth as of a field." It has all the bracing vigour and life of the young day, when, as old Chaucer says,

> "The sun looks ruddy and brode,
> Through the misty vapour of the morrowning;
> And the dew, as silver, shining
> Upon the green and soté grass."

> "My hounds (says Theseus) are bred out of the Spartan kind;
> So flew'd, so sanded, and their heads are hung
> With ears that sweep away the morning dew;
> Crook-knee'd, and dew-lapp'd like Thessalian bulls;
> Slow in pursuit, but match'd in mouth like bells,
> Each under each. A cry more tuneable
> Was never holla'd to nor cheer'd with horn."

It was a happy thought of the poet, in introducing the play within the play, got up by the "Athenian mechanicals," in honour of Duke Theseus's marriage, to make a travesty of the old tragic legend of "Pyramus and Thisbe," and thereby turning it, as it were, into a farce upon the serious and pathetic scenes that occur between the lovers in the piece—Demetrius and Helena, and Lysander and Hermia.

But what a rich set of fellows those "mechanicals" are! and how individual are their several characteristics! Bully Bottom, the epitome of all the conceited donkeys that ever strutted and straddled on this stage of the world. In his own imagination equal to the performance of anything separately, and of all things collectively; the meddler, the director, the dictator. He is for dictating every movement, and directing everybody—when he is not helping himself. He is a choice arabesque impersonation of that colouring of conceit which, by the half-malice of the world, has been said to tinge the disposition of actors, as invariably as the rouge does their cheeks. Peter Quince, although the delegated manager of the company, fades into a shadow, a cipher, a nonentity before him; for the moment Peter announces the commencement of proceedings with, "Is all our company here?"—in darts first tragedian, Bottom, "You were best to call them generally, man by man, according to the scrip." And when Quince does produce the scroll, the other instantly proposes something else. It is interesting to follow out this feature in Bottom's character—a perfect variety in the "class" "bumptiousness," ranging under the general "order" "conceit." Our "first tragedian" then interrupts the manager with: "First, good Peter Quince, say what the play treats on; then read the names of the actors; and so, grow to a point." And no sooner, again, does Quince proceed to read the title of the play, than Bottom bursts in with his comment: "A very good piece of work, I assure you, and a *merry*,"—merry!—it was high tragic in their estimation. And then he instantly resumes his dictation: "Now, good Peter Quince, call forth your actors by the scroll. Masters, spread yourselves." His own name coming first, he promptly replies: "Ready. Name what part *I* am for, and proceed." His part is the chief point. And when the part of Pyramus, the lover's part, is assigned to him, he announces that the audience "must look to their eyes; for that he will move storms"—"he will condole in some measure." Great, however, as Mr Bottom professes to be in the lover's vein, his "chief humour (he declares) is for a tyrant. I could play Ercles rarely; or a part to tear a cat in; to make all split." Then he will play Thisbe—the heroine—if he may hide his face; and he will "speak in a monstrous little voice." Then he will play the lion: "Let me play the lion, too. I will roar, that it will do any man's heart good to hear me. I'll roar, that I'll make the Duke say, 'Let him roar again! *let* him roar again!'" What an amusing caricature of self-esteem! The idea of a man pluming himself on the possibility of being encored in a roar. But the roaring is objected to, for that it would frighten the ladies; and that were enough to hang every mother's son of them. But when is true conceit ever put to a nonplus?—and so with our friend Bottom. Like a Chinese tumbler, however you may thrust him from his centre, he instantly regains his position; he is equal to all contingencies, and, therefore, he answers the objection to the roaring by the amendment, that he will so "*aggravate* his voice, that he will roar you as gently as any sucking-dove;" he will "roar you an 'twere any nightingale." Nothing is proposed, but an amendment comes from Professor Bottom. Quince says: "We will have a prologue; and it shall be written in eight and six:" that is, in alternate lines of eight and six feet. "No, make it two more, (rejoins the dictator); let it be written in eight and eight." What a happy example of opposition for opposition's sake; for Quince's was the better plan.

Peter Quince, by the way, displays the part of an experienced manager, in tickling the conceit of his first trout-tragedian, and moulding it to his purpose when he declares, "You can play no part but Pyramus: for Pyramus is a sweet-faced man: a proper man, as we shall see in a summer's day; a most lovely, *gentleman-like* man: therefore *you* must *needs* play Pyramus."

Roscius Bottom becomes suddenly mollified by this testimony, and he acquiesces: "Well, I will undertake it." And then he falls to discussing the all-important point—his costume.

"What beard were I best to play it in?"

"*Quin.* Why, what you will.

"*Bot.* I will discharge it in either your straw-coloured beard, your orange-tawny beard, your purple-in-grain beard, or your French-crown-colour beard, your perfect yellow."

I knew of an actor who summoned the whole green-room at a morning rehearsal to see his new dress for the part of Romeo. The glory of that sartorial achievement obliterated all consideration of the embodying the character of the prince of lovers. The part, nothing,—the satin, everything. So with our immortal Bottom: the professional complacency, and gravity of consideration with which *his* costume is debated, is accurately in character with a personage who feels confidently that the whole burthen of the piece is on his shoulders,—that upon him wholly rests its success,—that he is the mainspring and Atlantean support of the entire structure. Theatrical conceit was never better impersonated than by the great representer of Pyramus. Roscius Bottom is a type of that class of gentry who are illustrated in an admirable caricature-sketch which once appeared in *Punch,* where a certain Mr Walter Belville is represented looking up at the bust of Shakespeare in Stratford-on-Avon Church, and indignantly ejaculating in soliloquy: "Immortal bard, indeed! I should just like to know, my buck, where you'd have been if it hadn't been for—well—no matter."

The character of Bottom is well worthy of a close analysis, to notice in how extraordinary a manner Shakespeare has carried out all the concurring qualities to compound a thoroughly conceited man. Conceited people, moreover, being upon such amiable terms with themselves, they are ordinarily good-natured, if not good-tempered. And so with Bottom; whether he carry an amendment, or not, with his companions he is always placable; and if foiled, away he starts for some other point—nothing disturbs his equanimity. When Puck has transformed him into the ass, and his companions all scour away from him, exclaiming, "Bless thee, Bottom! thou art translated!" Snout comes in, and, in amazement, exclaims:—

"Oh, Bottom, thou art changed! What do I see on thee?
"*Bot.* What do you see? You see an ass's head of your own, do you?"

His temper and self-possession never desert him: "I see

their knavery. This is to make an ass of me, and fright me if they could: but I will not stir from this place, do what they can. I will walk up and down here, and I will sing, that they shall hear I am not afraid."

Combined with his amusing and harmless quality of conceit, the worthy Bottom displays no inconsiderable store of imagination in his intercourse with the little people of the fairy world. How pleasantly he falls in with their several natures and qualities; dismissing them one by one with a gracious speech, like a prince at his levee: "I shall desire of you more acquaintance, good master Cobweb. If I cut my finger I shall make bold with you. Your name, honest gentleman?" "Peas-blossom." "I pray you commend me to Mrs Squash, your mother, and to master Peas-cod, your father. Good master Peas-blossom, I shall desire of you more acquaintance too. Your name, I beseech you, sir?" "Mustard-seed." "Good master Mustard-seed, I know your patience well; that same cowardly giant-like ox-beef hath devoured many a gentleman of your house. I promise you your kindred hath made my eyes water ere now. I desire of you more acquaintance, good master Mustard-seed."

And how daintily epicurean the fellow shows when he is installed in the court of Queen Titania:—"Monsieur Cobweb: good monsieur, get your weapons in your hand, and kill me a red-hipped humble-bee on the top of a thistle. And, good monsieur, bring me the honey-bag. Do not fret yourself too much in the action, monsieur; and, good monsieur, have a care the honey-bag break not. I would be loath to have you overflown with the honey-bag, signior."

Also, under his transformation to the ass, his epicurean tendency runs into the brute nature: so, he becomes dainty in oats, and manifests a fastidious tooth for peas and beans. Titania says to him—

"Say, sweet love, what thou desirest to eat.

"*Bot.* Truly, a peck of provender: I could munch your good dry oats. Methinks I have a great desire for a bottle of hay: good hay, sweet hay hath no fellow.

"*Tit.* I have a venturous fairy, that shall seek the squirrel's hoard, and fetch thee new nuts.

"*Bot.* I had rather have a handful or two of dried peas."

We never lose the cock-a-whoop vein in Bottom's character. He patronises his brother-mechanics; he patronises the fairies: he even patronises himself: "If I had wit enough to get out of this wood, I have enough to serve mine own turn."

Then, there is Snug, the joiner, who can board and lodge only one idea at a time, and that tardily. He begs to have "the lion's part written out, because he is slow of study;" and is amazingly comforted by the intelligence, that he "may do it extempore; for it is nothing but roaring."

To him succeeds Starveling, the tailor, a melancholy man, and who questions the feasibility and the propriety of everything proposed. Being timid, he thinks the lion's part had better be omitted altogether: "Will not the ladies be afeard of the lion? *I* fear it, I promise you."

If, as some writers have asserted, Shakespeare was a profound practical metaphysician, it is scarcely too much to conclude that all this dove-tailing of contingencies, requisite to perfectionate these several characters, was all foreseen and provided in his mind, and not the result of mere accident. By an intuitive power, that always confounds us when we examine its effects, I believe that whenever Shakespeare adopted any distinctive class of character, his "mind's eye" took in at a glance all the concomitant minutiæ of features requisite to complete its characteristic identity. "As from a watch-tower," he comprehended the whole course of human action,—its springs, its motives, its consequences; and he has laid down for us a trigonometrical chart of it. I believe that he did nothing without anxious premeditation; and that they who really study—not simply read him, must come to the same conclusion. Not only was he not satisfied with preserving the integrity of his characters while they were in speech and action before the audience; but we constantly find them carrying on their peculiarities—*out* of the scene—by hints of action, and casual remarks from others. Was there no design in all this? no contrivance? no foregone conclusion?—nay, does it not manifest consummate intellectual power, with a sleepless assiduity?

And now, what can we say, worthy to be said, of those tiny beings of the elements—those substantial shadows of poetical fancy—those transparent and æther-like forms, that glanced hither and thither, as moonlight on the water's ripple?—now in the upper regions, bathing their wings in rainbow dews; or listlessly floating with the gossamer upon the summer air; or rousing the mole-cricket with their midnight roundels upon the pearly grass. What *can* we say of those lovely denizens of the fairy mythology? What of the feminine waywardness and sweet humanity of the little queen, Titania, with that pretty story of the Indian mother and her babe? And what of Oberon, with his ape-like mimicry of mortal royalty, grudging and restless, till he had beguiled her of her infant page? What of their sportive gambols on the ocean-marge, "chasing the ebbing Neptune;" or of their merry assiduity and swift obedience, glancing hither and thither on their errands, like the summer-fly?

"Over hill, over dale,
Thorough bush, thorough briar,
Over park, over pale,
Thorough flood, thorough fire,
I do wander everywhere,
Swifter than the moon's sphere:

And I serve the fairy queen,
To dew her orbs upon the green;
The cowslips tall her pensioners be;
In their gold coats spots you see.
Those be rubies, fairy favours,
In those freckles live their savours:
I must go seek some dew-drops here,
And hang a pearl in every cowslip's ear."

And oh! more than all, what of that madcap, will-o'-the-wisp—that spiritualisation of fun, frolic, and mischief—immortal Puck?

As Ariel was the etherealised impersonation of swift obedience, with an attachment perfectly feminine in its character—Puck, Robin Goodfellow, is an abstraction of all the "quips, and cranks, and wanton wiles," of all the tricks and practical jokes in vogue among the "human mortals." Puck is the patron saint of "skylarking." How prompt his spirit for carrying out a plot! "I'll put a girdle round the earth in forty minutes." He is the poet's anticipated personification of the electric telegraph:—

"I go, I go;—look how I go;
Swifter than arrow from the Tartar's bow."

And when his victims are well limed and caught, what infection in the outbreak of his mirth! We can fancy him scouring through the forest glades; outvieing the clatter of the woodpecker; scaring the hermit squirrel at his hoard; and perplexing the solemnity of the monastic owl:—

"I am that merry wanderer of the night.
I jest to Oberon, and make him smile,
When I a bean-fed horse beguile,
Neighing in likeness of a filly foal:
And sometimes lurk I in a gossip's bowl,
In very likeness of a roasted crab:
And when she drinks, against her lips I bob,

And on her wither'd dew-lap pour the ale.
The wisest aunt, telling her saddest tale,
Sometime for three-foot stool mistaketh me;
Then slip I from her bum, down topples she,
And 'Tailor' cries, and falls into a cough;
And the whole quire hold their hips, and laugh,
And waxen in their mirth, and neeze, and swear
A merrier hour was never wasted there."

But, like a true minion of waggery and mischief, while he assumed the office of Grand Inquisitor, and corrector general of slatternly menials and other household delinquents; while he pinched the lazy kitchen-wench black and blue; and beguiled the loitering hind into the mud-pool, and then would "whirr away laughing his ho, ho, ho!" yet was merry Robin also the coadjutor and hearty assistant of all industrious housewives and honest labourers; the former finding their "cream-bowls duly set" for them; and for the latter, "ere glimpse of morn, his shadowy flail would thresh their corn." He was the good genius of honest thrift; the household deity of order and cleanliness, as well as prologue and superintendent of the graver passages in the career of mortality:—

"Now the hungry lion roars,
And the wolf behowls the moon;
Whilst the heavy plowman snores,
All with weary task foredone.
Now the wasted brands do glow,
Whilst the screech-owl, screeching loud,
Puts the wretch that lies in woe
In remembrance of a shroud.
Now it is the time of night,
That the graves, all gaping wide,
Ev'ry one lets forth his sprite,
In the church-way paths to glide:
And we fairies that do run
By the triple Hecate's team,

From the presence of the sun,
Following darkness like a dream,
Now we frolic.—Not a mouse
Shall disturb this hallow'd house:
I am sent with broom before,
To sweep the dust behind the door."

This is the sedate and propitious feature in his attributes: but, as in the old Greek mythology, their gods were supposed to preside over the most contrarious qualities and passions; so with this fantastic offshoot of Celtic demonology, the character by which he is most familiarly recognised is that of a boisterous mischief-maker.

The echo of his laugh has reverberated from age to age, striking the promontories and headlands of eternal poetry: and to those whose spirits are finely touched, it is still heard through the mist of temporal cares and toils—dimly heard, and at fitful intervals; for the old faith in that fairy presence has ceased for ever, and exists only in the record of those other elegant fancies that were the offspring of the young world of imagination. We have passed into an age of practicality and demonstrative knowledge—great, and even wonderful in its results; but perhaps somewhat too exclusive in its occupation of the human faculties. We lack the Holy-day—the Sabbath of the Fancy. We have been divinely told that "man cannot live by bread alone;" the mind of man cannot go straining on from utility to utility, from practicality to practicality; nevertheless, as Keats says, "The poetry of earth is never dead:" poetry, like the fiery element, exists through all created Nature, animate and inanimate, waiting only for the Promethean touch of the magician's wand to give it form and action.

The Fairies are gone:—Oberon and Titania, with all their train, lie embalmed in the winding-sheet of the poet's fancy:—but he who contemplates his fellow-beings with the eye of imagination, will raise up to himself a vision of beauty and heart-stirring truth that will compensate him for all the turmoils of world-cares and anxieties. Look at those fairy beings of the material world—those tender buds of humanity—the little children around us. What creation of the poet's brain can compare with those lovely little creatures for tricksy waywardness and pretty caprices? Talk of Robin Goodfellow's laugh! what a genuine thing is the laugh of a child! it is as if sorrow never had been, and never could be, the companion of that soul. There we have the spirit of Puck in our homes and in our streets—the spirit of irrepressible and unaffected merriment.

The creative power of the fancy is a blessed gift in itself; but he substantiates that gift who converts it into the ordinary occurrences of daily life, drawing from them the honey-bag of sweet and joyous thought; and I am one who, having had my sorrows, can still believe that there is a sunny side to almost all the events of our life, if we will but turn to it with a sincere and trusting heart.

No fairy mirth ever surpassed the mirth of happy children. Only observe a bevy of them seated on a door-step, joining in tiny chorus to the directing melody of an elder precentor. The soul of music is there, for it is the music of the heart. The dance of fairies round a mole-hill of wild-thyme, footing it to the cricket's song, is a lovely object of the fancy; but look at a knot of infants, hand-in-hand, holding each other's frocks, dancing to a street organ. How absorbed are they in their pastime! how zealously they perform their little rites, totally unconcerned, and unconscious of observing eyes. Will any after occupation in life be more seriously entered upon by them, or more conscientiously fulfilled?

Then, for the gravity of children: how profound it is! I know of nothing more intense than the seriously inquiring face of an infant—the face of Newton, on the threshold of a discovery, not more eloquent. One might fancy it capable of solving the great mystery of life and death. Again;—observe two or three of those little creatures seated knee to knee, and one of them imparting to the assembly some recent event that has transpired in their neighbourhood; or are debating the propriety of electing a fourth to partake in their solemnities: no grave council of state can be more earnest, more occupied.

Yet again, if we are amused with the human jealousies and sparrings of the fairy Oberon and Titania, when each, to obtain possession of the little page, left in her care by the Indian woman—his tiny majesty commits himself by royal poutings, and upbraidings, and plots, and crooked chicaneries; while his consort asserts her prerogative by a consistent obstinacy of purpose to retain the boy; so that, as Puck says,

> "Now they never meet in grove or green,
> By fountain clear, or spangled star-light sheen,
> But they do square;—that all their elves, for fear,
> Creep into acorn-cups, and hide them there:"

have we no counterpart in the manœuvrings, and plots, and counter-plots, bickerings, and angers of our little human fairies—their *casus belli* turning, perchance, upon the possession of a doll, or the fee-simple of a doll's house?

Truly may it be said, "The poetry of earth is ceasing never;" for there *is* poetry, or the power of creative intellectual embellishment, to every action and substance throughout all nature; and we do not neutralise or destroy the action or substance by such process of the fancy—we sublimate, and present it in the most agreeable form to the senses. Poetry is the electricity of the intellectual world. It is the principle of life and movement, stirring the inert masses of mind-matter. "Poetry," says Hazlitt, "is the universal language which the heart holds with nature and itself. In all human beings the poetical faculty (or an apprehensiveness of the beautiful in Nature) exists in various degrees of intensity; but it still exists. The consummation of the faculty lies in producing those feelings in the form of winged words."

I repeat, therefore, that we have our little fairies of the material world—our graceful and lovely children; and he who contemplates them and their miniature ways with an eye of fancy will multiply his sources of pleasure, and, at the same time, amplify his own heart's benevolence.

In one sense the child may, indeed, be said to be the "father to the man;" for they read us many a wholesome lesson in sincerity and social wisdom. Little children are the bright emanations of omnipresent loving-kindness; they are the virgin snow, shed in the dawn, before the smoky atmosphere of day has tarnished its splendour.

When that miserable wretch, Corder, was hanged for the murder of a girl, I remember being deeply touched with one circumstance that transpired after his death. It was that of his having been noticed by his neighbours to be very kind and gentle towards the little children in the streets, usually having some dainty in his pocket to give them. Now, was this a movement of instinct in him,—that the aroma of innocence—the loveliness, the divine beauty of innocence would assuage in his heart the torment of the fire of bloodguiltiness? We cannot know what passed in that wretched man's mind after he had committed the murder—after he had killed the being who had given him her whole truth and self;—what throes! what spasms! what collapsings of the heart! what pangs of remorse! He used to stalk about his bed-room through the night-watches and the darkness, to the perplexity and dismay of his wife; for then the worm was gnawing his heart: and on the morrow he went among the children, and made himself meek and kind, hoping to wipe out the blood-spot by mingling with their white souls. And

God was merciful to that "cruel man of clay," who had himself "cut mercy with a sharp knife to the bone."

Experience has told us that our term of years is extended by a consociation with children; and I am sure that, next to a conscience void of offence, nothing more tends to keep the heart young, and fresh, and green, amid the winter-snows of age, than the habit of accustoming oneself to sympathise with and take delight in the actions of this fairy race of our own species. The habit itself keeps the mind young; and the mind imperceptibly acts upon the body. This, upon a very essential point, may be denominated "poetical utilitarianism."

Let me not be thought indiscreet, still less irreverend, when I say—for I do say it in the implicit adoration of the unbounded love that dwelt in the Divine Speaker—"Suffer little children to come unto me; for of such is the kingdom of heaven."

# V.

# Othello.

# V.

# OTHELLO.

---

UPON reading again this tragedy of Othello for my present purpose, two or three presumed discrepancies in the conduct of the principal character recur to me, which I will state as succinctly as possible, and then proceed to the main object of my Essay.

In the first place, then, we may state, without fear of contradiction, that the ruling moral principle in the character of Othello is an aristocratic pride, and a quick sense of honour, engrossing, and all but swallowing up every other emotion or passion of his heart. Every sentiment, every movement in his career, convinces us that, in his ordinary conduct, he would as soon turn his back in the day of battle as commit a single act of duplicity in the social transactions of life. That he is imbued with the true aristocratic feeling, is manifest in the first scene of the play, where, in conversation with Iago, he at once justifies his prerogative to claim alliance with the haughty nobles of Venice. He says :—

"'Tis yet to know,—
Which, when I know that boasting is an honour,
I shall promulgate,—I fetch my life and being
From men of royal siege ; and my demerits

> May speak, unbonneted, to as proud a fortune
> As this that I have reach'd."

That is, in modern parlance, "the bonnet being a badge of dignity in Venice, my merits of fortune (*un*-bonneted) are as high as those with which I have gained alliance." "Demerit" and "merit" had the same signification in Shakespeare—"mereo" and "demereo" having the same meaning in Latin.

By birth, then, to say nothing of his individual accomplishments, he places himself in a superior grade to the lineage of his father-in-law, Brabantio. But why does the Venetian lord and senator speak of him with aristocratic loathing—the man who is generalissimo of the armies of the state, and who is looked to with anxiety in every military emergency? Because he is a foreigner, (a noted ground of objection to the Italians,) a man of another clime; and more, of another colour; and, above all, of another faith. Othello being a Moor, was consequently a Mahometan—a religion hateful beyond all others to the bigoted among Catholics. Brabantio, speaking of the stolen alliance with his family, says:—

> "If such actions may have passage free,
> Bond-slaves and *pagans* shall our statesmen be."

He is strictly designated as a *Moor*, not a negro; Shakespeare never would have confounded the two classes, knowing what that extraordinary race of men had achieved in Spain. The Venetians knew little if anything of negroes; but they had frequent intercourse with the Moors. Shakespeare, too, who could have had no other association with the negro than as a slave, never would have made a negro talk of his "*royal*" birth. Besides, in the second scene of the fourth Act, Mauritania is spoken of as the *home* of Othello.

Our poet, then, as it appears to me, has placed himself in

this dilemma with regard to consistency in his principal character: he has either turned him from the faith of his forefathers, or he has forgotten the circumstance of his being a Mahometan; for it will be recollected, in his last speech, he says:—

> "When a malignant and a turban'd Turk
> Beat a Venetian, and traduced the state,
> I took by the throat the circumcisèd dog,
> And smote him thus."

As a Mahometan, Othello could not have used such a term; and, to preserve the high sense of honour and noble generosity in his nature, he would not have done so; for it is the distinguishing characteristic of magnanimity to be forbearing towards an opinion or creed that we have abjured. But we may be sure that Othello was a Mahometan, or whence the consistency and propriety of his father-in-law's (Brabantio's) protest, just quoted.

The next objection I have to hint, and which, I confess, lowers the proud and great-minded Othello in my estimation, is, when he consents to conceal himself, and become the spy upon the words and actions of Cassio. It would be difficult to reconcile such a proceeding with a nature like his, unless we admit the desire of confirming the guilt or innocence of Desdemona; or (which is the most probable) that the poet intended to show the towering intellect of Iago, in the passiveness of Othello to an act repugnant to his own open and direct character; for it is Iago who induces him to play the eavesdropper—a most subtle course of conduct. The scene, however, is judiciously omitted in the representation, for it certainly is not dramatic.

My last and heaviest count of inconsistency in the noble Moor's conduct is connected with the fatal handkerchief. The charge brought against him before the Senate by his father-in-law is, not only that he had seduced the affections of his daughter, but that he had violated a law of the State, in using the "arts inhibited" of sorcery and witchcraft to effect his purpose. We all remember that Othello concludes his defence with the simple statement, that it was the story of his life which had wooed and won the gentle Desdemona:—

> "She lov'd me for the dangers I had pass'd,
> And I lov'd her that she did pity them.
> This *only* is the '*witchcraft*' I have us'd."

Subsequently, however, when the handkerchief is missing, we find that a vital importance attaches to the possession of it:—it was a "*charmed* napkin," wrought by a Sibyl:—that with it the wearer would "entirely subdue the affections of her husband." And he afterwards repeats:—

> "There's magic in the web of it:
>
> . . . . .
>
> The worms were hallow'd that did breed the silk;
> And it was dy'd in mummy, which the skilful
> Conserv'd of maidens' hearts."

Now, from this discrepancy we must come to one of the following conclusions—either that the "noble Moor" told a deliberate lie, or that the potent love-charm was a present made subsequently to his marriage. Yet, when Emilia steals it, she says, "It was her first remembrance from the Moor," and that "he conjur'd her she should ever keep it." The latter benefit, however, that it was a gift made after marriage, I willingly extend to the poet; whose fame, after all, is only aggrandised by these puny exceptions—a fame which the acutest of critical intellects combined, for more than two hundred years, have not been able to reduce even to the standard of acknowledged *ordinary* supremacy. The fact is, whenever I am startled by some apparent oversight or discrepancy in Shakespeare, I have learned to pause, and always to suspect my own insufficient examination of all the possible *intentions* the poet may have had in any seeming error, rather than believe he has committed an actual one. In the present instance, for example, the dramatist probably intended to indicate, by these imperfections in the "noble Moor's" conduct that have been cited, how even the most high-minded nature may become warped into indirectness by the torturing passion of jealousy.

In turning to my task of noticing the inferior points and agents in the play, I would first glance at the naturalness, the ease, and propriety with which the conversation among the senators is carried on, relating to the Turkish fleet making for Cyprus. The Duke opens the discussion by doubting the authenticity of the news. "There is no composition in them," he says, "that gives them credit." The reports vary as to the number of the galleys. The Duke's letters say a hundred and forty; the 1st Senator's, a hundred and seven; and the 2d Senator's, two hundred. But he adds—

> "Though they jump not on a just account,
> (As in these cases when the aim reports,
> 'Tis oft with difference,) yet do they all confirm
> A Turkish fleet, and bearing up to Cyprus."

Upon this ensues a most natural discussion why the expedition should be intended for Cyprus rather than Rhodes. Had Shakespeare been bred a secretary for foreign affairs, he could not have treated the question with graver technicality. Then a messenger enters, confirming the news that the fleet was seen steering for Rhodes, for the purpose of joining an after-fleet intended to bear upon Cyprus. All this is no more than a note of preparation to introduce Othello, and impart a dignity to his character by his being selected, in the State's emergency, to supersede the "trusty and most valiant Montano."

Another circumstance of inferior action in this drama worthy of notice, is the scene that occurs in Cyprus upon the arrival of Othello and his suite, in different vessels, with the bustle, the description of the storm, and the uncertainty of the inhabitants whether it be the envoy of the republic, or the Turks. One of the gentlemen remarks:—

> "The town is empty; on the brow o' the sea
> Stand ranks of people, and they cry, 'A sail!'"

Who has not observed this, even upon ordinary occasions, in a sea-port town?—the inhabitants of which appear to have more leisure for gape and gossip than any others. The arrival of a strange vessel will bring them down to the beach; and there they stand patiently, as if they were Otaheitans, and Cook's ships had just cast anchor. No one being at hand to give them certain news, the same gentleman decides that the arrivals are "friends at least," for they "do discharge their shot of courtesy." How easy and natural all this! And what unity and consistency of thought in the poet, who never for a moment appears to slumber at his post, but constantly makes his action dove-tail with his circumstance and place.

Another minor point of attention to local knowledge and propriety. In order to annoy Brabantio, Roderigo tells him that Desdemona was "transported" from her home,

> "with no worse nor better guard,
> But with a knave of common hire, a gondolier."

Which is as if he had apprised a man like Lord Grey or the Marquis of Westminster, that his daughter had gone off under the protection of a cabman; with the additional horror conveyed to the mind of the senator: "The gondoliers of

Venice being the only conveyers of persons, and of a large proportion of the property of the city, they are thus cognisant of all intrigues, and the fittest agents in them; and are under perpetual and strong temptation to make profit of the secrets of society."

Shakespeare is remarkable, also, for the oaths that he puts into the mouths of his characters. They always suit both the persons and their country. That they should be appropriate in his English plays was to be expected from his familiarity with our traditions and national chronicles; for the oaths and exclamations of many of our kings have come down to us. Rufus used to swear by "the face of Luke!" Richard III., by "Holy Paul!" Henry VIII. adjured the same patron saint; and even the "virgin queen" had her distinctive and characteristic oath, and a tremendous one it was. In Venice, Shakespeare has more than once made his characters swear "by Janus!" Now, it is familiar to every traveller, that even in the present day the Italians retain their old Roman mythological adjuration, "Per Bacco!" or "Corpo di Bacco!" and which may be heard quite as often as our "by George!" or any other the commonest exclamation. His friars exclaim, "Jesu Maria!" an expression perfectly appropriate to the character, and never heard but in a purely Catholic country. I make no apology for dwelling upon these minutiæ of circumstance. The very sweepings of his genius are virgin gold.

The character of Cassio is a remarkable specimen of variety in the class of Shakespeare's military men. He displays the same frank, unsuspicious, and generous nature, but without their usual perception and appreciation of character. Cassio is a sensualist, quickly excited by stimulants, and, from their combined effects, is infirm of purpose; also, from geniality of disposition, swayed against his better reason. The very vices in Cassio's character would have made Iago a better man, who envies him for his social nature as much as for his having been advanced in rank above him. He says: "Cassio hath *a daily beauty in his life* that doth make me ugly." Nothing in the whole range of dramatic portraiture can be finer than the delineation of these two men. Cassio, from his excessive demonstrativeness—his sudden burst of piety in his drunken fit; and the bitterness of his self-reproach in his sobriety:—his utter prostration "upon the knees of his heart" (as Essex would say) to his offended and noble-minded friend and commander, are all the inevitable, and therefore natural results of his open and generous nature. But Cassio was the last man of the whole company who was fitted to supersede Othello in the government of Cyprus. His indiscriminate confidence was not the quality best adapted to sway a garrison-town, and would surely be his "rock a-head." No, no! with his constitutional infirmities, poor Cassio did not long succeed his general in the governorship; he was sure to commit some folly which would occasion his being recalled to Venice.

Another of the thousand instances which might be quoted of Shakespeare's regard to consistency of conduct in his delineations of character, occurs in the simple circumstance of Othello's deportment towards Cassio. Through the first two Acts, and before their estrangement, he uniformly calls him by the familiar and brotherly name of "Michael;" afterwards, when the poison of jealousy has entered his soul, he speaks of him always as "Cassio." It may appear trivial to notice these minutiæ; but in estimating character, "Trifles, light as air, are confirmations strong as proofs of holy writ."

Iago is the direct antipodes to Michael Cassio. Iago may be deemed the strongest of immoral philosophers—for he has a philosophy: its code is, that "Evil" is "Power;" that Good is a nonentity—that Vice is an acquisition—and that Virtue is a thing to be avoided, or to be taken advantage of,—in either case a weakness. Iago has no faith but in the intellectual supremacy arising from Will. He has no faith in mutual Love. Here is his confession: "I have looked upon the world for four times seven years; and since I could distinguish a benefit from an injury, I never found a man who knew how to love himself." No one among Shakespeare's men of intellect utters stronger axioms of social and moral philosophy than this remarkable character. The career which he had chalked out for himself furnished him the motive for this, and his mental power and energy were stimulants to his motive. That Iago's is a voluntary system—a deliberate choice and pursuit of wickedness—his own words prove in glaring and marvellous strength:—

"Virtue?—a fig! 'Tis in ourselves that we are thus or thus. Our bodies are our gardens; to the which our *wills* are gardeners: so that, if we will plant nettles, or sow lettuce; set hyssop, and weed up thyme; supply it with one gender of herbs, or distract it with many; either to have it sterile with idleness, or manured with industry; why, the *power* and corrigible authority of this lies in our *wills*."

Iago is essentially a self-lover—a self-worshipper. The poor fool Roderigo has more belief in good than he. In answer to Iago's disgusting calumny against Desdemona, he says: "I cannot believe that in her; she is full of most blest conditions." "Blest fig's-end!" is his reply. The loathsome opinions he entertains of human nature, arising out of his self-love and absorbing conceit in his own power, vent themselves in language more gross than is to be met in any character in all Shakespeare; and how frequently do we find this in our commerce with the world, that the self-lover and self-worshipper are prone to gross implications by reason of their utter obtuseness in perception of what is beautiful and good and true out of their own dark circle. I confess that I have rarely known a thoroughly selfish person who did not betray a beastly opinion of his species. And Iago's language and allusions are not merely gross, they are hard, and unfeelingly obscene. They do not even hint at a manifestation; they have not the redemption of self-enjoyment in their utterance; but are the vile fungus-growth of his malignant misanthropy. They are the rampant off-shoots of his hatred.

Iago's ambition partakes of his revengful nature. He ministers to the gratification of his malignant and resentful passions to the full as much as he does to the promptings of his ambition in the steps he takes to bring about his purposes. His character is true to the baser and coarser part of Italian nature—it is subtle and unforgiving; but it is also peculiarly his own individual character. It is based upon a firm conviction of his own intellectual superiority. That is the only thing in which he has faith—his commanding genius, his mastery of mind. It is that he may obtain what he conceives to be the due of that superiority, which makes him ambitious. The object of his ambition is military promotion. His ambition is that of his profession; it is that ambition which is almost a virtue—certainly the master-ingredient in making a soldier. It is that quality which Lord Bacon declares essential to the character, when he says, "To take a soldier without ambition is to pull off his spurs." His first speech of importance shows the quality of Iago's ambition—compounded of several ingredients. There is the conviction of his own merit; the hatred of Othello; and the envy of Cassio, while affecting to disparage him because of his having been promoted to the post which he himself covets. Here is a specimen of his paramount self-worship:—

> "If I were the Moor, I would not be Iago;
> In following him I follow but myself;
> Heaven is my judge, not I for love or duty,
> But seeming so, for my peculiar end."

Iago is essentially self-reliant. He has no accomplices; Roderigo is his mere puppet—his machine; his own brain is his sole resource; he needs no other; he feels *that* to be all-adequate to the compassing of his ends. He has thorough confidence in the force of Will, and in his own powers to carry out the dictates of his Will. The merest thread of circumstance will suffice to string his devices on. He never doubts the capacity of his wit to disturb and destroy matters, however seeming smooth; and to direct his crooked ends, events however straightly progressing. While watching the full content and the conjugal endearments of Othello and Desdemona, when they meet at Cyprus, he says, with the malignant confidence in future evil of the arch-fiend himself, contemplating the joy of our first parents:—

> "Oh, you are well tun'd now!
> But I'll set down the pegs that make this music,
> As honest as I am."

It is a substantive part of his craft to gain this reputation for "honesty." It is strongly insisted on; and, as a soldier, he cultivates bluntness, as harmonising best with his professional character; and this character is asserted in his behalf through the whole play. He is a magnificent illustration of the superficial advantage that the man of intellect merely—intellect without moral feeling, mind without soul—gains over the man of noble nature. The unsuspecting, generous Moor gives Iago implicit credit for the qualities he lays claim to. The man whose heart interferes nothing with the hard, cold action of his intellectual faculties, sways at will the man of fervour and impulse: the man who has no faith in goodness—neither himself inspired by goodness nor believing in its existence in others—has yet the power to impress his victim with the idea of his integrity of heart and clearness of judgment. At times my brain has been in a whirl of wonderment as I have penetrated into the marrow of this extraordinary character. Othello says of him :—

> " This fellow 's of exceeding honesty ;
> And knows all qualities with a learned spirit
> Of human dealings."

This is accurately the facility of belief and trust which unscrupulous knavery obtains from a guileless nature. It is precisely the dupery we appreciate; while we loathe and condemn the depraved ingenuity that has succeeded in triumphing over it. We estimate the deceiver, and despise the deluder—all the more for his superior talent, perverted to so vile a use.

In his conduct, too, and principle of action, how finely has the poet discriminated the deportment of Iago toward his victims. With Othello he is merely suggestive and deferential, and is satisfied with clinching the opinions and conclusions drawn by his jealous-poisoned prey.

> " Let me be thought too busy in my fears,
> As worthy cause I have to fear I am."

Also, of the handkerchief, which he says he saw Cassio " wipe his beard with,"

> " If it be that, [he concludes,] or any that was hers,
> It speaks against her, with the other proofs."

With Cassio he is patronising, and liberal of his advice. He knows the placability of his temper, and the demonstrative gratitude of his heart for proffered benefits.

With Desdemona he is sympathising :—

> " Can he be angry ?
> Something of moment, then : I will go meet him :
> There 's matter in 't, indeed, if he be angry."

Lastly, with Roderigo, he coolly sways the "snipe," (and what a happy term to give him!) as if he had ordained his destiny. Roderigo he does not admit even to a parley, but constantly enjoins him silence when he wants to talk him into obedience. "Lay thy finger thus, and let thy soul be *instructed.*" However superior he might feel to all the others, and that feeling was paramount, he never would have ventured upon that tone with any one of them. He even deems it a due concession to the majesty of intellect to account for his associating with such an imbecile as Roderigo:—

> "For I mine own gain'd knowledge should profane,
> If I would time expend with such a snipe,
> But for my sport and profit."

Besides the perversion of his intellect to minister to his malice, there is another odious feature in Iago's conduct. His ambition partakes of avarice—an execrable form of passion. He uses Roderigo as a means of obtaining money, as well as revenge: "Thus do I ever make my fool my purse." He cheats and robs the poor dotard of jewels, under pretence of gifts to win Desdemona to his suit. In short, Iago's ambition is compounded of still viler passions than the desire to rise unlawfully. It is made of hatred, malignity, revenge—nay, it is even subordinate to them; for we perceive it only occasionally lurking in the midst of them, as *but one* among the incentives that actuate him. He takes a keen pleasure in the pursuit of his villanies for their own sake, and for the sake of the exercise they afford to his intellectual ability. The recompence is but part of the sport, not its sole aim:—

> "I'll make the Moor
> Thank me, love me, and reward me
> For making him egregiously an ass,
> And practising upon his peace and quiet
> Even to madness."

The most consummate instance of his skill in machination appears, I think, in his recommending Cassio, after he has been cashiered by Othello, to induce the gentle Desdemona to intercede for him with her husband; by which show of interest and sympathy he hoodwinks all parties. He maintains his character for honesty; and, at this one cast of his net, encloses all his victims. This single move in the plot of this astounding play is in, and of itself, a piece of perfect mastery. Communing afterwards with himself, he says:—

> "How am I, then, a villain,
> To counsel Cassio to this parallel course,
> Directly to his good? Divinity of hell!
> When devils will the blackest sins put on,
> They do suggest at first with heavenly shows,
> As I do now; for while this honest fool
> Plies Desdemona to repair his fortunes,
> And she for him pleads strongly to the Moor,
> I'll pour this pestilence into his ear—
> That she repeals him for her body's lust;
> And by how much she strives to do him good,
> She shall undo her credit with the Moor;
> So will I turn her virtue into pitch;
> And out of her own goodness make the net
> That shall enmesh them all."

And the most awful instance of his fiend-like nature, is when he contemplates Othello, as he approaches, after he has poisoned his mind against his ill-starred wife:—

> "Look, where he comes!
> Not poppy, nor mandragora,
> Nor all the drowsy syrops of the world,
> Shall ever medicine thee to that sweet sleep
> Which thou owd'st yesterday."

The character of Iago alone, in this tragedy, is a profound subject for psychological study. M. Guizot, in his book entitled "Shakespeare and his Times"—(a remarkable production for a man who has passed the chief portion of his life in political activity, and one which proves him to be not only an elegant scholar, but one possessed of more candour, deference, and discrimination than have frequently marked the criticisms of his countrymen upon our poet)—M. Guizot has a fine passage upon the character of Iago, illustrative of the subject before us. He says:—"Iago is not merely an irritated enemy, desirous of revenge, or an ordinary rascal, anxious to destroy a happiness which he cannot contemplate with satisfaction; he is a cynical and reasoning wretch, who has made for himself a philosophy of egoism, and a science of crime; who looks upon men merely as instruments or obstacles to his personal interests; who despises virtue as an absurdity, and yet hates it as an injury; who preserves entire independence of thought while engaged in the most servile conduct; and who, at the very moment when his crimes are about to cost him his life, still enjoys with ferocious pride the evil which he had done, as if it were a proof of his superiority." To return: Iago is the wickedest man of intellect upon record; and, indeed, he would be an anomaly—a moral monster, but for one circumstance; which, although no extenuation in itself of such a career of enormity, would be ample apology to a man of his gross perceptions and selfish propensities. And here again we recognise Shakespeare's insight into human nature. No intelligent being could enter upon and sustain so systematic a career of diabolism, without a motive, although an insufficient one; and that motive was revenge, for the suspected injury he had received from both Othello and Cassio, with reference to his wife Emilia; but the unjust conduct (as he terms it) of Othello, in promoting Cassio over himself, perpetually rankles in his bosom, and is the sole spring of his action. Iago, then, is not an anomaly, a nondescript, as some have pronounced the character; but it is one of more stupendous contrivance, intricacy, and management, plausibility, rationality, and working up to a climax, than is, perhaps, to be parallelled in the whole range of the poet's *dramatis personæ.* He is an incarnation of the evil principle that threw a blight over the fairest flowers in Paradise.

Roderigo is a florid specimen of one of Shakespeare's simpleton lovers. He has placed his whole fortune at the disposal of Iago, to use for the purpose of winning favour for him with Desdemona, not having the courage and ability to woo for himself; or rather, having an instinctive knowledge of his own incompetence, with so profound and devout a respect for the talent of his adviser, as to leave the whole management of the diplomacy in his hands. Although Roderigo is a compound of vacillation and weakness, even to imbecility; although he suddenly forms resolutions, and as suddenly quenches them at the rallying contempt and jeering of Iago; and even, although being entangled in the wily villain's net, he is gradually led on to act unconsonantly with his real nature; yet withal, Roderigo has so much of redemption in him, that we commiserate his weakness, and wish him a better fate; for he is not wholly destitute of natural kindness: he really is in love with Desdemona, and was so before her marriage. Iago has had his purse, "as though the strings were his own," to woo her for him; and yet we find, with all Roderigo's subserviency to the superior intellect, that the very first words of the play announce his misgiving that his insidious friend has played him false, since he knew of the projected elopement of Desdemona with Othello, and did not apprise him of it. With this first falsehood palpable to him, he again yields to the counsel of Iago, who schools him into patience with the promise that he shall yet obtain his prize.

Next, after Othello's triumph with the Senate, and that he

has led off his bride, Roderigo, in blubbering despair, vows he "will incontinently drown himself." To mark the sway of intellect, we notice, that all through the play Roderigo has constant misgivings of Iago, and upon various occasions even revolts against his arguments, yet through incontinence and passiveness he uniformly yields to them. In this very scene his professing "friend" out-jeers him from "drowning;" urges him to "put money in his purse;" renews the promise that he shall possess his prize; and the scene ends consistently with Roderigo's counter-resolution—"*I'm changed.* I'll sell all my land."

Again, shortly after, we find him betraying his misgiving of his adviser. He says:—

"I follow here in the chase, not like a hound that hunts, but one that fills up the cry. My money is almost spent; I have been to-night exceedingly well cudgelled, [his friend's provision;] and I think the issue will be, I shall have so much experience for my pains; and so, with no money at all, and a little more wit, return to Venice."

The next scene presents the poor gull, in the full conviction that he has been thoroughly duped. He makes the one sensible resolution of his life. He says:—

"The jewels you have had from me would half have corrupted a votarist. You have told me she has received them, and returned me expectations and comforts of sudden respect and acquittance; but I find none. . . . I will make myself known to Desdemona. If she will return me my jewels, I will give over my suit, and repent my unlawful solicitation. If not, assure yourself *I will seek satisfaction of you.*"

Iago now finds him serious. He therefore shifts his tact of dictator, and praises his courage:—

"Why, now I see there's mettle in thee; and even from this instant do build on thee a better opinion than ever before. Give me thy hand, Roderigo. Thou hast taken against me a most just exception; but yet I protest I have dealt most directly in thy affair."

The interview concludes with the renewed promise that he shall still gain his Desdemona; but to that end, and for their mutual interest, that Cassio must be got rid of. Iago wins him over; he joins in the plot, and he himself falls by the hand of his tempter. A grand moral lesson to all who are able to distinguish between right and wrong, and good and evil, yet swerve to the evil path.

In the character of Montano we are presented with a welcome specimen of an honest-hearted soldier, devoid of all pettiness or jealousy. Montano, who is to be superseded by Othello, pays him the highest compliment of any of the other characters, and himself a still higher one in making the welfare of his native country subservient to his own individual interest. Alluding to the tempest in which Othello is sailing for Cyprus, he says:—

"Pray Heaven he be safe;
For I have serv'd him, and the man commands
Like a full soldier."

Then follows one of those charming pieces of scenic painting, that are as real in two or three words as the magic canvas of a Vandevelde or a Stanfield:—

"Let's to the sea-side, ho!
As well to see the vessel that's come in,
As to throw out our eyes for brave Othello;
Even till we make *the main and the aerial blue,*
*An indistinct regard.*"

Stevens, who, by the way, is not the most obtuse of the commentators, has misrepresented the conduct of Montano in the drinking-scene with Cassio and Iago. He says:— "He is not very characteristically employed where he is, tippling with people already flustered, and encouraging a subaltern officer, who commands a midnight guard, to drink to excess." In the first place, it was natural that a free, open-hearted soldier should welcome the arrival of his brother-officers with a rouse. And in the next, they had some warrant for a relaxation of discipline, seeing that the new governor, Othello, had issued a proclamation that there should be "full liberty" for revels, sporting, and feasting. It is scarcely worth while noticing such an objection, unless it be to show how constantly Shakespeare releases himself from the pick-thanking of his critics. But what a choice scene *is* that drinking-bout! The forced and artificial sociality of Iago, plying his victim with the liquor, feeding his vanity, and avoiding even the chance of offending him by the slightest contradiction, knowing his irascible nature. The piety of Cassio in his cups, so constantly witnessed in persons of a demonstrative tendency, and who are three-fourth roysterers, and one-fourth what, by correct people, is denominated "serious;" that is, persons who have an inkling that a profession of "*form*" is the "correct thing," and, in itself, substantive. His quickness to check the remotest disrespect towards himself. Iago, the Ancient, *may* be saved; but the Ancient must not be saved before the Lieutenant, who is his superior officer. The constant presence of his late promotion. His sudden recollection that they are committing a breach of discipline in this carouse:—

"Let us have no more of this: let's to our affairs. I hold him unworthy of his place who does these things. Forgive us our sins! Gentlemen, let's look to our business. Do not think, gentlemen, I am drunk: this is my Ancient; this is my right hand, and this is my left hand. I am not drunk now: I can stand well enough, and speak well enough."

No scene is more dramatically or more accurately detailed. Gratiano is one of the poet's "walking gentlemen" of the level standard. It is he who, as it were, represents the grief of Desdemona's friends on account of the calamity that has befallen her. Through him we hear of the death of her father, in those tender words :—

> "Poor Desdemona : I am glad thy father 's dead.
> Thy match was mortal to him, and pure grief
> Shore his old thread in twain : did he live now
> This sight would make him do a desperate turn ;
> Yea, curse his better angel from his side,
> And fall to reprobance."

The characteristics of Lodovico are calmness and caution. For the first quality, turn to the opening scene of the fourth Act, where he comes to summon Othello home to Venice. All his questions and observations are put with the most phlegmatic temper. Like a thorough-bred politician, he "neither loves nor hates." He has a dry duty to perform, and he executes it like a parliamentary report. Even when the Moor strikes his wife in his presence, the only observation he makes is, "This would not be believed in Venice." And, for his caution, we note that when Cassio is calling for assistance, after Iago has wounded him at night in the street, Lodovico says to Gratiano :—

> "Two or three groan ! it is a heavy night, [that is,
> dark night :]
> *These may be counterfeits ; let's think 't unsafe*
> To come in to the cry *without more help.*"

This is remarkable. And, again, in the last scene of the play, when Othello, in his paroxysm at being made so deluded a victim, wounds Iago, Lodovico *tells some one* "to wrench his sword from him ;" he does not attempt to do it himself. He is as collected and methodical as a surgeon at an operation.

The clown in Othello (and, probably, few readers recollect

that a clown is introduced in that play) comes in but for a minute or two; but he employs his time to advantage in mystifying the musicians whom Cassio has engaged to serenade the General :—

"Well, masters, here's money for you; and the General so likes your music, that he desires you, of all loves, to make no more noise with it. . . . . If you have any music now that may not be heard, to 't again; but, as they say, to hear music the General does not greatly care."

The character of Emilia has not, I think, hitherto been properly understood by either commentators or performers: the latter, among other misapprehensions of the poet's intention, always make her speak *at* her husband in the celebrated scene where Othello traduces Desdemona. She says :—

"The Moor 's abus'd by some most villanous knave,
Some base, notorious knave, some scurvy fellow:
O Heaven, that such companions thou 'dst unfold,
And put in every honest hand a whip,
To lash the rascal naked through the world."

That she had no thought of including Iago in that surmise is evident from her immediately adding :—

"Some such squire he was
That turn'd your wit the seamy side without,
And made you to suspect me with the Moor."

But, indeed, Emilia, who had the best means of knowing the character of Iago, is the last to believe him dishonest. She acknowledges him to be rough, blunt, and wayward; but she, with all the others, believes him to be a true friend. She urges Desdemona to intercede in behalf of Cassio with Othello :—"Good madam, do; I know it grieves my husband as if the case were his." She purloins the handkerchief solely "to please his fantasy;" the bare thought of his turning it to a dishonest purpose never enters her head. Moreover, in every subsequent emergency, and in Desdemona's distress, she constantly appeals to her husband; and, up to the very last scene, she bears him harmless of all suspicion. She says:—

> "Oh, are you come, Iago? you have done well,
> That men must lay their murders on your neck."

And, indeed, all through the same scene, she iterates in the most natural tone of surprise to all the charges crowding in against him, "My husband!" as if she could not possibly take it into her faculties that he was capable of a treachery. She is uniformly submissive to him, till his own lips have proclaimed his calumny of Desdemona's infidelity with Cassio; and only then is it that she throws off her allegiance to him.

> "*Emil.* Did you ever tell him she was false?
> "*Iago.* I did.
> "*Emil.* You told a lie; an odious, damned lie;
> Upon my soul, a lie; a wicked lie:—
> She false with Cassio! *Did* you say with Cassio?
> "*Iago.* With Cassio, mistress. Go to, charm your tongue.
> "*Emil.* I will not charm my tongue; I'm bound to speak:
> My mistress here lies murder'd in her bed."

And in answer to his order that she "go home," she says:—

> "Good gentlemen, let me have leave to speak;
> 'Tis proper I obey him, but not now."

The only expression that can convey any previous suspicion on her part of her husband is, when she exclaims, "Oh, villany! villany! *I thought so then;*" but this merely implies that she believed some treachery was on foot—by no means that her husband was the traitor; on the contrary, she is so overwhelmed, upon the discovery of his guilt, that she even says, "I'll kill myself with grief." Every step in the plot, up to the climax of his appropriating the handkerchief, goes to prove Emilia's love for, and confidence in, her husband. Even the very act of retaining it, and telling Desdemona the deliberate lie, that she knew nothing of it, may be quoted as a desire on her part to screen *him;* but it is likewise a glowing example not only of the mischief accruing from indirect conduct, but of the extraordinary compromise that common-minded people make with their sense of right and wrong. It is trite enough to say, that there could have been no catastrophe, no calamity, had Emilia told the truth in the first instance; but what a lesson does the great master teach us, in working out so disastrous a consequence from such an origin!—an *apparently* innocuous deception and falsehood on the part of Emilia, in the first instance;—thus tracking, in short, the murder of Desdemona to her friend and champion, and not to the arch-plotter, and her bitter enemy, Iago. This, I must say, appears to me the very sublime of social moral philosophy.

The whole character of Emilia is a perfect specimen of a free woman of the world, having no evil or malice prepense in her composition; at the same time, retaining her virtue only by a slip-knot. For an exquisite portraiture of the pure and holy truth of female delicacy and conjugal love, let any one read the conversation at the close of the fourth Act between Desdemona and Emilia, while the latter is undressing her mistress for bed, (a scene—that portion at least—never acted,) and then let him rival it, if he can, from the pages of any professor of social morality. This very scene, by the way, contains one of those surprising touches of nature which indicate the headlands and promontories of genius. When Othello, who has made up his mind for the murder, bids Desdemona go early to bed, Emilia (after he is gone) says, "How goes it now? He looks gentler than he did." Some one has truly said, "An inferior dramatist would have extended that thought over two pages." Yes, and have made a flat result of it.

Another artistical contrast, showing the triumphant beauty of conjugal love, is instituted between the conduct of Desdemona and that of the courtesan, Bianca, who, nevertheless, is no offensive specimen of her class, as she would have been delineated in the coarse pages of the contemporary dramatists. When I think how Bianca would have been exhibited by Beaumont and Fletcher, Etheridge, Dryden, and Wycherly, she is a positive purist in the hands of Shakespeare. Although her career of life, and intimacy with the vilest language, are suggestive of much that might legitimately be put into her mouth, she is an absolute vestal, both in heart and tongue, compared with Iago: and, indeed, Shakespeare seems to have been incapable of originating an atrocious female character. Even the harlot Bianca possesses a strong infusion of that kindliness which "makes the whole world kin." She shows an unselfish, animal love for Cassio; and the truth of this is only allowed to appear, in the poet's artful but prodigal way, by a side-wind observation from one of the other characters. When Cassio has been assassinated in the street at night, Iago says, "Prythee, Emilia, go know of Cassio where he supped to-night." Then turning suddenly upon Bianca, he adds, "What do you shake at?" pretending to criminate her, and knowing how easily suspicion attaches to her unhappy sisterhood, he himself having wounded Cassio. Bianca answers, "He supped at my house, but I therefore shake not." What an exquisite thought to show by *action*, and not by *profession*, that the peril of him she loved had unnerved her! Shakespeare had Divine authority for knowing that such as Bianca (deluded, and then misused beings) will be received where the Pharisees and hypocrites will be rejected.

"Othello," says Coleridge, "has no life but in Desdemona: the belief that she, his angel, had fallen from the heaven of her native innocence, wrought a civil war in his heart. She is his counterpart, and, like him, is almost sanctified in our eyes by her absolute unsuspiciousness, and holy entireness of love. As the curtain drops, which do we pity most?"

Schlegel designates the play of "Othello" as a "tragical Rembrandt." The main incident of the story is indeed "dark with fierce keeping;" and the reader must retain his imagination, and his feelings too, completely under control, who can rise from an absorbed attention to its steadily-accumulating and grievous catastrophe, without feeling harassed and exhausted by reason of its intense reality.

VI.

# Merry Wives of Windsor.

# VI.

# MERRY WIVES OF WINDSOR.

---

THE "Merry Wives of Windsor" is one of those delightfully happy plays of Shakespeare, beaming with sunshine and good humour, that makes one feel the better, the lighter, and the happier, for having seen or read it. It has a superadded charm, too, from the scene being purely English; and we all know how rare and how precious English sunshine is, both literally and metaphorically. The "Merry Wives" may be designated the "sunshine" of domestic life, as the "As You Like It" is the "sunshine" of romantic life. The out-door character that pervades both plays gives to them their tone of buoyancy and enjoyment, and true holiday feeling. We have the meeting of Shallow and Slender and Page in the streets of Windsor, who saunter on, chatting of the "fallow grey-hound, and of his being out-run on Cotsal;" and, still strolling on, they propose the match between Slender and "sweet Ann Page." Then Ann brings wine out of doors to them; though her father, with the genuine feeling of old English hospitality, presses them to come into his house, and enjoy it with a "hot venison pasty to dinner." And she afterwards comes out into the garden to bid Master Slender to table, where, we may imagine, he has been lounging about, in the hope of the fresh air relieving his sheepish embarrassment. When Doctor Caius bids his servant bring him his rapier, he answers, "'Tis ready, sir, here in the porch,"—conveying the idea of a room leading at once into the open air—such a room as used to be called "a summer parlour." Then we hear of Ann Page being at a "farm-house a-feasting;" and we have Mrs Page leading her little boy William to school; and Sir Hugh Evans sees people coming "from Frogmore over the stile this way;" and we find that Master Ford "is this morning gone a-birding." Even the very headings to the scenes breathe of dear, lovely English scenery—"Windsor Park"—"A field near Frogmore." They talk, too, of Datchet Lane; and Sir John Falstaff is "slighted into the river." And, with this, come thronging visions of the "silver Thames," and some of those exquisite leafy nooks on its banks, with the cawing of rooks; and its little islands, crowned with the dark and glossy-leaved alder; and barges lapsing on its tranquil tide. To crown all, the story winds up with a plot to meet in Windsor Park at midnight, to trick the fat knight beneath "Herne's oak." The whole play, indeed, is, as it were, a village, or even a homestead pastoral.

The *dramatis personæ*, too, perfectly harmonise, and are in strict keeping with the scene. They are redolent of health and good humour—that moral and physical "sunshine."

There are the two "Merry Wives" themselves. What a picture we have of buxom, laughing, ripe beauty! ready for any frolic "that may not sully the chariness of their honesty." That jealous-pate, Ford, ought to have been sure of his wife's integrity and goodness, from her being so transparent-charactered and cheerful; for your insincere and double-dealing people are sure to betray, some time or other, the drag that dishonesty claps upon the wheel of their conduct. The career of a deceitful person is never uniform. In the sequel, however, Ford does make a handsome atonement—that of a frank apology to the party whom he had abused by his suspicions; and he winds up the play with the rest, not the least happy of the group from having an enfranchised heart. He says well:—

> "Pardon me, wife. Henceforth do what thou wilt.
> I rather will suspect the sun with cold
> Than thee with wantonness. Now doth thy honour stand,
> In him that was of late a heretic,
> As firm as faith."

Shakespeare also says, "The husband is to blame if the wife do fall." But, good heaven! what a donkey a jealous man is, morally as well as politically! He is a donkey as regards his wife, if she *be* dishonest; for he gives her every advantage over him, by putting her on her guard to outwit him. But I think that, in ninety-nine cases out of the hundred, where the marriage-knot has been broken, we may depend upon one of two things,—either that the woman did not give her heart, only her hand; or that she has been chilled by coldness or want of confidence in her partner. For I assume it as an axiom, that, where a woman does love, nothing can shake the constancy of her attachment. The Duke in "Twelfth Night" says:—

> "However we do praise ourselves,
> Our fancies are more giddy and unfirm,
> More longing, wav'ring, sooner lost and worn
> Than women's are."

I confess that I have so little respect for a jealous man, and so much of the mischief of "old Harry" in me, that (but for the woman's peace) I would keep his steam at high pressure.

Then, there is Page, the very personification of hearty English hospitality. You feel the tight grasp of his hand, and see the honest sparkle of his eye, as he leads in the wranglers with, "Come, gentlemen, I hope we shall drink down all unkindness." If I were required to point to the portrait of a genuine, indigenous Englishman, throughout the whole of the works of Shakespeare, Page would be the man. Every thought of his heart, every motion of his body, appears to be the result of pure instinct; he has nothing exotic or artificial about him. He possesses strong yeoman sense, an unmistakable speech, a trusting nature, and a fearless deportment; and these are the characteristics of a true Englishman. He is to be gulled—no man more so; and he is gulled every day in the year—no proof, you will say, of his "strong yeoman sense;" but an Englishman is quite as frequently gulled with his eyes open as when they are hoodwinked. He has a conceit in being indifferent to chicanery. He confides in his own strength when it behoves him to exert it; and then he abates the nuisance. The English have never yet been fooled to their ruin; and my belief is, that they never will be. They go on bearing the most insolent injustice with an apathy that is inscrutable to foreigners, who know their character when they are opposed: at length they wake up, come to the sudden conclusion that this thing has lasted long enough, and then down it goes. Your true Englishman is confiding; and for that very reason he is an "awkward customer" when his confidence is betrayed. And yet, "nevertheless and notwithstanding," (as the lawyers say,) our brother John does at times contrive to make a prodigious Tom-noddy of himself. And he has lately been kicking up his heels in that fashion to a wonderful extent. I am not launching into politics. It is neither the place nor the occasion. But this, and no more, I will say:—When all the Frenchmen in the world are turned into gnats, we may then dread being taken unawares by an invasion of a million of them upon some fine, calm day, with a south wind—and not till then. And if they do come, not one will go back alive. But our revered brother John not only allows himself to be bamboozled, but, worse than that, to be hectored over by a very low and very presumptuous minority of his family. And he has a positively sleepless horror of that ubiquitous lady, "Mrs Grundy," who has only to stare him in the face, when he would do something without consulting her, and down will his whole soul, courage and all, sink into his shoes. I knew a fine hulking fellow, with limbs of iron, and a heart of honey, who could have tried a fall with Goliath—and he *did* belabour and half kill a first-class prize-fighter; yet that man's wife (a little, shrewd, waspish woman) so crowed over, and would so peck and spur him, that he was a totally different man when in her company, and seemed not to have a soul of his own. She was *his* "Mrs Grundy," and he was afraid of her. Now Page was of a better breed in the race than this. When Ford makes his almost abject apology to his injured wife, Page says:—

> "'Tis well, 'tis well; no more:
> Be not as extreme in submission
> As in offence."

The commentators have called Page "uxorious;" which, in plain-spun English, means that he is in love with his wife: it is a term of contempt, applied by men who are Turkish in their homes, and whose wives are their freehold servants. But, so far from seeing any disgrace in a man being thoroughly in love with his wife, I only hope the complaint may become more and more epidemic. What is fighting for our hearths but fighting for our wives? and what is a hearth worth without a wife? Where there is something at home worth struggling for, the whole world in arms, all the turbulent malcontents, and all the brood of zig-zag politicians will go screaming down the wind. Page was a thoroughly kind-hearted man. He joins in the hoax of the squabble between Sir Hugh and the Frenchman, but he says he "had rather hear them scold than fight." Mrs Quickly bears testimony to the transparency and unsuspecting kindness of his nature in that speech to Falstaff, wherein his generosity is inferred from the liberty of action he allows his wife. The woman Quickly says:—

"Truly, Master Page is an honest man. Never a wife in Windsor leads a better life than she does:—do what she will, say what she will, take all, pay all; go to bed when she list, rise when she list, all is as she will; and truly she deserves it, for if there be a kind woman in Windsor, she is one."

One word more upon Page and his wife before their dismissal. He has been strangely enough spoken of, in combination with his comely partner, as "the *foolish* Page and his no less *foolish* wife." These are the terms in which the worthy yeoman of "The Merry Wives of Windsor" is mentioned by a German critic; who resolves all in Shakespeare's writings into an æsthetic truism, or a mere technicality of art. Can the right worshipful and very ponderous Herr Doctor Ulrici see nothing else than the "folly" of Page, because he makes a mistaken plan for his daughter's bestowal in marriage? Can he see nothing of the "*wisdom*" of non-malice-bearing, and a cheerful acquiescence with things that have been done when they cannot be undone, in his prompt forgiveness of his child's young husband, when he finds they have stolen a match?—"Well, what remedy? Fenton, Heaven give thee joy! What cannot be eschewed must be embraced." Can he see nothing of the "wisdom" of frank English hospitality, with hearty English peace-making, and love of making quarrellers reconciled, in Page's "Come,—we have a hot venison pasty to dinner,—come, gentlemen, I hope we shall drink down all unkindness." Can he see nothing of the "wisdom" of Page's sturdy English confidence in his wife's honesty, where he says, upon hearing of Falstaff's proposed attempt upon her virtue,—"If he should intend this voyage towards my wife, I would turn her loose to him; and what he gets more of her than sharp words, let it lie on my head?" That the reliance is not a blind one, we have already learned from Mrs Page's own words, just previously, where she says of her good man,—"He's as far from jealousy as I am from giving him cause; and that, I hope, is an unmeasurable distance." Such a speech as that argues but little "foolishness" in the "no less foolish wife." But we have plentiful evidence, too, of Mrs Page being *no fool.* Witness the ready wit of her arch reply to Ford; when he says,—alluding to the strong attachment subsisting between herself and his own wife,—"I think, if your husbands were dead, you *two* would marry," she retorts, "Be sure of that—*two other husbands.*" This is no slight to her own lord and master; but only a smart rap on the knuckles for her friend's jealous-pated one. There is anything but "foolishness" in the brisk way with which she carries on the jest, in concert with her gossip, Mrs Ford, against the "greasy knight," as she calls Falstaff. There is anything but lack of wit in her exclamation, "Heaven guide him to thy husband's cudgel; and the devil guide his cudgel afterwards." And though, *in anticipation,* her sense of humour prompts this lively sally; yet, *at the time,* her sense of justice, and also her wise kind-heartedness, will not see him beaten too unmercifully.

Upon my life, I can see nothing "foolish" in all this; but, on the contrary, a sprightly, sensible, quick-witted woman, who deserves her husband's confidence—and has it—by her faithful, true-hearted allegiance to him; who secures and preserves his love by her cheerful spirits, and blithe good-humour; and who seconds her husband in all his hospitable, peace-making schemes; for, at the end of the play, she says, "Let us every one *go home,* and laugh this sport o'er by a country fire—*Sir John and all.*" In short, they are a perfectly worthy couple;—worthy of each other, in their good temper, good faith, and excellent good sense. To call them "the foolish Page, and his no less foolish wife," is no less than flat blasphemy against the "*wisdom*" of *good-nature.* But many persons confound good-nature with weakness—often, perhaps, with the hope of finding it weak enough to be taken advantage of. It is, doubtless, infinitely more easy to write a flippant, undervaluing word of one of Shakespeare's characters, than to discern and appreciate its multitudinous beauties. Both the Pages are people of kind-hearted common sense; which is as far removed from "foolishness"—quite as far removed—as a boring into the mere rules and strictnesses of dramatic art is from a clear perception of the poetry, the philosophy, the harmony, the consistency, the truth to nature, the knowledge of character, and a hundred things beside, that exist in Shakespeare's dramatic art.

And now, with a slight infringement of the plan of these Essays,—viz., that of giving extra discussion to "subordinate characters,"—I would speak a word of Falstaff—incomparable Sir John Falstaff!—for it would be an absolute indignity to this sunshiny play, (like flouting the sun itself!) to omit mentioning Falstaff when enumerating its characters. He, in himself, is *all* sunshine; for he is capable of dazzling the eyes with his brilliancy, even while they look upon roguery and vice. The desire to speak of him is in reply to what has frequently, nay, over and over, been asserted, that Falstaff, in the "Merry Wives," does not show to such advantage as in the plays of Henry IV. But if we call to mind some of his finest passages here, we shall find, I think, that he scarcely, if at all, comes short of himself in the other two dramas. For instance, what can exceed the insolent self-possession and sublime coolness, with which he throws overboard the accusations of Shallow and Slender? (in the opening of the play.) His entering, with that illustrious, bullying swagger—that lordly contempt and defiance of all objection:—"Now, Master Shallow; you 'll complain of me to the king?" Telling the poor flabby knight that he will only "be laughed at." Then, turning upon Slender:—"Slender, *I broke your head; what matter have you against me?*" His deciding the pick-pocket allegations of his rascally followers, who, of course, deny the charge of robbing Slender:—"You hear these matters denied, gentlemen—you hear it." The word of denial of such men to be taken for granted! and an appeal made for the truth of their asseveration! "*You hear it.*"

Then, for the adventure in the "buck-basket," and his being "slighted into the river!" No description in the previous plays exceeds this, both in wit and humour:—

"You may know, by my size, that I have a kind of *alacrity in sinking*. . . . I had been drowned, but that the shore was shelvy and shallow—a death that I abhor; for the water *swells* a man; and what a thing should I have been, swelled! I should have been a mountain of mummy!"

His very mishaps only furnish him with matter for jests and witty description. He goes on rioting in the detail of this same adventure—

"Crammed in with stinking clothes, . . . . think of that, a man of my kidney!—think of that; that am as subject to heat as butter—a man of continual *dissolution and thaw:* it was a miracle to escape suffocation. And in the height of this bath, when I was more than half stewed in grease, like a Dutch dish, to be thrown into the Thames, and *cooled, glowing hot, in that surge, like a horse-shoe:* think of that—hissing hot,—think of that, Master Brook!"

These are two or three bricks, for samples of the perfect structure.

There is a fine self-consciousness about Falstaff, which nevertheless is not so much *egoism* as "*Falstaffism*." If proof were wanting of Falstaff's being equal in this play to himself in the "Henry the Fourths," witness that single little speech of his, when Mrs Page affects to reproach him with his joint love-making to Mrs Ford. In the midst of his eagerness to make his escape, he says:—"I love thee, and none *but* thee: *help me away!*" His selfishness, glaring as it is, and gross as his illimitable person, has a *right* to exist; for is it not his own self—Jack Falstaff, that most unique and fine of individualities?

Moreover, his similes are none the less exquisite in wit and humour from their being elicited by his own calamities. It seems as if that very fact gave a keenness to their point, and set the edge of their sharp severity. And then, with what audacity of joke does his self-love take out its revenge against ill-fortune! Never was there a bolder jest than the one with which the following speech concludes. It forms a climax to Falstaff's daring impudence of wit. He says:—

> "I would all the world might be cozened; for I have been cozened, and beaten too. If it should come to the ear of the court how I have been transformed, and how my transformation hath been washed and cudgelled, they would mock me out of my fat, drop by drop, and liquor fishermen's boots with me. I warrant they would whip me with their fine wits, till I were as crest-fallen as a dried pear. I never prospered since I forswore myself at primero. Well, *if my wind were but long enough to say my prayers, I would repent!*"

"Mine host of the Garter" is one of the most original characters in the play. He is imbued with an eccentric fancy, and has the richest humour for a joke or a hoax. Moreover, mine host is the prince of good fellows. He feels perfectly easy whether Falstaff pay him "ten pounds a-week" or two; and he, good-naturedly, takes his "withered serving-man" (Bardolph) "for a fresh tapster." His self-conceit in his own skill and management is delicious:—"Am I politic? am I subtle? am I a Machiavel?" And again, "The Germans shall have my horses; but I'll make them pay—I'll sauce them." But he loses his horses, and then his "mind is heavy,"—the last thing we should expect from him. We do not, therefore, regret that his loss is made up in the "hundred pounds in gold" promised him by Fenton. There is no malice in mine host's "waggery;" and he manages the quarrel between Sir Hugh Evans, the parson, and Dr Caius in the best spirit imaginable. What rich drollery in his taking advantage of Caius's ignorance of English to befool him in the eyes of the company, while the Frenchman is waiting to fight with Sir Hugh. Shallow says:—

"Master Doctor Caius, I am come to fetch you home. I am sworn of the peace. You have showed yourself a wise physician, and Sir Hugh hath showed himself a wise and patient churchman. You must go with me, Master Doctor."

"*Host.* Pardon, guest Justice. A word, Monsieur Muck-water.

"*Caius.* Muck-vater! Vat is dat?

"*Host.* Muck-water, in our English, is '*valour*,' Bully.

"*Caius.* Be gar, den I have as much muck-vater as de Englishman. Scurvy, jack, dog, priest! Be gar, me vill cut his ears."

"*Host.* He'll clapper-claw thee tightly, Bully.

"*Caius.* Clapper-de-claw! Vat is dat?

"*Host.* That is, *he will make thee amends.*

"*Caius.* Be gar, me look he shall clapper-de-claw me; for, be gar, me vill have it.

"*Host.* And I will provoke him to it, or let him wag."

Next come Shallow and Slender,—specimens of imbecility run to seed. Choicely effete is the Justice's vapouring about his dignities! Not only is he "Coram," but he is "Custalorum"—ay, and "Ratolorum," too; and writes himself "Armigero in any bill, warrant, quittance, or obligation,—

Armigero." The very "totting up" of his qualifications creates a "real presence" of the man. Shallow's saturnalia is in the Second Part of Henry IV. He there exhibits in rampant folly. His gabble and his nonsense are superb. It is there that we have Master Shallow in his glory.

The reintroduction of these characters into the "Merry Wives of Windsor"—Shallow, and Bardolph, and Pistol, and Nym—is, in itself, a proof how thoroughly they were appreciated by the public upon their first appearance; and still more is it a proof of their author's power in investing them with unfaded vigour and interest; for we know by experience how rarely a second portraiture of a character has succeeded with the public. And yet, although they are identically the same people, not one of the whole party repeats himself. We have met them at the Boar's Head in East Cheap, and at Coventry; and here they are again in Windsor,—the same characters, but with a difference.

Slender comes out in this play with extraordinary force. He and Falstaff are the persons who at once present themselves to the imagination, when it is referred to. What a speaking portrait we have of Slender in the conversation between Mrs Quickly and his man, Simple! His "little wee face, with a little yellow beard—a cane-coloured beard." He is a "tall fellow, too, of his hands, as any is, between this and his head." The humorous, quaint, and witty old Fuller says:—"Your men that are built six stories high have seldom much in their cockloft." But Master Slender hath earned a reputation, at all events, with his serving-man; he hath "fought with a warrener." And he doth not hide his pretensions to valour, especially from the women, or his station in society. He takes care that Anne Page shall know he "keeps three men and a boy, till his mother be dead;" and that he lives like a "poor gentleman born." He says this before Anne, not to her.

It is interesting to note the distinction that Shakespeare has made in drawing the two fools, Sir Andrew Aguecheek and Master Slender. The difference between them seems to be, that Andrew is stupid, awkward, and incompetent, and fails in all cases from lack of ideas to help him in his need: if he had these, his stock of conceit would carry him through and over anything; but he is a coward, as well as a fool. Slender possesses not only the deficiencies of Aguecheek, but he is bashful, even to sheepishness. This quality makes him uniformly dependent on one or another for support. His spirit is so rickety that he cannot trust it alone; and yet, withal, in little non-essentials of conduct and character. Slender is not so perfect a fool but that he has the tact to display his accomplishments to win his mistress's favour. Some have not even that wisdom, who would, nevertheless, turn up their noses at Master Slender. Having insinuated his rank and "possibilities," what love-diplomacy can surpass the patronising, and the magnanimous indifference with which he introduces the subject of his courage? Anne is sent to entreat him to dinner:—

"I pray you, sir, walk in.

"*Slen.* I had rather walk here, I thank you. I bruised my shin the other day with playing at sword and dagger with a master of fence,—three veneys for a dish of stewed prunes; and, by my troth, I cannot abide the smell of hot meat since. Why do your dogs bark so? be there bears in the town?

"*Anne.* I think there are, sir; I heard them talked of.

"*Slen.* I love the sport well; but I shall as soon *quarrel* at it as any man in England. You are afraid if you see the bear loose, are you not?

"*Anne.* Ay, indeed, sir.

"*Slen. That's meat and drink to me now.* I have seen Sackerson loose twenty times, and have taken him by the chain; but, I warrant you, the *women* have so cried and shrieked at it, that it pass'd; but *women*, indeed, can't abide 'em; they are very ill-favour'd rough things."

Does not this precisely tally with Mrs Quickly's description of the man, that he "holds up his head, as it were; and struts in his gait." Again, be it said, Master Slender is not so great a fool, but that he is to be drawn by a thread where he has a dawning that his interests are conspicuous. He will not only marry Anne Page, with her "seven hundred pounds and possibilities," but he "will do a greater thing than that," upon "the request of his cousin Shallow, *in any reason*." That morsel of a scene is worth its weight in gold, where his uncle Shallow and Parson Evans have concocted the match between him and Anne Page, and are badgering him into an explicit declaration of his affection; and which, from sheepishness, he constantly eludes, by negative acquiescences. His concluding resolve is immortal:—

"I will marry her, sir, *at your request;* but if there be no great love in the beginning, yet Heaven may decrease it upon better acquaintance, when we are married, and have more occasion to know one another. I hope upon familiarity will grow more contempt; but *if you say,* 'Marry her,' that I am freely dissolved, and dissolutely."

All who have intercourse with the world can testify that the character of Master Slender is by no means an anomaly. The love-scene between him and Mistress Anne is a notable display of broad humour; and what a thought it was to make him ask his man Simple for his book of sonnets and love-songs, to woo with! for he has not a word of his own to throw to a dog; and a pretty girl frightens him out of his little senses. When he first sees her, he says in a faint fluster, "O heaven! this is Mistress Anne Page!" And when dragged to the wooing-stake, like a lugged bear, by his cousin Shallow, we hear him yearning, "I had rather than forty shillings I had my book of songs and sonnets here." In default of this, his book of riddles might serve. Riddles to make love with! But the book of riddles he had lent to Alice

Shortcake a week before "Hallowmas." So the poor soul stands gasping, like a stranded grampus. And when left alone in wretchedness with her, her very first question flabbergasts him. If she had not led off, he would have stood there till now :—

"Now, Master Slender.

"*Slen.* Now, good Mistress Anne.

"*Anne.* What is your will?

"*Slen.* My will? Odds heartlings, that's a pretty jest, indeed! I ne'er made my will yet, thank Heaven. I am not such a sickly creature, I give Heaven praise.

"*Anne.* I mean, Master Slender, what would you have with me?

"*Slen.* Truly, for mine own part, I would little or nothing with you. Your father and my uncle have made motions. If it be my luck, so; if not, happy man be his dole! They can tell you how things go better than I can."

Nothing can surpass this. Well might Anne, in despair, say :—

"This is my father's choice.
Oh, what a world of vile ill-favour'd faults
Looks handsome in three hundred pounds a-year!"

That is an excellent touch of worldly prudence on the part of Anne's father, by the way, brought in to justify his objection to the addresses of Fenton; whose "riots past, and wild societies;" his not only being "galled in his expense," and which he "seeks to heal" by an alliance with his daughter: but Page, moreover, being a plain, unaspiring yeoman, is also unfavourable to Fenton, on account of his being "*too great of birth.*" This simple, fleeting expression places the whole character of the father before us in perfect integrity and consistency; and is alone, and in itself, a refutation of Ulrici's charge against him, for folly,—"the foolish Page!" It is worth a whole scene of see-sawing and protesting. It also prepares us for Fenton's honest justification of himself. And here we have one of Shakespeare's lessons in wisdom—viz., in the matrimonial contract to avoid everything in the shape of duplicity and mental reservation—most especially before the fulfilment of it. This passage in Fenton's courtship is the only one which gives him an interest with us as a lover, because it raises him in our esteem; and with the confession, it is natural that Anne should promote his suit. In answer to his report of her father's objection to him, that "'tis impossible he should love her but as a property," like a sensible girl, she candidly replies, "May be he tells you true;" and he as candidly and fervently replies:—

"No, Heav'n so speed me in my time to come!
Albeit, I will confess, thy father's wealth
Was the first motive that I woo'd thee, Anne;
Yet, wooing thee, I found thee of more value
Than stamps in gold, or sums in sealed bags;
And 'tis the very riches of thyself
That now I aim at."

And the consummation of his good sense and steadiness of character appears at the close of the play; and Shakespeare's own matrimonial morality is displayed, where Fenton succeeds in carrying off Anne, in the teeth of Page and his wife, who each wanted to force her into a money-match. Fenton's rebuke is excellent; and the father and mother's reconciliation perfectly harmonises with their frank and generous dispositions. Fenton says:—

"Hear the truth of it.
You would have married her most shamefully,
Where there was no proportion held in love.
* * * * * *
The offence is *holy* that she hath committed;
And this deceit loses the name of craft,
Of disobedience, or unduteous title;

Since therein she doth evitate and shun
A thousand irreligious cursed hours,
Which forcèd marriage would have brought upon her."

Next in order comes the good-natured but peppery Welsh parson, Sir Hugh. Like the worthy Parson Adams, in Fielding's "Joseph Andrews," he is thrown into various undignified attitudes by the author; and although we laugh with, and sometimes at him, yet Shakespeare has never once committed his character in such a way that we should refuse cordially to grasp his hand. The country parish priests in those days were a different class of men from the present members of the Establishment: nevertheless, some scattered remnants of the old brotherhood may still be met with in those secluded villages where the high post and railroads swerve in the distance: men of almost indiscriminate sociality, taking an inoffensive part in the pastimes and homely mirth of the parishioners. I knew a gentleman who well remembered Dr Young, the eminent author of the "Night Thoughts," in his rectory of Welwyn, in Hertfordshire. He had dined at his table on the Sunday, when he and any of his school-fellows had acquitted themselves creditably during the week at the grammar-school. Among other personal anecdotes, he told me that he had constantly seen him playing at bowls on the Sunday, after he had preached the words of peace, and good-will, and eternal salvation to his flock. He not only tolerated, but even promoted that harmless recreation; at the same time he had a keen eye and a reproof for all who were truants at the hour of prayer.

Sir Hugh Evans stands not aloof from the plot to get Anne a good husband; and he is master of the band of fairies to pinch and worry the fat knight in the revelry under "Herne's oak."

"Trib, trib, fairies; come, and remember your parts; be

pold, I pray you; follow me into the pit; and when I give the watch-'ords, do as I pid you: come, come; trib, trib!"

And he was an actor, too, as well as manager of the revels; for Falstaff says while they are tormenting him:—"Heavens defend me from that Welch fairy! lest he transform me into a piece of cheese!" Even in the noted scene of the duel with Doctor Caius, although the honest preacher is forced into a ludicrous and "unhandsome fix" by the hoax of mine host of the Garter, yet our kindly feeling for Sir Hugh remains unimpaired. It is true, he waxeth into a tremendous Welch passion: he is full of "melancholies," and "tremplings of mind;" moreover, not being a professed duellist, his self-possession is not conspicuous: he sings a scrap of a madrigal and a line of a psalm, and mixes both.

"Pless my soul! how full of cholers I am, and tremplings of mind!—I shall be glad if he have deceived me. How melancholies I am! pless my soul! [*Sings.*
'To shallow rivers, to whose falls.'
Mercy on me! I have great dispositions to cry. [*Sings.*
'Melodious pirds sing madrigals,
When as I sat in Pabylon,—
And a thousand fragrant posies.'"

But when the belligerents *do* meet, and he finds that they have been fooled by the whole party, he is the one to preserve their mutual self-respect.

"Pray you, let us not be laughing-stogs to other men's humours; I desire you in friendship; and I will one way or other make you amends. He has made us his vlouting-stog; and let us knog our prains together, to be revenge on this same scall, scurvy, cogging companion, the host of the Garter."

And the way in which he revenges himself is—like a practical teacher of the "Sermon on the Mount"—to come and put the host on his guard against trusting the Germans with his horses.

"There is a friend of mine come to town, tells me, there is three cousin Germans, that has cozened all the hosts of Readings, of Maidenhead, of Colnbrook, of horses and money. I *tell you for good-will,* look you; you are wise, and full of gibes and vlouting-stogs, and 'tis not convenient you should be cozened. Fare you well."

Doctor Caius is one of those exotics, half professional, whole quack, whose chief source of attraction with John Bull is, that they are *not native.* The French Doctor, therefore, is always flourishing of his success at court. By the blessing of an impenetrable assurance, and a ball-and-socket morality—turning at will in every direction of their interest, and desire of their patrons; and above all, with that choicest and most needful of accomplishments for a quack—an utter unconsciousness of misgiving, or of diffidence with regard to their own talents, these same exotics are received by our easy, gullible brethren with "outstretched arms;" while "patient merit goes out sighing." This prejudice, however, in favour of foreign talent is not without its advantage to brother John, who would subside into an indolent animal if he encountered no opposition; but being put upon his mettle, and moreover, inheriting no small store of pugnacious obstinacy, with great and available talent, he contrives to keep pace with his rivals; and he will yet maintain his ascendancy in the civilised world. Real ability, like truth, must prevail; and though quackery may, and does succeed for a season, it is commonly but with the empty-skulled and the frivolous.

Pretty little Anne Page, who contributes no small portion of the "sunshine" in this delightful comedy, is not so deeply and anxiously enamoured of Master Fenton, but that she can afford to trifle and amuse herself with the single-speech courtship of Slender; and her very protestation against the suit of the Frenchman has in it such a spice of humour as makes one fall head-and-ears over in love with her.

> "Good mother, do not marry me to yond' fool! [Slender.]
> "*Mrs Page.* I mean it not; I seek you a better husband.
> "*Mrs Quick.* That 's my master, master doctor.
> "*Anne.* Alas! *I had rather be set quick in the earth, and bowled to death with turnips.*"

But although a "subordinate character," how very important a person in this play is Mistress Quickly, the housekeeper to Doctor Caius; or, as Sir Hugh designates her, "his nurse, or his dry-nurse, or his cook, or his laundry, his washer, or his wringer." What a perfect specimen she is of a fussy, busy-bodying old woman! "That foolish carrion, Mrs Quickly," as Mrs Page calls her; making herself necessary to all, by reason of her fussiness; and conspicuous, by reason of her folly. A large family,—the race of the Quicklies! Our Mrs Quickly, the type of the whole breed, meddles and "trepots" in every one's affairs: with the seriousness and sincere dealing of a diplomatist, she acts the go-between for Falstaff with the two merry wives; she courts Anne Page for her master, undertaking the same office for Slender. She favours the suit of Fenton; and if the Welsh parson had turned an eye of favour upon the yeoman's pretty daughter, she would have played the hymeneal Hebe to him too. Her whole character for mere busy-bodying, and not from any active kindness of heart,—for they who are sweet to all alike, have no principle worth a button;—her whole character is comprised in that one little speech in the 4th scene of the the 3d Act, when Fenton gives her the ring for his "sweet Nan." After he has gone out, she says:—

"Now Heaven send thee good fortune! [She would have uttered the same benediction for Slender.] A kind heart he hath: a woman would run through fire and water for such a kind heart. But yet, I would my master had Mistress Anne; or I would Master Slender had her; or, in sooth, I would Master Fenton had her. I will do what I can for them all three: for so I have promised, and I'll be as good as my word; but speciously for Master Fenton."

He was the last applicant to, and had paid her.

Some people are such idiots, and are so rabidly bent on match-making, that they would marry a girl to an ass rather than not marry her. Your match-making people are thought amusing, and are laughed at; and they have the character of being assiduous, and serviceable in their neighbours' affairs; but they come next to the tale-bearers for the mischief they frequently occasion. It is not the paramount concern with them, whether tastes and tempers assimilate, but whether the girl wants a housekeeper's place for life; and some marriages are no whit superior to that arrangement; or whether her jointure be worthy his, or his equal hers; and if so, they think it a mere flouting at the gifts of Providence if they do not snap the bait like gudgeons. They who have not witnessed some of this mischievous trumpery, have made but a select acquaintance in the world.

Mrs Quickly, however, is as much a professional as an amateur match-maker. She takes her fee of office; and it is observable that Fenton, the least capable of the three suitors to be disbursatory, is the only one liberal for her services. Her first introduction to us, in all the importance of housekeeping, the players would call "a hit." She patronises her fellow-servant, Jack Rugby:—

"What, John Rugby! I pray you, go to the casement and see if you can see our master, Master Doctor Caius, coming. If he do, i' faith, and find anybody in the house, here will be an old abusing of God's patience and the king's English. Go, and we 'll have a posset for it anon at night, in faith, at the latter end of a sea-coal fire. [*Exit* Rugby.] An honest, willing, kind fellow, as ever servant shall come in house withal; and I warrant you no tell-tale, nor no breed-bate. His worst fault is, that he is given to prayer; he is something peevish that way; but *nobody but has his fault.*"

She cross-questions Slender's man, Simple, (already quoted,) and receives her master with prepared alacrity, humming a tune of acted unconsciousness, having hidden Simple in the closet. Her first scene with Fenton is inimitable, where she goes on about a wart on his face :—

"Master Fenton, I'll be sworn on a book she loves *you.* Haven't your worship a wart above your eye?

"*Fent.* Yes, marry have I; what of that?

"*Quick.* Well, thereby hangs a tale. Good faith, it is such another Nan; but, I detest, an honest maid as ever broke bread. We had an hour's talk of that wart. I shall never laugh but in that maid's company; but, indeed, she is too much given to allicholy and musing. But for you—well, go to.

"*Fent.* Well, I shall see her to-day. Hold, there 's money for thee. Let me have thy voice in my behalf. If thou seest her before me, commend me.

"*Quick.* Will I? I'faith, that we will; and I will tell your worship *more of the wart* the next time we have confidence, and of *other wooers.*"

Like a true potterer, she interferes in every conversation, and elbows herself in wherever she sees business going on. Sir Hugh cannot even examine the little boy Page in his Latin exercise but she must put in her comments. That little scene, by the way, (the first of the 4th Act,) is an amusing specimen of what might be styled "*closet* comedy," and is an additional illustration of the farcical character of the woman.

Warton calls the "Merry Wives of Windsor" "the most

complete specimen of Shakespeare's comic powers." Had he said low comic, humorous, or farcical powers, we should perhaps acknowledge the dictum of the critic. But although there is as much broad fun in the "Twelfth Night," and in the "Much Ado About Nothing," there is also a considerably stronger infusion of the most refined and quintessentialised wit in those two plays,—an absolute desideratum in the legitimate comedy,—to say nothing of the poetry and the sentiment, sublimating and imparting the most delicate rainbow tints to all that is graceful, and passionate, and lovely in human nature. We do not expect, and we do not meet with these qualities in the present comedy. Yet the "Merry Wives of Windsor" is a wonderful production. It is all movement and variety, from the first scene to the very last; and the last ends in a rich piece of romance. Dr Johnson is right in his estimate when he says, "Its general power, that power by which works of genius shall finally be tried, is such, that perhaps it never yet had reader or spectator who did not think it too soon at an end."

# VII.

# King Lear.

# VII.

# KING LEAR.

---

THE play of King Lear—as, I think, must be apparent to every one who studies it psychologically—is a practical example of the calamities resulting from unbridled, unguided self-will. "*Will*," independent of, and irresponsible to, justice and rationality, is the pivot upon which turn all the disasters that befall its leading characters. Like a steam-engine without check or safety-valve, they destroy themselves, and scatter ruin and dismay among those within the range of its fury. Besides the leading character, Lear, the same principle of action—that of self-will—forms the leading feature in the characters of Gonneril and Regan: as witness their wolf-like grasping at power the moment it comes within their reach; the unrelenting spirit with which they exercise it over their father and husbands; their passion for Edmund, and which resolves itself as much into mutual struggle for the mastery over each other, and dominion, as in their lust of a criminal and riotous self-indulgence; and, lastly, their imperious bearing, up to the very close of their career. The tide of will in their minds is ever at the flood, rolling on without an eddy of misgiving or remorse, till it ends in a climax of fierce defiance. At the end of the 5th Act, when

Albany, Gonneril's husband, threatens her with the murderous letter found upon the steward, and which she had despatched to Edmund :—

> " Shut your mouth, dame,
> Or with this paper I shall stop it. . . . .
> No tearing, lady ;—I perceive you know it."

This is her answer :—

> " Say, if I do,—the laws are mine, not thine :
> Who can arraign me for it ?
> " *Alb.* Most monstrous !
> Know 'st thou this paper ?
> " *Gon.* Ask me not what I know."

And with this characteristic retort, she leaves the scene, and we hear no more of her, except that she destroys herself,—*self-willed* to the last.

The lust of " will " and of " power," again, is the mainspring of Edmund the bastard's character. Not content with the indulgent affection of his father, Gloster, and jealous of the rights of his legitimate brother, Edgar, he treacherously ejects him ; and in the sequel, compasses the disgrace of his father, in order that he himself may become " Earl of Gloster ;" and which title he at once assumes.

It may appear paradoxical to instance the conduct of the perfect Cordelia, when treating of the dominant passion which controls the progress of this drama ; but it is interesting to notice, that she inherits, in a degree and kind, the self-will and obstinacy of her father. Having once resolved to say, " Nothing," in answer to the old king's question, which of his three daughters " doth love him most," no leading questions, no inducements can make her qualify the tone of that reply. She resolves " to love, and be silent." She will love her father according to her bond ; no more nor less. " So young, and so untender," (says the old king)—" So young, my lord, and true," is her persistent answer. Another confirmation of the argument for the predominance of "will" in Cordelia's character appears in the 4th Act; she makes her *passion of grief subservient to dominion.* The passage is in a scene between Kent and a gentleman, and is one of matchless beauty and pathos:—

"*Kent.* Did your letters pierce the queen to any demonstration of grief?

"*Gent.* Ay, sir; she took them, read them in my presence;
And now and then an ample tear trill'd down
Her delicate cheek: it seem'd she was a queen
Over her passion; who, most rebel-like,
Sought to be king o'er her.

"*Kent.* O, then, it mov'd her.

"*Gent.* Not to a rage: patience and sorrow strove
Who should express her goodliest. You have seen
Sunshine and rain at once: her smiles and tears
Were like a better way: those happy smiles,
That play'd on her ripe lip, seem'd not to know
What guests were in her eyes; which parted thence,
As pearls from diamonds dropp'd.—In brief, sorrow
Would be a rarity most belov'd, if all
Could so become it.

"*Kent.* Made she no verbal question?

"*Gent.* 'Faith, once or twice she heav'd the name of 'father'
Pantingly forth, as if it press'd her heart;
Cried, 'Sisters! sisters!—Shame of ladies! sisters!
Kent! father! sisters! What, i' the storm? i' the night?
Let pity not be believ'd!'—There she shook
The holy water from her heavenly eyes,
And clamour moisten'd: then away she started
To deal with grief alone."

The conduct of Cordelia has been quoted to corroborate the position started with,—that the unyielding exercise of "will" forms the principle of moral unity which sways the course of action in all the leading characters of the drama—the good as well as the bad, and finally brings about the great catastrophe by the ruin of both parties. I am not unconscious, that by thus enlisting, as it were, this characteristic feature in the disposition of Cordelia, for the purpose of carrying out the general principle of the drama, I incur the charge of wire-drawing in criticism,—a charge I would certainly avoid. I am aware, too, that the admirers of Shakespeare are ever prone to seek out, and give him credit for intentions that probably never entered his head; nevertheless, I would say upon the present occasion, that, at all events, it forms a remarkable coincidence that *all* the offspring of the self-willed old king should, with certain modifications, have inherited his constitutional obstinacy; and that, if such were the foregone conclusion in the poet's mind, it only proves his contrivance, and comprehension of his subject, to be little less than perfect.

Besides the character of Lear, and that of the other prime movers in the play, I would quote, and lastly, Gloster, as another of the victims to the effects of an irresponsible "self-will," and of the selfishness inherent with it. His self-indulgence in early life, and scanty dispensation of justice to his natural son, Edmund,—one part of a vicious system in morals, and which proves to himself so bitter a scourge in the sequel, —and his blind rage against the legitimate son, both emanate from his ruling passion, and both concur in effecting his downfall. This is the grand and imperishable principle upon which Shakespeare's ethics are constructed. In his code of morality we have no epicene or doubtful virtues, and we have no amiable or elegant vices. He does not make seduction, or treachery of *any* sort, one of the indispensable properties of a gentleman; neither does he perk in our faces, like an Old Bailey pleader, the heroic disinterestedness of a midnight ruffian. In Shakespeare we have no Don Juan adulteries, and we have no Blueskin sentimentalities. Shakespeare has, indeed, written expressions that modern refinement rejects as indelicate; but he has nowhere given to virtue the hoof of a fiend, or to vice the golden wings of an angel. And, if ever the time should arrive that he is denounced for immorality,—and the spread of a liberal intelligence happily renders such a result problematical,—it may, indeed, be apprehended, (to use the words of Voltaire,) that "Virtue has left the heart and rested only on the lips."

The despotism of self-worship, then, in the irresponsibility of the "will," sways the chief characters of this play. Another feature in the consistency with which the poet has worked up to the spirit of the sketch from whence he took his plot, may be observed in the broad and strong colouring, and in the massive shadows he has used for the purpose of preserving a propriety in all its subordinate figures; and these, we must bear in mind, are all of them his own invention. Thus, the broad outline of the old ballad legend came to him, fraught with the simple, uncompromising, and exaggerated features of primitive history. The main incident, the characters of the principal agents, and their course of action being all strained to the utmost tension of probability, his naturally fine instinct at once prompted him, that to preserve a harmonious proportion throughout, it was necessary that he should aggrandise the moral qualities of the inferior persons in the *dramatis personæ.* We therefore notice that all the contrasted passions are thrown into high lights. The virtuous characters become glowingly conspicuous by their juxtaposition with the vicious ones; and not merely so, for by themselves, and uncontrasted, they are perfect specimens of truth, honour, disinterested love, and self-devotion, and these form the antagonist passion or principle in the plot to that of "self-will."

Thus, the daughters of Lear, the two elder and the youngest, form, in themselves, studies of contrasted character, harmonising with the whole construction of this sublime character-drama. The same strongly-marked features in evil nature, and high lights in virtuous nature, are visible through each. Cordelia is so forcibly drawn,—though with so few brief touches,—that we marvel at the masterly hand that could delineate a female figure known to us as perfectly as our own sister's, by means so succinct. There is a certain conciseness in all that is said of Cordelia, as well as all that she herself says, which consists singularly with her own character,—this being the extreme of reticence. Her father makes allusion to her having a soft, gentle, low voice; but it it is not only these,—it is seldom heard. Her very first words are uttered *aside;*—marking her habit of self-communing, rather than overt expression of thought. Her speeches throughout the play amount to but a small number, and they are for the most part composed of but sparing words. Essentially *condensed* is Cordelia's character. She is reserved, and, like many reserved people, has a fund of latent pride—the pride of rectitude—which takes refuge beneath an ultra-quiet exterior demeanour. Conscious of her rich hoard of filial love, of the sterling quality of her superiority to her hollow professing sisters, of her being perfectly undeserving her father's harshness, she is content to seem cold, passive, almost hard. There is a curious combination of loftiest dignity with lowliest humility in her nature, which combine to form the beautiful piece of womanhood known to us as Shakespeare's Cordelia. Observe the way—at once supreme in self-respect and simple in expression—in which she urges her father to clear her from imputation of real blameworthiness, and to "make known it is no vicious blot," &c., that has deprived her of his favour; with which she superbly dismisses the Burgundian Duke:—

> "Peace be with Burgundy.
> Since that respects of fortune are his love,
> I shall not be his wife;"

and with which she leaves her sisters, committing her father to their "*professed* bosoms." This condensedness, this intensity in Cordelia's temperament and utterance, is equally displayed in what she says of this kind, as in what she says of a gentle and tender kind. Few instances of concentrated disdain could be quoted as more pungent than Cordelia's "Shall we not see *these daughters,* and *these sisters?*" when she and her father are brought in prisoners; while her gentleness, her modesty, her meekness, are no less summarily indicated by the short quiet speeches she makes to the physician who is tending Lear in the crisis of his recovery. With the same subtle eloquence of brevity are Cordelia's emotions made visible through those one or two sobbed-out replies, "And so I am, I am," and, "No cause, no cause," as her old father pathetically endeavours to reassemble his wandering ideas and fix them in recognition upon her. As much as by her own words, is Cordelia made known to us by what others speak of her. Through the Fool having "much pined away;" through Kent's fine appreciation and firm attachment; and through inferences to be drawn from Lear's conduct, we gather that thorough knowledge of Cordelia's character which we possess; and which—were it not for this magical art of the poet—we could not, from the very nature of the reticent character itself, obtain. How evident is her father's experience of her untalked but not unevinced love in his first address to her, when he turns to her, saying, "Now, our joy, although our last, not least," &c., and when he soon after, in the very midst of his wrath, betrays how rooted is his trust in her proved affection, by the words, "I lov'd her most, and thought to set my rest on her kind nursery." Very noteworthy, too, is the point, that Lear *at first* talks of filial ingratitude generally; afterwards, he says, "*two* pernicious daughters," asks, "Hast thou given all to thy *two* daughters?" In the scene where he arraigns them of cruelty, he speaks only of Gonneril and Regan. What he deemed of Cordelia's undutifulness never recurs to him; for he has already long ago recognised the fact of its having been a delusion. Very affecting—just one of Shakespeare's exquisite touches of hinted suggestion, speaking volumes of heart-history—is that casually-dropped, muttered sentence of Lear's, while he is half-listening to the Fool's prattle, and attempting to keep up response to it, (in the 5th scene of the 1st Act): "I did her wrong." And again, how wonderfully is the loveliness of her nature indicated in the remorse felt by Lear when his eyes are opened to the truth of his having wronged it; in the shame he feels, in the sense he shows of the injury he has done her, by kneeling to her for forgiveness when he recognises her for his "child Cordelia." Even the very terms in which he addresses her, on first awaking, serve to impress upon us the pure look, the angelic spotlessness of Cordelia, where he says, "Thou art a soul in bliss," and, "You are a spirit, I know." Few of Shakespeare's women are more consummately depicted (although she is so tersely characterised) than "fairest Cordelia."

In following our course of the "contrasted characters" in this drama, the sisters of Cordelia immediately and naturally present themselves. And having already observed that the whole legend came to our poet with the full credentials of ballad history, he was bound to enter no party questions against the chronicler,—to assert no prerogatives for Dame Nature; but, according to his subject and "brief," to display with ogre-like hideousness the anomalous, unmixed, and unredeemed cruelty of an offspring (and a female, too,) towards her aged parent. There is no motive for the barbarity and wanton ingratitude that Regan and Gonneril exercise towards their father; therefore, their whole conduct is a violation of nature: for (unless there be insanity in the case) motive is to action what cause is to effect; and hence the revulsions that our senses undergo when we read some of the monstrosities of character that we meet in the elder dramas,—mere gratuitous exhibitions of hideousness and horror; and so "out of drawing," as to be caricatures of enormity, results without principles, conclusions without ratiocination.

In the case of Regan and Gonneril, then, Shakespeare clung implicitly to his subject; and, as if to show his mastery over *himself*, as well as his principles, he has carried the anomaly of unredeemed moral deformity to a pitch of terrible perfection. History presents no parallel in criminality to the conduct of the two elder daughters of Lear; and the poet, with unerring instinct in ethics, has extended their hard and cruel undutifulness towards their husbands, as well as their parent. In this part of their conduct will again be recognised that "harmony" in the poet's mind, heretofore so frequently referred to. Children who could leave a fond and too indulgent father to perish, would scarcely be faithful and affectionate to those with whom they had formed a merely civil compact—an alliance for convenience, if not for interest. We therefore find them plotting against each other, and against the lives of their husbands, in order that they may riot in criminal intimacy with the bastard Edmund.

Throughout their career of wickedness, we cannot fail to be struck with the tact and feeling of the poet, in toning down the *externals* of their natures upon those occasions when they are brought into communion and contact with their father. Then we find that their speeches are subdued, and delivered with a certain air of deference, as though the paternal authority were not wholly extinct in their minds. The unfilial deportment bursts forth, and is displayed when he has quitted the scene. Gonneril expostulates with him upon the riotous conduct of his attendants; but she has previously instructed her steward to neglect, and even insult him. Shakespeare has made the unkindness of Gonneril and Regan to their father to be neuter-passive in its character and action.

Their constraint upon his conduct lashes him into fury, and he scours from one to the other in helpless resentment.

There is also another point in which the two characters attract attention, and that is in their individuality. It has frequently been observed that there is no distinction or predominance in the cruelty of the two daughters of Lear. They are twins in wickedness, and yet there is a characteristic difference in the *mind*-manner of the two women. Gonneril is more towering and haughty in her deportment. She never, for a moment, loses sight of her descent—she never forgets the aristocrat. Her conduct towards her husband is uniformly that of one who has descended from a higher sphere to ally herself with, and to tolerate a husband; and whom (when she encounters a person more agreeable to her fancy) she plots to assassinate.

Her corollary of defiance upon being shown her treasonable letter, with her climax of criminality, have been noted.

Regan is only equal to her sister in undutifulness. Her mind is of a coarser grain. There is a ribald ferocity in her nature which one would suppose it impossible to transcend. When she and Cornwall, her husband, her really "other self," act the frightful scene of tearing out Gloster's eyes, Regan's behaviour and language bear the character of a butcher in a slaughter-house, jesting at the resistance and contortions of his tethered victim. They are choice illustrations of cruelty by nature.

Turn we from this "smell of the sin," to that gracious emanation of all that is gentle, and constant, and cheerful, and true—the Fool; certainly the one of all Shakespeare's, or of any other dramatist's, Fools with whom we have the most sympathy. In the character of this most illustrious creation we recognise a tender, fondling nature,—a passive dependence on, and attachment to his old master,—an active affection for Cordelia, when she is expelled by her father, his sorrow taking the character of sickness. This—with the exception of a line indicating Lear's care for the lad—is the first we hear of him; and an exquisite thought to adopt such a course for the means of begetting an interest in his character with the reader.

It is in the 4th scene of the 1st Act, when the king begins to be disturbed at the waning duty and incipient disrespect of his daughter Gonneril's servants. He repeatedly calls for his fool, that he may divert the current of his thoughts. He says, "I have perceived a most faint neglect of late; which I have rather blamed as mine own jealous curiosity, than as a very pretence and purpose of unkindness,—I will look farther into it. But where's my fool? I have not seen him this two days." His attendant knight answers, "Since my lady's going into France, sir, the fool hath much pined away." "No more of that; I have noted it well." And after, through all his melancholy wanderings, his thought for and care of the Fool are both gentle and constant. In the crowd of all his vehement reproaches, and explosions of rage and invective, he constantly turns with affecting tenderness to provide for his faithful companion. The unkindness of his daughters, the bitter fruits of misplaced confidence, the unpitying elements,—all cannot quench this spark of love in the corner of his old heart. In the midst of the storm, when the hovel is pointed out to him, his first thought is for the Fool.

"My wits begin to turn.—
Come on, my boy: how dost, my boy? Art cold?
I am cold myself.—Where is this straw, my fellow?
The art of our necessities is strange,
That can make vile things precious."

And then, in the depth of his misery, and in the rage of the storm, he turns from his own sufferings to think of his Fool:—

"Poor fool and knave, I have one part in my heart
That's sorry yet for thee."

M

—"Knave" is of Saxon origin, and signifies neither more nor less than "boy." In Chaucer's story of "Griselda," she gives birth to a "knave child." The constancy of attachment between the two opposite natures of Lear and his Fool is one of the most masterly, as well as beautiful creations that ever entered the mind of any poet. At one time of their companionship the Fool is alone with him. In the opening scene of the storm on the heath, Kent asks of a Gentleman, "Where is the king?" who replies:—

"Contending with the fretful elements;
Bids the wind blow the earth into the sea,
Or swell the curlèd waters 'bove the main,
That things might change or cease; tears his white hair,
Which th' impetuous blasts, with eyeless rage,
Catch in their fury, and make nothing of;
Strives in his little world of man to outscorn
The to-and-fro conflicting wind and rain.
This night, wherein the cub-drawn bear would couch,
The lion and the belly-pinchèd wolf
Keep their fur dry, unbonneted he runs,
And bids what will take all.
"*Kent.* But who is with him?
"*Gent.* None but the fool; who labours to out-jest
His heart-struck injuries."

And this is the strong point in his character; all his faculties are strained to cheer and divert his master. He never gives way: and here again we recognise Shakespeare's application of the "sweet uses of cheerfulness in adversity;" and which, not only keeps alive, but constantly brings out the kindly qualities of the king's heart.

It is, perhaps, the most masterful combination of the humorous and the pathetic that ever poet achieved. The character itself contains a singular union of the two; and its position in the tragedy affords as wonderful a concomitant source of the two emotions. The Fool's own struggles between his *heart's sadness* and his *duty's jesting*, form one powerful self-contrast; and the way in which Shakespeare has used this humour of the Fool, as a forcible heightening of the mournful and the tragic in the play, forms another. There is an admirable poetic harmony in the jarring of the Fool's words against the old king's words, with the tumult of the elements, and the fearful moral discord that reigns through all. No one but so great a genius as Shakespeare would have dared to place the grotesque levity of the Fool's expressions against the sublime of Lear's passion. He knew that they only served to render more terrible that storm of grief in appeal, with their affecting attempts at pleasantry in the midst of distress. Their very licence makes them only the more startling in their effect of forced mirth, as the poor Fool "labours to out-jest" his master's "heart-struck injuries." The mingled humour and pathos in the Fool's speeches, with their effect upon the reader's mind, recall that exquisite sentiment of Bacon's, where he speaks of alternated impression. He says:—"Is not the precept of a musician, to fall from a discord or harsh accord upon a concord or sweet accord, alike true in affection? Is not the trope of music to avoid or slide from the close or cadence, common with the trope of rhetoric in deceiving expectation? Is not the delight of the quavering upon a stop in music, the same with the playing of light upon the water?" Thus with the Fool in Lear; our sympathies are no sooner attuned to the key-note of affectionate tenderness in the lad's character, by hearing just before his first entrance, that since Cordelia's "going into France the fool hath much pined away," than we see him come in with a playful manner, assumed to hide his concern from his old master; and from that time to the close, maintaining a constant endeavour by sportive words to veil his profound interest in all that takes place. How well, for instance, does the sorrow with which he beholds Lear's paternal blindness betray itself beneath those apparently careless words :—

"Canst tell how an oyster makes his shell?

"*Lear.* No.

"*Fool.* Nor can I neither : but I can tell why a snail has a house.

"*Lear.* Why?

"*Fool.* Why, to put his head in; not to give it away to his daughters, and leave his horns without a case."

At another time he says :—

"Pr'ythee, nuncle, keep a schoolmaster that can teach thy fool to lie; I would fain learn to lie.

"*Lear.* If you lie, sirrah, we'll have you whipped.

"*Fool.* I marvel what kin thou and thy daughters are: they'll have me whipped for speaking true; thou'lt have me whipped for lying; and sometimes I'm whipped for holding my peace. I had rather be any kind o' thing than a fool: and yet I would not be thee, nuncle: thou hast pared thy wit o' both sides, and left nothing i' the middle."

Again, when Lear resents his daughter Gonneril's demeanour toward him: "How now, daughter! Methinks you are of late too much i' the frown;" the Fool says, "Thou wast a pretty fellow when thou hadst no need to care for her frowning;—Now thou art an O, without a figure. I am better than thou art now. I am a fool,—thou art nothing."

The bitter meaning couched in that very witty sentence is farther confirmed in an after one he makes, still more pregnant of significance: "He that has a house to put his head in, has a good head-piece." Well may Kent exclaim :— "This is not altogether fool, my lord." No, he was a fool of Shakespeare's generating.

It is the fidelity and attachment of the Fool that beget the respect and kindly consideration of Kent, who includes him when preparing to bear the king under shelter. He says :—

> "Oppressed nature sleeps.
> *   *   *   *
> [*To the Fool*] Come, help to bear thy master;
> Thou must not stay behind."

This, again, is one of those supernumerary, but inestimable touches which the poet is constantly throwing in, to give force to character;—hints and byeplays of action, telling more than meets the ear; and showing also that he forgot nothing.

The next in the list of the contrasted characters is Kent the good, the mediator, the peace-maker. Kent is the personification of a brave, uncompromising, all-enduring friendship. What in almost any other writer would appear like a crude melo-drame friendship, by the force of genius, assumes the air of a perfectly natural course of action. We are surprised at no sacrifice on the part of Kent in behalf of his master: we feel that he would have gone to his death to have rescued him from his miseries; and this, not from a blind, serf-like obedience; for Kent is a reasoning man, and in the day of Lear's power is the only one who stands between him and his perversity, and endeavours to protect him against himself. The blunt, rough-speaking of many honest friends is not altogether free from an impertinent conceit of superiority that we reluctantly resent: in Kent it is the manifestation of disinterested love and fidelity; with a sense to foresee the consequences of the king's headlong career, and the power to rescue him from its consequences: and this he would have done with as little ceremony of speech as he would in act, had his master been about to cast himself into a torrent. The future promise of the man is indicated in his first speech. He attempts to mitigate the fury of Lear against his daughter, Cordelia :—

"Good, my liege,—
"*Lear.* Peace, Kent!
Come not between the dragon and his wrath.
I lov'd her most, and thought to set my rest
On her kind nursery."

With this, he portions out his kingdom; and Kent again deprecates, and protests:—

"Royal Lear!
Whom I have ever honour'd as my king,
Lov'd as my father, as my master follow'd,
As my great patron thought on in my prayers,—
"*Lear.* The bow is bent and drawn, make from the shaft."

Then follows the noblest vindication of the true principles of friendship that ever was uttered in the same compass of speech:—

"*Kent.* Let it fall rather, though the fork invade
The region of my heart: be Kent unmannerly
When Lear is mad. What wouldst thou do, old man?
Think'st thou that duty shall have dread to speak,
When power to flattery bows? To plainness honour's bound,
When majesty stoops to folly. Reverse thy doom;
And, in thy best consideration, check
This hideous rashness; answer my life my judgment,
Thy youngest daughter does not love thee least;
Nor are those empty-hearted, whose low sound
Reverbs no hollowness.
"*Lear.* Kent, on thy life, no more.
"*Kent.* My life I never held but as a pawn
To wage against thine enemies; nor fear to lose it,
Thy safety being the motive.
"*Lear.* Out of my sight!
"*Kent.* See better, Lear; and let me still remain
The true blank of thine eye."

No speech can surpass this in magnanimity—the grandest magnanimity—that of self-subjugation and depreciation, with disinterested loyalty and devotedness.

In this first act of his career he has vindicated his title to an unflinching friend; and at every stage his character dilates, and strengthens with the motive for exertion. So large a promise in the outset, required no common sequences of devotion; we therefore find him, after the king's sentence of banishment against him, returning in disguise to watch over and serve his old friend. And here may be remarked the judgment of the poet, in causing him to adopt a blunt, plain-speaking character when he assumes the semblance of a serving-man, as the one most easily to be supported, from its giving scope to the habit of command, and ease, that are native to his real rank and station. The quaint character he gives himself when he comes to be hired by the king:—

"I can keep honest counsel, ride, run, mar a curious tale in telling it, and deliver a plain message bluntly; that which ordinary men are fit for, I am qualified in, and the best of me is diligence."

This honesty of manner naturally attracts Lear; who, with that instinct which has been remarked in monarchs, judges at once of his character, and in answer to Kent's reply respecting his own age, ("Not so young, sir, to love a woman for singing; nor so old as to dote on her for anything,") Lear says, "Follow me; thou shalt serve me: if I like thee no worse after dinner, I will not part from thee yet."

Shortly after this, his active service begins; and we find him sharing with his master the brunt of his unparallelled reverses; watching over him with a care and tenderness almost womanly; constantly and actively alive to the interests of the absent Cordelia; fiercely resenting any indignity offered to those he loves, (as witness the rough handling with which he salutes the steward;) the constant cheerfulness of his temper, most prominent when subjected to indignities for his master's sake,—and the gravest men in the conscious exercise of kindness are always cheerful. While sitting in the stocks,—a punishment applied to brawling drunkards,—Gloster sympathises with, and says he will entreat for him; but he replies—

> "Pray do not, sir;—I have watch'd and travell'd hard;
> Some time I shall sleep out, the rest I 'll whistle.
> A good man's fortune may grow out at heels."

And as the old king's career draws to a close, his pathetic endeavour, during a lucid interval, to make himself known to him; and when dead, his wise and humane appeal to those who would detain him from his last long sleep—

> "Vex not his ghost:—O let him pass! he hates him,
> That would upon the rack of this tough world
> Stretch him out longer;"—

a complete answer in itself to the presumption of that man, Tate, whose unhallowed ignorance converted this sublime effort of passion, endurance, and poetical justice consummated, into the vulgar finale of a holiday tale:—"And so, they were all married, and lived very happy afterwards." But, as Charles Lamb, in that fine Essay upon the Tragedies of Shakespeare, has said:—"As if the childish pleasure of getting his gilt robes and sceptre again, could tempt Lear to act over again his misused station; as if, at his years, and with his experience, anything were left but to die." To which might be added: as if, at his years, Lear could become another man; as if he could become unwilful, and even pliable. Theatrical enormities enough have, indeed, been perpetrated, but no one sacrilege has ever yet equalled Tate's mutilation of the tragedy of "King Lear." And Garrick, of whom some *acute* critic said, that he possessed "a *kindred mind* with Shakespeare," not only seconded, but confirmed, the new version, by performing it. It were charitable to hope that Garrick had never read the original text of Lear ; for if he had, it would make his acquiescence in Tate's profanation the more contemptible. A "kindred mind!" Heaven help us! In its incongruity, one is reminded of William Cobbett's powerful, and as coarse reply, when some one had boasted of being a friend of the excellent old Major Cartwright. "That man," said Cobbett, "call himself a '*friend*' of Major Cartwright! Why, a bug may as well call itself a man's bedfellow."

It has so frequently formed the subject of observation and comment, that I will simply allude to, and so dismiss it;—I mean, that no discriminative development of character in the drama of "King Lear" appears more clearly distinguished and defined, than in that of the feigned madness of Edgar, and the real mania of Lear. The speeches of Edgar are quaintly fantastical; mere strings of incongruous images, and no more; void of reason, as they should be, but full of intention. They have the fault, which they should have, and which feigning maniacs uniformly commit, that of extravagant nonsense. Those of Lear, on the other hand, are mingled with flights of fancy, uncontrolled imagination, and sudden acute sarcasms, familiar to all who have been acquainted with the victims of that awful malady. As Polonius says of Hamlet, "How pregnant sometimes his replies are! A happiness that often madness hits on which reason and sanity could not so prosperously be delivered of." It is noticeable, too, that Shakespeare has not unfrequently given to Lear that strange mixture of cunning, and love of stratagem, with irrationality in the contrivance, so remarkable in insane people. For instance; "I will have a troop of horse shod with felt, and steal upon them unawares, and kill, kill, kill!"

It is observable, that the first indication which Lear gives of his madness having become palpable—and an affecting indication it is—is when Edgar enters disguised as the "Tom of Bedlam." He says, "Didst thou give all to thy two daughters? And art thou come to this?" Kent replies, "He hath no daughters, sir." "Death, traitor! nothing could have subdued nature to such a lowness but his unkind daughters." And what a stroke of pathos in the speech that Edgar makes (*aside*) upon encountering the forlorn wreck of the poor old man's mind:—"My tears begin to take his part so much, they 'll mar my counterfeiting."

In the character of the steward to Queen Gonneril, Shakespeare has given an impersonation of blind feudal attachment. He is the reverse of Kent. He, from the mere servility of slavish obedience, would perpetrate any enormity of vice or of good service with the implicit punctuality and passiveness of a machine. It is no question with him whether an act be just or unjust, merciful or cruel. Kent speaks of him to this effect when he indignantly describes him as one of those who "turn their halcyon beaks with every gale and vary of their masters; knowing naught, like dogs, but following." He is, in short, a serf, and carries out the will of his mistress, as an axe obeys the hand of an executioner. The spirit of active and passive fidelity was never more aptly contrasted than in the two characters of Kent and Oswald the steward. The whole world would not stand between Kent and his zeal to serve his friend; and he has given proof that the whole world would not bring him to commit an unjust act, or to approve of it. The steward goes to his death in the service of his mistress, and with his dying breath entreats Edgar, who has killed him, to deliver the treasonable letter, upon his person, from Gonneril to Edmund. He is accurately the character that Edgar gives him: "A serviceable villain, as dexterous to the vices of his mistress as badness would desire."

Among the mistakes that Dr Johnson has made in commenting upon Shakespeare, may, I conceive, be included his summary of the character of the steward. He deems it inconsistent in the poet to give to this man, whom he styles "a mere factor of wickedness," so much "fidelity." As if "fidelity" were the *accident* of his character, and "wickedness" the *basis;* whereas, it is his serf-like fidelity to his mistress which is his leading characteristic, and which, in fact, is the cause of, and produces his evil deeds; they being merely her promptings or commands carried into action. The poor wretch is base enough in all conscience, but it is the baseness of servility and dogged servitude. His very reply to Lear, which gives the old man so much offence, is the epitome of his whole world of action :—

[*Enter Steward.*]

"*Lear.* O, you, sir, you ; come you hither, sir. Who am I, sir ?

"*Stew.* My lady's father."

He at once carries out the intention of his mistress, in stripping him of all quality but that of being the simple progenitor of Queen Gonneril, who has just before instructed him as to the bearing she wishes him to observe towards her father :—

"If you come slack of former services,
You shall do well; the fault of it I 'll answer.
* * * * * *
Put on what weary negligence you please,
You and your fellows; I 'd have it come to question :
If he distaste it, let him to my sister,
Whose mind and mine, I know, in that are one,
Not to be overruled."

Another feature in this play, worthy of attention : a reiterated confirmation of the poet's watchfulness in maintaining the *extrinsic* properties as regards the condition and quality of the subordinate members of the *dramatis personæ,*—in other words, the principle of "harmony." The plot, and prime agents in it, being all eminently aristocratic, the same high tone of rank and civility is preserved throughout. There is Curan, a courtier, introduced merely for the purpose of displaying the retinue, and to ask the question of Edmund, whether he has heard of no "likely wars toward, 'twixt the Dukes of Cornwall and Albany." Then we have the attendant and messenger between Kent and Cordelia, who is styled "A gentleman." His description of her receiving the intelligence of the old king's ill treatment, and that of his houseless condition in the storm, have been already quoted. What little we have of this character is developed with exquisite taste and gentleness. His general bearing and fulfilment of his mission, perfectly harmonise with the nature of his calling, and the sphere in which he moves. The rich eloquence put into his mouth is at once consistent with his station, and it also displays the prodigality of the poet in investing so unimportant a character with such language. But no one less than Shakespeare reserved himself to make "points," in technical phrase. What was due to a character, however subordinate, he gave in "imperial measure," regardless, or rather, not fearing to make the inferior diminish the lustre of the superior. He had no trick, but the trick of unsophisticated nature, with his own consummate instinct and perception of propriety. Then, we have the "Old Man," who leads in Gloster after his eyes have been put out. He is among the lowest with regard to rank of all the characters, and he has been fourscore years a tenant of the Earl and of his father. He is a first-class yeoman. Even the menial servants in Gloster's establishment sustain the poetical dignity of the story. After Cornwall, with his own hands, has perpetrated the horrid mutilation of the old Earl, by tearing out his eyes; and Regan, with a ferocious ribaldry, orders him to be turned out of doors, that he may "*smell* his way to Dover," the servants make the following characteristic reflection upon the scene they have just witnessed :—

> "2 *Serv.* I'll never care what wickedness I do
> If this man come to good.
> "3 *Serv.* If she live long,
> And, in the end, meet the old course of death,
> Women will all turn monsters.
> "2 *Serv.* Let's follow the old Earl, and get the Bedlam
> To lead him where he would : his roguish madness
> Allows itself to anything.
> "3 *Serv.* Go thou. I'll fetch some flax, and whites of eggs,
> To apply to his bleeding face. Now, Heaven help him!"

Good domestic surgery that,—whites of eggs to stop a bleeding wound. Some authority has said that he could not have chosen a finer immediate remedy.

The revolting scene of tearing out Gloster's eyes has been protested against by some critics—Coleridge among the number—as being the "tragic urged beyond the uttermost mark and *ne plus ultra* of the dramatic." I have no more wholesome defence to set up for the poet, than to refer to the period of civilisation in which all the events of the story were transacted ;—a period when mutilation, and even homicide produced not more excitement, than in our day would ensue upon seeing one man knock down another in the street. In all young states of society we recognise a remarkable prodigality and contempt of life. Sir Walter Scott, in his Preface to the "Border Minstrelsy," alluding to the outrages in some of the old ballad catastrophes, says that "a murder was not merely a casual circumstance, but in some cases an exceedingly good jest." It is also worthy of remark, that in all barbarous ages, one of their pet revenges is to punch out the eyes of an adversary. It is one of the mutilating feats of tar-and-feathering ruffians in America. It is an effectual method of putting a troublesome party in "a fix," to gouge out his eyes. You cut off his resources; while you yourself keep on the windy side of assassination and murder—which is convenient. The "Cutting and Maiming Act" had not passed in the reign of Queen Regan; her husband, therefore, busied himself with the simple question, to extinguish his adversary, without murdering him; and no plan was so suggestive as that of quenching his sight.

> "Go, seek the traitor Gloster,
> Pinion him like a thief, bring him before us.
> [*Exeunt Servants.*
> Though well *we may not pass upon his life*
> *Without the form of justice,* yet *our power*
> *Shall do a courtesy to our wrath, which men*
> *May blame, but not control.*"

The incorporation of the story of Gloster and his sons upon the old legend of King Lear has also met with its censurers upon the ground that the "unity"—that preposterous bug-a-bo, the "unity"—of the action has thereby been compromised: but one of the good commentators upon our poet—the German critic, Schlegel—appears to have satisfactorily annulled the objection. He says:—

"Whatever contributes to the intrigue, or unravelment, must always possess unity. And with what ingenuity and skill the two main parts of the composition are dovetailed into one another! The pity felt by Gloster for the fate of Lear becomes the means which enables his son Edmund to effect his complete destruction, and affords the outcast Edgar an opportunity of being the saviour of his father. On the other hand, Edmund is active in the cause of Regan and Gonneril; and the criminal passion which they both entertain for him, induces them to execute justice on each other,—and on themselves. The laws of the drama have therefore been sufficiently complied with; but that is the least: it is the very combination which constitutes the sublime beauty of the work."

But, after all, bring the question to the test of *feeling*,—a criterion worth a folio of argument upon the unities: Who would forego the coadjutor story of Gloster and his sons, in order to fulfil the tyranny of a conventional code in criticism? And what would be the condition of the original plot without its powerful, and even indispensable alliance?

VIII.

# Twelfth Night.

# VIII.

# TWELFTH NIGHT.

---

If any proof were wanting to convince us of Shakespeare's "sweetness of nature," and his tenderness of conscience in asserting the laws of moral and poetical justice, we need only turn to and note the principle of retribution he has carried out in the person of every agent in the comedy of "Twelfth Night."

With the serious and sentimental lovers, their web of life is one ravelled yarn—a perpetual check—a system of cross-stitch, (like a perplexing dream,) ending, nevertheless, in a bright and golden tissue of priceless joy. These are the principal, and almost sole conductors of the plot; and these, therefore, I shall dismiss very cursorily, with simply referring to those scenes which they occupy, for some of the most exquisite imagery, impassioned protestation, and chivalrous ardour (verging, mayhap, upon the fantastic) to be found in the whole range of the poet's wonderful stories of human life.

"It is impossible," as Mr Knight has truly observed, "for one of ordinary sensibility to read through the 1st Act of this play without yielding himself up to the genial temper in which the whole is written." We may, indeed, say that the "sunshine of the breast" spreads its purple light over the whole champaign, and penetrates into every thicket and dingle. From the very first line to the last,—from the Duke's, "That strain again, it had a dying fall," to the Clown's song, "With hey-ho, the wind and the rain,"—there is not a thought or a situation that is not calculated to call forth pleasurable feelings. The love-melancholy of the Duke is a luxurious abandonment to one pervading impression; not a fierce and hopeless contest with one over-mastering passion. It delights to lie "canopied with bowers;" to listen to "old and antique songs," which dally with its innocence; to be "full of shapes" and "high fantastical." The love of Viola is the sweetest and tenderest emotion that ever informed the heart of the purest and the most graceful of beings, with a spirit almost divine. Perhaps in the whole range of Shakespeare's poetry there is nothing which comes more unbidden into the mind, and always in connexion with some image of the ethereal beauty of the utterer, than Viola's celebrated speech to the Duke in her assumed garb of the page, having hired herself into his service: "She never told her love," &c., (*Act* ii., *sc.* 4.)

Viola's disguise, by the way, in the habit of page to the Duke, and the involution and perplexity in the plot, occasioned by her strong resemblance to her brother Sebastian, although conducted in the most delightful manner, and with the most artist-like ingenuity, nevertheless requires the implicit faith of childhood to receive without a misgiving of belief. But he who reads Shakespeare in the *true* spirit, reads him with kindred simplicity of heart, blended, or rather powerfully impregnated, with a relish for the romance of life, combined with the profoundest of all sciences—the philosophy of human action. The characters thus lightly glanced at, with that of the Countess Olivia, Sebastian, Viola's brother, and Antonio the sea-captain, comprise the serious agents in the play.

No one but Shakespeare, with his reverence for what is

due to *real* refinement in the female character, could have redeemed Olivia from the charge of violating the principles of delicacy inherent in women; for, instead of being the retiring and attracting, she is the seeking party. The love of Olivia, however, wilful as it is, is in no one instance masculine in character or repulsive in manner. So strictly does she maintain the proprieties of her sex, that our sympathies constantly accompany her perplexities, and we rejoice in her ultimate happiness.

In the position of Olivia, as a countess in her own right, and from her position in the world, (to a certain extent independent of general opinion,) the poet's course was a comparatively easy one. Yet, in her case, as in that of Helena, in "All's Well that Ends Well," he has retained the two women from the remotest charge of unfeminity, at the same time that he has demanded, and gained for them, intense sympathy and interest from every worshipper of a true *heart*-love.

The character of Sebastian presents no "mark or likelihood" for especial notice. He is the "counterfeit presentment" of his sister in external favour, and no more. Let us hope that he made as kind a partner to the Countess as the loving and lovely page, Viola, would have done under similar circumstances.

Antonio, the sea-captain, is a delightful specimen of that frank, open, and prodigal nature so common in the nautical character—at all events, in the English sailor. His offering Sebastian the use of his purse is done in the best manner; for it is homely, natural, and without ostentation:—

"Hold, sir, here's my purse.
In the south suburbs, at the Elephant,
Is best to lodge. I will bespeak our diet,
Whiles you beguile the time, and feed your knowledge,
With viewing of the town: there shall you have me.
"*Seb.* Why I your purse?

"*Ant.* Haply your eye shall light upon some toy
You have desire to purchase; and *your store,*
*I think, is not for idle markets, sir.*"

In this short scene (the third of the 3d Act) it is interesting to note how the general character and previous career of the seaman respond to this unaffected proffer of a bounteous loving-kindness.

The secondary movement, or plot, in the drama, is one round of fun, and hoaxing, and carousing, and mad waggery. There never was, perhaps, a larger store of wit, and humour, and roguish "larking," (unmingled with coarseness or malice,) condensed within the same space of writing; and a rare choice of materials are brought together for the purpose.

There is the roaring blade, Sir Toby Belch, and his butt and tool, Sir Andrew Aguecheek; the former, so complete a John Bull in character and habits, that we wonder how he came to be domiciliated in Illyria, of all places, and to be a kinsman (cousin) of the rich Countess Olivia; but we need not rigidly scrutinise his genealogy. Her mother we may assume to have been an Englishwoman.

Then, there is the king of all clowns, a fellow that would leave an atmosphere of fun behind him wherever he had been for one hour; and of shrewd and worldly sense, too. And Fabian, the servant to the Countess, who possesses wit and spirit enough to accomplish fifty gentlewomen's servants.

And lastly, that terrible little gadfly—that Robin Goodfellow in petticoats—the waiting-woman, Maria. This phalanx proved formidable odds to bring against the poor pragmatical self-worshipper, Malvolio, the Countess's steward, who draws on himself the mischief of their contrivances by his over-estimation of himself, with a too rigid exaction from those ranking below him in the household. He keeps no measure in his contempt for them; and they, in return, (as the vulgar phrase has it,) "pay him out."

There is an inherent propensity in mankind to upset a self-worshipper; and if he be also a detractor, Heaven have mercy on him, for no mortal will. We notice, however, that all their teazing, notwithstanding the animal spirits exciting and carrying it on, is attended by no malice, no ill-nature, no vulgarity. At the close of the play, when their mistress, Olivia, rebukes them for the extremity to which they had carried their hoax, Fabian apologises for it all:—

> "Good madam, hear me speak:
> Most freely I confess, myself and Toby
> Set this device against Malvolio here,
> Upon some stubborn and uncourteous parts
> We had conceiv'd against him.
> How with a *sportful* malice it was follow'd,
> May rather pluck on laughter than revenge,
> If that the injuries be justly weigh'd
> That have on both sides pass'd."

Of all the subordinate persons in the "Twelfth Night," no one character is more finely conceived and more thoroughly followed out, than that of Maria. She is by nature of the most boisterous spirits, irrepressible, outpouring. Her delight is teazing; her joy a hoax; her happiness a good practical jest. Worrying is her element, and she gambols in it, "dolphin-like;" tormenting is her beatitude on this earth, and she would scarcely desire a new earth, and to live in it, if debarred of her darling joke-inquisition, of which she is grand inquisitor, arch-judiciary, and executioner. She has no female companion, no associate of her own sex but her mistress, and she (the Countess) is a recluse, shutting herself out from society, musing over her brother's death. This circumstance naturally throws one of Maria's temperament into fellowship with the men of the household; and her conduct takes a colour from that association. Her fun is all but masculine; and yet her gaiety is of the most inspiring kind, but still perfectly feminine; so impulsive, so breathlessly eager, so unmisgiving! No one escapes her; not one, even, of her hoax-fellows. She rates Sir Toby, and soundly, about his late hours; twitting him with his jollifications, and scoffing at his gull-companion, Sir Andrew Aguecheek. And when this last enters, she has a tilt at him, jeering, joking, mystifying, obfuscating him.

We next see her, head-over-ears, in a plaguing-bout with the Clown, whom she threatens with her lady's displeasure for some misdemeanour, of which she is curious to discover the secret. But Feste is the only one who is a match for her; and he brings her *two* Rolands for her Oliver. He has a secret of her own, and this gives him the whip-hand of her. But she is never content except when plying the teazle upon one hapless pate or other; and her talent is unmisgiving and untiring.

Viola, disguised as the Duke's page, has an interview with Olivia, and Maria hovers about like a gnat, watching her opportunity to have a gird at the youth; and on the first symptom of her lady dismissing him, she steps forward with an impertinence of alacrity to show him the door. She manifests her delight in making him believe that she would gladly shut it in his face. And yet, with all her impudence, there is such a relish of fun, such a gusto of waggery in her, in the midst of all her sauciness, that no one can be angry with her; no one but the grave self-worshipper, Malvolio, takes offence at her sallies. He has the natural instinct of dislike towards that which threatens to upset his pomposity. To such a man, this grig of a girl, ever on the alert for roguery, sleepless for mischief, on tip-toe for a prank or pert speech, is an absolute abomination. He avoids her as a quicksand, perilous to the stately bark of his dignity; and he is right. Her vivacity loathes his ponderous sedateness, and she resolves to scuttle it. His own peculiarities furnish her with the ready means;

and to one of her disposition, the temptation to use them is irresistible. How like the woman is the language of her relish with which she devises the trick against the steward:—

"For Monsieur Malvolio, let me alone with him. If I do not gull him into a nay-word, and make him a *common recreation,* do not think I have wit enough to lie straight in my bed. I know I can do it."

How like the kind of woman is that phrase! She originates and concocts the letter intended for him; and when he has fallen into the snare, we have the whole picture of her manner: flitting hither and thither like a bat; rushing in and out in a breathless ecstasy as her plot thickens and her mischief begins to ferment. She watches her prey, lynx-eyed, unwinking upon him, and yet contriving to possess her fellow-conspirators, from time to time, with all the particulars of his behaviour. She is in a perpetual chuckle of merry malice the whole time their trick is being played. Her zest in the game is infectious, and we have caught the taint. At one time she darts in with those immortal words:—

"If you desire the spleen, and will laugh yourselves into stitches, follow me. Yond' gull Malvolio is turned heathen, —a very renegado; for there is no Christian that means to be saved by believing rightly, can believe such impossible passages of grossness. He 's in yellow stockings!

"*Sir To.* And cross-gartered?

"*Mar.* Most villainously—like a pedant that keeps a school i' the church. *I have dogged him like his murderer.* He does obey every point of the letter that I dropped to betray him. He does *smile his face into more lines than are in the new map, with the augmentation of the Indies.* You haven't seen such a thing as 'tis. *I can hardly forbear hurling things at him.* I know my lady will strike him; and if she do, he 'll smile, and take 't for a great favour."

The little toad's hunting and badgering of the poor "gull," (as she calls him,) are performed with a zest, and exquisite relish for tormenting, that are perfectly characteristic, and as infectious. The men are noodles to her. Following up the hoax, to the pretence that he is going mad, she says :—

"Get him to say his prayers, Sir Toby, get him to pray.
"*Mal.* [*turning angrily.*] My prayers, minx?
"*Mar.* Oh, Lord! No, I warrant you, he'll not hear of godliness."

And even when Fabian begins to relent, with, "Why, we shall make him mad indeed," her only answer is, "The house will be the quieter." Her hand is constantly in to help any hoax. She zealously joins Toby and Fabian in urging Sir Andrew to challenge Viola, the page. She is like the stormy peterel, and mischief is her element. In her appetite for teazing, she does not even spare her mistress the Countess :—

"If you will see the fruit of the sport, [that is, the effect of the letter upon Malvolio,] mark his first approach before my lady. He will come to her in yellow stockings, and 'tis a colour she abhors ; and cross-gartered, a fashion she detests ; and he will smile upon her, which will now be so unsuitable to her disposition, being addicted to melancholy as she is, that it cannot but turn him into a notable contempt."

Maria's intimacy with Sir Toby is more than implied two or three times during the play. When the Clown hints his suspicion to her, she says, "Peace, you rogue, no more of that; here comes my lady." Sir Toby, however, performs the honourable part in the conclusion, and wisely marries her. They were well calculated for each other. Nothing he could do would quell her spirit ; and she would surely comb his head for him. Her little, sprite-like figure is constantly alluded to in the course of the play. Good taste this in the poet, to keep the externals of the feminine character in the mind's eye of the reader ; for a man-statured woman, a horse-godmother, acting in the way that Maria did — hail-fellow with the men—would be a vision too horrible to contemplate. With a strapping Amazon playing the same fantastic tricks, there would be no alternative but to call in the whole constabulary force, with the *posse comitatus,* — the military being in reserve,—and at once, and for ever, put her down. As it is, we feel that we could have been pleased, almost, to have been the object of her mischievous sallies—certainly to have shared in their merriment. But besides inspiring us with this feeling respecting Maria, by letting us know that she is a little creature, Shakespeare has, as is usual, evinced his perception of the natural. Large women, with a feminine instinct of what is graceful and becoming in their sex, seldom indulge in pranks of this character; whereas little women are instinctively skilled in feats of tormenting; they are "powerful" at it, because they know, perhaps, that from them it is not wholly unpalatable. Thus, of Maria, we think as of a marmoset, or a mischievous fairy. Viola calls her Olivia's "giant." Sir Toby says, "Good-night, Penthesilea," —Penthesilea being an Amazon, a man-woman. And again, "Here comes the little villain. How now, my nettle of India?" And lastly, "Here comes the youngest wren of nine:" the wren, the smallest of our European birds; and the youngest bird in a nest being always the smallest of the brood.

Sir Andrew Aguecheek is not only the foil of Sir Toby, his butt and his tool, but he is his shadow—his echo. No one, like Shakespeare, has portrayed the *conceit* of fatuity. Other dramatists have drawn imbecile characters, but they have ordinarily been objects, either revolting from their mental degradation, or so overstrained and buffoon-like in the colouring, as to be anomalous and monstrous. Shakespeare always ranges within the worldly experience of us all. There are few persons in commerce with society who cannot, in their own experience, identify a Shallow, a Slender, or an Aguecheek;

but then, the wonder is, that although they are all of one family, yet that the characteristic gradations in each should have been retained with such accurate distinctness. Shallow is iterative; he repeats and repeats, from lack of idea and mere love of gabbling. Slender is bashful and conscious, with a glimmering, and but a glimmer, of his own importance. He hovers about the suburbs, and lives in the twilight of intellect. Aguecheek is an unadulterated fool, without even good nature to redeem his folly. He is chiefly imitative in character. He apes Sir Toby, echoing all his phrases. Toby is dictatorial and bullying, and Sir Andrew must mimic him in that, although a coward to his heart's root: and being a coward, there is every chance of his being a boaster; he therefore announces, that at a bout of fence he has "the back trick, simply, as strong as any man in Illyria." Maria, however, in the opening of the play, tells us of him:—"Besides that he's a fool," she says, "he's a great quarreller; and but that he hath the gift of a coward to allay the gust he hath in quarrelling, 'tis thought among the prudent he would quickly have the gift of a grave." Toby *knows* him, and says, "If there be so much blood in his liver as will drown a flea, I will eat the rest of the anatomy." He is fooled into the courage to challenge the page Viola; and Fabian says, "Oxen and wainropes will not drag them together." He joins in the plot against Malvolio, as a baboon would. He has received no offence from him; yet, through mere stupidity, and aping of mischief, he would do him harm; and admirably is the poltroon character maintained throughout. Maria says of Malvolio, "Sometimes he's a kind of Puritan." "Oh! if I thought that," says Andrew, "*I'd beat him like a dog.*" "What, for being a Puritan?" Toby answers; "thy exquisite reason, dear knight?" "I have no exquisite reason for it, but I have reason good enough." The cowardly fool had just *sense* enough to keep that to himself. The Puritans being a suffering class; and, in doctrine, at all events, preaching the return of "good for evil," Sir Andrew thought he could buffet Malvolio with impunity. How flabby, and ineffectual too, are his outbreaks of indignation! "'Slight, I could so beat the rogue!" And again, "Fie on him, *Jezebel!*" The very misapplication of that term was a happy thought. Then his inane admiration of Viola's phrases: stupidly longing to ape them, completes the consistency of his character. When she, disguised as the Duke's page, says to Olivia, "Most excellent, accomplished lady! the heavens rain odours on you!" he mutters to himself, "That youth's a rare courtier! 'rain odours!' Well!" Again, she says, "My matter hath no voice, lady; but to your own most pregnant and vouchsafed ear." He repeats—"'Odours,' 'pregnant,' and 'vouchsafed.' I'll get them all three ready"—for paying his court to the Lady Olivia. But the full meridian blaze of his folly shines forth when he is mimicking Sir Toby. Throughout the whole play he never originates one single idea; or scarcely makes one observation which is not suggested to him. Toby says, "Maria is a beagle true bred, and one that adores me; what o' that?" Echo replies, "I was *adored* once too." The iteration of that word is worth a mint. Again, after the success of Maria's plot against Malvolio, Toby comes rolling in:—

"I could marry this wench for this device.

"*Sir And. So could I, too.*

"*Sir To.* And ask no other dowry with her but such another jest.

"*Sir And. Nor I neither.*

"*Fabian.* Here comes my noble gull-catcher.

"*Sir To.* Wilt thou set thy foot on my neck?

"*Sir And. Or on mine either?*

"*Sir To.* Shall I play my freedom at tray-trip, and become thy bond-slave?

"*Sir And. I'faith, or I either?*

"*Sir To.* To the gates of Tartar I 'll follow thee, thou most excellent devil of wit.

"*Sir And. I'll make one too.*"

With such a fool as this, one feels no repugnance at Toby's making a nose of wax of him; moreover, he merits all the usage he receives. Fabian says, with a knowing wink, "This is a dear manikin to you, Sir Toby." And he replies, "I have been '*dear*' to him, lad, some two thousand strong, or so." None but such a character as Toby, who has a strong spice of Falstaff's roguery as well as waggery, could so pigeon and roast him.

Feste, the clown in this most delicious play, succeeds Touchstone in especial favour—he is a capital fellow. Blest with the most indomitable cheerfulness, the most elastic and untiring spirits, nothing vexes him; nothing makes him anxious, or even grave; not even the threat of his mistress's displeasure; nay, not hanging itself has any terrors for him. If the Lady Olivia turn him away, he is prepared to rough it in the open air, and consoles himself with the warmth of the season: "Let summer bear it out." If he is to be hanged, why, then, he philosophically reflects, "Many a good hanging prevents a bad marriage." The fact is, he knows he has the fee-simple of his lady-mistress's partiality for his merry "quips and cranks." He hugs himself upon his power over her, in being able to joke away her disapprobation; for he says, "Well, God give them wisdom that have it; and those that are fools, let them use their talents." As Olivia appears, he mutters the aspiration, "Wit! an 't be thy will, put me into good fooling!" and he goes on strengthening himself in self-encouragement, saying, "Those wits that think they have thee, do very oft prove fools; and I, that am sure I lack thee, may pass for a wise man: for what says Quinapalus,—'Better a witty fool than a foolish wit.'" His pleasant foolery, and his cheerful temper together, soon win back his lady's favour, as he has calculated. She cannot long withstand his playful retorts. At first, we see the half frown with which she says :—

"Go to ; you are a dry fool ; I 'll no more of you. Besides, you grow dishonest.

"*Clown.* Two faults, Madonna, that drink and good counsel will amend. For, give the dry fool drink, then is the fool not dry ; bid the dishonest man mend himself—if he mend, he is no longer dishonest ; if he cannot, let the botcher mend him. Anything that 's mended is but patched. Virtue that transgresses is but patched with sin ; and sin that amends is but patched with virtue. If that this simple syllogism will serve, so ;—if it will not, what remedy ?"

Malvolio, who is sick of self-love, is the only person in the play who does not affection the gay and sweet-spirited jester. The Duke likes him, welcoming him to his palace, and getting him to sing sweet old songs, that soothe his love-melancholy. There is choice taste and feeling in the modicum of colloquy that ensues between Duke Orsino and cheerful-hearted Feste at the conclusion of his song :—

"*Duke.* There 's for thy pains.

"*Clo.* No pains, sir ; I take pleasure in singing, sir.

"*Duke.* I 'll pay thy pleasure, then.

"*Clo.* Truly, sir, and pleasure will be paid one time or other."

Pithy philosophy that ! the philosophy of doing pleasant things for pleasant things' sake. No surer self-contained repayment.

Master Feste's humour is strictly and professionally legitimate. It spares no one, gentle or simple, chick or child. He has a gird or two at Viola, in her apparent character of Cæsario, the Duke's page. When she asks him, "Art not thou the Lady Olivia's fool ?" he replies, thinking (it will be remembered) that Cæsario is likely to wed his lady-mistress—

"No, indeed, sir; the Lady Olivia has no folly. She will keep no fool, sir, till she be married: and fools are as like husbands as pilchards are to herrings—the husbands are the bigger. I am, indeed, not her fool, but her corrupter of words.

"*Vio.* I saw thee late at the Count Orsino's.

"*Clo.* Foolery, sir, does walk about the orb like the sun; it shines everywhere."

Shakespeare has given to Feste a mechanical skill in music, as well as a "sweet breath" for singing. In one scene he brings him in with a tabor. There is a portrait of Dick Tarlton, the actor, and jester to Queen Elizabeth, which represents him with a tabor in his hand. That Feste enters playing, we find from Viola's address: "Save thee, friend, and thy music; dost thou live by thy tabor?" Upon which the Clown jokingly answers, "No, sir, I live by the church." Will it be credited that one of the commentators should confess that this reply of the Clown's is "*not intelligible*" to him? Why, the forlorn owl! not to see that the humour is of the same character as that which lay in the answer of the wounded man, who, when asked by the surgeon, if he had received his wound "near the vertebræ," said, "No, sir, near the obelisk."

Fabian, the man-servant, is artistically introduced to assist Maria, and to restrain the impetuosity and rage of Toby and Andrew, while they are all concealed in the garden watching the effect of their plot against Malvolio. He is a blithe young fellow, with sound sense, perfectly comprehending, as we have just seen, the slip-shod honesty of Sir Toby; and joining as heartily to hoax Sir Andrew, as to "fool Malvolio black and blue." He helps to reconcile us to their usage of the steward, by showing how offensive he has contrived to make himself to the whole household. Fabian, being the most sound-sensed man of the group, is the least bitter against him—Shakespeare's consistency, as usual. But, indeed, a valuable moral is to be drawn from the conduct of Malvolio, and the treatment he encountered. He is honest and zealous in his stewardship, and is so far estimable; and he has his reward in the confidence and favour of his mistress. But his honesty is bitter, and his zeal is overweening: and being so dragon-like and "virtuous," he would banish all the "cakes and ale" from good fellowship. He is a moral teatotaller, a formalist, a pragmatist, and a self-worshipper. His gravity is that of decorum, of punctilio; he is solemn in observance; sober, sedate, and inflexible in ceremonial. He would suffer amputation of a limb rather than that of a ceremony. He cannot perceive the entertainment of jesting, either spoken or listened to, and marvels that his mistress can tolerate, far more take delight in the sallies of her jester—the fooleries of the fool. He has measureless and acrid contempt for those who can endure such toys of mirth. He says, "I protest, I take these wise men, that crow so at these set kind of fools, no better than the fools' zanies." He is so steeped in, so saturated with the idolatry of decorum, as the one thing needful, that he far outstrips his mistress's injunctions in the control of her household; and exercises his office with a bitterness of rectitude, even a malignity of precision, that may be resolved into a compounded love of power and love of propriety. Even in such a trifle as the execution of her commission respecting the restoration of the ring to Viola, as the page, he goes far beyond his duty. Olivia simply bids him hasten after the messenger, and return the ring, which she feigns was left with her: but Malvolio, when he overtakes the page, represents his mistress as highly incensed: he exaggerates her message, and *flings* the ring back. There was no question of throwing it; but Malvolio says, "Come, sir, you peevishly threw it to her, and her will is, it should be so returned. If it be worth stooping for, there it lies in your eye; if not, be it his that finds it." All this fluster may have arisen from a horror of the steward, in the idea that his darling formula of "decorum" had been violated in the page's having made an extempore love-declaration to the Lady Olivia. Certain it is, that he nurses his own disdain, while pretending to be the medium of his mistress's displeasure. So also, when interrupting the night-revel of Sir Toby and his co-mates, we feel that he is quite as much venting his ill-temper at the hilarity and the roistering, as that he is conveying her reprobation of their obstreperous merriment. With austere relish of his rebuke, he says:—

"My masters, are you mad? or what are you? Have you no wit, manners, nor honesty, but to gabble like tinkers at this time of night? Do ye make an ale-house of my lady's house, that you squeak out your coziers' catches, without any mitigation or remorse of voice? Is there no respect of place, persons, nor time, in you?

"*Sir To.* We did '*keep time*,' sir, in our catches. Sneck up!

'Three merry men we be.'"

Perfect is this scene and situation! with the pompous man in authority, surrounded, and bated by the hubbub of the roisterers: they persisting in bawling their wine-songs, as a note of his indignation; and, in answer to his remonstrances, screaming a chorus. His gravity has no odds against their ungovernable mirth; his sobriety is fairly upset and smothered in their drunken uproar. He has nothing for it but retreat; and this he makes in as dignified ill-humour as need be, and a threat into the bargain: "My lady shall know of it, by this hand!" [*Exit.*]

The fact is, Malvolio was intended to represent a member of that class, the main features of whose character betrayed an ostentatious moral vanity. Not satisfied with having obtained the privilege to act according to the dictates of their own consciences, and of having confirmed, in their own behalf, the right of private judgment, they proceeded to wrench that power to the restraining of all dissentients within their own pinfold. When we consider that these men had begun to influence the legislature to restrict the players in their performances; and that, if they could have instituted a puritanical autocracy, every description of dramatic entertainment, every quality of music, psalms only excepted, and they *unaccompanied*, would have been swept from the earth: when these provocations to resentment are considered, it is with no slight pleasure that we turn to the forbearance of our Shakespeare in drawing the character of the overweening Malvolio. He has greatly justified him at the close of the play. With his unswerving sense of even-handed justice and righteous dealing, he will not suffer us to cast away our respect for the *solid* qualities in the steward's character, whatever encouragement he may give to our laughing at his pragmatisms and solemn coxcombry. The last impression he gives us of him is that of respect and sympathy; and this, too, I take to be sound morality, as well as a fresh confirmation of the innate sweetness of the poet's nature.

The slight and third-rate character of Fabian the servant, contains some of Shakespeare's rich waifs and strays, worthy of the first-rate of any ordinary dramatist. These are the things that suggested the taking for my subject the inferior members of his *dramatis personæ*. There is that fine simile, for instance, at the close of Fabian's speech to Sir Andrew, whom he is rallying and hoaxing for allowing the Duke's page to cut him out in his pretensions to the hand of Olivia. Every line in it contains a figure or a metaphor. He says—

"She did show favour to the youth in your sight, only to exasperate you, to awake your dormouse valour, to put fire in your heart and brimstone in your liver. You should then have accosted her; and with some excellent jests, fire-new from the mint, you should have banged the youth into dumbness. This was looked for at your hand, and this was baulked:

the double gilt of this opportunity you let time wash off, and *you are now sailed into the north of my lady's opinion, where you will hang like an icicle on a Dutchman's beard.*"

In Fabian's mouth, too, occurs one of the instances, out of numbers that might be quoted, of Shakespeare being always up to the high-water mark in any appeal that is made from one character to another. When Sir Toby desires to bring on the duel between Aguecheek and the page, and defers to Fabian whether the latter is not a coward, he replies, with a spice of wit quintessentialised—" A coward ?—a most devout coward, religious in it!" Fabian, as I said, is the balance-wheel between the other two, to keep them in check, while they are all watching Malvolio during the famous soliloquy and letter-scene in the garden: and to this I refer you, feeling persuaded that it will lead (although for the fiftieth time) to the reading and revelling over the whole play.

IX.

# Antony and Cleopatra.

# IX.

# ANTONY AND CLEOPATRA.

---

IN these "Characters," Friend Reader, my main object has been to contribute to your intellectual recreation: to consider myself in the light of your "Poetical Remembrancer;" not your teacher, not your pedagogue, but your companion, your brother botanist, culling the simples of beauty, and wisdom, and truth—and this is the highest wisdom—from that rich terrene of anthology, the pages of Shakespeare;—our Shakespeare—the whole world's Shakespeare. And, indeed, a bare recurrence to the ample wisdom and bland morality of such a humanist as Shakespeare, brings with it both recreation and improvement; for what is his mind but a transmission in daguerreotype of the created world, animate and inanimate? and who that is endowed with the reflective faculty, ever looks that creation in the face without an accompanying thought that brings him into communion with the Author of all that is great, and good, and fair?—the deep solemnity of the blue firmament, "fretted with gold;" the restless expanse of ocean; the green earth, and the mountains bare; the waving forests; and the unchartered wind, that "bloweth where it listeth,"—all preach to us a lesson of "wisdom" and "beauty," of "truth" and peace, "beyond whate'er was spoken."

And he who has told us that we may find "books in the running brooks, sermons in stones, and good in everything," does but square his moral code with the grand principle of legislative wisdom promulgated in the book of universal nature; for there is "good in everything," even in "things evil;" which, like the "primal curse," may be converted into inestimable blessings: and he who studies the principle of human action in a philosophical spirit, must come to the same conclusion. So with the writings of a genius like Shakespeare; that man must have a limited or perverted vision, who does not perceive in them a whole Macrocosm—a Great World of human knowledge, in which the principles of Good and Evil are no more confounded than we find them in nature; and this axiom should be invariably asserted with reference to his moral philosophy—indeed, the main point on which he is to be studied for improvement, as well as recreation; and I shall have fulfilled my intention if I succeed in impressing this truth,—one not sufficiently recognised by the casual reader of his wonderful productions.

What a world of associations does not the fancy conjure up, as we enter the precincts of the picturesque career of Antony and Cleopatra! The mind runs back through the remote vista of scenes and events connected with the theatre and arena on which they ran their wilful and tragical course. Those long pageants and swart dynasties, the Pharaohs, the Ptolemies, and the Sesostrises, with all the drums and tramplings of a thousand conquests and depopulations,—kings in their triumphal chariots borne home upon the tide of a conquered and captive people,—all pass in shadowy, silent review before the mind's eye: and we stretch on in thought to that most strange era, when the young Hebrew redeemed his tribe from the bondage of their hard task-masters, and led them forth to freedom, as on "dry land in the midst of the sea."

No region of the world is more fruitful in local and historical interest than the country of Egypt:—its monumental mounds and mountain sculptures; its gigantic and unique architecture; its pyramids, "so doting with age," (as old Fuller quaintly describes them,) that they have forgotten not only the "names of their founders," but even their intention; its extraordinary river, which periodically sends forth its great throbbing pulse of vitality over the parched earth; and lastly, its curious and infant-like picture literature;—all is mysterious, and all is interesting because of the mystery; and it is like nothing else in the whole world.

This was the stage of Cleopatra's voluptuous and reckless career; and this point in the world's history Shakespeare has touched with his magician's wand, and the characters start into light, life, and identity. I cannot think that in any one of his historical dramas, he has more grandly conveyed the ideal, with the implicitly accurate in the historical, than in the play now under consideration.

The *historical* character of Cleopatra may be briefly summed. She was the grandest coquette that ever lived. Cæsars were her fit slaves, for she had *imperial* powers of captivation. She was a gorgeous personification of female fascination,—of bewitching womanhood in regal magnificence. She used her female graces as enhancements of her queenly state; and made her power of pleasing, a crown to her royal power. She was born a princess, reigned a queen, won an emperor, swayed a hero, and defeated a conqueror; while her personal blandishments live, in the imagination of posterity, as far outweighing the facts of her fortune. We think of her as the queen of enslavers, more than as queen of Egypt. She stands conspicuous to fancy in might of allurement.*

* As the earnings of the wife are, by law, the property of the husband, I lay claim to this summary of Egypt's queen from the pages of "World-noted Women."

She overcame Julius Cæsar by placing herself in his power,—thereby trusting to her own,—and relying on his magnanimity and chivalry. She overcame Antony by dictating to him, and then displaying the full panoply of her charms before him. He had summoned her (as Triumvir of Rome—and of the world) to appear before him, and answer certain accusations that had been brought against her. She made so light of his summons, as not to answer one of his letters; but set forward in her barge (gorgeously furnished beyond all Eastern romance of luxury) to meet him. The whole population came forth to see her in her state; while Antony was left totally alone, in the market-place, waiting for her;—the summoning judge,—the inquirer into her conduct,—left to abide her coming. This was her first advantage over Antony.

When she had landed, and he had beheld her, and had had an interview, he sent to invite her to supper with him. She returned for answer, (having, at a glance, seen him through and through,) that he would do better to come and sup with her; and Plutarch says, "He, to show himself courteous to her on her arrival, was contented to obey her, and went to sup with her; where he found such sumptuous fare, that no tongue can express it." Step the second—his invitation set aside, hers accepted; and the delinquent, instead of being entertained of the judge, becoming his entertainer. And afterwards, when he did entertain her, she found his feast so gross and soldier-like, that (as the historian continues) "she gave it him finely; and, without fear, taunted him thoroughly." Here was she already installed as rater of *his* conduct, instead of rendering him an account of hers; and, in the end, she drew him completely within the spell of her witchery;—the fact being that she saw, at one review, that her victim was weak in judgment, and, in every sense, a sensualist; she therefore baited for, and caught her prey.

Cleopatra is said to have been not remarkable for beauty; but that she had so matchless and inexpressible a *charm* of face, and that her company and conversation were so sweet, that a man could not possibly *but* be taken.

Shakespeare has made her appear, speak, move, breathe, and live again before us: he has caused us to behold her in all that marked individuality, in those minute betrayals of character, which only either personal knowledge or Shakespeare's page enables us to witness. Diversified, yet complete; inconsistent, yet in keeping; whimsical, yet direct of purpose; replete with jarring elements, yet in perfect consonance with itself. In what is said of her, in what is said to her, in what she says of herself, he makes us equally behold the actual woman—Cleopatra—compounded into one gorgeously vivid impersonation.

To conclude in a dozen words: Cleopatra is enthroned enchantress of the world. She captivated Julius Cæsar; entranced the heart and senses of Mark Antony; and succeeded in beguiling the wary Octavius. She, of all her sex, in her person gave to the unworthy art of coquetry, a something of magnificent and lustrous in its so potent exercise. Hers was indeed the *poetry* of *coquetry.*

With Plutarch's life of Antony, and with Sir Thomas North's noble translation for his text-book, Shakespeare has availed himself of every dramatic point in the narrative, and invested it with an air of unpremeditated ease and verisimilitude, that is as enchanting as it is wonderful. All the scenes laid in Egypt, where the regal paramours are engaged, are instinct with the wayward caprice and indecision of the voluptuary,—the very atmosphere is heavy with inertness and indolence. We have the resolute tone, and heroic promise of the old and practised soldier, Antony; with the prostrate thraldom, and imbecile performance of Antony the enervated Sybarite.

In the full confidence of experience and power, he goes into the sea-fight against Octavius; and while the "'vantage" is in his favour, he

> "Claps on his sea-wing, and like a doting mallard,
> Leaving the fight in height, flies after 'Cleopatra.'"

Nothing can be finer than the skill with which the poet has contrived to give us the natural character of Antony in contrast, in order that he might rescue him from the debasement into which he had sunk, after he became entangled in the folds of his "serpent of old Nile;" for Antony was really in heart and compound the noblest and most generous of the Triumvirate who succeeded the greatest man Rome ever saw —the "mightiest Julius." Octavius was cold, calculating, and treacherous: his heart was a stone, and his blood "very snow-broth." Lepidus was merely cruel and sensual,—sensual, too, in his cruelty:—he was gross, and brute-like, even in his sanguinary indulgences. Antony had that in his nature which might have turned to a better account. He had prodigious constancy in adversity: Octavius bears testimony to his power of endurance in that passage of vigorous diction, where he is contrasting his soldierly accomplishments and constancy in trial, with his prone vassalage to the regal courtezan. Without this testimony, Antony's qualifications to be the hero of a high-swelling tragedy would be questionable; and here the poet has converted a historical fact into a lofty theme in morality. Antony might have swayed the world had he not been a sensualist and a voluptuary—he might have walked the earth with dominion; but he dragged a fine nature through the common sewer of licentiousness; and consequently he lost the world's, and, what is worse, his own respect. This is the moral read to us; and this it is to assert the real privilege of the drama,—"to show virtue her own feature, vice her own scorn."

This is the testimony alluded to, put into the mouth of Octavius:—

"Antony,
Leave thy lascivious wassails. When thou once
Wast beaten from Modena, where thou slew'st
Hirtius and Pansa, consuls, at thy heel
Did famine follow; whom thou fought'st against,
Though daintily brought up, with patience more
Than savages could suffer: thou didst drink
The stale of horses, and the gilded puddle,
Which beasts would cough at: thy palate then did deign
The roughest berry on the rudest hedge;
Yea, like the stag, when snow the pasture sheets,
The barks of trees thou browsedst; on the Alps,
It is reported thou didst eat strange flesh,
Which some did die to look on: and all this
(It wounds mine honour that I speak it now)
Was borne so like a soldier, that thy cheek
So much as lank'd not."

It is not the cue to linger upon the character of Antony, farther than to link him with the other characters of the drama.

The next to him in importance, though not in interest, is Octavius Cæsar. The ruling passion in the character of Octavius was the paramount lust of dominion; but even that never seems to have excited him to enthusiasm. His command over others, and his command over himself, were asserted with the calculated precision and determination of a machine. He was the only one whom Cleopatra could not ensnare. His passionless nature enabled him to withstand even her, who had fascinated and nearly destroyed the great Julius. Octavius is a perfect exemplar of a politician and commander. In various features of his character and career, and, which is curious, even in his aspect, he reminds one of the first Napoleon Buonaparte. He was the man, of all others, fitted to sway and direct the Roman people at the critical juncture of their running into faction upon the assassination of Julius Cæsar. Like Napoleon, too, he skilfully released himself from the coalition of the Triumvirate, and made himself perpetual dictator, and then emperor. Again, like Napoleon, under the ostentation of liberty, he was a selfish, imperious, and unrelenting tyrant, because (like a pattern politician) he had not one spark of feeling unconnected with his own individual and personal ambition and advantage; no sympathy but for vulgar glory, as centring in, and emanating from himself. And lastly, like Napoleon, he knew the value of being beforehand with an enemy. Canidius, one of Antony's officers, says, "This speed of Cæsar's carries beyond belief;" and a soldier adds—

> "While he was yet in Rome,
> His power went out in such distractions as
> Beguil'd all spies."

He took by surprise even the veteran Antony, who says—

> "Is it not strange, Canidius,
> That from Tarentum and Brundusium
> He could so quickly cut the Ionian sea,
> And take in Toryne?"

Cleopatra answers with a sneer, "Celerity is never more admired than by the negligent." The laboured consistency, and the accuracy with which Shakespeare has borne out the historical character of Octavius, might be discussed and confirmed at considerable length. The cool and artful manner in which he assumes the sole command, is, in itself, as remarkable as it is consistent. To Lepidus, who is his equal in the dictatorship, he says—

> "Assemble *me* immediate council; Pompey
> Thrives in our idleness."

In the celebrated scene, too, of recrimination and exculpation between himself and Antony, his language and manner are ably contrasted with those of his compeer, which are frank, open, and generous; Octavius constantly keeping in the foreground of the conference that *he* has been compromised by the others' negligences—not the Triumvirate—not the Commonwealth, but *he*, Octavius, dictator *in futuro*. The scene is the second of the 2d Act. Throughout he shows himself to be the better, because the cooler politician; but Antony is the man in whom a vanquished enemy would confide. Shakespeare never once loses sight of this calculating spirit in Octavius. In the last Act, when he desires to obtain possession of the person of Cleopatra, (he had created a jealousy and division between her and Antony,) in order that he might make a show of her in his triumphal return to Rome, he says—

"Come hither, Proculeius. Go and say,
We purpose her no shame: give her what comforts
The quality of her passion shall require;
Lest in her greatness, by some mortal stroke
She do defeat us; for her life in Rome
Would be eternal in our triumph."

The nearest approach that Octavius makes to a demonstrative enthusiasm is when the news is brought in of Antony's death; and very grand it is. He says—

"The breaking of so great a thing should make
A greater crack: the round world
Should have shook lions into civil streets,
And citizens to their dens. The death of Antony
Is not a single doom; in the name lay
A moiety of the world."

There is a prejudice that your cold and calculating men are mainly fortunate in enterprises of chance; the fact being, that as success is the attendant upon deliberation, with skill and method, we are apt to associate "luck," as it is called, with the prudent man; because failure with him is the exception. Even upon this point, therefore, Shakespeare has given to the career of Octavius the air of a charmed fortune. Antony's soothsayer dissuades him from remaining in the same sphere of action with Octavius, giving his reason for the advice :—

"Thy demon—that 's thy spirit which keeps thee—is
Noble, courageous, high, unmatchable,
Where Cæsar's is not ; but, near him, thy angel
Becomes a fear, as being o'erpower'd : therefore
Make space enough between you.
* * * * * *
If thou dost play with him at any game,
Thou art sure to lose ; and of that natural luck
He beats thee 'gainst the odds : thy lustre thickens
When he shines by : I say again, thy spirit
Is all afraid to govern thee, near him ;
But he away, 'tis noble."

Here, the superstition of the Pagan mythology is artfully blended with the experience of this observer of human nature ;—the man of impulse being always at a disadvantage with the passionless man of talent. When the soothsayer has left him, Antony confirms his judgment ; and says—

"Be it art, or hap,
He hath spoken true ; the very dice obey him ;
And in our sports, my better cunning faints
Under his chance : if we draw lots, he speeds ;
His cocks do win the battle still of mine,
When it is all to naught ; and his quails ever
Beat mine, inhoop'd, at odds."

Certain it is, that all men are more or less influenced by luck. The celebrated Edmund Burke lays it down as a *sine quâ non,* that one qualification to constitute a prosperous commander is, that he should be lucky, and have the reputation for being so.

There is little to be added to what has been already said respecting the character of the third triumvir, Lepidus. He is the pottering peace-maker between his coadjutors, Octavius and Antony. Before their meeting, he says to the friend of Antony :—

"Good Enobarbus, 'tis a worthy deed,
And shall become you well, to entreat your captain
To soft and gentle speech.
"*Eno.* I shall entreat him
To answer like himself: if Cæsar move him,
Let Antony look over Cæsar's head,
And speak as loud as Mars. By Jupiter,
Were I the wearer of Antonius' beard
I would not shave 't to-day.
"*Lep.* 'Tis not a time
For private stomaching.
"*Eno.* Every time
Serves for the matter that is then born in 't.
"*Lep.* The small to greater matters must give way.
"*Eno.* Not if the small come first.
"*Lep.* Your speech is passion;
But, pray you, stir no embers up."

Lepidus was a peace-botcher from timidity; moreover, he was stupid, sensual, and swinish. We have these his characteristics epitomised in the one scene, where the young Pompey entertains the triumvirate at a feast on board his barge. As Lepidus waxes drunk, Antony hoaxes him. Lepidus asks—

"What manner of thing is your crocodile?

"*Ant.* It is shaped, sir, like itself; and it is as broad as it hath breadth;—it is just so high as it is, and moves with its own organ. It lives by that which nourisheth it; and the elements once out of it, it transmigrates.

"*Lep.* What colour is it of?

"*Ant.* Of its own colour, too.

"*Lep.* 'Tis a strange serpent.

"*Ant.* 'Tis so. And the tears of it are wet.
"*Cæsar* to *Ant.* Will this description satisfy him?
"*Ant.* With the health that Pompey gives him, else, he's a very epicure."

We have no more of Lepidus—he's "down among the dead men;" for, after, when Pompey pledges him, Antony interferes, saying, "Bear him ashore. I'll pledge it for him, Pompey." And at the close of the entertainment, Enobarbus, pointing to Lepidus, as he is being carried out on an attendant's back, says—

"There's a strong fellow, Menas.
"*Men.* Why?
"*Eno.* He bears the third part of the world, man."

But the whole of this drinking-scene, with the actors in it, is admirably maintained. Their several characteristics become, of course, more apparent as the men are steeped in the wine. Antony would have swamped them all. Octavius backs out: his caution and reserve come to his rescue. "Strike the vessels, ho!" cries Antony. "Here's to Cæsar." Octavius replies—

"I could well forbear't.
It's monstrous labour, when I wash my brain,
And it grows fouler."

And after they have had the dance of Egyptian Bacchanals, and roared the song, "Come, thou monarch of the vine!" Octavius is the one to break up the carouse:—

"What would you more?—Pompey, good-night. Good brother,
[*To Antony, who had married Octavia.*
Let me request you off; our graver business
Frowns at this levity. Gentle lords, let's part;
You see we have burnt our cheeks: strong Enobarbe
Is weaker than the wine; and mine own tongue
Splits what it speaks."

The scene was evidently a favourite with the poet; and he gives us over-measure in another touch of nature. At the commencement of the triumvirate's interview with Pompey, the latter has reproached Antony with having possessed himself of his father's, the elder Pompey's, house at Rome; but at the breaking up of the carousal—all in drunken good humour, and shaking hands—Pompey, recurring to a question in the early part of the conference, determines to fight the Triumvirate by land: in taking leave, therefore, of Octavius, he says—

> "I'll try you on the shore.
> "*Ant.* And shall, sir. Give us your hand."

Pompey, who is the weakest-headed of the party, has a touch of the half-maudlin: "O Antony! *You have my father's house.* But what? *we* ARE FRIENDS! Come down into the boat."

Never was drinking-scene conducted with more spirit and less vulgarity.

Some French critic upon Shakespeare, when discussing this very scene, says,—"It is no doubt sufficiently ridiculous to make valets talk like heroes; but it is still more ridiculous to make heroes talk in the *language of the people.*" The Frenchman, in his homage to the "classicism" of the Gallo-Greek drama, and in his horror of Anglo-Gothic vulgarity, would in all probability have had the Bacchanalian carouse omitted altogether: nevertheless, as kings and heroes will get drunk, and as, when drunk, their language and behaviour are rarely elevated above those of their butlers, the poet of all human nature has put the best face on the business, and has, at all events, invested the scene with a poetical, not to say a patrician dignity.

It were edifying to speculate upon the manner in which this "classic" would have conducted the revel on board of

Pompey's barge. With what metred decorum the triumvirate would have bandied the festal amenities! Think, too, of the Tuileries etiquette; the conventionalisms that would have been promulgated; the powdered and embroidered politesse of the guests, with the discretion and *bienséance* of their host. How the velvets would have escaped with uncorrugated pile, and laced ruffles have rejoiced in their wonted starch. This school of writing has still its "latter-day" admirers; but I confess to a meek preference of the Nature of Shakespeare to the Art of the Petit Trianon. Hazlitt might well call the French "the Cockneys of Europe." I wish he had said the *Parisian* French.

In the character of the younger Pompey, it should seem that Shakespeare had purposely represented the soldier of fortune; a man possessing a bright spark of gratitude and generosity in his composition; but, at the same time, not united with the most austere sense of justice. Individually, and in their private capacities, Pompey would have offered no personal wrong to Octavius and his coadjutors; but he would have sanctioned the most barefaced treachery towards them, perpetrated by one of his own officers. While he is feasting the triumvirate on board his own vessel, his confidential friend, Menas, proposes to him, aside, that he should entrap the three, and sail away with them. He says:—

"These three world-sharers, these competitors,
Are in thy vessel; let me cut the cable;
And, when we are put off, fall to their throats:
All there is thine."

With how easy a running-knot Pompey held in his conscience, is a fair sample of political orthodoxy. He answers—

"Ah, this thou shouldst have done,
And not have spoke on't! In me, 'tis villainy;
In thee, 't had been good service. Thou must know
'Tis not my profit that does lead mine honour;

> Mine honour, it! Repent that e'er thy tongue
> Hath so betray'd thine act: being done unknown,
> I should have found it afterwards well done;
> But must condemn it now."

The conduct of Pompey is by no means solitary in the political world. A commoner who shall commit murder, and attempt the abduction of an heiress, will become an outcast, and surely be hanged. The man at the head of a nation—the administrator of justice—who may perform the same feat, (*by deputy*,) will hold himself irresponsible. Thus it is, "robes and furred gowns hide all." Beautifully has it been said by the same master-spirit, "Our life is but a mingled yarn, of good and ill together;" so, the character of Pompey exhibits features of attractive quality—frank and generous, with all those sanguine aspirations that render the season of youth the most apt for great accomplishments.

All the soldiers, indeed, in this tragedy, are favourable specimens of their class. In the opening of the 3d Act, the introduction of Ventidius and Silius, returning from a victory over the Parthians, has given Shakespeare an opportunity, of which he has not unfrequently availed himself, of throwing into his military characters a dash of that worldly prudence which, from their intercourse with mankind of every grade, is not inconsistent with their romantic and fortuitous profession. In the flush of triumph, Silius urges his superior officer to follow up his success; adding—

> "So thy grand captain, Antony,
> Shall set thee on triumphant chariots, and
> Put garlands on thy head."

His companion replies with this unexpected piece of wisdom and military diplomacy:—

> "O Silius, Silius,
> I have done enough. A lower place, note well,
> May make too great an act; for learn this, Silius,

Better to leave undone, than by our deed acquire
Too high a fame when him we serve 's away.
Cæsar and Antony have ever won
More in their officer than person. Sossius,
One of my place in Syria, his lieutenant,
For quick accumulation of renown,
Which he achiev'd by the minute, lost his favour.
Who does i' the wars more than his captain can,
Becomes his captain's captain : and ambition,
The soldier's virtue, rather makes choice of loss,
Than gain which darkens him.
I could do more to do Antonius good,
But 'twould offend him ; and in his offence
Should my performance perish."

Silius rejoins,—

"Thou hast, Ventidius, that,
Without the which a soldier, and his sword,
Grants scarce distinction. Thou wilt write to Antony?
" *Ven.* I 'll humbly signify what in his name,
That magical word of war, we have effected ;
How, with his banners, and his well-paid ranks,
The ne'er-yet-beaten horse of Parthia
We have jaded out o' the field."

It is from among the underwood of these stately productions (for these are very subordinate characters in the drama) that we bring to remembrance gems of practical wisdom : as in the great natural world, knowledge is scattered with the prodigality of beneficence for the admiration and improvement of the investigator.

While upon the character of the soldiers in this play, I will conclude with one or two points in their conduct worthy of revision. The first is the lesson that is read to us against mere obstinacy ; and obstinacy may be distinguished from firmness, as being a persistence in act, in defiance of self-conviction.

All his companions in arms are opposed to Antony's fighting Cæsar by sea; but Cleopatra was for the sea: nothing, therefore, but a sea-fight would the dotard commander listen to. The debate upon the occasion is a perfect example of what mere dogged self-will is capable, as opposed to wholesome reason. Enobarbus (the close friend of Antony) is the first to object—

"Why will my lord do so?
"*Ant.* For that he dares us to it.
"*Eno.* So hath my lord dared him to single fight.
"*Canid.* Ay, and to wage this battle at Pharsalia,
Where Cæsar fought with Pompey: but these offers,
Which serve not for his 'vantage, he shakes off;
And so should you.
"*Eno.* Your ships are not well mann'd,
Your mariners are muleteers, reapers, people
Ingross'd by swift impress; in Cæsar's fleet
Are those that often have 'gainst Pompey fought:
Their ships are yare; yours heavy: no disgrace
Shall fall you for refusing him at sea,
Being prepar'd for land.
"*Ant.* *By sea, by sea.*"

To the earnest expostulation, again, and experience of Enobarbus, his only reply is, "*I'll fight at sea.*" Then a private soldier enters, hearing of his general's determination—

"O noble emperor, do not fight by sea;
Trust not to rotten planks: do you misdoubt
This sword, and these my wounds? Let the Egyptians,
And the Phœnicians, *go a-ducking:* we
Have us'd to conquer standing on the earth,
And fighting foot to foot."

He leaves them, resolving on the sea-fight. Then, exclaims the veteran soldier—

"By Hercules, I think I am i' the right.
"*Can.* Soldier, thou art; but his whole action grows
Not in the pow'r on 't: so, our leader 's led,
And we are women's men."

Contempt and insubordination are the natural consequence of mere stubbornness of will in a superior, when opposed by plain sense. These feelings, therefore, become seriously demonstrative after Antony's shameful defeat and flight. Scarus exclaims—

> "The greater cantle of the world is lost
> With very ignorance; we have kiss'd away
> Kingdoms and provinces."

Reproach follows upon reproach, and Canidius ends by declaring his resolution to "render his legions and his horse to Cæsar."

This defection in his officers is one of the most painful circumstances in the story, and Shakespeare has enlisted our sympathies in favour of its hero, by immediately after exhibiting him as wholly absorbed in his own unworthiness, and, with affecting self-abasement, impeaching the wretched prostitution of his finer nature. Misery, sorrow, reverse of fortune, treachery, violence, and assassination, are all qualities of high tragic event; but no circumstance, or emotion of the mind, makes a stronger appeal to our sympathy than the bitterness of self-reproach in a noble and generous nature. The wisest of kings has said, "The spirit of a man can sustain itself; but a wounded spirit who can bear?"

Few scenes are more touching than the speech of Marc Antony to his attendants after his defeat, beginning, "Hark! the land bids me tread no more upon it:" and the chief cause of its pathetic character is, that in the front of all his self-reproaches and disasters, the provision for his followers stands most apparent in his thoughts.

> "Friends, come hither:
> I am so lated in the world, that I
> Have lost my way for ever. I have a ship
> Laden with gold; take that, divide it; fly,
> And make your peace with Cæsar."

It is this generosity of disposition, this unselfishness, coming against his grosser animal propensities, that redeem what would otherwise be an undignified subject for the chief character in a heroic drama.

Scarus alone, of his principal officers, remains attached to him. And it is worthy of notice, that Shakespeare, true to his own happy philosophy, has made Scarus the most energetic and the most cheerful of them all. In the last battle, Antony says to him—

"Thou bleed'st apace."

He replies—

"I had a wound here, that was like a T,
But now 'tis made an H. . . .
We'll beat them into bench-holes; I have yet
Room for six scotches more."

Eros enters to announce that the enemy are routed, and Scarus answers—

"Let us score their backs,
And snatch 'em up, as we take hares, behind;
'Tis sport to maul a runner."

Antony says to him—

"I will reward thee
Once for thy sprightly comfort, and tenfold
For thy good valour. Come thee on.
"*Scar.* I'll halt after."

Upon searching into the minutiæ of these characters, one would suppose that Shakespeare had passed all his days in a camp, so thoroughly has he imbibed the manner, as well as matter of the men.

But of all the subordinates in this great drama, none makes so powerful an appeal to the *feelings* as Enobarbus. Poor, unstable, unhappy Enobarbus! had you but held fast your integrity to your master, you had been a guiding star for all generations to steer their course by; as it is, we set thee as a lone beacon on a promontory to warn wayfarers through the sea of life from the shoals and the sunken rocks of inconstancy, remorse, and self-abandonment.

Let us, however, tread tenderly upon the memory of poor Enobarbus, for amply did he extenuate his fault; and all the reproaches we could devise would come far short of the pitiless scorn with which he himself judged his own infirmity.

Enobarbus stands in the record of those who deserted a kind master in the winter of his fortunes; but he also numbers with the few who have expiated to the uttermost the baseness of their ingratitude. Here, again, we perceive that Shakespeare, in the sweetness of his nature, could not bring himself utterly to cast out one who, up to the eleventh hour, had run so fair a course: besides, he knew that it would be offering an undue violence to humanity to introduce at so momentous a point of the story a moral anomaly, a fellow-being with a Janus-nature, bluntly and sincerely honest up to a certain stage in his career; and then, with the suddenness of a pantomime trick, convert him into a remorseless, callous self-seeker. Such men are not of this world, and Shakespeare drew men as he found them, and not as they may, perchance, be in the moon, (with the lunatics,) or any other planet.

In portraying the defection of Enobarbus, he has, with unusual care even for him, and, of course, with accurate truth, represented him as oscillating between inconstancy and steadiness, with the gradual and stronger leaning to inconstancy. Upon the first occasion, when Canidius resolves to desert to Cæsar, Enobarbus says—

> "I 'll yet follow
> The wounded chance of Antony, though my reason
> Sits in the wind against me."

Here's the first motive which shakes him: his reason and self-interest begin to oppose his fidelity. We next see him with Cleopatra after the sea fight, and their disgraceful flight from it. This conversation is finely characteristic of a rough and brave soldier, whose wounded honour has forced him into lukewarmness towards the cause in which he was embarked. In the absence of all plan and purpose, she helplessly inquires of him, "What shall we do, Enobarbus?" to which his bluff answer is, "Think, and die!"

> "*Cleo.* Is Antony, or we, in fault for this?
> "*Eno.* Antony only, that would make his will
> Lord of his reason.

[Referring to his obstinate determination against the counsel of his followers.]

> What though you fled
> From the great face of war, whose several ranges
> Frighted each other; why should he follow?
> The itch of his affection should not then
> Have nick'd his captainship; at such a point,
> When half to half the world oppos'd, he being
> The mer'd question: 'twas a shame, no less
> Than was his loss, to course your flying flags,
> And leave his navy gazing."

As another instance of Shakespeare's consistency in propriety, we note that Enobarbus, unlike the other officers of Antony, never takes cause against Cleopatra. He was more about her person than they. He has, with them, the same excuse for bitterness, yet he never censures her; he never calls her coarse names, as the others do. He fixes the blame where it ought to rest—upon the stronger party—Antony. All this harmonises with his voluptuous description of her in the barge, (in the 2d scene of the 2d Act,) while it preserves his own integrity of character as a brave and generous warrior.

Immediately after the above conversation with Cleopatra, Antony enters, and thinks to patch up his desperate fortune by challenging Octavius to a single combat. When he has left the scene, we note that the respect of Enobarbus is rapidly verging towards contempt; and he gives utterance to one of those acute reflections upon human action, that keep us in a state of perpetual wonderment as we scrutinise these great compositions.

For instance,—what art is thrown into the following speech that we may be gradually prepared for the infidelity of Enobarbus, and that it may receive some meed of qualification. It is his own reflection upon Antony's resolution to challenge Octavius. He says—

> "Yes, like enough, high-battled Cæsar will
> Unstate his happiness, and be staged to the show
> Against a sworder! I see *men's judgments are*
> *A parcel of their fortunes; and things outward*
> *Do draw the inward quality after them,*
> *To suffer all alike.* That he should dream,
> Knowing all measures, the full Cæsar will
> Answer his emptiness! Cæsar, thou hast subdu'd
> His judgment too!"

Close on the heels of this summary of Antony's position, we find Enobarbus debating his own; and, with a natural vacillation between honesty and self-interest, concluding upon adopting the higher and loyal course. I know of nothing in dramatic history surpassing in artistic skill the gradual development of declension, and final secession in the conduct of Enobarbus. It is like one of those subtle *physical* changes which come over the human structure. His next self-debating is—

> "Mine honesty and I begin to square,
> The *loyalty well held to fools does make*
> *Our faith mere folly:* yet he that can endure
> To follow with allegiance a fallen lord,
> Does conquer him that did his master conquer,
> And earns a place i' the story."

This counter-resolution in favour of Antony is ingeniously introduced as a foil to the insane proposal of the latter to spend the night in feasting, when his fortunes are drained to their lowest dregs. How the contempt of Enobarbus strengthens even into disgust, at the unsoldier-like (though, under the circumstances, most natural) boasting of his master in his desperate extremity. Antony says—

> "Call to me all my sad [steadfast] captains;
> . . . . . to-night I'll force
> The wine peep through their scars. Come on, my queen;
> There's sap in't yet. The next time I do fight,
> I'll make death love me; for I will contend
> Even with his pestilent scythe."

When they are gone out, Enobarbus says—

> "Now he'll outstare the lightning! To be furious
> *Is to be frighted out of fear;* and, in that mood,
> The dove will peck the estridge; and I see still,
> A diminution in our captain's brain
> Restores his heart; *when valour preys on reason,*
> *It eats the sword it fights with.* I will seek
> Some way to leave him."

Shakespeare makes out the strongest case for Enobarbus —under the circumstances. He leaves his master; but he takes nothing away with him. The conduct of Antony, too, upon hearing of his desertion, rises into magnanimity:—

> "Go, Eros, send his treasure after; do it;
> Detain no jot, I charge thee; write to him
> (I will subscribe) gentle adieus and greetings;
> Say, that I wish he never find more cause
> To change a master.—Oh, my fortunes have
> Corrupted honest men!—Despatch!—Enobarbus!"

Pathetically natural is that ejaculation of Antony,—comprising a volume of wonderment and sorrow, at the defection of his old friend and companion in arms. The celebrated exclamation of Julius Cæsar, in the drama—"Et tu Brute!"—sounds pedantic when compared with that simple sigh of Antony.

Poor Enobarbus! his infidelity soon rises up against him; but the news of all his treasure being sent after him puts the finishing stroke to his remorse. In bitterness of spirit, he exclaims—

"I am alone the villain of the earth,
And feel I am so most. O Antony,
Thou mine of bounty, how wouldst thou have paid
My better service, when my turpitude
Thou dost so crown with gold! This blows my heart;
If swift thought break it not, a swifter mean
Shall outstrike thought; but thought will do't, I feel.
I fight against thee!—No!—I will go seek
Some ditch wherein to die; the foul'st best fits
My latter part of life."

His last speech in the field, at night, before the battle, is perhaps the most affecting ever penned or uttered by man, under similar affliction; for what affliction can equal a self-reproving heart? What yearning, what desolation in the eloquence!—

"Be witness to me, O thou blessed moon!
When men revolted shall upon record
Bear hateful memory, poor Enobarbus did
Before thy face repent.
O sov'reign mistress of true melancholy!
The poisonous damp of night disponge upon me,
That life, a very rebel to my will,
May hang no longer on me: throw my heart
Against the flint and hardness of my fault;
Which, being dried to grief, will break to powder,
And finish all foul thoughts. O Antony!
Nobler than my revolt is infamous,
Forgive me in thine own particular;

> But let the world rank me in register
> A master-leaver, and a fugitive,—
> O Antony!—O Antony!"

His heart breaks.

The origin of the character is to be seen in Plutarch, occupying about six or seven lines. Shakespeare saw at once that it was an occasion for dramatic susceptibility and development of action; and, in consequence, he perhaps never more satisfactorily constructed and completed a character than this secondary one of Enobarbus. We can be at no loss to recognise another type from whence the poet mainly drew this portrait of an attendant, remorse-stricken upon abandoning a kind master in his adversity.

Octavia—the wife of Antony—with her sweet, and very womanly qualities; with her still and holy meekness; her dignity, and perfect discretion, was not the character to be brought into the same sphere of action with her meteor-like rival. Universal opinion has therefore applauded the poet's judgment in not bringing them together; since the result must have been detrimental to one party; and this, neither the historic nor the dramatic law would have sanctioned, by reason of the pre-eminent, and totally opposite qualities in the two women: the restless, dazzling brilliancy, and overweening coquetry of the one; with the calm, sensible, and sensitive deportment of the other.

The parting scene between Octavius and his sister, upon her marriage to Antony, is very pretty and affectionate; his gentle speeches to her, and her full heart at the leave-taking,—

> "The swan's down feather,
> That stands upon the swell at the full of tide,
> And neither way inclines,"—

furnish a perfect picture of fraternal love, and give us an interest in the first emperor of the world, beyond all his ambition and his conquests.

The characters of Charmian and Iras, Cleopatra's women, exhibit no prominent marks of character deserving exclusive notice. Their devotion to their mistress is instinctive and Hindoo-like. They know no motive but obedience; and the superadded kindness excites them to the prodigality of self-sacrifice with her.

But the most powerful, or rather the most genuine piece of individual portraiture among the insignificant actors in this drama, is that of the country clown who brings Cleopatra the serpent—the asp. The utter indifference and boorish obtuseness dawning into an expression of humour, thrown into this character, is excessively happy. There is no human animal more stupidly regardless of death and its consequences than your genuine country lout. He is, indeed, "of the earth, earthy." As he has sprung from the clod, so the soil of his nature adheres to him, and he returns to his primary element with congenial stupidity. Only observe the grinning brutishness with which the fellow discusses the merits of the reptile he has provided. And how correctly in keeping with the character his giving the creature its most common generic name—that of "worm." He does not call it snake, serpent, or asp: there would be some hint of knowledge and refinement had he done that; so he has no other idea connected with it than that of "worm." It was, indeed, a consummately artistic and altogether picturesque idea to place that primitive lump of humanity in juxtaposition with the gorgeous Eastern magnificence, the rich fancy, the voluptuous beauty, the sensuous languor, the fervid graces, the regal grandeur, and yet greater regality, conscious of feminine charm and sway, which pre-eminently distinguish the royal paramour, that "caught the world's great hands." The Egyptian queen, in her potency of will, choosing to die rather than to swell the triumph of Octavius;—thereby setting the crowning act to her many subtle subjugations of men's resolves to her own purposes ;—attired in imperial robes and jewels, no less arrayed in majesty of adornment, than in majesty of womanly determination,—stands a picture of striking glowing historic portraiture, still farther heightened by the attendant figure of the loutish countryman. There is something in the contrast of this lump of life's commonest clay with the superb ore of golden Cleopatra, which wonderfully harmonises the whole scene. It is, indeed, a scene of harmony in contrast throughout. There is the simple basket of figs concealing deadliest venom ; the small dark aspic, and the coiled splendour of the "Serpent of old Nile ;" the obtuse jokings of the boor, and the refined ease, with haughty composure, of the imperial woman, firm in her dread intent. No element could have been introduced so effectively, in enhancement of the impression created by Cleopatra's death-scene, as the clown's earthy brutality. And what a perfect morsel of a scene it is! He forms, as it were, an emblem of that common mould to which all worldly splendour must come. He enters, and Cleopatra says—

"Hast thou the pretty worm of Nilus there,
That kills and pains not?

"*Clown.* Truly I have him; but I wouldn't be the party that should desire you to touch him, for his biting is immortal: those that do die of it do seldom or never recover.

"*Cleop.* Remember'st thou any that have died on 't?

"*Clown.* Very many, men and women too. I heard of one of 'em no longer ago than yesterday;—a very honest woman, but something given to lie; as a woman shouldn't do, but in the way of honesty. How she died of it; what pain she felt: truly, she makes a very good report of the worm. But he that will believe all they say, shall never be saved by half that they do. But this is most fallible; the worm 's an odd worm.

"*Cleop.* Farewell. [*Clown sets down the basket.*]

"*Clown.* You must think this, look ye, that the worm will do his kind. [That is, will obey its nature.]

"*Cleop.* Ay, ay; farewell.

"*Clown.* Look ye, the worm is not to be trusted but in the keeping of wise people; for, indeed, there's no goodness in the worm.

"*Cleop.* Take thou no care; it shall be heeded.

"*Clown.* Very good. Give it nothing, I pray you, for it isn't worth the feeding.

"*Cleop.* Will it eat me?

"*Clown.* You mustn't think I am so simple, but I know the devil himself will not eat a woman. I know that a woman is a dish for the gods, if the devil dress her not. But truly, these same whoreson devils do the gods great harm in their women; for in every ten that they make, the devils mar five.

"*Cleop.* Well, get thee gone; farewell.

"*Clown.* Yes, forsooth. *I wish you joy of the worm!*"

Constant occasions occur of Shakespeare's natural piety, and of his unaffected reverence for holy rites and observances. During the reign of Augustus Cæsar the Messiah came into the world. Historians and poets have signalised that epoch as being divinely accompanied by a universal peace among the civilised nations of the earth. Milton, in his young and noble poem on the "Nativity," says—

"No war, or battle-sound
Was heard the world around:
The idle spear and shield were high up-hung;
The hook'd chariot stood
Unstain'd with hostile blood:
The trumpet spake not to the armed throng;
And kings sat still with awful eye,
As if they surely knew their sovran Lord were by."

And Guthrie, in his "Universal History," makes this simply pathetic record of the event—"Peace now reigned over the whole earth, and Jesus Christ came into it."

Shakespeare, availing himself of the same impressive circumstance, causes Octavius to proclaim, as in an involuntary prophecy, "The time of universal peace is near."

X.

# All's Well that Ends Well.

# X.

# ALL'S WELL THAT ENDS WELL.

---

THE story or plot of "All 's Well that Ends Well" is one of the most interesting of Shakespeare's comedies. The main incident, which turns upon the circumstance of a young maiden becoming the wooing party, and claiming the royal prerogative to bestow upon her the hand of the man she is in love with, as a reward for the service she has rendered to her sovereign in administering to him a prescription hereditary in her family, and thereby restoring him from a painful distemper that the faculty had considered incurable; the circumstance, again, of the youth to whom she had attached herself being the son of the lady who had afforded her protection in her orphanhood, and who was her superior in point of rank; his yielding to the power of the king, and, although he wedded her, resolving never to fulfil the duties of a husband; his quitting her to follow the Florentine war; her tracing him in the disguise of a pilgrim, and succeeding in winning the confidence and friendly offices of the young maiden, Diana, whom he has attempted to seduce, and who is the sole means of causing him to render justice to his discarded wife, is all brought about with a force of ingenuity, and delicacy of feeling, that are perfectly admirable.

The character of the heroine, Helena, is one of rare sweetness, blended with high romantic fervour. She is placed in the singularly critical position of courting her husband, both as a maiden and a wife; and the glorious testimony to the transparent beauty of virtue is fully borne out, and a triumph achieved, by her not committing one single violation of the laws of the most scrupulous modesty.

I must take leave to say a few words in behalf, and, I hope, in justification of Helena, whose principle of action appears to have been wonderfully mistaken, and whose mental structure to have been—I will not say, unappreciated, but not even recognised by the general reader. Of all Shakespeare's heroines, it strikes me that Helena is the one that is most philosophical, both in temperament and in speech and conduct. When I say "philosophical in temperament," I do not mean that she is either stoical or resigned. She is the very reverse of either. But she is reflective, she is observant, and she is essentially *remedial.* An apparently hopeless passion has taught her reflection, introspection, and humility of spirit. It has taught her to think conscientiously, to reason justly, to weigh her own and others' claims carefully. She has discernment, and she has warmth of heart: the first teaching her to perceive accurately, the latter impelling her to decide generously. She, therefore, estimates herself and her own value at modest rate, while to Bertram she awards all the superiority that loving worship takes delight in imputing to its chosen idol. But at the same time that Helena's affection prompts her to *over*rate the man she loves, and to *under*rate herself, her disposition will not let her sink beneath the sense of disparity. Her own character will not let her do this; for, besides its diffidence of self, it possesses uncommon self-reliance and moral courage,—a combination less rare than is generally believed. Womanly gentleness and modesty, together with womanly firmness and fortitude, are far from incompatible ; and in Helena of Narbonne they co-exist to a remarkable degree. The kind of gentleness which consists of mere prone and passive yieldingness, oftener degenerates into weakness, ending in obstinacy and slyness, than Helena's kind of gentleness, which is self-modesty without self-distrust. She is conscious, to an acutely-sensitive degree, of her own inadequate pretensions; but she is also conscious—involuntarily conscious, as it were—of her own powers to win through patient trial, earnest attempt, and devoted endeavour. It is this that makes Helena's philosophy so "remedial" a one. Ever ready to acknowledge her lack of *personal* merit, she is inwardly aware of a *moral* merit, that requires but time and opportunity to obtain for her that which her own simple attractions are unable to command. She does not feel herself formed to inspire regard, but she knows herself worthy to gain regard; and this she diligently and faithfully dedicates her whole thoughts and energies to achieve. Observe here with what mingled fervour and humility her loving thoughts clothe themselves in thoughtful words :—

"'Tis pity,
That wishing well had not a body in 't,
Which might be felt;—that we, the poorer born,
Whose baser stars do shut us up in wishes,
Might with effects of them follow our friends,
And show what we alone must think ; which never
Returns us thanks."

Helena, with the true courage born of a practical and remedial philosophy, is eager to find resources in her own sense of resolve. She says—

"Our remedies oft *in ourselves* do lie
Which we ascribe to Heaven : the fated sky
Gives us free scope ; only doth backward pull
Our slow designs, when *we ourselves* are dull."

She gathers confidence from inborn consciousness of steadfastness and ardour of perseverance, exclaiming—

> "Impossible be strange attempts to those
> That weigh their pains in sense; and do suppose
> What hath been cannot be. Who ever strove
> To show her merit that did miss her love?"

The same characteristic earnestness, with faith in the philosophy of *endeavour*, marks the whole of her arguments with the king during the interview where she seeks to persuade him of the efficacy of her father's medicine. She thus modestly, yet ardently, urges him to essay its effect—

> "What I can do, can do no hurt to try,
> Since you set up your rest 'gainst remedy.
> HE that of greatest works is finisher,
> Oft does them by the weakest minister.
> So holy writ in *babes* hath judgment shown,
> When judges have been babes. Great floods have flown
> From simple sources; and great seas have dried,
> When miracles have by the greatest been denied.
> *Oft expectation fails; and most oft there,*
> *Where most it promises; and oft it hits*
> *Where hope is coldest, and despair most fits.*"

This is perfectly the language of one accustomed to reason hopefully in the midst of discouragement, and to reap fruit for trust out of the most unpromising occurrences. Helena has a spirit of fervent reliance, the offspring of her very meekness and innocent humility. When the king waves her proffered help, she thus gently, yet warmly, meets his refusal. Her speech is at once femininely diffident and devoutly earnest:—

> "Inspired merit so by breath is barr'd.
> It is not so with HIM that all things knows,
> As 'tis with us that square our guess by shows:
> But most it is presumption in us, when

The help of Heaven we count the act of men.
Dear sir, to my endeavour give consent :
Of Heaven, not me, make an experiment.
I am not an impostor, that proclaim
Myself against the level of mine aim ;
But know I think, and think I know most sure,
My art is not past power, nor you past cure."

No wonder such eloquent persuasion succeeds in its desired effect upon her royal listener. He replies, "Art thou so confident? Within what space hop'st thou my cure?" And then Helena answers his words full of her characteristically humble, yet trustful spirit—rising into poetic beauty with her own mounting hope—

"The greatest grace lending grace,
Ere twice the horses of the sun shall bring
Their fiery torcher his diurnal ring ;
Ere twice in murk and occidental damp
Moist Hesperus hath quench'd his sleepy lamp,
Or four-and-twenty times the pilot's glass
Hath told the thievish minutes how they pass ;
What is infirm from your sound parts shall fly ;
Health shall live free, and sickness freely die."

The essence of Helena's philosophy, in its practical energy, which prefers deeds to speech, and its hopeful nature, ever looking to the possibility of good, as well as facing the existence of evil, is contained in those few words of hers where she interrupts something she was going to say, thus—

"But with the word, the time will bring on summer ;
When briars shall have *leaves* as well as *thorns*,
And be as *sweet* as *sharp*. We must away.
Our waggon is prepar'd, and time revives us :
All 's well that ends well. Still the fine 's the crown ;
Whate'er the course, the end is the renown."

Helena's remedial philosophy supplies her with one invaluable resource—unflinching courage against disappointment. When on her journey homewards, hoping to meet the king at Marseilles, and, arriving there, finds him just gone, with what promptitude and cheerfulness she prepares to follow him. No time wasted in weak lamentation and regret, but active resolve and steady perseverance. This is precisely the kind of courage—*moral* courage—which women of Helena's nature and philosophy possess. It is the noblest, the sublimest courage; and it is essentially *feminine* courage. Fortitude of spirit against discouragement—bravery of heart and mind amidst disappointment, disaster, and defeat—constitute womanly valour; and we see that the gentlest, at the same time the firmest, among women, are those most distinguished by this heroic attribute. So much for Helena's philosophy.

But Helena has been tacitly impeached, if not openly arraigned, of an unseemly forwardness in the proffer of herself and her affections. She has had high justice done her, it is true, at the hands of several critics: Coleridge calling her upon one occasion, "Shakespeare's *loveliest* character;" Hazlitt saying, "She is placed in circumstances of the most critical kind, * * * yet the most scrupulous nicety of female modesty is not once violated;" Charles Lamb ascribing to her "the full lustre of the female character;" and lastly, one of her own sex, Mrs Jameson, in her "Characteristics of Women," having written a noble vindication of her character and conduct. Yet still, there has been a prevailing feeling—an impression—that Helena is guilty of unfeminine want of delicacy and reserve in the manifestation of her passion for Bertram; and the very zeal of her defenders in pleading her cause, evinces the consciousness that such impression exists. How this impression has arisen, I think I can show. In the first place, Helena, as has been already said, is a remarkable union of moral force and courage, with gentleness and tenderness of heart; and there are many men who cannot believe in—nay, who cannot see—gentleness and softness in a woman's nature, if it be accompanied with *strength of character.* There is a favourite cant phrase in Noodledom (as Sydney Smith calls the region of numskulls) about "strong-minded women," which seems to preclude the possibility of strength in co-existence with gentleness of feeling and softness of manner. As "strong-minded women" are frequently spoken of, one would think a "strong-minded" woman must necessarily have the figure of a horse-guard, the swag of a drayman, and the sensibility of a carcase-butcher. Helena, in her energy of purpose, in her quickness of intelligence to discern a means of fulfilling her object, and in her spirited pursuit of those means, may give the idea of unfeminine will and decision to those who confound passiveness with gentleness, helplessness with retiring delicacy, and incapacity with modesty; a confounding of qualities which characterises the opinion of one class of men, about women, of the present day. But to those who know how entirely consistent with unaffected diffidence of self, is the utmost heroism of self-devotion and self-exertion, in women distinguished by all their sex's grace of person, sentiment, and behaviour, will perceive nothing but truest feminine beauty in all that Helena does. She has that absence of self-conceit, with reliance upon her sense of right, which abates no jot of modest feeling and demeanour, while it leads to the most courageous endeavour. No difficulty daunts her; because she has confidence in the *motive* which impels her, rather than *in her own power* to accomplish its ends,—a characteristic distinction deserving of notice.

The modesty—with force—of her appeal, in the interview with the king, has been discussed: in all that regards her love, not only is she modest, but she is humble—that is, she has the modesty and humility of true passion; which takes pleasure in debasing its own estimate and pretensions, in exact proportion to its eagerness to exalt and deify the merits of the object beloved. Musing upon her passion for Bertram, she says—

> "It were all one
> That I should love a bright particular star,
> And think to wed *it*—he is so above me."

And nothing can surpass in modesty, with ardour of worship, her famous *impelled confession* to the Countess Roussillon; it is the very prodigality of loving humility and humble love:—

> "Then I confess
> Here on my knee, before high Heaven and you,
> That before you, and next unto high Heaven,
> I love your son:
> My friends were poor, but honest; so 's my love.
> Be not offended; for it hurts not him
> That he is lov'd of me: I follow him not
> By any token of presumptuous suit;
> Nor would I have him till I do deserve him,
> Yet never know how that desert should be.
> I know I love in vain, strive against hope;
> Yet in this captious and intenible sieve
> I still pour in the waters of my love,
> And lack not to lose still; thus, Indian-like,
> Religious in mine error, I adore
> The sun, that looks upon his worshipper,
> But knows of him no more. My dearest madam,
> Let not your hate encounter with my love,
> For loving where you do; but, if yourself,
> Whose aged honour cites a virtuous youth,
> Did ever, in so true a flame of liking,
> Wish chastely, and love dearly, that your Dian
> Was both herself and love; oh! then, give pity
> To her, whose state is such, that cannot choose
> But lend and give, where she is sure to lose;
> That seeks not to find that her search implies;
> But, riddle-like, lives sweetly where she dies."

These last lines are in the perfect spirit of a self-sacrifice that characterises a genuine and modest love.

Then, at the very moment when she attains the summit at which she has aimed and has the royal privilege to choose her husband—no triumph—no exultation—no welcoming of success marks her manner; but meekest words, and gentlest deference:—

> "I dare not say, I take you; but I give
> Me and my service, ever while I live,
> Into your yielding power."

And when this chosen husband bluntly and contemptuously rejects her, she relinquishes her claim; turning to the king, and saying—

> "That you are well restor'd, my lord, I am glad;
> Let the rest go."

The whole scene of their parting, when Bertram leaves her, (the 5th of the 2d Act,) is exhibited, as ONE writer *only* could have done, without descending into coarseness and over-painting, And, in the climax of the plot, she is not only justified in the scheme as regards herself personally, but she saves her husband from a dissolute act of profligacy, the almost natural consequence of a constrained wedlock—of a marriage into which the man is forced, against both will and inclination; and lastly, by its means, she protects the young maiden, Diana, from the lawless suit of a seducer, and preserves her virtue from the snare laid for it. And now I hope that I have rescued the severely-judged Helena from the charge of "forwardness" and "immodesty." Certainly, a finer specimen of moral fortitude, with feminine true delicacy of sentiment, I do not think is to be found in all the Shakespeare gallery of heroines.

But the story of "All's Well that Ends Well" is a specimen of one of the curses of a feudal tyranny, where the dearest privileges, and dearest of earthly blessings—a free choice in marriage—was prostrate to the caprice of the sovereign: and Shakespeare has, with his ample and humane philosophy, manifested the folly, as well as injustice of that prerogative; and this may have been the reason why he has created so great a disproportion between the moral qualities of Helena and Bertram. Had they both been estimable persons, there could have been little scope for romance in the plot; it must per force have taken a commonplace character. Had she not been endowed with the highest qualities of devotion and virtuous principle,—or say, even had she betrayed a questionable purity,—he could at once (being the stronger party) have righted himself by a forcible separation. The incongruity of the law, therefore, was forcibly displayed, by his availing himself of the man's conventional privilege of desertion, seeing that he could not bring his affections to respond to the disposing will of his feudal lord. This, therefore, again must be the reason why the poet has so laboured the character of his hero, in order that he might become a foil to the excellent Helena; and, moreover, we again recognise Shakespeare's knowledge of the human heart, inasmuch as every day affords us testimonies of the extraordinary endurance, devotion, and attachment of women in the midst of repugnant qualities, and even of savage treatment; for Helena is conscious of, and proves the infidelity, with other disreputable propensities, of her husband. But Bertram is, really, a dirty dog—a thoroughly dirty dog: he is an aristocrat, not of the "first water," but of the last—the lowest water—sewer-water. He has the pride of birth, with scarcely a virtue to give dignity to, and warrant that pride. He is weak in judgment; for he is the last to perceive the scoundrel character of the wretch Parolles. He is imperious and headstrong, treacherous, a liar, and a coward. One of the commentators (Dr Johnson, I think) denies that he is a coward, assuming that he must have distinguished himself in the Florentine war, since he received the favour of the duke; but I mean that he was a moral coward; as proof, there is scarcely a scene wherein he appears, (but more especially in the 3d of the last Act, when he infamously traduces the character of Diana,) that he does not exhibit himself a despicable, and even a loathsome coward. And this, forsooth, is a man for the pure and high-minded Helena to woo, and win, and think to convert into a respectable companion for life! But, indeed, we may find occasion for wonder at the matrimonial alliances concocted in more than one of Shakespeare's dramas; in which it should seem, that if the woman were but legitimately united with the man, and according to ecclesiastical law, and was provided with an establishment for life, it was expected of her to become profoundly grateful and complacent, whatever may be the character, or have been the previous conduct of the man. In the feudal ages the women were scarcely a grade higher in the scale of creation than the live-stock on the estates: because they administered to the vanity and sensual gratification of their lords, these deigned to make a fuss with them, and talk prodigiously of the imperial dominion of ladies' eyes and ladies' favours; but they possessed no more real power than the selected female in a Mussulman's harem: it remained for Shakespeare to assert in behalf of his sisterhood a claim to the higher endowments of intellectuality, with the most serenely beautiful of all the active virtues—those of loving-kindness, and steadfastness of heart.

I judged it allowable to say thus over much, perhaps, of Bertram and Helena, although the principal characters in the play, because it is one not frequently turned to by the casual readers of the poet. To such, therefore, the foregoing remarks have been addressed; as, indeed, I may say I have done throughout these Dissertations.

Another fact in this play, and in which Shakespeare marks his estimation of Bertram's false aristocracy, (for nobility of birth and rank, without nobleness of nature, is a melancholy contradiction,) may be recognised in the foil that has been given to his character in that of the two young lords in their honest and hearty denunciation of his unchivalrous conduct in his amours. Their conversation about him is not tainted with envy on account of his prowess in the campaign, but it conveys a high-minded disgust at his heartless intrigues. The one young nobleman, after confiding to the other that Bertram hath "perverted a young gentlewoman of a most chaste renown," and hath even given her his "monumental ring,"—that is, the family jewel,—follows up his detestation of the act by adding, in a fine spirit of philosophy, "We are merely our own traitors. And, as in the common course of all treasons, we still see them reveal themselves, till they attain to their abhorred ends; so he, that in this action contrives against his own nobility, in his proper stream o'erflows himself." And immediately after, when it has been noticed that the war was over, and the one inquires whether Bertram will return to France, the other replies, "I perceive, by this demand, you are not altogether of his counsel." To which the former retorts, "Let it be forbid, sir! So should I be a great deal of his act." Then, again, when speaking of Bertram's having received intelligence of the death of Helena, his wife, the second young lord sums up his cold-blooded nature in these ten words—"I am heartily sorry that he will be glad of this." And he adds—"How mightily, sometimes, we make us comforts of our losses:" to which the other rejoins, "And how mightily, some other times, we drown our gain in tears. The great dignity that his valour hath here acquired for him, shall, at home, be encountered with a shame as ample." And then comes the well-known golden reflection: "The web of our life is of a mingled yarn, good and ill together: our virtues would be proud if our faults whipped them not; and our crimes would despair if they were not cherished by our virtues."

It cannot be too often repeated, that some of the very finest of Shakespeare's aphorisms are, as precious seed, scattered on the by-ways of his dramas; and this circumstance enforces the necessity that none but persons of imagination and quick feeling should presume to impersonate any of his characters; and yet more, that his plays never will be worthily represented till the theatrical professors are so imbued with that ambition for its best interests, that they shall consider a strenuous exertion to give the utmost effect to an inferior part allotted to them paramount to all squabbles and intrigues for the more prominent ones. The characters of these young lords, for instance, are capable of much development, and should be intrusted only to persons of pronounced refinement, both of mind and education. They are not mouthing young men, see-sawing the axioms of a college tutor, (which half our groundling actors would make of them,) but high and gallant spirits, ready to distinguish themselves in the romance of a warrior's life, and incapable of a compromise, either of their own honour or that of another. This is the true "aristocracy" of human nature; and this is the lesson that Shakespeare intended for his audience, by placing them as contrasts to the young lord Bertram, who, at the time that he was insisting upon the dignity of his "order," was soiling it by rascal vices and meanness. Who will say that this is not pure morality?

Monsieur Lavatch, hereditary household jester to the counts of Rousillon, is a lively and pleasant fellow, with very strong touches of nationality about him. He has French quick-wittedness, French good temper, French good spirits, French light-heartedness; and, sooth to say, French light-headedness, in many points. He is light-minded, being inconsequent and uncontinuous, which is very French. He is light-mannered, being somewhat free in his talk, and frolic in his demeanour, very French also. He is light-moraled, loose-conscienced, fickle, and inconstant; and if these be not French characteristics, I have made a mistake. He thinks of marrying Isbel, the Countess's waiting-woman, *before* he leaves Rousillon, but the gaieties of Paris, the fineries of the court, dazzle his weathercock fancy, and when he comes home he has "*no* mind to Isbel," and coolly owns that the "brains of his Cupid are knocked out." The fact is, that his own teetotum brain is upset, for it has no steadiness, no stability in it. He not only makes love to please himself, and he gives up his mistress for the same reason—under the name of "gallantry," (perfectly French that, they having pretty names for all kinds of unhandsome proceedings!) but he has flippant speeches against the sex; such as many dissolute gentlemen, who assume the privilege to misuse it, and then abuse it, are in the habit of uttering. Lavatch banteringly replies to his lady the Countess of Rousillon:—

"One good woman in *ten*, madam! Would that Heaven would serve the world so all the year! We'd find no fault with the tithe-woman if I were the parson. One in ten quotha? An we might have a good woman born at every blazing star, or at an earthquake, 'twould mend the lottery well: a man may draw his heart out ere he pluck one."

Among his snip-snap word-catching, he lets fall one or two good things; as where he says, "Though honesty be no Puritan, yet it will do no hurt; it will wear the surplice of humility over the black gown of a big heart." The reasons he gives to the Countess why her son (and his master) should be a "melancholy man," are neat, apprehensive, and witty; but he does not give his mother the real reason of her son Bertram's "melancholy;" which was, that he was ill at ease with himself, having lost his own self-respect. He was in an exalted station in society, and he possessed a rascal soul; quite enough to make any man "melancholy," who had a glimpse of self-knowledge and self-respect. The Clown says to the Countess—"By my troth, I take my young lord to be a very melancholy man."

"*Count.* By what observance, I pray you?

"*Clown.* Why, he will look upon his boot, and sing; mend the ruff, and sing; ask questions, and sing; pick his teeth, and sing. I know a man that had this trick of 'melancholy,' sold a goodly manor for a song."

His idea of what is requisite to make a presentable appearance at court is entertaining from its appreciation of the all-sufficiency of *external* politeness as a passport into worldly society:—

"Truly, madam, if Heaven have lent a man any manners, he may easily put it off at court. He that cannot make a leg, put off his cap, kiss his hand, and *say nothing*, has neither leg, hands, lip, nor cap; and, indeed, such a fellow, to say precisely, were not for the court: but for me, I have an answer will serve all men."

And this answer, comprised in three words, "O Lord, sir!" uttered in every variety of the modest, the disclaiming, the ingratiatory, and the simpering tone, forms an agreeable satire upon the efficiency of a meaningless sentence in the mouth of an effete man of the world.

Lavatch's retort upon the wordy braggadocio Parolles (whom he thoroughly appreciates, and, consequently, as thoroughly despises) is one of his best speeches. Upon the fellow's exclaiming, "Why, I say *nothing*," the Clown replies, "Marry, you are the wiser man; for many a man's tongue shakes out his master's undoing. To say nothing, to do nothing, to know nothing, and to have nothing, is to be a great part of your title, which is within very little of nothing."

Even the Steward in this play, although a part containing not more than half-a-dozen speeches, is a character so nicely discriminated, that no ordinary-minded player could sufficiently appreciate it, to give full effect to that deference of behaviour due from him to the Countess, his mistress, combined with his own consciousness of the dignity of his situation, from its responsibility; and none but a man of nice sentiment, with tasteful associations, could rehearse the soliloquy of Helena upon her love for Bertram, which he had overheard. It is in the 3d scene of the 1st Act. And the allusion to this circumstance introduces an exquisite passage, in the same scene, between her adopted orphan, Helena, where she is proving the report of the steward, and testing her own suspicions:—

"You know, Helen,
I am a mother to you.
"*Hel.* Mine honourable mistress.
"*Count.* Nay, a mother:
Why not a mother? When I said, a mother,
Methought you saw a serpent: what's in mother,
That you start at it? I say, I am your mother;
And put you in the catalogue of those
That were enwombed mine: 'tis often seen,
Adoption strives with nature; and choice breeds
A native slip to us from foreign seeds:
You ne'er oppress'd me with a mother's groan,
Yet I express to you a mother's care;—
God's mercy, maiden! does it curd thy blood
To say, I am thy mother? What's the matter,
That this distemper'd messenger of wet,
The many-colour'd Iris, rounds thine eye?
Why?—that you are my daughter?
"*Hel.* *That I am not.*"

Then follows the fine confession of her love, already quoted: but the delicacy and ingenuity of the above equivoque are couched in the purest and most refined sense of womanly modesty, conscious of not possessing a requited love; for she has already confessed to herself the hopelessness of her passion, in that felicitous image of despondency—

"It were all one
That I should love a bright particular star,
And think to wed it—he is so above me."

There is one feature in this play as regards the female portion of the *dramatis personæ*, which may be said to form an exception to Shakespeare's usual custom of contrasting his characters. Every one of these women is exemplary, every one good ; and yet we recognise no monotony, no satiety, in the progress of the plot. The development of character proceeds with an ease and naturalness of manner that are enchanting. They are all in league to befool the traitor, Bertram, in his immoralities, and they carry their point triumphantly. The man who thinks to outwit *three* women, who are aware of his purpose, must indeed be a stupendous ass ; and had not Bertram been that ass, and knave to boot, he must have seen that Diana intended to throw him over. In the scene where she defends herself from his illicit suit, (the 2d of the 4th Act,) she affords an instance of how well Shakespeare's women know how to vindicate their own good sense by sensible argument, and without becoming mere dogged debaters. There is always in the reasoning of his women a certain modest dignity, which preserves the feminine propriety, while it enhances the impressive effect of what they adduce in support of their own opinion. Notwithstanding the unmistakable tone of Diana's appreciation of Bertram's honour and moral integrity, he persists ; and, at length, during the torrent of his protestations, she asks him for the ring on his finger, which he declines, giving as his reason—

> "It is an honour 'longing to our house,
> Bequeathed down from many ancestors ;
> Which were the greatest obloquy i' the world
> In me to lose."

Her reply to this is a clincher :—

> "Mine honour 's such a ring :
> My chastity 's the jewel of our house,

> Bequeathed down from many ancestors,
> Which were the greatest obloquy i' the world
> In *me* to lose."

Well, he scatters "the honour of his house," the bequest of his ancestors, and the "greatest obloquy in the world" to all the winds, and parts with the ring to her; and she, in return, makes an assignation with him; and, like a true-hearted woman, contrives that his own wife shall keep the appointment. When he has gone, she gives us a touch of womanly insight into character:—

> "My mother told me just how he would woo;
> As if she had sat in his heart."

But all the subordinate characters in this play are so well conceived and carefully developed, that they are interesting in and for themselves, and independently of the general story. The common soldiers, for instance, who entrap and hoodwink Monsieur Parolles, are complete specimens of their class; and, indeed, we shall have occasion to notice in other of Shakespeare's plays, where he has introduced the private soldier, in how accurate a manner he has varied the features of the individual, maintaining all the while the integral identity of the species. Under whatever aspect he introduces the soldier, he uniformly makes him a man of the world, bearing about him an atmosphere of manner belonging to those who have quartered in various countries, and among varieties of customs. He never gives a homely, or home-loving character to his soldier. He appears to be, and he is, as happy anywhere as at home. His quarters and his rations are all his care; and where he fares best, that place is his home. He is always prepared for hard service; and is not more careless and light-hearted when he is joining his comrades in a "lark." He will head a forlorn hope, or entrap and badger a poltroon with the like sedateness and determination of purpose. To unmask a battery—or a braggart, he will set about in the same business-like style. Both are duties of honour, and both he fulfils to the utmost of his faculties. Nothing can be more complete than the conduct of the soldiers in this play. They *know* Parolles to be a coward; but as he is a man holding rank above them in the army, they do not proffer their opinion, or forget their station. He is their captain, yet they join heart and hand in the plot with his brother-officers, who keep no terms with his reputation. Be it repeated again and again,—the *minutiæ in character* that Shakespeare has left to be inferred—that he has not expressed, as well as those that he has directly suggested, supply ample material, alone, and in themselves, for admiration at his intuitive perception of propriety.

Schlegel has an agreeable as well as just remark upon one of the prevailing characteristics of this play. He says:—"In it *age* is exhibited to singular advantage; the plain honesty of the king, the good-natured impetuosity of old Lafeu, the maternal indulgence of the Countess Rousillon to Helena's love of her son, seem all, as it were, to vie with each other in endeavours to conquer the arrogance of the young count."

The character of the old king is indeed one of a graceful placidity and sweet gravity, seasoned, moreover, with a high tone of severity against the least manifestation of baseness or duplicity. His dismissal of the young lords, who are departing for the war, is delivered in the purest spirit of chivalry:—

> "Farewell, young lords;
> Whether I live or die, be you the sons
> Of worthy Frenchmen: let higher Italy
> (Those 'bated, that inherit but the fall
> Of the last monarchy) see that you come
> Not to woo honour, but to wed it; when
> The bravest questant shrinks, find what you seek,
> That Fame may cry you loud. I say, farewell!"

But the finest point in the old king's conduct lies in his rebuke of Bertram, who objects to the union with Helena, solely on the score of her being a "poor physician's daughter." This is at once distinguished by its dignity, and by its noble distinction between the two qualities of true and false honour. Moreover, the calm and fine tone of reasoning is brought in with admirable relief against the irrational pride of the youth, who is neither touched by the argument, nor by the condescension of an old man and a king reasoning with his subject. He says—

"'Tis only *title* thou disdain'st in her, the which
I can build up. Strange is it, that our bloods,
Of colour, weight, and heat, pour'd all together,
Would quite confound distinction, yet stand off
In differences so mighty. If she be
All that is virtuous, (save what thou dislik'st,
A poor physician's daughter,) thou dislik'st
Of virtue for the name; but do not so:
From lowest place when virtuous things proceed,
The place is dignified by the doer's deed:
Where great additions swell, and virtue none,
It is a dropsied honour: good alone
Is good, without a name; vileness is so:
The property by what it is, should go,
Not by the title. She is young, wise, fair;
In these to Nature she's immediate heir;
And these breed honour: that is honour's scorn,
Which challenges itself as honour's born,
And is not like the sire: honours thrive,
When rather from our acts we them derive,
Than our foregoers: the mere word's a slave,
Debosh'd on every tomb; on every grave
A lying trophy; and as oft is dumb,
Where dust and damn'd oblivion is the tomb
Of honour'd bones indeed. What should be said?
If thou canst like this creature as a maid,
I can create the rest: virtue and she
Is her own dower; honour and wealth from me."

A finer reproof to arrogant assumption, from the mere accident of birth, it would take some trouble to quote. The old king combines in his character the greatest, indeed, the only qualities that constitute an honourable man: an incompetence to commit a base action, a placable and even magnanimous temper, (refer to his conduct in the last Act,) with a lively sense of gratitude for benefits received,—for he never for one moment compromises his debt of health to Helena.

Of the Countess Rousillon, little more need be said, than that she is a specimen of a gentle and motherly, and even a grand woman. Her farewell speech to her son, Bertram, on his quitting home for the court, is scarcely inferior in wisdom of counsel to the one which Polonius addresses to his son, Laertes; it has, too, precisely that characteristic difference which the dramatist so well knew how to present—being a mother's, instead of a father's parting advice. It is the maternal exhortation of a noble-minded woman and high-souled lady—

"Be thou blest, Bertram! and succeed thy father
In manners as in shape! thy blood and virtue
Contend for empire in thee, and thy goodness
Share with thy birthright! Love all, trust a few,
Do wrong to none: Be able for thine enemy
Rather in power than use; and keep thy friend
Under thy own life's key:—be check'd for silence,
But never tax'd for speech. What Heaven more will,
That thee may furnish, and my prayers pluck down,
Fall on thy head!—Farewell!"

Then, turning to the old lord, Lafeu, we have a natural touch of the mother's solicitude:—

"My lord,
'Tis an unseason'd courtier; good, my lord,
Advise him."

In those few words,—"Love all, trust a few, do wrong to

none," is condensed the whole code of social duty from man to man, in one golden rule.

But the Lord Lafeu is the greatest character in the play. He is the very model of an aristocratic soldier: "quick in honour, sudden in quarrel;" acute in appreciating character —a quality remarkable in military men, from their habit of command, and of watching the dispositions of their subalterns. He is a steady friend, impenetrably brave, greatly magnanimous, and possessing a vein of scornful humour admirably in keeping with his profession, as well as his impetuosity of character. He is the type of his countryman, Bayard, the knight *sans peur et sans reproche.*

It is Lafeu who first smokes the real character of the poltroon-scoundrel Parolles; and the moment he has made up his mind to it, he worries him as a mastiff would a mongrel. He sums up his character in one line—

"That fellow's soul is his clothes."

The art of the poet is here noteworthy in preparing the reader for Lafeu's disgust at Parolles. It is their first interview, and Lafeu is addressing his conversation to Bertram respecting the sudden recovery of the king from his dangerous malady. Although not one word is addressed (in the first instance) by Lafeu to Parolles through the whole scene, yet the fellow, with the uneasy impudence and restless vulgarity of a swaggering dependant and fortune-hunter, struggling to bring himself upon a level with his company, contrives to take the word, and interrupt every observation made by the old nobleman. Uninvited, he persists in taking his share in the talk, and Lafeu as steadily cuts him, finishing his own sentences to Bertram. The scene is a curious one, corroborating, among hundreds of others, how, by inferences from the *conduct* of *other* characters in his plots, Shakespeare contrives to insinuate his own design and intention. This is one feature of what I mean by the "harmony" and "just proportion" of his mental faculty.

Immediately after this scene, upon their second interview, when Parolles has been gasconading prodigiously, and Lafeu has had a gird at him, the Captain signifies that the veteran has the "privilege of antiquity," and, but for that, he might— "Oh, ho! [bounces Lafeu] do not plunge thyself too far in anger, lest thou hasten thy trial—which if—Lord have mercy on thee for a hen! So, my good window of lattice, fare thee well; thy casement I need not open, for I look through thee!" He afterwards promises, for Bertram's sake, to be friends with him; but the instant he enters, his disgust returns, and he again insults him. Bertram attempts an extenuation—

> "It may be you have mistaken him, my lord.
>
> "*Laf.* And shall do so, even though *I took him at his prayers!* Fare you well, my lord Bertram; and believe this of me, there can be no kernel in this light nut. Trust him not in matter of heavy consequence. I have kept of them tame, and know their natures. Farewell, Monsieur! I have spoken better of you than you have, or will deserve at my hand; but we must do good against evil."

Lafeu was a true prophet. Parolles betrays his master; and afterwards, in the abjectness of poverty, the old nobleman is the only one to whom he applies for relief. He knows, by instinct, that Lafeu, being a man of honour and true courage, is superior to the common motion of a low resentment. In reply, therefore, to his petition, he says, "Sirrah! inquire farther after me. I had talk of you last night. Though you are a fool and a knave, *you shall eat.*" Unconsciously we speak of these persons in conversations as though they had been characters in history; and they have existed, and they will exist, through all time; the privilege of every master-spirit who draws his resources from that deep well, the human heart. We identify his creations, and give them a "local habitation" in our memory and experience. One beautiful circumstance stands forth in the composition of Lafeu's character; and that is, that with the goodness of his nature, he possesses the youngest heart in the company. Moreover, he brings enthusiasm enough for them all; and enthusiasm will keep the heart young even though it overtax the rest of the body. Read the 1st scene of the 2d Act, where he comes in to apprise the king of the arrival of his fair young physician, Helena. His delight at the approaching relief to his master's malady causes him to run on in such a strain of boyish rhapsody that he is compelled to check himself, in order (as he says) that he may "seriously convey his thoughts in that light deliverance."

If Lafeu is the finest character in the play, Parolles is the most complete and original. Parolles is the type of all the cowards that have been introduced on the stage since his time. Doctor Johnson, again, in comparing him with Falstaff, manifested that he could have had but little perception of even the broadest distinctions in human character. There is as strong and as marked a distinction between Falstaff and Parolles, as between an impudent witty cheat—a fellow who will joke and laugh the money out of your pocket—and a dull, hard, sordid, and vulgar swindler. The cowardice of Falstaff arose quite as much from his constitutional love of ease, sociality, and self-enjoyment, as from an inherent want of principle and self-respect; it was the cowardice of fat and luxuriousness. Falstaff possessed qualities which attached to him friends of each sex. We all know the speech uttered by Bardolph after the fat knight's death, "Would I were with him, wherever he is, in heaven or in hell." A more genuine apotheosis to the social qualities of a man never was uttered. Even the women hated Parolles; and, upon my life, that man has little enough to recommend him whom women dislike. The Countess Rousillon speaks of him as a "very tainted fellow, full of wickedness;" and that her son "corrupts a well-derived nature with his inducement." He held the respectable office of toad-eater, and something worse, to the weak young lord. Mariana, too, whom he had addressed in love-terms, says of him, "I know the knave!—hang him!—a filthy officer he is in those suggestions for the young earl." And lastly, Helena describes him as a "notorious liar, a great way fool, and solely a coward." She, too, although of a gentle nature, cannot forbear girding at him for being a palpable and transparent poltroon. In taking leave of her, to go to the court with his master, he says, with the insolence natural to a braggart, "Little Helen, farewell. If I can remember thee, I will think of thee at court." She answers with the sarcasm of a well-bred female—

"Monsieur Parolles, you were born under a charitable star.
"*Par.* Under Mars, I.
"*Hel.* I especially think, under Mars.
"*Par.* Why under Mars?
"*Hel.* The wars have so kept you under that you must needs be born under Mars.
"*Par.* When he was predominant.
"*Hel.* When he was retrograde, I think, rather.
"*Par.* Why think you so?
"*Hel.* You go so much backward when you fight.
"*Par.* That's for advantage.
"*Hel.* So is running away when fear proposes the safety. But the composition that your valour and fear make in you, is a virtue of a good wing, and I like the wear well.
"*Par.* I am so full of businesses I cannot answer thee acutely."

If Parolles had not been a fool as well as knave, he would not have answered Helena's first reply. He did not know when to drop the dialogue, and at last does so like a fool.

It was a pleasant thought in the poet, when the troops were returning victorious, and content with their triumph, to make Parolles, the boaster, the only one who is dissatisfied: and what a cause for his displeasure; because they had lost a drum! the only thing in a battle "full of sound and fury," without result; the emblem of his precious self—empty, noisy, and urging on others to the fight. For the loss of this drum, therefore, he swells and fumes with infinite humour. While he is marching in procession, and the women inquire of each other why that "French jackanapes, with the scarfs, is so melancholy;" we hear him ejaculate, "Lose our drum! WELL!"—and we find afterwards how he has been blowing and storming about this drum; for the young lords, when they are resolved that Bertram shall open his eyes to his purblind confidence in the knave, lay the plot to surprise him, one of them advises, "Oh, for the love of laughter, let him fetch his drum; he says he has a stratagem for it." And the other echoes, "For the love of laughter, hinder not the humour of his design; let him fetch off his drum in any hand." Bertram assents to the plot for the hoax; and Parolles coming in, he calls out to him—

"How now, Monsieur; this drum sticks sorely in your disposition.

"2 *Lord.* Oh, the deuce take it; let it go; 'tis but a drum.

"*Par.* But a drum! Is 't but a drum? A drum so lost!"

The parley ends by Bertram promising, that if he will undertake the recovery of the drum, the whole merit of the enterprise shall be awarded to him. "Then, by the hand of a soldier," answers Parolles, "I will undertake it;" adding, "I love not many words."

The scene of the plot which ensues (the opening of the 4th Act) is long, and, perhaps, the most humorous of its class ever penned; not untainted, however, with painfulness, as we contemplate the shocking self-prostration and debasement of a fellow-mortal. It opens with his famous soliloquy; which, for self-knowledge, with baseness, has never been surpassed, not even, perhaps, equalled :—

"*Par.* Ten o'clock: within three hours 'twill be time enough to go home. What shall I say I have done? It must be a very plausive invention that carries it. They begin to smoke me; and disgraces have of late knocked too often at my door. I find my tongue is too foolhardy; but my heart hath the fear of Mars before it, and of his creatures, not daring the report of my tongue. . . . . What the devil should move me to undertake the recovery of this drum, being not ignorant of the impossibility, and knowing I had no such purpose?

"I must give myself some hurts, and say I got them in the exploit. Yet, slight ones will not carry it; they will say, 'Came you off with so little?' and great ones I dare not give." . . . .

Then follows one of those profound reflections that give one pause in studying these fine pictures of human nature. One of the young lords says, aside, "Is it possible he should know *what* he is, and be *that* he is?" Well, the whole party sally from their ambush, seize, and blindfold him, jabbering all the while to each other in gibberish. One of the soldiers volunteers the office of interpreter between them; and to him, through fear of present death, he betrays the secrets of his party, and even traduces his friend and benefactor; the only one, by the way, of whom he speaks the truth. At this juncture, when he has blown himself up, and is left, the last of the party, the common soldier, reviles him in a farewell speech—"If you could find out a country where but women were, that had received so much shame, you might begin an impudent nation." And when all are gone, and he is alone, he gives utterance to another remarkable prompting of self-knowledge :—

"*Yet* am I thankful. If my heart were great,
'Twould burst at this. Captain I'll be no more;

> But I will eat, and drink, and sleep as soft
> As captain shall: simply the thing I am
> Shall make me live."

In the sequel, however, we find the poor wretch paying the extreme penalty of misery and starvation. He introduces himself to the Clown, whom he formerly had insulted, and now calls "Sir;" another instance of propriety in the poet's characters, into whatever position they may be thrown—

"Good Monsieur Lavatch, give my Lord Lafeu this letter. I have, ere now, sir, been better known to you, when I have held familiarity with fresher clothes; but I am now, sir, muddied in fortune's mood, and smell somewhat strong of her strong displeasure.

"*Clown.* Truly, fortune's displeasure is but sluttish if it smell so strongly as thou speak'st of. I will henceforth eat no fish of fortune's buttering. *Prithee, allow the wind.*

"*Par.* Nay, you need not stop your nose, sir. I spake but by a metaphor.

"*Clown.* Indeed, sir; if your metaphor stink, I will stop my nose; or against any man's metaphor. Prithee, *get thee farther.*"

Old Lafeu comes in, inquires after his drum, and crowns his contempt of the reptile by telling him, that "though both fool and knave, he shall eat."

Two conclusions, among others, we must come to in reading this delightful play; one—that nobility of birth, without nobleness of character, is naught; and the other—that virtue and self-respect bring their own reward of peace and satisfaction within, with esteem and benevolence from all who are worthy to bestow them.

XI.

# Tempest.

# XI.

# TEMPEST.

IN the play of the "Tempest" Shakespeare has combined all the resources of his wonderful imagination; and in it has with consummate skill displayed the vast variety of his powers. In this latter quality—that of his variety—the play may be pronounced the most original, as well as the most complete of his productions. It is at once instinct with grace and beauty, grandeur and sublimity, mirth, cheerfulness, and broad humour. It is not more natural in its human passion than it is in its spiritual emotion and affection; and such is the power of the poet's "so potent art," that his *ideal* beings, however wild and fantastic, possess as complete an individuality and identity, with show of verisimilitude, (or, in plainer words, they are as *natural*,) as his most ordinary and everyday characters. Such, too, is his skill in exciting our sympathies with them all, that we take no more interest in the crowning of Miranda's happiness with her lover, than we do in the emancipation and unchartered liberty of the delicate Ariel; nay, so consociated have we the "gentle spiritings" of that sweet little angel with his master's missions,—they have been so long together, ruler and ministrant, that I know not whether their final separation does not ensue with a feeling of regret on our part. Well may Prospero say, at leave-taking, "I shall miss thee, my delicate Ariel!" To be sure he would,—and why should they have parted? Who would not rather have remained lord of that enchanted island, with its "sounds and sweet airs, that delight, and hurt not," than have returned common-place Duke of Milan? Ferdinand and Miranda might have instituted a very pretty patriarchal government; and what an heirloom to the estate would they have possessed in the faithful Ariel as their prime minister—*in perpetuo!* But it was necessary to dissolve that lovely vision, and resign its aerial creatures to their primitive elements.

It has just been said that the "Tempest" is the most "varied," as well as the most "original, of Shakespeare's productions." In it, and it alone, he has brought together, in their several stages of progression, human beings, and beings possessing human impulses, affections, and aspirations; from the earthly Caliban—part clod, part witch-born, an impersonation of the grosser and lower propensities of the human animal, up to the most attenuated form, that has no more substance than the fleeting air or the tinted rainbow.

The subject of Shakespeare and his power of invention are never, or rarely, alluded to, without an instancing of his creative power in producing such contrasted perfections of character as Lear and Falstaff, Hamlet and Aguecheek, Othello and Malvolio,—and so we may go on with the enumeration, heaping wonderment on wonderment, till we are exhausted; for his mind intellectual plumb hath never yet sounded. In the play now under consideration, what exquisite discrimination and consistency are evinced in the two creations alone, of Ariel and Caliban! Caliban, the essence of primitive grossness,—redeemed, however, as Hazlitt has excellently observed, from every particle of "vulgarity" in his composition; adding, with his own fine talent at definition, "Vulgarity is not natural coarseness, but conventional coarseness, learned from others, contrary to, or without an entire conformity of, natural power and disposition; as fashion is the common-place affectation of what is elegant and refined, without any feeling of the essence of it." In no one point, indeed, does Shakespeare more signally manifest his power, than in the approximating shades and minute discriminations in those of his characters that are congenial in complexion—whatever may be said of his skill in contrast—and which, after all, is not so high in quality, if it be of more startling achievement. Great, therefore, as is the contrasted effect between the refined and the imaginative, and the gross and the sensual persons in this play, that effect does not appear to exhibit so elevated a design in invention and detail, as in the manner in which he has discriminated between, and, indeed, has brought into relief, the common working-day coarseness of Trinculo and Stephano, against the wild and romantic brutishness of Caliban. What a gusto there is in the latter's remembrance of "water with berries in it;" and what a dash, too, of poetry in it, compared with the riotous bawlings of the others' wine-songs. Again, his remonstrance to Trinculo,—"Thou dost me yet but little hurt; thou wilt anon, I know it by thy trembling," compared with that of Stephano, in his drunkenness,—"Prithee, do not turn me about, my stomach is not constant." Again, Caliban says:—

> "I pr'ythee, let me bring thee where crabs grow;
> And I with my long nails will dig thee pig-nuts,
> Show thee a jay's nest, and instruct thee how
> To snare the nimble marmoset: I'll bring thee
> To clust'ring filberds, and sometimes I'll get thee
> Young sea-mells from the rock. Wilt thou go with me?"

Stephano says,—"He shall taste of my bottle." The drunkard butler has no higher notion of earthly bliss than the wine-cask. Caliban, it is true, upon tasting it, calls it "celestial liquor," which only proves that Stephano has aggravated the poor monster's brutality. Even his gloating exclamations, revolting as they are, by reason of his bestial conformation, are higher, and more true to the natural animal, than the vulgar worldliness of the city-bred one. His exultation to Prospero, who reviles him with ingratitude in attempting the violation of his daughter—

> "Oho! Oho!—would it had been done!
> Thou didst prevent me; I had peopled else
> This isle with Calibans."

And afterwards, to Stephano, when proposing to him the murder of the father, and seizure of the daughter, he says:—

> "She will become thy bed, I warrant,
> And bring thee forth brave brood."

The other, in the true spirit of "vulgarity," and consequently of inferiority to the monster, replies,—"His daughter and I will be king and queen, (save our graces!) and Trinculo and thyself shall be viceroys." And lastly, Stephano's obtuse, worldly comment upon the aerial symphony which they hear; he says,—"This will prove a brave kingdom to me, where I shall have my music *for nothing;*" in answer to Caliban's exquisitely poetical description of those wandering sounds in the air:—

> "The isle is full of noises—
> Sounds and sweet airs, that give delight, and hurt not.
> Sometimes a thousand twangling instruments
> Will hum about mine ears; and sometimes voices,
> That, if I then had wak'd after long sleep,
> Will make me sleep again: and then, in dreaming,
> The clouds, methought, would open, and show riches
> Ready to drop upon me; that, when I wak'd,
> I cried to dream again."

To which beautiful piece of imagination, one of the other two merely replies,—"The sound is gone away; let's follow it, and after *do our work*,"—that is, commit the murder of Prospero.

Caliban says,—"I pray you, tread softly, that the blind mole may not hear a foot-fall." At the cave of Prospero, Caliban shows himself to be the superior being. They are grumbling for the loss of their wine-bottles, and are captivated by the gaudy dresses hung up to lure them: he rejects all they offer him,—"I will have none on't; we shall lose our time; and all be turned to barnacles, or to apes with foreheads villainous low." In short, the poet has made out a glowing case for the hybrid monster; and, in the comparison, the natural animal, whether considered poetically or morally, assumes a dignity in our minds over the artificial and conventional animal,—"The vulgar knaves of the civilised world," as Schlegel well calls them; adding, "The whole delineation of this monster is inconceivably consistent and profound; and, notwithstanding its hatefulness, by no means hurtful to our feelings, since the honour of human nature is left untouched."

In one of his early lectures, Coleridge drew a humorous comparison between Caliban and a modern Radical. This was subsequent to that period in his career when Mr Coleridge was a private soldier, and preached Jacobinism to his brethren militant. He would then, in all probability, have done full justice to Caliban, by acknowledging him *proprietor* of the land *inherited* from Sycorax, his mother; and Prospero, then, would have been pronounced an aristocrat—probably a Tory. But, really so to speak, with all our admiration of and sympathy with the illustrious magician, we perforce must acknowledge Prospero to be of a revengeful nature. He has not the true social wisdom; and he only learns Christian wisdom from his servant Ariel. By nature he is a selfish aristocrat. When he was Duke of Milan he gave himself up to his favourite indulgence of study and retired leisure, yet expected to preserve his state and authority. When master of the Magic Island, he is stern and domineering, lording it over his sprite-subjects, and ruling them with a wand of rigour. He comes there, and takes possession of the territory with all the coolness of a usurper ; he assumes despotic sway, and stops only short of absolute unmitigated tyranny. His only point of tender human feeling is his daughter ; and his only point of genial sympathy is with the dainty being Ariel. And yet withal, beneath Prospero's sedate experience, we find there lie real kindness and affection for the little embodied Zephyr ; for when, with a sportive question and child-like, Ariel says, "Do you love me, master ? No ;" the master replies, "Dearly, my delicate Ariel." And again, afterwards, "I shall miss thee ; but yet thou shalt have thy freedom," showing that he has a heart to comprehend the eagerness of the airy sprite to be at liberty amidst the boundless elements of which he is the creature. The best of Prospero's social philosophy is, that it consists not in so obstinate an adherence to its tenets, but that it suffers itself to be won over to a kindlier and more tolerant course when convinced that it has hitherto held too strict a one. His purpose of revenge gives way to mercy when assured that his injurers repent.

Ariel is the extreme opposite of Caliban. Ariel is the ethereal personification of will and accomplishment, with the lightning's speed. When despatched on an errand by Prospero, and desired to make good speed, he answers, "I drink the air before me!" What an idea do those six words convey of compassing time and space! With a refinement of his art, Shakespeare has contrived to secure our interests in and sympathies with this exquisite being, by imbuing it with the frolicsome and wayward fancies of a petted child. We incline to take part with Ariel in his little fretfulnesses and longings to be as unfettered as the winged winds. His desires to be set free, (for freedom is his nature,) and his pretty frowardness under the constraint of the mighty magician, who, although his liberator, is still his master, even his tyrant, is more excusable than the latter's tetchy reproaches :—

"Is there more toil? [says the little libertine.] Since thou dost give me pains,
Let me remember thee what thou hast promis'd,
Which is not yet perform'd me.
"*Pro.* How now! moody?
What is 't thou canst demand?
"*Ari.* My liberty.
"*Pro.* Before the time be out? no more!
"*Ari.* I prithee,
Remember, I have done thee worthy service;
Told thee no lies, made no mistakings, serv'd
Without or grudge or grumblings; thou didst promise
To bate me a full year.
"*Pro.* Dost thou forget
From what a torment I did free thee?
"*Ari.* No.
"*Pro.* Thou dost; and think'st it much to tread the ooze of the salt deep,
To run upon the sharp wind of the north,
To do me business in the veins o' th' earth
When it is bak'd with frost.
* * * * * *
If thou more murmur'st, I will rend an oak,
And peg thee in his knotty entrails, till
Thou hast howl'd away twelve winters."

All this enlists our sympathy with the little "featureless angel," as he has been happily called; but Shakespeare has gone yet farther upon this point, by giving to Ariel a feeling of tender commiseration for the interests of those whom he is commanded to punish and torment. Here the poet's own sweet nature steps in, and he makes the being with feelings and notions foreign to the human, read his master a lesson upon forbearance and forgiveness. Is not the following little dialogue between them a practical homily upon the first great principle of social humanity?—

"Your charm so strongly works them,
That if you now beheld them, your affections
Would become tender.
"*Pro.* Dost thou think so, Ariel?
"*Ari.* Mine would, sir, were I human.
"*Pro.* And mine shall.
Hast thou, which art but air, a touch, a feeling
Of their afflictions; and shall not myself,
One of their kind, that relish all as sharply,
Passion as they, be kindlier mov'd than thou art?
Though with their high wrongs I am struck to the quick,
Yet, with my nobler reason 'gainst my fury
Do I take part. The rarer action is
In virtue than in vengeance; they being penitent,
The sole drift of my purpose doth extend
Not a frown farther. Go, release them, Ariel."

Whenever and wherever Shakespeare speaks from the movement of his own mind, and not from traditional authority, we invariably find him swayed by the highest and most refined principle of magnanimity; the common and heathenish notion of revenge seems to have been utterly foreign to his nature. Magnanimity, in its most extended sense, was the characteristic of his mind.

I believe that we may search through the fields of fancy and discover no imaginative being equalling, in beauty of conception, the creation of Ariel in the "Tempest."

The "Ideal" may indeed be said to constitute the main feature of this matchless composition. In addition to the imaginary beings that have just been alluded to, the young Prince Ferdinand, upon his first introduction to Miranda, "Most sure, the goddess on whom these airs attend!" not only is prepared, but is eager to receive her as a supernatural creation; and also, in alluding to the aerial music, he says, "This is no mortal business, nor no sound that the earth owes;" but he, moreover, discovers that he had always previously held a faith in the unknown, which led him to be fastidious with regard to the persons moving around him:—

"Full many a lady
I have ey'd with best regard; and many a time
The harmony of their tongues hath into bondage
Brought my too diligent ear: for several virtues
Have I liked several women; never any
With so full soul, but some defect in her
Did quarrel with the noblest grace she ow'd,
And put it to the foil; but you, O you!
So perfect and so peerless, are created
Of every creature's best."

His abrupt and eager belief in her worth, in the third speech only that he makes to her—

"Oh, if a virgin,
And your affection not gone forth, I 'll make
Thee queen of Naples;"

and again, his prodigal acquiescence in *any* plan which may lead to their union—even to the abandonment of all his worldly advantages, and to live with her in the island:—

"Let me live here ever.
So rare a wonder'd father, and a wife,
Make this place paradise;"

all proclaim his ardent imagination and thorough faith in goodness: only the good know the full truth of goodness; this very faith forms a feature of the "Ideal," and it is the characteristic of all the worthy persons in this play. All this, be it observed, harmonises with the first grand outline of the story—being in itself an idealised conception and construction. Here again appears the dominant feature in the poet's mind—that of "keeping," and consistency.

The full and entire confidence of these two young creatures (Ferdinand and Miranda) in each other's integrity of love is an absolute type of the primitive innocence and bliss of Paradise. Her answer to his question, "Wherefore weep you?" and which is the result of her happiness upon hearing his love-protestation, is one of the most perfect specimens that can be produced of womanly trustingness, with innocence of motive. She says, I weep

> "At mine own unworthiness, that dare not offer
> What I desire to give; and much less take
> What I shall die to want. But this is trifling;
> And all the more it seeks to hide itself,
> The bigger bulk it shows. Hence, bashful cunning!
> And prompt me plain and holy innocence!
> I am your wife, if you will marry me;
> If not, I'll die your maid; to be your fellow
> You may deny me; but I'll be your servant,
> Whether you will or no."

Here we have an epitome of what alone can sublimate and consolidate the social compact between the sexes,—viz., the non-conceit in our own power to please: the promptness to receive, and the gratification in receiving and imparting pleasure, constitute the true cement of a pure and passionate love; a cement that hardens rather than crumbles with use.

The good old lord, Gonzalo, in his disposition, also carries out the "Ideal" principle insisted upon in this play. He, too, partakes of the faculty of imagination, and it may be remembered how tenderly he employs it to amuse and cheer his sorrowing master, the King Alonzo. His utopian scheme for a commonwealth, if he were master of the island, is quite in character with a merry and crotchety old man. He says:—

"I' the commonwealth, I would by contraries
Execute all things; for no kind of traffic
Would I admit; no name of magistrate;
Letters should not be known; riches, poverty,
And use of service, none; contract, succession,
Bourn, bound of land, tilth, vineyard, none;
No use of metal, corn, or wine, or oil;
No occupation; all men idle, all;
And women, too, but innocent and pure;
No sovereignty."

The worthy old nobleman had been reading Florio's translation of Montaigne's essay "Of the Cannibals;" for this, his scheme to construct a commonwealth, he had adopted, almost literally, from the delightful and most merry old Frenchman. Gonzalo is a most sweet and gentle character. How placidly he bears the hard quizzing of the other lords; with a worldly wisdom of indifference, as befits a counsellor and courtier, but full of a chirping spirit and happy feeling, springing out of a pure conscience, that causes him to turn to the sunny side of things in misfortune. With the true generosity of genuine goodness, too, he rebukes the reproaches which the others, in their selfishness, heap upon the king for bringing them into trouble:—

"My Lord Sebastian,
The truth you speak doth lack some gentleness,
And time to speak it in. You rub the sore
When you should bring the plaster."

And then he turns to divert the king from his grief at the supposed death of his son Ferdinand. He does this, too, in the full knowledge of Alonzo's former guilt; for, after the thunder and lightning, with the dreadful forms raised by Ariel to terrify them, and they rush out distracted, Gonzalo says:—

"All three of them are desperate: their great guilt,
Like poison given to work a great time after,

Now 'gins to bite the spirits. I do beseech you,
That are of suppler joints, follow them swiftly,
And hinder them from what this ecstasy
May now provoke them to."

It is in this scene that the conscience-struck Alonzo makes confession of his crime in those grand lines:—

"Oh, it is monstrous! monstrous!
Methought the billows spoke, and told me of it:
The winds did sing it to me; and the thunder,
That deep and dreadful organ-pipe, pronounc'd
The name of Prosper: it did bass my trespass."

We note also the pious gratitude in the conduct of Gonzalo. He is the only one whose speech assumes that tone upon the happy reconciliation of the families. With gentle pathos, upon contemplating the scene, he says:—

"I have inly wept,
Or should have spoke ere this. Look down, you gods,
And on this couple drop a blessed crown!
For it is you that have chalk'd forth the way
Which brought us hither."

It is to be observed that the good people, old Gonzalo and the two lords, Adrian and Francisco, maintain throughout an unaffected cheerfulness, and evince a gay desire to discover all that is pleasant and agreeable in their wanderings through the island. Their principle is to make the best account of everything they encounter. And here, again, we note the uniform tendency of Shakespeare's moral philosophy, while Antonio and Sebastian, the two bad ambitious brothers, indulge in hollow jests and flippant sneers at the others, and are, moreover, querulous and unhappy. Coleridge has truly said—"Shakespeare has shown the tendency in bad men to indulge in scorn and contemptuous expressions as a mode of getting rid of their own uneasy feelings of inferiority to the good, and also of rendering the transition to wickedness easy, by making the good ridiculous. Shakespeare never puts habitual scorn into the mouths of other than bad men." So with Antonio and Sebastian; and he must be a superficial reader who does not perceive in their hollow jests and bullying deportment a sense of unreality. Moreover, they lose their presence of mind in the storm, and betray their fear in abusing the captain of the vessel. They abuse him as though he had raised the tempest; and they reproach the king of Naples for being the cause of their leaving home. How true to nature all this selfishness! Whereas, on the other hand, and all through, the worthy characters busy themselves to turn every casualty into a grace and a benefit. Adrian says, "Though this island seem to be desert, the air breathes upon us here most sweetly." And Gonzalo follows him up with, "How lush and lusty the grass looks! how green!" And it is Francisco who consoles the king in those justly-celebrated lines, descriptive of the young Prince Ferdinand swimming to shore:—

"Sir, he may live.
I saw him beat the surges under him,
And ride upon their backs: he trod the water,
Whose enmity he flung aside, and breasted
The surge most swoln that met him: his bold head
'Bove the contentious waves he kept, and oar'd
Himself with his good arms in lusty stroke
To the shore, that o'er his wave-worn basis bow'd
As stooping to relieve him. *I not doubt*
*He came alive to land.*"

Let no one say that all this contrast in character-painting of the foregone individuals is not true to nature in her course of action. We cannot tell the deepest thoughts of men from their betrayals of feature-expression; but we may be sure that bad men are not happy. The celebrated "Junius," who certainly knew something of mankind, makes the following affirmation :—"After long experience of the world, I affirm before God, I never knew a rogue who was not unhappy."

The manly and dreadnought character of the seafaring man—at all events, of the English sailor—is admirably hit off in the conduct of the boatswain in the midst of the terror and confusion of the sea-storm. His perfect manifestation of true courage—fully appreciating the danger they were threatened with, (and it is no "courage," but stupidity, that does not "appreciate" the danger which is imminent,) and yet maintaining an animated and encouraging tone:—"Heigh, my hearts!—cheerly, cheerly, my hearts! yare, yare; take in the topsail; 'tend to the master's whistle. Blow till thou burst thy wind, if *room enough!*" The perfect ejaculation of a seaman,—"Blow till thou burst, *so long as we are off shore.*" And then the rough and contemptuous check he gives the king and his courtiers, who endeavour to assume authority over him :—

"I pray you now keep below.

"*Gonz.* Nay, good, be patient.

"*Boats.* When the sea is.—Hence!—What care these roarers for the name of king? To cabin—silence; and trouble us not.

"*Gonz.* Good, yet remember whom thou hast aboard.

"*Boats.* None that I more love than myself. You are a counsellor; if you can command these elements to silence, and work the peace of the present, we will not hand a rope more: use your authority. If you cannot, give thanks you have lived so long, and make yourself ready in your cabin for the mischance of the hour, if it so hap."

Gonzalo's reflection upon this blunt fellow harmonises with his own lively temper and honest life :—

"I have great comfort from this fellow; methinks he hath no *drowning* mark upon him,—his complexion is perfect gallows. Stand fast, good fate, to his hanging. Make the rope of his destiny our cable, for our own doth little advantage! If he be not born to be hanged, our case is miserable."

And true to his character, when they are all in extremity, and the ship is going down, he maintains his humour to the last—

"Now would I give a thousand furlongs of sea for an acre of barren ground.—Long heath, brown furze, anything. The wills above be done! but I would fain die a dry death."

The Boatswain's rough and straightforward speech at the end of the play comes in the midst of the poetical winding-up like a well-contrasted colour in a picture. He is asked, "What news?"

"The best news is, that we have safely found
Our king and company; the next, our ship,
Which but three glasses since we gave out split,
Is tight, and yare, and bravely rigg'd, as when
We first put out to sea."

Upon the technical orders and manœuvrings of the vessel during the storm, Lord Mulgrave, Captain Glascock, and Sir Henry Mainwaring—all eminent naval tacticians—have borne testimony to Shakespeare's accuracy. Lord Mulgrave says that the poet "must have drawn his knowledge of seamanship from accurate personal observation, or have had a remarkable power of applying the information of others." And Captain Glascock says, "The Boatswain in the 'Tempest' delivers himself in the true vernacular style of the forecastle." Doctor Johnson—preferring pickthanking to approbation—says, "The scene of the shipwreck exhibits some inaccuracies and contradictory orders." Whom does the critic show to be at fault?

There is still the "Mask" to speak of in this enchanting drama. As if he had not heaped beauty on beauty, rapture-high, the poet yet "throws a tint upon the rose, and adds a perfume to the violet." Only observe how, in a mere show—a casual and fleeting pageant—Shakespeare, with a prodigal hand, scatters some of his most sparkling gems! Here, too, where there is more simple description, and where other poets can with better chance compete with him, than in his transcendent power of dramatic passion, yet, even here, see how he surpasses them all—all the professors of Mask composition. Shall we in any of them find more pure rythmical harmony, or poetic diction to compare in chaste adherence to rustic nature, with Iris's invocation to Ceres?—

"Ceres, most bounteous lady, thy rich leas
Of wheat, rye, barley, vetches, oats, and peas;
Thy turfy mountains, where live nibbling sheep,
And flat meads thatch'd with stover, them to keep;
Thy banks with peonied and lilied brims,
Which spongy April at thy hest betrims,
To make cold nymphs chaste crowns; and thy broom-groves,
Whose shadow the dismissed bachelor loves,
Being lass-lorn; thy pole-clipp'd vineyard;
And thy sea-marge, sterile, and rocky-hard,
Where thou thyself dost air: the queen o' the sky,
Whose wat'ry arch and messenger am I,
Bids thee leave these; and with her sov'reign grace,
Here on this grass-plot, in this very place,
To come and sport. Her peacocks fly amain:
Approach rich Ceres, her to entertain."

And what poetry, in its class, is more fanciful and elegant than the reply of Ceres to this invocation of Iris?—

"Hail, many-colour'd messenger, that ne'er
Dost disobey the wife of Jupiter;
Who, with thy saffron wings, upon my flowers
Diffusest honey-drops, refreshing showers;
And with each end of thy blue bow dost crown
My bosky acres, and my unshrubb'd down,
Rich scarf to my proud earth; why hath thy queen
Summon'd me hither, to this short-grass'd green?"

Rich and gorgeous as Spenser is in his mythological displays, he has nothing finer or more true than this pageant.

> "Highest queen of state,
> Great Juno comes; I know her by her gait,"

is like Homer; or, as the commentators would say—after trying to prove that he had no classical learning—"this phrase Shakespeare found in Homer." And what poet but the poet of poets would have thought of that lovely epithet—"ever-harmless looks," as applied to those gentle imaginary beings, the Naiads? and how gracefully elegant is the manner of their summoning!—

> "You nymphs, call'd Naiads, of the winding brooks,
> With your sedg'd crowns, and ever-harmless looks,
> Leave your crisp channels, and on this green land
> Answer your summons: Juno does command.
> Come, temperate nymphs, and help to celebrate
> A contract of true love: be not too late.
> You sun-burnt sicklemen, of August weary,
> Come hither from the furrow and be merry:
> Make holyday: your rye-straw hats put on,
> And these fresh nymphs encounter every one
> In country footing."

They who can turn aside from the hard and macadamised road of dry duty and daily labour, to wander amid the glades and flowery knolls of the imaginary world of never-dying poetry, are privileged beings; for they have a sense and a sensation superadded to the ordinary dispensation of their fellows. They are, for the time, lifted "above the smoke and stir of this dim spot called earth;" they are in another world, and they revel in unworldly thoughts and unworldly associations; they become denizens of the golden sphere of romance; and romance is the salt in the ocean of life, keeping its waters sweet and fresh amidst the turmoiling and common-places of every-day action.

XII.

# Much Ado About Nothing.

# XII.

# MUCH ADO ABOUT NOTHING.

I NEVER knew any one object to the nature and conduct of Beatrice in "Much Ado About Nothing," who was not either dull in faculty, ill-tempered, or an overweening assertor of the exclusive privileges of the male sex.

The late Thomas Campbell, in an edition of the poet, denounces her as "an odious woman." I never saw Mr Campbell, and knew nothing of him personally; I can say nothing, therefore, of his temper, or of his jealousy as regards the privileges claimed by the stronger party in the human world; and most certain am I that he was not a man of "*dull* faculty," for I do know his intellectual character. But I should be inclined to draw a conclusion from the epithet used by that elegant poet and cultivated scholar, that he was a man subject to strong impulses, and to a high degree of nervous irritability; and that he had risen from his task of editing this enchanting play, annoyed and excited by the sparring between Beatrice and Benedick, in which word-encounters she certainly is no "light weight" to him; but to call her "odious" was an injudicious comment, and only true as regards his own individual temperament and feelings. In the general estimation of the world, Beatrice is one of those who wear their characters inside out. They have no reserves with society, for they require none. They may, perhaps, presume upon, or rather forget that they possess a mercurial temperament, which, when unreined, is apt to start from its course and inconvenience their fellow-travellers; but such a propensity is not an "odious" one—it is not hateful; and this is the only feature in the character of Beatrice that Mr Campbell could object to. She is warm-hearted, generous; has a noble contempt of baseness of every kind; is wholly untinctured with jealousy; is the first to break out into invective when her cousin Hero is treated in that scoundrel manner by her affianced husband at the very altar, and even makes it a *sine quâ non* with Benedick to prove his love for herself by challenging the traducer of her cousin.

This last fact, by the way, leads to a natural digression when speaking of the career of Beatrice; and that is, that the very circumstance of her embroiling her lover in a duel for another person is of itself a proof that the *sensual* passion of love had no predominant share in her choice of Benedick for a husband; and in this insignificant—apparently insignficant—but momentous point of conduct, we again, and for the thousandth time, recognise Shakespeare's unsleeping sense of propriety in character. A woman, personally and passionately in love, has been known to involve her lover where her own self-love has been compromised; and even then I should question the quality of the passion; that, however strong it might be, it was weaker than her own self-worship; for the sterling passion of love, by the law of nature, is all-absorbing, all-engrossing, and admits no equal near the throne. But no woman, so enamoured, would place her lover's life in jeopardy for a third party; and this leads me to retrace my position and observe, that the union of Beatrice and Benedick was only a "counterfeit presentment" of ninety-nine hundredths of the marriages that take place in society, and which are the result of friendly concoction. There was no "love," no sexual love, between Benedick and Beatrice; but the self-love of each being fanned into a flame from hearing, through the plot of their friends, that they were mutually, though unknowingly, an object of attachment to each other,—this "self-love," with an emotion of gratitude, exalted their reciprocal respect into the conventional love of every-day society; but there was not a spark of passion in the whole affair. The very discovery that each is an object of supposed interest with the other produces not one word in avowal of passion; and here again Shakespeare is on his guard; and in how masterly a manner has he sustained the several characteristic peculiarities of the two individuals upon that discovery. Beatrice, with her lively demonstrativeness of nature, rushes from the arbour after hearing the conversation of Hero and Ursula respecting her being the object of Benedick's affection. She has fallen into the trap they have laid for her, and she exclaims:—

> "What fire is in mine ears? Can this be true?
> Stand I condemn'd for pride and scorn so much?
> Contempt, farewell; and maiden pride, adieu!
> No glory lives behind the back of such.
> And, Benedick, love on: I will requite thee;
> Taming my wild heart to thy loving hand.
> If thou dost love, my kindness shall incite thee
> To bind our loves up in a holy band."

There is no avowal of passion, methinks, in that speech. It is merely an acquiescent one,—"If thou *dost* love, my *kindness* shall incite thee" to tie the knot. On the other hand, Benedick, being a man of the world, a soldier, too, and not wholly a child to stratagems, comes forward sedately questioning the dialogue respecting himself and Beatrice, between Don Pedro, Claudio, and old Leonato. To give full force to the doubt and caution of Benedick, and at the same time to enrich the plausibility of the plot against him, he would have suspected his young companions, but old Leonato being of the party staggers him. He says to himself, "I should think this a gull, but that the white-bearded fellow speaks it; knavery cannot sure hide himself in such reverence." And never was soliloquy more naturally penned than his communing with himself upon the dialogue he had just heard:—

"This can be no trick; the conference was sadly borne. [That is, sedately, seriously borne.] They have the truth of this from Hero. They seem to pity the lady. It seems her affections have the full bent. Love me! why, it must be requited. I hear how I am censured; they say I will bear myself proudly if I perceive the love come from her. They say, too, that she will rather die than give any sign of affection. *I did never think to marry.* I mustn't seem proud. Happy are they that can hear their detractions and put them to mending. They say the lady is fair: 'tis a truth, I can bear them witness;—and virtuous; 'tis so, I cannot reprove it: and wise, but for loving me! by my troth, 'tis no addition to her wit; nor no great argument of her folly; for I will be horribly in love with her. I may chance to have some odd quirks and remnants of wit broken on me, because I have railed so long against marriage; but doth not the appetite alter? A man loves the meat in his youth that he cannot endure in his age. Shall quips and sentences, and these paper bullets of the brain, awe a man from the career of his humour? No! The world must be peopled. When I said I would die a bachelor, I did not think I should live till I were married."

Will any one say that there is any expression of love in its exclusiveness in that speech?

I would devote a few more words upon the two characters of Benedick and Beatrice, and principally upon the latter, who is one of our favourites among the heroines in Shakespeare.

Beatrice is not without consciousness of her power of wit;

but it is rather the delight that she takes in something that is an effluence of her own glad nature, than for any pride of display. She enjoys its exercise, too, as a means of playful despotism over one whom she secretly admires, while openly tormenting. Her first inquiries after Benedick show the sort of interest she takes in him; and it is none the less for its being veiled by a scoffing style; while what she says of their mutual wit-encounters proves the glory she has in out-taunting him. When her uncle observes to the Messenger, in reply to one of her sarcasms, "There is a kind of merry war betwixt Signior Benedick and her; they never meet, but there is a skirmish of wit between them;" she replies—

"Alas! he gets nothing by that. In our last conflict four of his five wits went halting off, and now the whole man is governed by one; so that if he have wit enough to keep himself warm, let him bear it for a difference between himself and his horse; for it is all the wealth he hath left to be known for a reasonable creature."

She is suspiciously anxious to point her disdain of him; for when the Messenger remarks,—"I see, lady, the gentleman is not in your books;" she retorts, "No; an he were, I would burn my study." Her native hilarity of heart is evidenced constantly, and in the most attractive manner; for it serves to make the blaze of her intellect show itself as originating in a secret blitheness of temperament. The prince, Don Pedro, says,—"In faith, lady, you have a merry heart;" to which she replies,—"Yea, my lord, I thank it, poor fool, it keeps on the windy side of care." And when, following this up by some smart banter, she gracefully checks herself,—"But I beseech your grace, pardon me; I was born to speak all mirth and no matter:" he rejoins—"Your silence most offends me; and to be merry best becomes you; for out of question you were born in a merry hour." Whereto she answers, "No, sure, my lord, my mother cried; but then there was a star danced, and under that was I born." Well may the prince remark after she has gone out, "By my troth, a pleasant-spirited lady!" To which her uncle, Leonato, replies:—

"There's little of the melancholy element in her, my lord; she is never sad but when she sleeps; and not ever sad then; for I have heard my daughter say she hath often dreamed of unhappiness, and waked herself with laughing."

The fact, is, like many high-spirited women, Beatrice possesses a fund of hidden tenderness beneath her exterior gaiety and sarcasm,—none the less profound from being withheld from casual view, and very seldom allowed to bewray itself. As proofs of this, witness her affection for her uncle, Leonato, and his strong esteem and love for her,—her passionate attachment to her cousin Hero, and the occasional, but extremely significant, betrayals of her partiality for Benedick; her very seeking out opportunities to torment him being one proof (especially in a woman of her disposition and breeding) of her preference; for women do not banter a man they dislike,—they mentally send him to Coventry, and do not lift him into importance by offering an objection, still less a repartee, or a sarcasm. The only time we see Beatrice alone, and giving utterance to the thoughts of her heart,—that is, in soliloquy, which is the dramatic medium of representing self-communion—(already quoted)—her words are full of warm and feminine tenderness,—words that probably would not seem so pregnant of love-import, coming from another woman, more prone to express such feeling; but, from Beatrice, meaning much. It is the very transcript of an honest and candid heart. Then the poet has given her so potent an antagonist in her wit-fencing, that her skill is saved from being thought unbefitting. Benedick's wit is so polished, so manly, so competent, that her womanhood is spared the disgrace of bearing away the palm in their keen encounters. He always remains victor; for we feel that he voluntarily refrains from claiming the conquest he achieves; and he is ever master of the field, though his chivalrous gallantry chooses to leave her in possession of the ground—that "ground" so dear to female heart, "the last word." Benedick is a perfect gentleman, and his wit partakes of his nature; it is forbearing in proportion to its excellence. One of the causes which render Benedick's wit more delightful than that of Beatrice, is, that it *knows when to cease.* Like a true woman, (don't "condemn me to everlasting redemption," ladies!) Beatrice is apt to pursue her advantage, when she feels she has one, to the very utmost. She does not give her antagonist a chance; and if she could upset him, she would pink him when he was down: now, Benedick, with the generosity of superior strength, gives way first. His mode at the last of checking her mettlesome wit, when he finds it again about to curvet unseasonably against him, is worthy of Benedick's manly spirit. It is a gallant rebuke; at once gentle and conclusive, it is the most effectual, as it is the most fit, close that he could put to the lady's arch pertinacity. At the close of the drama, when they all come in masked, and the scene of Claudio's second betrothal takes place, Benedick comes forward, saying—

"Soft and fair, Friar.—Which is Beatrice?

"*Beat.* [*Unmasking.*] I answer to that name. What is your will?

"*Bene.* Do not you love me?

"*Beat.* No; no more than reason.

"*Bene.* Why, then, your uncle, and the prince, and Claudio, have been deceived; for they swore you did.

"*Beat.* Do not you love me?

"*Bene.* No; no more than reason.

"*Beat.* Why, then, my cousin, Margaret, and Ursula, are much deceived; for they did swear you did.

"*Bene.* They swore that you were almost sick for me.

"*Beat.* They swore that you were well-nigh dead for me.

"*Bene.* 'Tis no such matter. Then you do not love me?

"*Beat.* No, truly; but in friendly recompence.

"*Leonato.* Come, cousin; I am sure you love the gentleman.

"*Claud.* And I'll be sworn upon it he loves her; for here's a paper written in his hand,—a halting sonnet of his own pure brain, fashioned to Beatrice.

"*Hero.* And here's another, writ in my cousin's hand, stolen from her pocket, containing her affection unto Benedick.

"*Bene.* A miracle! here's our own hands against our hearts! Come, I will have thee; but, by this light, I take thee for pity.

"*Beat.* I would not marry you; but, by this good day, I yield upon great persuasion, and partly to save your life; for I was told you were in a consumption.

"*Bene.* Peace! I will stop your mouth."—[Which he does, with a kiss.]

One of Beatrice's best pieces of wit is her reply to her uncle's wish:—

"Well, niece; I hope to see you one day fitted with a husband.

"*Beat.* Not till God make men of some other metal than earth. Would it not grieve a woman to be over-mastered with a piece of valiant dust? To make an account of her life to a clod of wayward marle? No, uncle, I'll none: Adam's sons are my brethren; and truly I hold it a sin to match in my kindred."

One of Benedick's pleasantest as well as wittiest speeches is that wherein he complains of Beatrice's maltreatment at the masquerade. It is the only time when he seems to be earnestly irritated with her; and no wonder. He says of her behaviour—

"Oh! she misused me past the endurance of a block; an oak, with but one green leaf upon it, would have answered her. My very vizor began to assume life, and scold with her. She told me (not thinking I had been myself) that I was the prince's jester, that I was duller than a great thaw, huddling jest upon jest, with such impossible conveyance upon me, that I stood like a man at a mark, with a whole army shooting at me." . . . . "I would not marry her though she were endowed with all that Adam had left before he transgressed."

Benedick, being a man of acknowledged wit, as well as of a blithe temperament, has no fancy to be considered a jester, —a professed "jester." His brilliant faculties render him a favourite associate of the prince; but his various higher qualities, as a gentleman and a scholar, give him better claims to liking than those of a gay companion only. It is this that makes Beatrice's calling him the "prince's jester" so intolerable a gibe. She knew it, the hussy! with her woman's shrewdness in finding out precisely what will most gall the man she prefers; and he shows that it touches him to the quick, by reverting to it in soliloquy, and repeating it again to his friends when they come in. A man of lively humour who is excited by his native gaiety of heart to entertain his friends by his pleasantry, at the same time feeling within himself that he possesses yet stronger and worthier grounds for their partiality, has a peculiarly sensitive dread of being taken for a mere jester or buffoon. Benedick's buoyancy of spirit is no effect of levity or frivolity. His humour has depth of feeling as well as mirth in it. His wit has force and geniality, no less than intellectual vivacity. That little sentence, with all its sportive ease, is instinct with moral sound sense—"Happy are they that hear their detractions and can put them to mending." Benedick's wit has penetration and discernment in it. With all his mercurial temperament, too, yet in a grave question this fine character can deliver himself with gravity and a noble sedateness; as where he says, "In a false quarrel there is no true valour."

And throughout the challenge-scene he expresses himself with gentlemanly dignity and manly feeling; while we find, from the remarks of the prince upon his change of colour, that he is as deeply hurt as he has temperately spoken. He characterises his own wit, in its gentleness and gallantry towards women, when he says to Beatrice's attendant, "A most manly wit, Margaret; it will not hurt a woman." There is heart in Benedick's playfulness. His love-making, when he is love-taken, is as earnest as it is animated. That is a fine and fervent bit of his wooing-scene with Beatrice, where she asks him if he will go with her to her uncle Leonato's to hear the news, he answers, "I will live in thy heart, die in thy lap, and be buried in thine eyes; and moreover, I will go with thee to thy uncle's." Shakespeare has, with lustrous perfection, vindicated the sound sense and sweet heart that may accompany wit, in the character of Benedick. And after having discussed the mental sparrings and fit-fayings of the two creatures, turn to their first wooing, and see them each displayed to the best advantage—Beatrice, certainly; who in the course of it shows one of those genuine touches of womanly feeling that have been alluded to as redeeming her character from the unfounded as well as ungracious charge of unfeminine hardness. Here is the pith of the scene. When she and Benedick are left alone in the chapel,—the rest of the company having quitted it, after the public shame and scandal heaped upon poor Hero by the mean-spirited Claudio,—Benedick approaches his lady, saying:—

"Lady Beatrice, have you wept all this while?

"*Beat.* Yea, and shall weep a while longer.

"*Bene.* I will not desire that.

"*Beat.* You have no reason; I do it freely.

"*Bene.* Surely, I do believe your fair cousin is wronged.

"*Beat.* Ah, how much that man might deserve of me that would right her!

"*Bene.* Is there any way to show such friendship?

"*Beat.* A very even way, but no such friend.

"*Bene.* May a man do it?

"*Beat.* It is a man's office; *but not yours.*

"*Bene.* I do love nothing in the world so well as you; is not that strange?

"*Beat.* As strange as the thing I know not. It were as possible for me to say, I loved nothing so well as you; but believe me not,—and yet I lie not; I confess nothing, nor I deny nothing. *I am sorry for my cousin.*

"*Bene.* By my sword, Beatrice, thou lovest me.

"*Beat.* Do not swear by it, and eat it.

"*Bene.* I will swear by it that you love me; and I will make him eat it that says I love not you.

"*Beat.* Will you not eat your word?

"*Bene.* With no sauce that can be devised to it. I protest I love thee.

"*Beat.* Why, then,—God forgive me!

"*Bene.* What offence, sweet Beatrice?

"*Beat.* You have staid me in a happy hour; I was about to protest I loved you.

"*Bene.* And do it with all thy heart.

"*Beat.* I love you with so much of my heart, that none is left to protest."

I am mistaken in my taste of true wit and of true feeling if there be not a charming display of both in this very natural, very easy, and very graceful little scene. I wished to urge some extenuation in behalf of Beatrice, because it is not unusual to designate her (as well as Portia) as a "masculine woman." I can only say that every man who expresses this opinion commits a piece of egoism, for both women are endowed with qualities, moral and intellectual, that any man might be proud to inherit. And here again, it is impossible to forego a passing remark upon the generous, indeed, the chivalrous conduct of Shakespeare in portraying his heroines. Of all the writers that ever existed, no one ought to stand so high in the love and gratitude of women as he. He has indeed been their champion, their laureate, their brother, their friend. He has been the man to lift them from a state of vassalage and degradation, wherein they were the mere toys, when not the she-serfs, of a sensual tyranny; and he has asserted their prerogative, as intellectual creatures, to be the companions, (in the best sense,) the advisers, the friends, the equals of men. He has endowed them with the true spirit of Christianity and brotherly love, "enduring all things, forgiving all things, hoping all things;" and it is no less remarkable, that with a prodigality of generosity, he has not unfrequently placed the heroes in his stories at a disadvantage with them. Observe, for instance, the two characters of Hero and Claudio in this very play. She is the absolute perfection of sweetness and generosity, quenching in forgiveness all the injuries she has received, and bestowing her heart and confidence where she had every reason to be mistrustful. Claudio, on the other hand, is a selfish manœuvrer. He tells the prince that he is in love with Hero, but he opens the conversation about her by inquiring of him whether Signor Leonato *has a son;* he had an eye to the cash first, and then the girl, and the circumstance of her being an only child confirms him in his suit. Claudio is a fellow of no nobleness of character, for instead of being the last, he is the first to believe his mistress guilty of infidelity towards him, and he then adopts the basest and the most brutal mode of punishment by casting her off at the very altar. Genuine love is incapable of revenge of any sort, that I assume to be a truism, still less of a concocted and refined revenge. Claudio is a scoundrel in grain. This question is too ample to be discussed upon this occasion; but I would merely quote in confirmation of my remark, the characters of Bertram in "All's Well that Ends Well," of Posthumus Leonatus in "Cymbeline," of Leontes in "The Winter's Tale," of Othello, (who, indeed, advances much claim upon our extenuation, and even commiseration, for he was of a noble nature,) and, lastly, of

Proteus in "The Two Gentlemen of Verona." All these characters appear not only at a disadvantage by, but they are unworthy of the women with whom they are consorted. Shakespeare has himself put into the mouth of a man this honest confession. The Duke in "Twelfth Night" says—

> "However we do praise ourselves,
> Our fancies are more giddy and infirm,
> More longing, wav'ring, sooner lost and worn
> Than women's are."

Again, therefore, Shakespeare is the writer of all others whom the women should most take to their hearts; for I believe it to be mainly through his intellectual influence that their claims in the scale of society were acknowledged in England, when, throughout what is denominated the civilised world, their position was not greatly elevated above that of the drudges in modern low life. And have not both parties been gainers by the reformation?—not but that much yet remains to be modified—nevertheless, the moral philosophy of Shakespeare, anticipated by another code, which I am perfectly sure he would have been the first to recognise and avow, has exalted our social system beyond that of the rest of the world.

Plotters, malignants, slanderers, among others, may derive advantage and instruction from the study of the play; most important advantage to them, seeing that it touches the vital principle of their vocation—that of working mischief during the night of men's senses, when observation and watchfulness are off their guard—of sowing tares among the corn of a man's peace and comfort while he sleeps in apparent security. If liars need long memories, slanderers, manœuvrers, and workers in mystery require the watchfulness of Cerberus, and the hands of Briareus to keep all the strings, and springs, and wheels of their plot in full play; and be they wary as they may, some small unanticipated obstacle will intrude among the works, and blow up the plotter with all his mischief. That gratuitous villain, Don John, was triumphantly carrying on his scheme of treachery against the peace and happiness of poor Hero; she was driven from society; her whole family and friends were thrown into grief and dismay, and all were wretched, except Don John. Neither the prince, the father, nor the uncle, not even the quick-witted Beatrice, (and you may trust a woman to unearth a plot, if she set seriously to work,) could discern the mover in it. Benedick is the only one who casually hints at Don John. It was left to the drunken Borachio and his comrade to blab it by night in the hearing of the foolish watchmen. Dogberry was the man who "comprehended those arrant knaves," and committed them upon the charge of "flat burglary." Borachio, in his confession to the prince, says: "I have deceived even your own eyes; what your wisdoms could not discover, these shallow fools have brought to light." The ease, yet ingenuity and agreeable surprise in the development of this plot, with the variety of characters engaged in it, have made the comedy one of the greatest favourites on the stage.

The character of the father, Leonato, has no prominent feature in it deserving particular consideration, unless it be to notice the consistency of the poet in tracing the ebbs and flows of a temper that yields to every wind of passion sweeping over it. Leonato is a re-fusion of old Capulet, but without his fussiness and dollying. In the first blush of the charge against his daughter, he rashly casts her off, and is only brought to reason by the friendly and sagacious old friar, and his own brother, Antonio; and then he becomes equally furious against Claudio, denouncing him as the slanderer of his child; and, like a true specimen of a man of strong passions and weak judgment, he sinks into a mere negation before the consistency and equanimity of the Friar and

Benedick. He says, in reply to their reasoning with him, "Being that I flow in grief, the smallest twine may lead me." How true to nature all this! and how apt, as well as choice, that metaphor!

The quarrel of these old men with the young ones, stung by the injury inflicted on their family reputation, is eminently fine. Leonato says to Claudio:—

> "Tush, tush, man, never fleer and jest at me;
> I speak not like a dotard nor a fool,
> As under privilege of age to brag
> What I have done being young, or what would do
> Were I not old. Know, Claudio, to thy head,
> Thou hast so wrong'd mine innocent child and me,
> That I am forced to lay my reverence by,
> And with gray hairs and bruise of many days,
> Do challenge thee to trial of a man.
> I say, thou hast belied mine innocent child;
> Thy slander hath gone through and through her heart,
> And she lies buried with her ancestors;
> Oh! in a tomb where never scandal slept,
> Save this of hers fram'd by thy villainy."

At the close of this scene, Shakespeare has again taken up the hard nature of Claudio. The prince, who is only an acquaintance of the father, Leonato, and his brother, Antonio, nevertheless manifests a gentlemanly consideration, and even tenderness in their family disaster; but Claudio is wholly untouched by the anguish of the old men at the loss of their child (she his own mistress too!) and at the stain upon their house. He has no word of sympathy or commiseration; but wraps himself up in contempt of their aged and feeble defiance: and immediately after they have gone out, upon Benedick's entering, he jests upon the danger that he and the prince have escaped of having "their noses snapped off by two old men without teeth." Thus Shakespeare carries out a principle. He does not talk or parade it about, he pays you the compliment of allowing you to perceive his intention. Unlike many play-writers, he does not bring in his characters as choruses to themselves: "Now, I am going to turn out a villain or a hypocrite;" but we find out that they are those characters. So, in this of Claudio, we have no prologue to his nature, but, as events convene, he gradually develops into an unfeeling and selfish man of the world. It is observable that he utters no speech of regret, no speeeh at *all*, unless it be upon what *he* has lost, when he is informed that Hero has died broken-hearted. Now, is not all this in keeping with the man who *commences* his suit by inquiring about his chance of having money with her?

It may not be irrelevant here to notice, that in both the plays of "Romeo and Juliet," and "Much Ado About Nothing," the plots being of Italian origin, a main point in the conducting of them consists in the assumed death and interment of the heroines; a deception perfectly feasible, and not very improbable in Italy, where it has always been the custom not only to dispose of the corpse within a few hours after death, but to convey it openly on a bier, richly dressed with flowers, as for a festival, and even the flesh coloured to counterfeit life. Death is awful enough, take what shape he may, but so fruitless a mockery of vitality is hideous when thrust forth in impotent defiance of the mighty abstraction; and after all, nature, in her truth, and under any form, when contemplated in a spirit of resignation and submissiveness, will read us homilies upon peace, and happiness, and eternity, beyond all the contrivances and subterfuges of art and illusion. As Leigh Hunt has somewhere grandly said, "The face of a dead man appears as if it had suddenly arrived at the knowledge of all truth, and was, in consequence, profoundly at rest."

Shakespeare has, I think, never introduced a friar in any of his plays but he has made him an agent to administer consolation and provide the means for securing domestic peace. All his friars are characters implicitly commanding love and respect. Now, living as he did, in the early period of our rupture with the Church of Rome; and when, to lend a helping hand towards pulling down and bringing into disrepute that hierarchy, was considered an act of duty in every proselyte to the Reformed Church, it is not a little remarkable that he should have uniformly abstained from identifying himself with the image-breakers. To this may be retorted, that in the plays where he has introduced the friar, the scene was laid in Catholic countries, and where that religion was paramount; that he was a painter of nature and character, not a sectarian, civil or ecclesiastical; and lastly, that it was not his cue to be controversial, either actively or implied. But as the mental bias in every writer will casually bewray itself; so we find, that when Shakespeare has introduced a member of the *Low*-Church party—such as the Oliver Martexts, the Sir Hughs, the Sir Nathaniels, and the Sir Topazes—he has usually thrown him into a ludicrous position: for, like his brother poet, Spenser, and other master-intellects of the day, he was disgusted with the unimaginative interfering spirit, and gross intolerance of Puritanism, which had then come in, and, indeed, was prevailing. In the play of "King John" he has, it is true, with sufficient explicitness denounced the intolerance of the Papal dominion; but there (like the majority of his countrymen) he was but testifying a long-existing opprobrium; and could he now return to us, doubtless he would sanction those ten thousand priestly signatures praying for the remission of the Papal temporalities—*in order that the spiritual supremacy may be preserved;* for if those be not yielded, assuredly both will go together.

But there is every appearance that Shakespeare was essentially a "Quietist." He would remove no land-marks of precedent or existing faith; and this spirit pervades his writings. He would have allowed formulæ that had suited the temperament of society to continue in their integrity. He has put into the mouth of Imogen that piece of social wisdom—"Breach of custom is breach of all;" the axiom of a bland nature and native gentleman, and apparently the master-key to his own rule of moral conduct. His morality of principle and action appears to have been a practical fulfilment—so far as an imperfect being can fulfil it—of the "Sermon on the Mount." He not only inculcates the doctrine, "Whatsoever ye would that men should do unto you, do ye also unto them;" but he as frequently illustrates the still grander principle of returning unkindness with gentle deeds and forbearance.

Upon the question of his *non-avowal* of any point of faith or doctrine, Thomas Carlyle, in his "Hero-worship," says,—"That was the fruit of his greatness withal; his whole heart was in his own grand sphere of worship—we may call it such; these other controversies, vitally important to other men, were not vital to him."

Returning to my former notion of his perfect gentility and tolerance of spirit,—and, from that even tenor of spirit, I rest upon one of the following conclusions: either he had a latent respect and preference for the old-established form of religion, or (and this should raise him in our esteem) he was too magnanimous to join in the common cry of hounding out doctrines and opinions which, in their *primitive spirit,* at all events, had afforded consolation to millions of his fellow-mortals.

The Friar in this play is as amiable and intellectual a character as the one in "Romeo and Juliet"—quiet, observant, patiently biding his time to speak, until his silent comment shall have enabled him to deliver judgment upon the case before him. His close noting of the belied Hero's demeanour having convinced him of her innocence, he advises the plan of reporting her sudden death, and thus sagely explains his motive :—

> "It so falls out,
> That what we have, we prize not to the worth
> Whiles we enjoy it ; but being lack'd and lost,
> Why then we rack the value ; then we find
> The virtue that possession would not show us
> Whiles it was ours : so will it fare with Claudio ;
> When he shall hear she died upon his words,
> The idea of her life shall sweetly creep
> Into his study of imagination ;
> And every lovely organ of her life
> Shall come apparell'd in more precious habit,
> More moving-delicate, and full of life,
> Into the eye and prospect of his soul,
> Than when she liv'd indeed. Then shall he mourn,
> (If ever love had interest in his liver,)
> And wish he had not so accused her ;
> *No, though he thought his accusation true.*"

A line instinct with touching knowledge of human charity. Pity attends the faults of the dead ; and survivors visit even sin with regret rather than reproach.

The characters of Conrad and Borachio are such as may be met with in all populous communities,—fellows who are purveyors of moral filth to those who have wherewith to pay them for such hire. Men who generally end their career under a rug in the corner of a loft or garret, unless chance have given them a very high commission indeed for scoundrelism, and then they are perchance destined to close their revered existence in a "cottage ornée."

Margaret and Ursula may come under the denomination of "pattern waiting-women,"—that is, the patterns somewhat surpassing the order of the women. Margaret has perhaps too accomplished a tongue for one of her class ; she, however, evidently apes the manner of Beatrice, and, like all imitators of inferior mind, with a coarse and exaggerated character.

She forms an excellent foil to her mistress from this very circumstance; and both domestics are samples of that menial equality that exists between mistress and dependant still common in Italy.

But what shall we say to you, O Dogberry and Verges, Hugh Oatcake and George Seacoal? Why, that among his other crystallisations of animated nature,—there you are, you "most ancient and quiet watchmen," in all your integral conceit and imbecility of character, physical, mental, and moral; full-fledged specimens of your order, preserved for all time in the imperishable amber of his genius, when your race and calling have passed away from the earth. Civil government and social order in constant progress, protection and security have succeeded to inefficiency and fatuity.

> "The bellman's drowsy charm,
> To guard our doors from nightly harm,"

has become silent for ever, or lives only in the echo of the poet's line. The thin ghost of the departed watchman flits by us in the streets unconscious, his querulous wail inaudible to ears of flesh and blood. Now the policemen are in the ascendant, and the "Charlies" are fading even from the memory of man. Sergeant A of the B division stalks forth in the zenith of suburban dominion, and the lantern of Goodman Verges has "paled its ineffectual fire." *Troes fuimus—Troja fuit.* Let no one speak of Dogberry and his tribe as being caricatures of their class. As Macbeth says, "There is no such thing!"

Have any of you, my very respected readers, ever been "pulled up" before a constable of the night? Neither have I; we cannot "own that soft impeachment." Nevertheless, he must be a minim of a historian who confines himself to those facts only which he has seen and can testify. The daily police reports of the first half of the present century bear record that no invention of the most ludicrously-florid fancy can surpass in incongruous ideality the real, and substantial, and solidly-stupid old watchman: caricature "toils after him in vain." Nothing but himself *could* be his own parallel. With him caricature merges into fidelity, and inevitably commits an anticlimax. Dogberry, in himself, is not so much a caricature as he is a satire upon all who are intrusted with duties for which neither nature nor art ever destined them. The public instructor who cannot conceal his jealousy at the increase of knowledge among the commonalty, is a Dogberry in his vocation. The civil functionary who declaims upon the omnipotence and impartiality of statute law, yet swerves in his decision when the rich and powerful become amenable to its penalties, is no more or less than a Dogberry among magistrates. Every jackanapes with more sail than ballast is a Dogberry full blown. Every public officer who can command no more respect than attaches to his two gowns, whose "soul," as my Lord Lafeu says, "is his clothes," is a Dogberry in grain. Asses—conceited and stolid, pragmatists, sneaks, bullies, and grovellers, are but "the varied Dogberry." "Sweet are the uses" of old Dogberry! "he weareth a precious jewel in his head:" for he readeth a homely lecture to all of us:—viz., to elevate ourselves by moral worth in the station to which God has called us; and constantly to bear in mind that the office only adds lustre to the man, when he conscientiously and efficiently discharges the duties of it. It has been prudently recommended that no man should be without a corkscrew in his pocket; he had better always have a Dogberry. Should he be blest with one grain of self-knowledge, it will assist in drawing off his ignorance and conceit.

In one sentence, in conclusion, I would draw attention to another amiable quality in our poet's disposition, and that is his magnanimity in revenge. This item in his philosophy frequently crosses us in our progress through his dramas. Upon the present occasion it is accompanied with his own innate love of cheerfulness. In the last sentence of the 5th Act, a messenger comes to say that the contriver of all their late sorrow, the malignant Don John, is taken in flight, and brought with armed men back to Messina. "Oh! think not of him till to-morrow, [says the happy Benedick ;] I'll devise thee brave punishments for him! Strike up, pipers!"

In rising from the perusal of this enchanting play, we are impressed with three axioms: That people truly and deeply enamoured, are not only not suspicious, but are the last to be convinced of their lovers' transgressions, and the first to receive atonement for them. Secondly, That the union of two such beings as Beatrice and Benedick, although an amiably fraudulent one, in which there exists no more than a mutual esteem, offers an infinitely happier prospect to the woman, than the cold-blooded, hard conduct of Claudio can ever promise to her whom he so cruelly punished. And, lastly, That almost all the poison of unhappiness in this life is the result of our own want of judgment, or of faith in goodness, and that sooner or later it will engender its own antidote.

XIII.

# King John.

# XIII.

# KING JOHN.

---

IN what I have said upon the tragedy of "Lear," the master-movement of that composition was designated as being a "practical example of the calamities resulting from unbridled, unguided self-will; that 'will,' independent of and irresponsible to justice and rationality, is the pivot upon which turn all the disasters that befall its leading characters." It is no unusual circumstance with Shakespeare to take some master-passion, as for a text to those dramatic sermons of his, many of them being (without the ostentatious denotement) really dramas of some individual passion; and having so taken the text, or thesis of his discourse, he will work out his case in detail, and relieve, and heighten, and strengthen his argument by the grandest and most superb contrasts.

The prevailing characteristic both of the plot and of the chief personages in the play of "King John" is that of "craft." The poet, it is true, has taken—as he found it in the monkish record—the *historical* character of the king; but he has, with his own supreme genius, worked it out from the first scene to the last with undeviating consistency, and a revolting determination of purpose. He has shown him to us, seizing with unscrupulous hand the birthright and throne belonging to another, and that other his own orphan nephew. He has shown him to us preparing to pour forth the blood, and peril the lives of his subjects in support of this bad, unjust cause, in a war with France, when it disputes his usurping claim. He has shown him to us revolving in his selfish expediency how extortion and oppression at home shall supply the expenses thus incurred abroad. "Our abbeys and priories shall pay this expedition's charge," he mutters to himself, on the departure of the ambassadors.

We next see him paltering and sophisticating with the truth in the matter of Robert Falconbridge's heritage, preparing to wrest the estate from the legitimate son, and to bestow it on the illegitimate one—contrary to the will of the bequeather—on a plea false in spirit, though plausible in letter.

His next appearance is on the shores of France, making wheedling speeches to his nephew, Arthur, specious ones to the citizens of Angiers, patching up hollow compacts with the French king, followed by sudden breach of faith, and reckless plunge into the carnage of the battle-field.

Then comes his dark purpose against his young kinsman distilled into Hubert's ear: and then his return to his own kingdom, where we find him employed in warily seeking to ingratiate himself with his nobles, in striving to avert their but too-well-founded suspicions of his blood-guiltiness, and in sneakingly proffering them all sorts of rotten promises and lying declarations.

Next, we behold him shrinking with craven, selfish forebodings from the consequences of his own craft and cruelty, watching with coward eye the increasing disaffection at home and approaching danger from abroad, and studying how, by new guile, he may ward off the inevitable issue of old untruths and misdeeds. The picture of his base and dastard soul trembling in all the alarm of awakened, conscious guilt, with its dreaded results, is a revelation terrible in its bare and naked deformity. We turn, as from a hideous reptile-thing, from the spectacle of this despicable royal murderer, liar, and villain, alone with his own conscience and its fears; and we find him next trying, with loathsomest subterfuge, to fasten upon the factor of his monster-crime its responsibility and retribution. The shuffling sophistry and meanness of reproach with which he turns upon Hubert in this scene, throwing upon him the whole blame of a deed which he himself originally conceived, and had instigated Hubert to perpetrate, is the very flagrance and crassitude of baseness. It is scoundrelism—not dreading to *be* scoundrel, but to be *proved* scoundrel, and to meet scoundrel's due. The scene is the 2nd of the 4th Act, and commences with this remarkable sentence—

> "Why seek'st thou to possess me with these *fears?*
> Why urgest thou so oft young Arthur's death?
> *Thy hand hath murder'd him: I had a mighty cause*
> *To wish him dead, but thou hadst none to kill him.*"

And he goes on, in fine scoundrel-keeping,—

> "Hadst not thou been by,
> A fellow by the hand of nature mark'd,
> Quoted, and sign'd to do a deed of shame,
> This murder had not come into my mind;
> But taking note of thy abhorr'd aspèct,
> Finding thee fit for bloody villainy,
> Apt, liable to be employ'd in danger,
> I faintly broke with thee of Arthur's death;
> And THOU, *to be endearèd to a king,*
> *Mad'st it no conscience to destroy a prince.*"

This surely is the "ultima thule" of base wickedness. And yet, in this "lowest deep," there is still a "lower deep" in the character and conduct of this pitiful king; most of all does he appear vile and ignoble in the act of truckling and stooping to priestly tyranny. Here he not only degrades himself, but his whole people in his own person. By servilely seeking to fawn and cringe into the good graces of the Vatican, he compromises the honour of his throne and nation; and in lifting the golden symbol of sovereignty from his own head, he shamefully places the crown of England beneath the foot of Rome, to be spurned or forborne by Papal toe. But, to sum the conduct of this hateful king, he is hideous in his crimes, hideous in his hypocrisy, and hideous even in his remorse, because that arises from fear, and not from repentance of his foul deeds. A bold bad man, like Richard III., rises into an object of absolute admiration, compared with the crawling, abject wickedness of such a being as John.

Throughout the play every step that John makes is a step of guile—his every action is a manœuvre. His very first speech betrays his wary and cat-like circumspection. He watches the counsel of others before he enters into a resolution—" Silence, good mother; hear the embassy"—and almost the last speech he makes, cunningly and sneakingly involves the interests of those whom he is addressing.

> "I do not ask you much,
> I beg cold comfort; and you are so strait
> And so ingrateful, you deny me that."

The same principle of "craft" also distinguishes the conduct of his mother, Elinor, who puts the leading question to the illegitimate Falconbridge in his dispute with his brother Robert upon the question of heritage She says—

> "Whether hadst thou rather be a Falconbridge,
> And like thy brother, to enjoy thy land,
> Or the reputed son of Cœur-de-Lion,
> Lord of thy presence, [that is, taking priority of
> rank,] and no land beside?"

Betraying by this artful suggestion that she herself has at

once recognised the value of so brave an adherent to the cause of her son John, and thus linking him to it by fostering his own ambitious designs.

Again, in the 1st scene of the 2d Act, in the contest with Constance upon the question of her son Arthur's inheritance to the crown, by reason of his being issue of John's elder brother, Geffrey,—Constance, indignant at Elinor's slander, that her son is base-born, retorts—

> "By my soul, I think
> His father never was so true begot:
> It cannot be, an if *thou* wert his mother."

With the sly spite of a low-minded and crafty woman, Elinor says to the boy Arthur, "There's a good mother, boy, that blots thy father," meaning by this comment to throw the brand of discord between mother and child. And shortly after, with the true art of a politician, she insinuates that she can "produce a will that bars the title of her son," Arthur. And again, in the same crafty spirit of manœuvring, she astutely points out to her son, John, the advantages to be reaped from the union between the Dauphin, Lewis, and his own niece, Blanche of Castile. Her reason for urging this measure is a master-piece of diplomacy. She says—

> "Son, list to this conjunction, make this match,
> Give with our niece a dowry large enough;
> For by this knot thou shalt so surely tie
> Thy now unsur'd assurance to the crown,
> That yond' green boy shall have no sun to ripe
> The bloom that promiseth a mighty fruit."

It will be recollected that the French king had recognised Arthur's claim to the English crown. She continues—

> "I see a yielding in the looks of France,
> Mark how they whisper; urge them while their souls
> Are capable of this ambition,
> Lest zeal, now melted by the windy breath

Of soft petitions, pity, and remorse,
Cool and congeal again to what it was."

This is counsel not unworthy of a Richelieu or a Mazarin. Mrs Montague's was a felicitous illustration of the genius of Shakespeare when she compared him to that dervis who possessed the power of trajecting his soul into the body of any individual that suited his purpose.* The mind that conceived the spirit of Ariel, and the spotless innocence of Miranda, is here equally at home in describing the crooked and thorny policy of a court-intriguer.

The same ruling principle of "craft" is to be recognised—although with a difference and variety—in the weak, vacillating, and would-be policy of the French king, Philip, who ostentatiously would adhere to the letter, while he gives the spirit of his promises to the winds.

Then we have the prudent, compromising suggestions of the wary citizens of Angiers, whose "*words,* in the emergency, buffet better than a fist of France." And, lastly, there is the bold, open, asserting policy of the Legate, Pandulph, the representative of the assumed right to sway all things—even government itself. How finely does all this serpent-like tortuous policy contrast with the whirlwind passion of Constance, whose deep sense of wrong and unflinching spirit cause her to spurn all caution, all concealment of feeling; who vehemently urges her fancied friends and adherents to assist her in vengeance on her enemies, heaping unreserved and unmeasured contumely, and invoking loud curses on the heads of those who injure her.

Constance is a sublime personification of the maternal character, lashed into frenzy by the potency of will, but

* "Essay on the Writings and Genius of Shakespeare," p. 37. "Shakespeare seems to have had the art of the dervis in the Arabian Tales, who could throw his soul into the body of another man, and be at once possessed of his sentiments, adopt his passions, and rise to all the functions and feelings of his situation."

impotence of power to right herself of the injustice with which she is surrounded. She is a lioness at bay, her resources failed, and her retreat cut off. In the blind desire to secure her child's birthright, and in her wrath at his oppression, she fatally loses sight of the great privilege of his existence. How true to nature all this, and how accurately do we trace the gradual subsiding of her spirit of fury and resentment into an outpouring of tenderness and deprecation, as all her hopes and prospects of success fade away. What majesty in her reply to the French king when she refuses to attend his summons and accompany his messenger :—

"*Salisbury.* Pardon me, madam,
I may not go without you to the kings.
"*Const.* Thou may'st, thou shalt ; I will not go with thee ;
I will instruct my sorows to be proud ;
For grief is proud, and makes his owner stoop.
To me, and to the state of my great grief,
Let kings assemble ; for my grief's so great,
That no supporter but the huge firm earth
Can hold it up ; here I and sorrows sit ;
Here is my throne, bid kings come bow to it."

Magnificent as this is, it is even surpassed in beauty by the tearful passion of tenderness in that passage where she addresses the cardinal, when the little prince is taken from her :—

"O father cardinal, I have heard you say
That we shall see and know our friends in heav'n.
If that be true, I shall see my boy again ;
For since the birth of Cain, the first male child,
To him that did but yesterday suspire,
There was not such a gracious creature born.
But now will canker sorrow eat my bud,
And chase the native beauty from his cheek,
And he will look as hollow as a ghost,
As dim and meagre as an ague's fit ;
And so he'll die ; and rising so again,

When I shall meet him in the court of heav'n
I shall not know him; therefore, never, never
Must I behold my pretty Arthur more.
"*K. Philip.* You are as fond of grief as of your child.
"*Con.* Grief fills the room up of my absent child,
Lies in his bed, walks up and down with me,
Puts on his pretty looks, repeats his words,
Remembers me of all his gracious parts,
Stuffs out his vacant garment with his form;
Then have I reason to be fond of grief."

And she concludes with those affecting ejaculations of maternal anguish—

"O Lord! my boy, my Arthur, my fair son!
My life, my joy, my food, my all the world!
My widow's comfort and my sorrow's cure!"

I know of nothing in dramatic contrast surpassing in grandeur that of Constance with the other characters in this tragedy—open, direct, vehement action, with bravery, but without judgment; opposed to cunning, treachery, and cruelty, without courage—moral or physical.

Again, while upon the subject of "contrast," we find the obtuse ranting and vulgar bravadoes of the bully, Austria, brought in to relieve the craft of King John; and still more finely, the noble, unsuspicious nature of the young Dauphin, whose heart sickens at discovering the wickedness that meets him at every turn, and who is rebuked by the wary and cold-blooded politician, Pandulph. The young prince says:—

"There's nothing in this world can make me joy;
Life is as tedious as a twice-told tale,
Vexing the dull ear of a drowsy man;
And bitter shame hath spoil'd the sweet world's taste,
That it yields naught but shame and bitterness."

And now observe the practical wisdom that the poet has put into the mouth of the old embassador. Here is a maxim to encourage all those who undertake the cure of prevailing abuses and crying wrongs in a state. Pandulph replies by an illustration in an axiom. He says :—

> "Before the curing of a strong disease,
> Even in the instant of repair and health,
> The fit is strongest. Evils that take leave,
> On their departure most of all show evil."

And then, after explaining to the Dauphin how John's cause will be injured through his having obtained the possession of young Arthur's person, he winds up with this commiseration of the Dauphin's inexperience :—

> "How green you are and fresh in this old world!
> John hath seiz'd Arthur; and it cannot be
> That whiles warm life plays in that infant's veins
> The misplaced John should entertain an hour,
> One minute—nay, one quiet breath of rest.
> A sceptre snatch'd with an unruly hand,
> Must be as boisterously maintain'd as gain'd;
> And he that stands upon a slippery place
> Makes nice of no vile hold to stay him up.
> That John may stand, then Arthur needs must fall:
> So be it, for it cannot be but so."

Thus, like a thorough-bred politician, he calculates the chances and changes of government by violence and murder, as though the objects of them were no more than chessmen. This is all true to the very letter; and I think the position has been established—that "craft," with its usual companion, unkindness, forms the ruling passion of this play.

There are few of Shakespeare's or of any other poet's dramas that exhibit more strikingly the philosophy of war, than this of King John. What can be more palpable and more touching than the comment upon the utter worthlessness—even the folly of all strife and contention, than is comprised in that one affecting appeal of the little Arthur to his mother, Constance, in the midst of the tumult of the bad passions? Could anything tend more effectually to rebuke the worldly ambition of the mother, the aged spite of Elinor, the wily villainy of John, the interested vacillation of France, "whose armour conscience buckled on—whom zeal and charity brought to the field as God's own soldier," than this morsel of instinctive wisdom from the mouth of an innocent child? "Out of the mouth of babes and sucklings hast Thou ordained praise;" and here is a babe preaching, in spirit, the gospel of Christianity to the callous and case-hardened of the old world—the professing vicegerent of that Being who pronounced that "All they that use the sword shall perish by the sword;" the intriguing and strife-fomenting cardinal shows foully by the Christian humility of the royal child.

"Good, my mother, peace!
I would that I were low laid in my grave;
I am not worth this coil that's made for me."

Do we not feel deeply in our hearts, too, the instinctive yearning for sympathy and affection—a blessing so priceless, so far above worldly honour and conventional rank and distinction—which prompts the little prince to say to Hubert—

"Is it my fault that I was Geffrey's son?
No, indeed, is't not; and I would to Heav'n
I were your son, so you would love me, Hubert."

The childlike sweetness and simple beauty of that appeal surely never were exceeded. The gentle nature and innate perception of the folly of ambition—the "*low* ambition," as Pope finely calls it—of dominion, again appears in that simple speech—

"Mercy on me!
Methinks nobody should be sad but I:
Yet, I remember, when I was in France,

> Young gentlemen would be as sad as night,
> Only for wantonness. By my Christendom,
> So I were out of prison, and kept sheep,
> I should be as merry as the day is long."

Afterwards, he uses his rank as a plea, when reminding Hubert of his tender care of him, when he (Hubert) had an illness:—

> "Many a poor man's son would have lain still,
> And ne'er have spoke a loving word to you;
> But you at your sick service had a prince.
> Nay, you may think my love was crafty love,
> And call it cunning: do, an if you will:
> If Heaven be pleas'd that you must use me ill,
> Why then, you must."

This honest disclaiming of cunning, as being the basest of injurious imputations, comes with artistical contrast and relief to the main spirit of the play—the spirit of "craft" and treachery.

But the grandest carrying out of the author's intention in displaying the "philosophy of war," is to be found in the character of Falconbridge. It forms throughout, as it were, a *moral chorus* to the tragedy, embodying Shakespeare's own sentiments as to the worthlessness of strife and contention, and proving the medium of forcing this conviction upon his audience. The way in which the character is first introduced is in correct costume and keeping throughout. We behold a young and fiery spirit grasping at the earliest chance of what he deems honour, even at the expense of the honour of his mother, wherein he eagerly seeks to derive his descent from Cœur-de-Lion—not so much as being *King* Richard, but as the *war*-like monarch, the renowned military leader, the by-word and terror of the East, the plume in the helmet of Christian chivalry. He pants for distinction, come it how it may; and perceiving the cant of "craft" to be the court-fashion, he immediately announces his intention of adopting that course; adding—

> "For he is but a bastard to the time,
> That doth not smack of observation.
> And so am I, whether I smack or no;
> And not alone in habit and device,
> Exterior form, outward accoutrement,
> But from the inward motion to deliver
> Sweet, sweet, sweet poison for the age's tooth:
> Which, though I will not practise to deceive,
> Yet, to avoid deceit, I mean to learn;
> For it shall strew the footsteps of my rising."

And this lesson he instantly puts in practice by his sophistical speech to his mother, in allusion to her amour with Cœur-de-Lion, whereby he himself was descended:—

> "Some sins do bear their privilege on earth,
> And so doth yours. Your fault was not your folly:
> Needs must you lay your heart at his dispose,
> Subjected tribute to commanding love,
> Against whose fury and unmatchèd force
> The awless lion could not wage the fight,
> Nor keep his princely heart from Richard's hand.
> He that perforce robs lions of their hearts,
> May easily win a woman's."

On his first battle-field his tornado spirit hurries him at once into a quarrel with the Duke of Austria, against whom (with the instinctive dislike that men of courage entertain towards a blusterer and a bully) he at first sight conceives an antipathy. His disgust, moreover, is hereditary; for in Austria he hates the traitor to his own father, Cœur-de-Lion, whom he had kidnapped and imprisoned. No sooner, therefore, does the Duke utter one word commanding silence, than in bursts the jeering Falconbridge with, "Hear the crier!" "What the devil art thou?" rejoins the Duke.

> "One that will play the devil, sir, with you,
> An a' may catch your hide and you alone.

> You are the hare of whom the proverb goes,
> Whose valour plucks dead lions by the beard.
> I'll smoke your skin-coat, an I catch you right:
> Sirrah, look to't; i' faith, I will, i' faith!"

Throughout this scene,—nay, through the whole part, his warlike enthusiasm flares like a meteor. He whoops on the kings with a "View-holla!" to the battle:—

> "Why stand these royal fronts amazèd thus?
> Cry havoc, kings! back to the stainèd field,
> You equal potents, fiery-kindled spirits!
> Then let confusion of one part confirm
> The other's peace; till then, blows, blood, and death."

His aristocratic spirit and soldierly contempt of the artisan citizens could not fail to be registered among his other characteristics by the poet—

> "By Heav'n, these scroyles of Angiers flout you, kings:
> And stand securely on their battlements,
> As in a theatre, whence they gape and point
> At your industrious scenes and acts of death."

Even his leaning to the temporising system of policy which he had proposed to himself, by recommending to the kings the scheme of uniting their forces against Angiers, knowing it will win him their favour; and then his quick perception of the advantages to be reaped to his own party by the choice of situation made by France and Austria; chuckling to himself contemptuously, he says:—

> "O prudent discipline! From north to south,
> Austria and France shoot in each other's mouth.
> I'll stir them to it;"—

all these points bespeak him the young and eager soldier, whose sole thought is glory and military ambition; and all, too, display the master-mind that conceived and perfected the character with so undeviating a truth and consistency.

But then comes the soliloquy on "commodity," ("interestedness,") and how finely the better nature of the man revolts against the hollowness and want of good faith which he detects in the French king; yet Shakespeare, ever watchful, ever consistent, causes his eyes to open only by degrees; and Falconbridge concludes this very speech with adhering to his former resolution of pursuing his fortunes, keeping "commodity" as his lode-star. The soliloquy is remarkable for its vigorous worldly sense, as well as for the felicity with which the poet sustains his metaphor, in comparing self-interest, or "commodity," to the bias in the ball used by the player at bowls. When the assembly have gone out, having patched up the hollow compact between the French and English sovereigns, Falconbridge being left alone, he breaks forth:—

"Mad world! mad kings! mad composition!
John, to stop Arthur's title in the whole,
Hath willingly departed with a part;
And France (whose armour conscience buckled on,
Whom zeal and charity brought to the field
As God's own soldier,) rounded in the ear
With that same purpose-changer, that sly devil;
That broker, that still breaks the pate of faith;
That daily break-vow; he that wins of all,
Of kings, of beggars, old men, young men, maids,
Who having no external thing to lose
But the word maid, cheats the poor maid of that;
That smooth-faced gentleman, tickling commodity,—
Commodity, the bias of the world;
The world, who of itself is peised well,
Made to run even upon even ground,
Till this advantage, this vile drawing bias,
This sway of motion, this commodity,
Makes it take heed from all indifferency,
From all direction, purpose, course, intent;
And this same bias, this commodity,
This bawd, this broker, this all-changing word

Clapp'd on the outward eye of fickle France,
Hath drawn him from his own determin'd aid,
From a resolv'd and honourable war,
To a most base and vile-concluded peace.
And why rail I on this commodity?
But for because he hath not woo'd me yet:
Not that I have the power to clutch my hand,
When his fair angels would salute my palm;
But for my hand, as unattempted yet,
Like a poor beggar, raileth on the rich.
Well, whiles I am a beggar, I will rail,
And say, 'There is no sin, but to be rich;'
And being rich, my virtue then shall be,
To say, 'There is no vice but beggary.'
Since kings break faith upon commodity,
Gain be my lord; for I will worship thee."

But the important and decided change that takes place in the character of Falconbridge is when he first hears of the death of little Arthur, and at the same time hears it ascribed to John, to whom he himself is deeply indebted. His speeches after this event are still those of the courageous, high-spirited man, but they are distinctly those of the man of *moral* courage as contrasted with his previous *physical* courage. Like one of truly noble nature, he scorns to fall off from the patron to whom he owes so much; but the discovery of that patron's baseness and treachery acts like a talisman to unseal his eyes to the vain-glory and wickedness of "vaulting ambition" and low cupidity. He still cleaves to the cause of the king, and endeavours to screen him from the indignation of his revolting nobles; but he now discourses with a calm dignity totally unlike the rash impetuosity of Falconbridge in the opening of the play. And when Pembroke says, in justification of their revolt from King John, "Sir, sir, impatience hath his privilege," Falconbridge sedately and finely answers, "'Tis true: to hurt his master, no man else." And to Salisbury, who openly proclaims the blood-guiltiness of the king, he calmly replies, "Whate'er you *think*, good words, I think, were best." And Salisbury's rejoinder to this dignified rebuke does not quicken his pulse—"Our griefs, and not our manners, reason now;" he retorts, "But there is little reason in your grief; therefore 'twere reason you had manners now." All this is very different from his former bearing; and how the genius of the poet is displayed in quelling the fiery spirit of the man only by the chilling mist of suspicion and misplaced confidence. This is a beautiful tribute to the character of Falconbridge. The only time after this that his old impetuosity returns is when Salisbury threatens him—"Stand by, or I shall gall you, Falconbridge!" Then he flares out:—

"Thou wert better gall the devil, Salisbury;
If thou but frown on me, or stir thy foot,
Or teach thy hasty spleen to do me shame,
I 'll strike thee dead. Put up thy sword betime,
Or I 'll so maul you and your toasting-iron,
That you shall think the devil is come from hell."

The staring fact of the death of the little Prince Arthur is before him, he cannot blink that; he is pushed to a corner and hedged in, and yet he evades the charge, with the object pointed at. How natural all this; and how like a thorough and determined partisan. He is compelled to acknowledge thus much; he does confess—

"It is a damned and a bloody work;
The graceless action of a heavy hand,
*If* that it be the work of any hand."

He makes no farther concession to the rebel lords. When, however, they have left the scene, and he is alone with Hubert, he turns round upon him in a strain of sublime vituperation—

"Knew you of this fair work?
Beyond the infinite and boundless reach

Of mercy, if thou didst this deed of death,
Art thou damn'd, Hubert.
"*Hub.* Do but hear me, sir.
"*Falc.* Hey! I'll tell thee what:
Thou art damn'd as black—nay, nothing is so black;
Thou art more deep damn'd than Prince Lucifer:
There is not yet so ugly a fiend of hell
As thou shalt be if thou didst kill this child.
* * * * * *
I do suspect thee very grievously."

With the exception of the explosion with the nobles, (and this arose only from his valour being chafed,) throughout the whole scene, (the last of the 4th Act,) we discover working in him that divine maturer insight into the rottenness of contest and strife, which gradually takes the place of his young ambition, and which finds words at length in that grand and solemn soliloquy—closing the scene—where he bids Hubert bear away the little dead prince:—

"I am amaz'd, methinks, and lose my way
Among the thorns and dangers of this world.
How easy dost thou take all England up!
From forth this morsel of dead royalty,
The life, the right, and truth of all this realm
Is fled to heav'n, and England now is left
To tug and scamble, and to part by the teeth
The unow'd interest to proud-swelling state.
Now, for the bare-pick'd bone of majesty
Doth dogged war bristle his angry crest,
And snarleth in the gentle eyes of peace.
Now powers from home, and discontents at home,
Meet in one line; and vast confusion waits,
As doth a raven on a sick-fall'n beast,
The imminent decay of wrested pomp."

After this scene we find him bravely fighting for John, showing a valiant front to his enemies, and supporting him in his death-agony; but the moral perfectioning of his own character is wound to a climax in the closing words of the play:—

> "This England never did, nor never shall
> Lie at the proud foot of a conqueror,
> But when it first did help to wound itself.
> * * * * * *
> Come the three corners of the world in arms,
> And we shall shock them. Naught shall make us rue,
> If England to itself do rest but true."

Was I not correct in saying that the character of Falconbridge forms a "moral chorus" to the play to reveal to us the hidden skeleton beneath the veil and roses of war and ambition?

I have frequently recurred to Shakespeare's ingenuity in contrasting his characters in his dramas; great as this is, however, both this talent and effect are surpassed by the wonderful skill and ease with which he *contrasts characters with themselves*, as in this one of Falconbridge. The graduated manner in which he contrives to make one master-passion supersede another, and each in turn to become the dominant, still retaining the integrity, and even plausibility of the original construction, is in itself a profound metaphysical study.

One more remark upon this grand personation. Upon the question that the reign of King John was deficient in characters fully answering the demand for the *dramatic* interest in the play, and that in consequence the instinct of our poet perceiving the necessity for a supply of *representative* characters to meet that demand, the fine character just dismissed,—certainly one of the very finest in the whole gallery of Shakesperian *inventive* portraits,—is precisely the "representative" character required. Thoroughly Gothic in features and proportions, and as thoroughly English in temper and spirit, his presence rays life and manliness into every part of the drama, where they would else be wanting. "Is it strange," says well the Boston editor of our poet, "that a nation which could grow such originals, should have surpassed the rest of the world in all that is vigorous, and useful, and great?"

Beautifully conceived, too, is the career of Hubert. It would seem that no circumstance in his deportment, up to the period of his temptation by the king, could harmonise with his fulfilling the horrid mission he had undertaken; nevertheless, his being a court-retainer, and a pliant and assiduous one, justifies his being selected by John as the tool for his cruel purpose. In the last Act, Hubert nobly clears himself from suspicion of having murdered the child; and his scene in the prison, with the little prince pleading for his eyes, can barely receive the due estimation of its tenderness and genuine pathos. The opening of the 4th Act.

As an instance of the caution with which Shakespeare conducts and fills up the design in his dramas, and contrives to make even the most subordinate parts accord with the main outline, and constitute a portion and necessary adjunct to the consummated plot, may be noticed the introduction on the scene of the dying French lord, Melun,—with the sublime lesson put into the mouth of a man, "right in whose eyes are seen the cruel pangs of death." At that solemnest moment of all the junctures in a man's life, it was especially fine in the poet to place truth, and honour, and fidelity in contrast with dissimulation, fraud, and treachery. The revolted English nobles have gone over to the French king, and Melun warns them to fly; for that his sovereign, if victorious, means to recompense their services to him by cutting off their heads. Well might Salisbury exclaim, "I'm stifled with this smell of sin!" The dying speech of this French lord—one of the least important agents, be it observed, in the history—is scarcely to be exceeded in effect by any other in the play. He says :—

"Have I not hideous death within my view,
Retaining but a quantity of life,
Which bleeds away, ev'n as a form of wax
Resolveth from his figure 'gainst the fire?
What in the world should make me now deceive,
Since I must lose the use of all deceit?
Why should I then be false; since it is true
That I must die here, and live hence by truth?
I say again, if Lewis do win the day,
He is forsworn if e'er those eyes of yours
Behold another day break in the east.
But even this night, whose black contagious breath
Already smokes about the burning crest
Of the old, feeble, and day-wearied sun,
Even this ill night, your breathing shall expire,
Paying the fine of rated treachery
Even with a treacherous fine of all your lives,
If Lewis, by your assistance, win the day."

These revolted nobles, too, are sketched with the same propriety and distinctness that mark all the poet's characters, however slight the portion of words they have to deliver. Thus, we have the Lord Salisbury, generous and gentle, sympathising with the Lady Constance in her sorrows,—the text to his character being traceable in her words, as is frequently the case in Shakespeare: thus, it is imperative upon all actors studying their parts, to study likewise all the other characters in the piece, for hints as to their own characters and by-play; so artfully, and, withal, so naturally do they dove-tail, and carry out and explain each other. Thus Constance, in her address to Salisbury, upon hearing that her professing ally, the French king, had joined issue with John against the claim of her son Arthur :—

"What dost thou mean by shaking of thy head?
Why dost thou look so sadly on my son?

> What means that hand upon that breast of thine?
> Why holds thine eye that lamentable rheum,
> Like a proud river peering o'er his bounds?
> Be these sad signs confirmers of thy words?"

And again, in the scene with the Dauphin, (the 2d of the 5th Act,) we find him bewailing his own disloyalty in a beautiful strain of regret and self-reproach.

In the scenes at the court of King John, he is distinguished by a graceful flow of courtier-like eloquence; for his is the oft-quoted speech that he utters upon the *second* coronation of the king, which he says is,—

> "To gild refined gold, to paint the lily,
> To throw a perfume on the violet,
> To smooth the ice, or add another hue
> Unto the rainbow; or with taper light
> To seek the eye of heaven to garnish."

This eloquence is ingeniously contrasted with Pembroke's more blunt and straightforward utterance; and the characteristic diversity between these two lords is consistently maintained throughout the play.

In Pembroke's mouth is appropriately put one of those sly, side-wind girds at the French that, as an Englishman, Shakespeare could not restrain. In one of the skirmishes, Pembroke says,—

> "Up, once again; put spirit in the French:
> If they miscarry, we miscarry too."

He and Salisbury having gone over to the French party. In concluding my remarks upon the characters in this play of King John, I would subjoin a few upon the style of its reproduction at Drury Lane Theatre in 1842, under the management of Mr Macready.

In the first place, the difficulty of representing the skirmishes and alarms of battle on the stage—till then historically and proverbially ludicrous—was on that occasion triumphantly overcome. The siege of Angiers was a serious event. Also, the whole department which is technically styled the "getting-up," the scenery, and the costume, were absolutely perfect: it was a gorgeous pictorial illustration of a great dramatic poem. But what I would principally distinguish as the crowning talent displayed in that very fine revival, was the conception of the character of King John himself. It was the more artistical, inasmuch as the peculiar moral features of that bad king are rather to be suggested to the imagination than palpably and broadly developed. The stealthy watchfulness, the crafty caution, and the want of faith in human goodness, are all features that demand acute discrimination to perceive, and refined and delicate touches to embody.

It requires subdued deportment, self-mistrust, or rather the want of self-confidence—nice points of character to study, and all which few actors dare to personate with fidelity, because, unless they be understood and appreciated by an audience, it is frequently thought to be tame or under acting.

The whole character and bearing of John, in the version of Shakespeare, form a striking contrast to those of Henry V.* The one is ardent, brave, confident in the love and support of his people—the true English king; the other, wily, artful, making every movement by a stratagem, and feeling that he holds his subjects by no other tenure than the right of might, and an appeal to the baser passions of their nature.

They who call to mind those two brilliant and impetuous speeches—those rousing appeals to the zeal of his people in Henry V.—beginning, "Once more unto the breach, dear friends," in the 3d Act; and, "What's he that wishes so? my

* Mr Macready had previously revived the play of "Henry V." at Covent Garden Theatre, with prodigal magnificence and splendour.

cousin Westmoreland?" the celebrated speech upon the eve of the Agincourt fight; and then draw a parallel between them and the speech that King John makes to the citizens of Angiers, in the 2d Act,—

"These flags of France that are advanced here,
Before the eye and prospect of your town,"

sneaking his way, as it were, and feeling the pulse, as he proceeds, of those whom he is addressing,—they, I repeat, who institute a comparison between these speeches in the two plays, will perceive my meaning. These words may be taken as keys to the two characters. In John we have no confiding appeals, no "dear friends;" but the extortionate tyrant to his people appears in such phrases as—

"Ere our coming, see thou shake the bags
Of hoarding abbots; imprison'd angels
Set at liberty: the fat ribs of peace
Must by the hungry now be fed upon:
Use our commission in its utmost force."

Compare this with Harry Monmouth's courageous and magnanimous reflection:—

"There is some soul of goodness in things evil,
Would men observingly distil it out;
For our bad neighbour makes us early stirrers,
Which is both healthful and good husbandry:
Besides, they are our outward consciences,
And preachers to us all; admonishing,
That we should dress us fairly for our end.
Thus may we gather honey from the weed,
And make a moral of the devil himself."

And then note his playful intercourse with his soldiers, and those sprightly exclamations to his faithful old adherent, Sir Thomas Erpingham, "God 'a mercy, old heart, thou speakest cheerfully." Compare his confident reliance on his English bosoms, with John's misgivings and doubts, as of a man conscious and feeling that he has no right to the love of his subjects in the scene of his recoronation: "And looked upon, I hope, with cheerful eyes." And again, "I have a way to win their loves again;" as well as his storm of reproach and remorse, and base endeavour to shift the ponderous load of his guilt on to the shoulders of his instrument, Hubert.

After this comparison, they who fortunately witnessed the two performances, will not forget the manner in which Mr Macready impersonated the two kings, and the artistical way in which he demonstrated the unhappiness of wickedness throughout his King John; the gradual and constant declension of his spirit, its tide being always at the ebb; his small amount of confidence, his suggested consciousness of meanness, guilt, and the loss of all respect; his bearing latterly as that of a man who felt that indignant eyes were flashing on him, and his gait as if surrounded by pitfalls; in short, the general substratum of wretchedness which pervades the whole character, and yet is only known and felt, not blazoned; all this unprotruded demeanour, and which the million do not appreciate, greatly surpassed in merit the conception, even of his dying scene, terrifically real as that was.

Alexander placed the poems of Homer in a jewelled casket of inestimable price, the shrine being an emblem only of the offering; and the late theatrical regenerator presented the public with illuminated editions of the world's poet; superb, indeed, and wholly worthy of the text, were it only by reason of the zeal with which they were executed.

XIV.

# The Winter's Tale.

# XIV.

# THE WINTER'S TALE.

THE general plot and incidental circumstances of "The Winter's Tale" are more varied, exciting, and sensuously appealing than perhaps any other of Shakespeare's plays.

The jealousy of Leontes, which occasions the distressful portion of the story, is not, like the jealousy of Othello, cautiously and gradually introduced, artfully developed, fanned, heightened, and exasperated to its awful climax of assassination and suicidal punishment; but it bursts forth at once with a sudden explosion, it partakes more of the character of a paroxysm of disease; and it as quickly subsides into the humility of self-reproach, and the very abandonment to a meek and pliant repentance. The character of Leontes is essentially that of a weak man; his contrition is not more extreme and pitiable than his rage; and no one knew better than Shakespeare that the one is almost invariably the consequent of the other. In these contrasted impulses, nothing can be more opposed than the two natures of Leontes and Othello. Both are jealous men, both pursue the same cruel course, both are touched with remorse; yet, from their several intellectual conformations, as the one (Othello) never wholly loses our sympathy, not to say even our respect; the other (Leontes) never commands them.

In the laying forth of this character, some writers have objected that the jealous change brought forth in his disposition and conduct is too sudden and too extreme, and that there appears no previous indication to render plausible so complete a subversion of his ostensible ordinary nature.

It is, no doubt, an unusual course with Shakespeare to introduce abrupt, as well as violent antagonisms in character; he more commonly, nay, indeed, he almost constantly allows a dormant passion to germ and sprout forth, and effloresce by slow degrees, so that we recognise and accompany the alteration from its first development to its conclusion. Nature herself, however, has her anomalies, her freaks, her caprices; and that person's observation and knowledge of character have made no great strides in acquirement, that cannot verify the most remarkable as well as sudden transformations in the conduct of certain individuals, and which, not unusually, have arisen from some casual and slight inducement. Such mental transfigurations almost uniformly take place in highly excitable and impulsive natures; and it is to be observed that this was precisely the component of the mind of Leontes, whose every action betrays the weak and unstable man. As, therefore, there was not the time allowed in the progress of the drama for his passion of jealousy to be *gradually* pre-indicated, we may fairly give the poet the advantage of its extempore explosion. We are to bear in mind that the passion of Othello forms the great master-feature of that tragedy, and there is *no episode to sever its interest;* it is one integral history. The episode in "The Winter's Tale"—the history of Perdita and her Florizel—bears almost equal sway of importance with the serious and pathetic portion; the original cause of it, the jealousy of Leontes, could not therefore have been brought to occupy a larger space in the combined plot.

Upon the causes and consequences of Leontes's passion,

Schlegel makes the following remark. He says:—"It is a passion with whose effects the spectator is more concerned than with its origin, and which does not produce the catastrophe, but merely ties the knot of the piece. In fact, the poet might perhaps have wished to indicate slightly that Hermione, though virtuous, was too active in her efforts to please Polixenes, and it appears as if this germ of an inclination first attained its proper maturity in their children." But the German critic should have perceived that Hermione's "efforts to please Polixenes" were all made at the immediate instigation of her husband, and that it was, in fact, to *please Leontes*, that she endeavoured to please Polixenes, and induce him to prolong his stay. Any one carefully perusing that opening scene, will discern, from Hermione's words and bearing—playful, gracefully winning, the lady-hostess persuading a guest to remain—that she is merely acting in consonance with her husband's expressed wish. The very constancy of her reference to *him* through all her speech to their visitor, bears testimony to the pure singleness of his noble wife.

The character of Hermione is that of the truly classical heroine of a tragic drama; she is worthy of the Greek Muse, a perfectly regal woman, who claims our homage, respect, and esteem by reason of her station, conduct, and social virtues, and, of course, our sympathy on account of the persecution she endured, and her unmerited sufferings. I know not, however, whether this feeling be not enhanced by the one indication she manifests of being a really feminine creature—that of forgetting her own individual affliction, and falling senseless at the news of the death of her son, Mamillius. But the pervading and substantive quality in Hermione's character is that of a grand and unqualified magnanimity, taking the course of invincible firmness and constancy. Wronged by her husband's hideous suspicions, outraged by a public attainder, mock trial, and imprisonment, wounded through the persons of her children by his inhuman decrees, she consigns herself to a living grave. Finding remonstrance worse than fruitless, seeing that it exasperates him, she takes refuge in a proud, indignant silence, sternly willing it to be eternal. Her conduct throughout is consistent in lofty courage and self-respect. Her first emotion, upon finding herself the object of her husband's wild accusations, is sheer surprise and incredulity. "What, is this sport?" she exclaims. Her second is honest, indignant refutation of the groundless charge, and reliance upon her husband's belief in her word:—

> "But I'd say he had not,
> And I'll be sworn you would believe my saying,
> Howe'er you lean to the nayward."

Her third a burning denial of the calumny, checked by a remembrance of what is due to him who is her accuser:—

> "Should a villain say so,
> The most replenish'd villain in the world,
> He were as much more villain: you, my lord,
> *Do but mistake.*"

Her next speech is a mingling of implied conscious innocence and resolute patience—a patience which can afford pity for its mistaken impugner:—

> "How will this grieve you,
> When you shall come to clearer knowledge, that
> You thus have publish'd me! Gentle my lord,
> You scarce can right me throughly then, to say
> You did mistake."

And her concluding words, as she withdraws, are full of the most lofty self-assertion, with magnanimity of quiet rebuke:—

> "Beseech your highness,
> My women may be with me; for you see
> My plight requires it. [*To them.*] Do not weep, good fools,
> There is no cause; when you shall know your mistress

Has deserv'd prison, then abound in tears
As I come out. This action I now go on
Is for my better grace. [*To him.*] Adieu, my lord,
I never wish'd to see you sorry; *now,*
*I trust I shall.*"

This is accurately the utterance of a woman with whom the usual feminine resource of tears and lamentings forms no part of her character. Hermione is peculiarly self-concentrated, self-reliant, and uncomplaining. She says of herself:—

"Good, my lords,
I am not prone to weeping, as our sex
Commonly are—the want of which *vain dew*
Perchance shall dry your pities; but I have
That honourable grief lodg'd here, which burns
Worse than tears drown."

A weeping woman would not have fallen senseless on hearing of the death of her child; but Hermione is exactly and entirely the woman to make that grand speech of self-justification which she does upon her trial, pleading her own cause, courageously maintaining her innocence, calmly and confidently appealing to her husband's own conscience for her honourable acquittal: and, when all is useless, bowing to the full tide of her misfortunes, and shrouding herself beneath self-imposed death-in-life as the sole reprisal upon his injurious, his heinous treatment.

As an extraordinary piece of consistency in character-painting, it were well noted that in the concluding scene of the play, when Hermione is restored to her husband Leontes, her reconciliation with him is marked by *silent action,* not by words. We learn from the bystanders that she "embraces him," and "hangs about his neck," on coming down from the pedestal where she has enacted her own statue—but *she utters no syllable.* Words of tenderness and fond sentences were not for the mouth of a woman who had shown her enduring consciousness of the injuries she had sustained, by a sixteen years' sequestration of herself from his side. For Hermione there was nothing but a demeanour that should speak for itself; and she accordingly throws herself mutely into his arms, that his heart may comprehend all that hers would say to it. This is the eloquence of magnanimity in tacit evidence, perfectly befitting the majesty and self-respective dignity of Hermione's character.

The slight and fleeting sketch of the little prince, Mamillius, is remarkably beautiful both in character and treatment. His conversation with his father, whose jealous ravings he cannot comprehend, is conceived in the perfection of dramatic incident; and what a touch of art, and of nature too, at the moment when the king, his father, is writhing with suspicion of his queen's dishonesty, to put those words into his little, unconscious mouth, "*I am like you,* they say." In that simple scene, too, (the 1st in the 2d Act,) with his mother and her ladies, Shakespeare seems to have got at the very heart of childhood-nature—as he did of all other nature. The child says to one of the ladies who invites him to come and be her playfellow—

"No, I 'll none of you ;
You 'll *kiss me hard, and speak to me as if*
*I were a baby still.*"

As a set-oft against the pathetic incidents in the play, we have the bright creation of the enchanting Perdita, than whose love with her Florizel (the young prince, and son of Polixenes) we shall scarcely find anything more fresh and youthful, and nothing more pastoral, yet princely and refined. The grouped scene at the sheep-shearing is like a Grecian bass-relief; and her speeches to the guests are finer than anything of the kind, either in the old or the new world of poetry. Such is the address to her lover, accompanying the presentation of a coronal of flowers, and which, though familiar as household words, should never be alluded to without reviving:—

"Now, my fairest friend,
I would I had some flowers o' the spring that might
Become your time of day. * * * *
* * * * * O Proserpina,
For the flowers now, that, frighted, thou let'st fall
From Dis's waggon! daffodils,
That come before the swallow dares, and take
The winds of March with beauty; violets dim,
But sweeter than the lids of Juno's eyes,
Or Cytherea's breath; pale primroses,
That die unmarried, ere they can behold
Bright Phœbus in his strength—a malady
Most incident to maids; bold oxlips, and
The crown-imperial; lilies of all kinds,
The flower-de-luce being one. Oh, these I lack
To make you garlands of; and, my sweet friend,
To strew him o'er and o'er!
"*Flo.* What! like a corse?
"*Per.* No, like a bank, for love to lie and play on;
Not like a corse; or if,—not to be buried,
But quick, and in mine arms."

Well might the enraptured Florizel exclaim, "What you do still betters what is done!" He has already told her—

"I bless the time
When my good falcon made her flight across
Thy father's ground."

In the same scene with these two young princely creatures, (the 3d of the 4th Act,) there is another touch of loveliness and natural emotion. The old lord, Camillo, and Polixenes, Florizel's father, have attended the sheep-shearing, disguised, and are watching the love-making of the young couple. Camillo says:—

> "*He tells her something*
> *That makes her blood look out.*"

With his usual thought and consistency in the classification of character, it is to be observed that in that of Perdita, Shakespeare never compromises—he never even loses sight of her royal descent; and the manner in which he has indicated that self-assertion and wilfulness of nature (the usual concomitants of royalty) are as remarkable as they are amusing. Polixenes makes the observation—

> "This is the prettiest low-born lass that ever
> Ran on the greensward; nothing she does or seems
> But *smacks of something greater than herself,*
> *Too noble for this place.*"

Her first self-betrayal occurs at the sheep-shearing feast, where, like a true scion of the class administered *to*, and the *not*-administering class, she neglects the guests, and receives the rebuke from her old foster-father, the Shepherd:—

> "Fie, daughter! when my old wife liv'd,
> Upon this day she was both pantler, butler, cook;
> Both dame and servant; welcom'd all, serv'd all;
> Would sing her song, dance her turn; now here,
> At upper end o' the table; now i' the middle;
> On his shoulder, and on his—her face o' fire
> With labour; and the thing she took to quench it,
> She would to each one sip. You are retir'd
> As if you were a feasted one, and not
> The hostess of the meeting."

Here we have the royal instinct of dignity in "exclusiveness." Again, in the conversation with Polixenes upon the culture of the "streaked gillyflowers," of which she cares not to "get slips for her garden;" when he asks, "Wherefore, gentle maiden, do you neglect them?" She answers,—

> "For that I have heard it said,
> There is an art that, in their piedness, shares

With great creating Nature.
"*Polix.* Say there be,
Yet Nature is made better by no mean,
But Nature makes that mean: so, over that Art,
Which you say adds to Nature, is an Art
That Nature makes. You see, sweet maid, we marry
A gentler scion to the wildest stock;
And make conceive a bark of baser kind
By bud of nobler race. This is an art
Which does mend Nature,—change it rather: but
The art itself is Nature.
"*Per.* So it is.
"*Polix.* Then make your garden rich in gillyflow'rs,
And do not call them bastards.
"*Per.* *I'll not put*
*The dibble in earth to set one slip of them.*"

Here we have a specimen of royal and—with the meekest deference be it suggested—of *womanly* obstinacy. She has not an argument to face the king's; but having once said she cared not to grow them, she sticks to her text:—

"I'll not put
The dibble in earth to set one slip of them."

Very regal, too,—the giving no reason for her resolution.

Lastly, for the royal instinct as conveyed in her self-assertion of equality—and this the most remarkable example. When King Polixenes has forbidden their union, and then threatens her with death if she "open their rural latch to her lover's entrance;" after the king has gone, she says:—

"I was not much afear'd; for once or twice
I was about to speak, and tell him plainly,
The self-same sun that shines upon his court,
Hides not his visage from our cottage, but
Looks on alike."

Shakespeare never would have put that speech into the mouth of a commoner. Scan him and sift him as we may, we always detect a "foregone conclusion" in his most evanescent shades of character.

The finest indication that Perdita gives of her greatness and constancy of heart, is in the quiet answer she makes to the old lord, Camillo, who is setting before the two young lovers the trials of adversity they must encounter in their projected flight from Bohemia. The old friend concludes his dissuasion with these words:—

> "Prosperity's the very bond of love;
> Whose fresh complexion, and whose heart together,
> Affliction alters."

Perdita simply replies:—

> "One of these is true:
> I think affliction may subdue the cheek,
> But not take in the mind."

That is true heroism; and it is the heroism of a young heart. But not only the queen-mother's steadfastness of temper with repose of manner are renewed in Perdita's speech and conduct, but the personal likeness to Hermione is denoted by an exquisite touch that Shakespeare could not fail to add upon a favourable occasion. In the 1st scene of the 5th Act, where Leontes is looking upon his daughter, unconscious that she is such, and standing there in maiden youth and loveliness, the faithful Paulina recalls him to himself, with the half rebuke:—

> "Sir, my liege,
> Your eye hath too much youth in't: not a month
> 'Fore your queen died, she was more worth such gazes
> Than what you look on now.
> "*Leon.* I thought of *her*,
> *Even in these looks I made.*"

There is a parallel scene in the 1st scene of the 5th Act of "Pericles," even more touching in its eloquence, where the king, staring upon his daughter, Marina, has his belief in her worth confirmed by the living picture she presents to his soul of his dead wife, Thaisa.

The glorious old poet Chaucer—and it is delightful to bring two such natures in unison—has a passage, in his own simple beauty of style, indicating the like creed of native sympathy in resemblance.

It is where Constance's little son is brought into his father, King Alla's presence; and we have the vivid sketch of the incident in two lines:—

> "Before Allà, during the meatè's space,
> *The child stood, looking in the kingè's face.*"

The father is struck by the child's look; and we all know the pertinacious gaze of a child; and he inquires:—

> "Whose is that faire child that standeth yonder?"

Obtaining no satisfactory answer to his question, the story goes on to say:—

> "Now was this child as like unto Constance
> As possible is a creäture to be:
> This Alla hath the face in remembrance
> Of Dame Constance, and thereon musèd he,
> If that the childè's mother were aught she
> That is his wife; and *privily he sight,* [sighed,]
> *And sped him from the table that he might.*"

That touch of his sighing, and hurrying from the room to hide his emotion, is in the true dramatic feeling of nature and passion.

Paulina, the attendant and companion of the Queen Hermione, is an example of what might be adduced as an "end-on" partisan. An American would call her a "go-ahead" friend. She never for one moment has a misgiving with respect to the conduct of her injured queen and mistress; neither does she pause to consider the critical nature of her own position in the court, or to swerve one jot from her purpose, when denouncing to the king his purblind jealousy and barbarous persecution of his consort. Paulina is a specimen of those headstrong women who, taking up the broad principle of a question or a cause, allow no minor point to sway or interfere with their course of action. It is this wedge-like character in women which makes them such perplexing opponents in a party-question. Shakespeare knew this quite as well as we do; and he had witnessed some remarkable examples of its truth in the party-feuds that arose out of the bloated injustice visited upon the worthy Katherine of Aragon, and the heart-burning triumph of Anne Boleyn, with the Protestant succession, to say nothing of the kidnapping and execution of the Scottish queen. There were "end-on" partisans enough in his time; and Margaret Lamburn, who in open court aimed a dagger at the heart of Queen Elizabeth, was a specimen of the Paulina species.

There is another point in the female character that Shakespeare has exemplified with his usual felicity, in the conduct of Paulina. When a woman has once got the right end of the staff in a contest with a man, and has quelled her opponent, she does play the tattoo upon his skull with an amazing vivacity—and after he is down, too. When Leontes has come to a sense of his barbarity towards his queen, and is wallowing in the very slough of mean despondency, Paulina cannot forego the gratification of punching him in his maundering distress. He says:—

> "Whilst I remember
> Her and her virtues, I cannot forget
> My blemishes in them: and so still think of
> The wrong I did myself, which was so much,
> That heirless it hath made my kingdom, and
> Destroy'd the sweet'st companion that e'er man
> Bred his hopes out of."

Paulina answers :—

"True, too true, my lord :
If one by one you wedded all the world,
Or, from the all that are, took something good
To make a perfect woman, she you kill'd
Would be unparallell'd."

His reply displays the very prostration of self-abasement :—

"I think so. Kill'd!
She I kill'd! I did so; but *thou strik'st me*
*Sorely to say I did;* it is as bitter
Upon thy tongue as in my thought; now, good now,
*Say so but seldom.*"

It is observable that the only person in the play who encounters the severity of retributive justice is the lord Antigonus; and we scarcely regret his fate since he lent himself to the king's cruelty (however unwillingly and by oath) to leave the infant Perdita on the desert sea-shore of a strange country; a savage hire,—and the wages he receives are as dispiteous, for he is devoured by a beast. This scene, which first introduces the old shepherd and his son, is distinguished by that mixture of the horrible and the ludicrous which no one ventures upon but Dame Nature and Shakespeare. The old man, who has been wandering about the sea-shore in the storm, searching for a stray sheep, stumbles upon the babe, and in his astonishment at the circumstance, calls out to his son, who immediately echoes his summons :—

"What, art so near? [says the old shepherd.] If thou 'lt see a thing to talk on when thou art dead and rotten, come hither. What ailest thou, man?

"*Clown.* I have seen two such sights by sea and by land! but I am not to say it is a sea, for it is now the sky; betwixt the firmament and it you cannot thrust a bodkin's point."

It will be remembered how this same effect of a storm is described in Othello, where the persons talking are gentlemen and scholars. One speaks of the "wind-shak'd surge with high and monstrous mane;" and the other speaks of the "main and the aerial blue becoming an *indistinct regard.*"

The clown, with his rustic imagination, has none but homely comparisons, and afterwards he talks of the "yeast and froth as you'd *thrust a cork into a hogshead.*" These are minutiæ of consistency that have been often alluded to.

The Clown goes on :—

"Oh, the most piteous cry of the poor souls! *Sometimes to see 'em, and not to see 'em:* now the ship boring the moon with her main-mast. * * * And then for the land-service,—to see how the bear tore out his shoulder-bone—and how he cried to me for help, and said he was Antigonus—a nobleman!"

"What care these roarers for the name of king?" says the Boatswain in the "Tempest;" but how horribly natural is this scene! The fact which was uppermost in the Clown's mind —the tearing up of the man's shoulder-blade—he speaks of first, and without any preface, and afterwards describes his name and quality. Then he goes on :—

"But to make an end of the ship, to see how the sea flap-dragoned it; but first, how the poor souls roared, and the sea mocked them, and how the poor gentleman roared, and the bear mocked *him*, both roaring louder than the sea or weather.

"*Shep.* Name of mercy, when was this, boy?

"*Clown.* Now, *now!* I haven't winked since I saw these sights; the men are not yet cold under water, nor the bear half dined on the gentleman; *he's at it now!*"

Well, they turn to the infant Perdita, and lifting up their hands and eyes at the golden treasure that Antigonus has left with her, the old man proposes to his son to take the "next way home;" and here Shakespeare cannot close the scene without a parting touch of rustic humanity, which he puts into the mouth of the Clown :—

"Go you the next way with your findings; I'll go see if the bear be gone from the gentleman, and *how much he hath eaten.* They are never curst [mischievous] but when they are hungry. *If there be any of him left I will bury it.*"

This, in itself, is a trifling incident to notice, but a natural one, for the common people have a reverence, even to superstition, for the decencies of sepulture.

Among the subordinate characters in "The Winter's Tale," the noblemen about the court of Leontes do not offer any distinguishing characteristic worth dwelling upon, unless it be the unparallelled one of their all taking side with their brother-courtier, and against the king! Camillo is a fine honest fellow, who mainly assists to bring the estranged parties to a union; and there is a naturally and artistically-contrived conversation among some "Gentlemen" in the 2d scene of the 5th Act, who are describing to each other the meeting of the two kings, the discovery of Perdita to be the daughter of Leontes, and, in short, the hurrying of the plot to its climax of efflorescence. The whole dialogue is perfectly graphic; and immediately upon the heels of it we have the introduction of the old shepherd and his son, who have received honourable preferment for their faithful nurture of the little princess—a capital specimen of low comedy. The bumpkins absolutely reel under their promotion and fine clothes. The son talks of the "kings and princes—*our kindred*"—and, like a true lout, he does not see that they have condescended to him, but he instantly rushes on to their level, and so, with delightful humour, he rattles away:—

"I was a gentleman born before my father, for the king's son took me by the hand and called me brother, and the two kings called my father brother, and then the prince *my brother* called my father father, and so we wept, and there was the first gentleman-like tears that ever we shed."

Mopsa, one of the country wenches—and she and Dorcas are sisters of a class—is a type of that fraternity of women—

both high and low—who have just sufficient brains to see their own mercenary interest in all they do, and not one jot else; who are just so acute as to turn to gain, to profit, all that they possess, while to their truest and most real advantages and privileges they are as obtusely blind as earthworms. A trinket, a bauble, engrosses such a woman's soul to the exclusion of aught beside. She will go through any amount of meanness to wheedle a man into purchasing it for her, while, with it, *he* may beguile *her* of any amount of unworthy submission. The pedlar's knacks and gaudy trash absorb Mopsa's whole gloating vision; she never ceases pestering her swain to "buy" for her; she even gives up the darling delight of bickering and squabbling with Dorcas for the dearer delight of coaxing all she can out of her soft-skulled gallant. That he finds his account in "treating" her we gather from her own obtuse betrayals. In Mopsa's eagerness for the pedlar's tawdry laces and ribbons, with the fool's price she blindly pays for them, believing that she gets them for "*nothing*"—that eternal pitfall of the fool-buyer!—"Getting a bargain for nothing!"—in Mopsa's cupidity we have a symbol of those of her sex who, for a shawl, a bracelet, or a silk dress, sacrifice their dignity of spirit, their honesty of truth, their self-respect. They calculate that it costs them only a few fawning words—"only!" when in these are comprised the abandonment of women's just claims to be the friend and "equal" of man, which they are everlastingly talking about, and using such miserable means to accomplish.

And now talk we of that prince of quicksilver rogues—Master Autolycus. O thou type of all the nimble-fingered race that have plied in their vocation since the gallies and the gallows were instituted to teach men the principles of equitable adjustment, and accurately to know the distinction between "meum and tuum," and not to confound and misapply the "golden rule of proportion."

Master Autolycus!—that rogue of rogues! that *arch*-rogue! that knave of knaves! that inexhaustible wag of a pedlar! that scampering rip of a wayfaring huckster! With what a light hand he disposes of momentous considerations! with what an easy style he settles questions of conscience! "Beating and hanging [he says] are terrors to me;—for the life to come, *I sleep out the thought of it.*" How skimmingly he relates that, "having flown over many knavish professions, he settled down in rogue;" and he is an adept in the profession he has settled down in, having made its principles his earnest study, and having taken his degree, F.F.D., ("Professor and Doctor of Thieving,") thus he delivers to them "ex cathedra"—"To have an open ear, a quick eye, and a nimble hand is necessary for a cutpurse; a good nose is requisite also to smell out work for the other senses."

His ineffable disinterestedness in refusing donations is on a par with his dexterity in "raising the supplies;" for, upon having helped himself to what he wanted from the country fellow's pocket, what ludicrous earnestness, and what sincerity, too, in declining the proffered bounty:—"Offer me no money, I pray you; that kills my heart." What a zest, what intense relish he has in trickery! and what solemn horror of rectitude! when he has filched the shepherd's purse, exclaiming after him:—"I'll be with you at your sheep-shearing, too. If I make not this cheat bring out another, and the shearers prove sheep, let me be unrolled, and *my name put in the book of virtue.*" And then, at the prospect of mischief, he falls into a merry song, for very jollity of heart; the *fun* of the mischief being his "primum mobile"—his main principle of action.

He has a positive and unmitigated contempt for right and justice, as being indeed poor and very shallow affairs—and dull;—so, with what a twinkle of the eye, and irrepressible drollery beneath all, he shows that the *humour* of the thing is to him the main point. Laughing, he shouts, "What a fool Honesty is!—and Trust, his sworn brother, a very simple gentleman." He plumes himself upon his high-bred rascality in a strain of devout thankfulness, as he contemplates the simpleton-innocence of the two shepherds:—"How blest are we that are not simple men! Yet Nature might have made me as these are;—therefore I'll not disdain!" What delicious gusto and relish! and what wit! Again—defending himself from the charge of rectitude—*except by accident*—"Though I am not naturally honest, I am so sometimes *by chance*." And when he quits his pedlar clothes, and pedlar deportment, and has been promoted, with what magnificence of rebuke he charges the others not to misbehave themselves:—"And let me have no *lying; it becomes none but tradesmen!*" (O my beloved Willie! what a cordial philosopher wast thou!)

Gines de Passamonte was a callous and vulgar prig compared with thee, *my* Autolycus; for, of a surety, thou wouldst have respected the romantic benevolence of La Mancha's knight;—never wouldst thou, with a rascal ingratitude, have pashed that venerable face with the rude flint-stones, after he had delivered thee out of the hands of the ruthless alguazil. Compared, too, with thee, the renowned and much-belauded Du Val was a coxcomb and a dandy. He was a dancing-master plunged into an ungenial element—the younger brother, mayhap, of some sleek do-nothing; and so he inherited the instinct of living by faith upon his species,—"taking no more thought than lilies" for the morrow,—sufficient for the day being the plunder thereof. That such a kiddy should have made his public exit from the Tyburn stage in an embroidered dress, bag-wig, ruffles, and fringed gloves, was befitting his "exquisite" nature. He walked his minuet in life, and he danced out of it with a caper and a "galop à la corde."

Happy for thee, my merry Autolycus, that thou wast not merely a natural rogue—a rogue in grain, thoroughbred from a long and legitimate ancestry; but that, with all thy small filchings—thy "quips, and cranks, and wanton *wiles*"—the serene villainy of thy face—the solemnity of thy adjurations, and the glib-earnestness of thy protestations—thy romantic cheats—thy florid lies—thou hadst therewithal a lurking grain of good nature in thy composition;—that "salt preserved thee." Thou wast, it is true, a confirmed and a solid thief; but then thou wast *born* as well as *bred* to that branch of the "conveyancing" profession; and couldst thou have changed the Ethiop skin of thy nature, thou mightst have become a distrainer for rent, or a surcharger of taxes—possibly, an informer; and then we should have missed all thy merriment.

I am glad thou wast not hanged, my Autolycus! Such a destiny would have been a sorry climax to thy uncruel misdemeanours. Who but a churl could stop that throat, of which the shepherd's hind, who comes running in, says, in an ecstasy of delight:—

"O master! if you did but hear the pedlar at the door, you would never dance again after a tabor and pipe;—no, the bagpipe couldn't move you. He sings several tunes faster than you'll tell money. He utters them as though he had *eaten* ballads, and all men's ears grew to his tunes. He hath songs for man or woman, of all sizes: no milliner can so fit his customers with gloves. He hath the prettiest love-songs for maids; * * * with such delicate burdens of "dildos" and "fadings," "jump her" and "thump her," [burdens of song-writers of the time.] And he hath ribands of all the colours i' the rainbow; points, more than all the lawyers in Bohemia can handle, though they come to him by the gross; inkles, caddises, cambrics, lawns:—why, he sings them over as they were gods or goddesses. You would think a smock were a *she-angel,* he so chants to the sleeve-hand, and the work about the square on't."

Perdita, the lady innate, says:—"Forewarn him that he

use no scurrilous words in his tunes." Then in he comes singing:—

" Lawn as white as driven snow;
Cyprus black as e'er was crow;
Gloves as sweet as damask roses;
Masks for faces and for noses;
Bugle bracelet, necklace amber,
Perfume for a lady's chamber;
Golden quoifs and stomachers,
For my lads to give their dears;
Pins and poking-sticks of steel,
What maids lack from head to heel;
Come, buy of me, come; come buy, come buy;
Buy lads, or else your lasses cry:
Come buy."

Go thy ways, thou merriest of vagabonds! I could better spare a much better man than thou, Autolycus, my pet thief.

The probabilities and the possibilities, the imputed anachronisms, and the geographical blunders in "The Winter's Tale," have, I confess, never disturbed my rest—they never kept me awake at night. I leave the technical prudery of such objections to those dilettanti coxcombs in criticism, who, when they are contemplating Raphael's cartoon of the Miraculous Draught of Fishes, pass over the *face* of the Messiah, and proceed to measure the proportions of the *boat* in which He is seated; and then triumphantly tell us, that to be able to sit in that boat were a miracle equal to the one that had just been performed. The delineations of character and passion in this play; the decoration of the poetry, consorting in tender beauty with the rural simplicity of the subject, always transport me back to that golden age when the imagination ran loose amid the odorous glades of poetry, unfretted and unjaded by the burrs and briers of low-thoughted cares and carking anxieties. He who takes us from the smoke and stir of everyday toil, and laps us in the Elysium of our boyish days—blood-stirring and hopeful—is a benefactor to his species; and to no mortal do I more owe this reminiscence, and gratitude for it, than to

WILLIAM SHAKESPEARE.

# XV.

# Richard the Second.

## XV.

# RICHARD II.

---

THE dramatic poet could scarcely have desired two finer subjects to fulfil all the requisites of contrasted character than are to be found in the historical play of "Richard II." It would be difficult to describe two natures more opposed to each other at all points than those which really existed in the unhappy son of the Black Prince, and of his crafty cousin and deposer, the offspring of "Old Gaunt." Richard, whose faults almost wholly arose from defect of judgment—the elements of which, notwithstanding, were estimable, and whose affections were active and overflowing;—who, if he *did* lavish his favours upon unworthy creatures, could nevertheless appreciate the virtues and the love of his first consort—the "Good Queen Anne," as she was called; and who, while she lived, exercised an angelic influence over his conduct; and when she died, such was the transport—not to say the insanity—of his grief, that he destroyed the palace where they had lived in happiness together;—who in his single person, and during his nonage, quelled a formidable insurrection; and yet, in his last struggle for his crown, abandoned the contest with a facility—even an imbecility—wholly irreconcilable with his early character and deportment;—who was himself a singular contradic-

2 A

tion—weak and irresolute, when he should have been stable and firm, and consistently heroic—even to a Spartan endurance —where universal humanity dictates a surrender;—who abandoned, and then mourned over, the loss of his patrimony; and yet, in his adversity, (if one plausible tradition of the mode of his death speak correctly,) he had the strength stubbornly to die of starvation. In short, Richard was a creature of impulse, unhappily for himself, misdirected in after life; but who, for various qualities that he inherited, claims and receives our sympathy, even to the holding of our sterner judgments in abeyance. The natural emotions of his nature were kind, and noble, and generous, even to a childish profuseness; his acts of injustice and oppression were the result of flattery, weakness of judgment, and the misuse of irresponsible power,—an anomaly in civil government not likely to occur again in the history of the world, at all events, in our world of Britain.

Of a totally reverse character to Richard's was that of Bolingbroke: cold, crafty, determined, persevering, designing, and treacherous; politically plausible, and insolently unjust; an oppressor with a heart of ice,—and there is no tyrant like that;—a demagogue, a traitor, and a violator of his oath. He swore by the tomb of his grandfather, Edward III., (an impressive and solemn oath in that age,) that he had no design upon the crown; yet, as it were, in the same breath, he assumed the prerogative of royalty, condemning to death the favourites of Richard; and in a few weeks after he deposed and imprisoned his relation and sovereign.

Bolingbroke had doubtless strong ground of complaint against Richard, who had banished him, and had seized and converted to his own use the personal estate of the Duke of Lancaster, Bolingbroke's father, and who had died during the exile of his son.

If the dramatic history, however, of the period, as recorded by Shakespeare, be received for any authority, it should seem clear that the sentence of banishment passed upon Bolingbroke and Mowbray was an act of political expediency; more especially as regards Bolingbroke, and only was made to refer ostensibly to their mutual impeachment of treason and subsequent trial by battle. Richard, in one of his speeches, supplies us with the key to his sudden and arbitrary course of punishment; the fact being that his wily relative and near pretender to the crown had begun to take advantage of his cousin's unpopularity with the nobles as well as the commonalty, by acting the demagogue and courting their favour. Richard here supplies us with the motive for his course of action:—

> "Ourself and Bushy, Bagot here, and Green
> Observ'd his courtship to the common people;
> How he did seem to dive into their hearts
> With humble and familiar courtesy;
> What reverence he did throw away on slaves;
> Wooing poor craftsmen with the craft of smiles
> And patient underbearing of his fortune,
> As 'twere to banish their affects with him.
> Off goes his bonnet to an oyster wench;
> A brace of draymen bid God speed him well,
> And had the tribute of his supple knee,
> With, 'Thanks, my countrymen, my loving friends;'
> As were our England in reversion his,
> And he our subjects' next degree in hope."

In every movement, every act of Bolingbroke, throughout his career, both in this play and the subsequent one of "Henry IV.," Shakespeare has detailed the man with perfect consistency. Here, as hereafter, he is the aspiring and mounting politician; the thorough enthusiast—at the same time the imperturbable, self-composed, and unfailing ruler; and this self-possession—with sagacity, promptitude, and energy of fulfilment—brought every obstacle to the footstool of his will. The leading features in the character of this consummate dictator have been thus condensed by Hazlitt with his usual apprehensiveness of faculty and charm of diction:—"Patient for occasion, and then steadily availing himself of it; seeing his advantage afar off, but only seizing on it when he has it within his reach; humble, crafty, bold, and aspiring, encroaching by regular but slow degrees, building power on opinion, and cementing opinion by power."

These are the two chief personages in the drama; and having thus briefly introduced them, I proceed to the less exalted characters.

After the king, the next in historical, though not in the present instance of dramatic consequence, is the eminent John of Gaunt, Duke of Lancaster, who was also King of Castile, by virtue of his marriage with the daughter of Peter the Cruel. Godwin, in his masterly history of the life and times of Chaucer, has gone into considerable detail in recording the progress of events as connected with the personal career of John of Gaunt, who was evidently a pet character with him; for he has exerted his patient and logical talent in exculpating his hero from all the charges brought against his political conduct; and, indeed, he may be said to have composed a eulogium on his career, rather than an impartial history of it,—as Middleton also did in his celebrated life of Cicero. The balance of opinion, however, is, I believe, opposed to Godwin in his barrister-like defence of the Duke of Lancaster: who, notwithstanding, appears to have been an intriguing, in addition to his being an inordinately-ambitious man; nor do I find that he is wholly cleared from the charge of an attempt to divert the succession of the monarchy into his own line. That he was a temporising character, is unequivocal, from his having taken the popular, not to say the factious, side in the great religious Wickliffe-controversy; encouraging the first seceder from the Roman Catholic dogmas by his countenance and promise of support; and even at the celebrated convocation at St Paul's, in a fierce personal contest with the Bishop of London, swearing that he would drag that prelate out of the church by his beard; yet, when the hierarchical party proved too strong for Wickliffe, Gaunt suddenly fell away from him, like the latter snow, and quitting the kingdom, left him naked to the tender mercies of his priestly enemies.

It is not the object here to enter into a history of the period, but by this introduction to the character of "Old Gaunt" to show that this is precisely the light in which it was viewed by Shakespeare. With more excitability of nature than his son Bolingbroke, he displays the same compromising tendency:—as witness the dialogue between him and the Duchess of Gloucester, in the 2d scene of the 1st Act, where she is endeavouring to engage him to be of her party to revenge Richard's execution of her husband, who was his own brother. The scene is too long to quote, but concludes by commending her quarrel to Heaven; adding:—

"For Heaven's substitute,
His deputy anointed in his sight
Hath caused his death: the which, if wrongfully,
Let Heaven revenge; for I may never lift
An angry arm against his minister."

Again, his after encouragement of his son, reconciling him to the sentence of banishment passed upon him, is of the same complexion:—the advice also combines the merit of exhibiting the phlegm and indifference of cold-blooded old age. He thus calmly argues with his own son, whose face he is never more likely to see, and indeed never did see again:—

"All places that the eye of Heaven visits,
Are to a wise man ports and happy havens.
Teach thy necessity to reason thus;
There is no virtue like necessity.

Think not the king did banish thee,
But thou the king: woe doth the heavier sit,
Where it perceives it is but faintly borne.
Go, say I sent thee forth to purchase honour,
And not the king exil'd thee; or suppose
Devouring pestilence hangs in our air,
And thou art flying to a fresher clime:
Look, what thy soul holds dear, imagine it
To lie that way thou go'st, not whence thou com'st:
Suppose the singing birds musicians,
The grass whereon thou tread'st the presence strew'd,
The flowers fair ladies, and thy steps no more
Than a delightful measure or a dance;
For gnarling sorrow hath less power to bite
The man that mocks at it and sets it light."

The answer which Bolingbroke makes to his father's argument has been transferred to the first scene of "Richard III.," as it is now represented on the stage, in the contemptible alteration of Colley Cibber:—

"Oh, who can hold a fire in his hand
By thinking on the frosty Caucasus?
Or cloy the hungry edge of appetite
By bare imagination of a feast?
Or wallow naked in December snow
By thinking on fantastic summer's heat?
Oh, no! the apprehension of the good
Gives but the greater feeling to the worse:
Fell sorrow's tooth doth never rankle more
Than when it bites, but lanceth not the sore."

Notwithstanding the unfavourable quality here alluded to and instanced, there is much stateliness and classic grandeur in Shakespeare's portraiture of John of Gaunt; and his dying scene is as sublime as the heavenward flight of some old prophet in sacred history. The tattered and dishevelled condition of his native country, under the misrule of an imbecile and luxurious monarch and his worthless minions,

suggested to the poet a noble opportunity to compliment the land of his birth, by sounding its praise in the deathless hymn of the dying son of the conqueror of France: and in the whole range of poetic diction it stands forth, distinct and alone, for sincerity and lustrous imagery, with glowing patriotism. Happy the land to be so eulogised; happy the land to deserve the eulogy; and still more happy in possessing such a laureate to hymn its fame. The passage is in the opening of the 2d Act. Speaking of his nephew Richard's wanton and reckless conduct, the dying seer breaks forth:—
"Methinks I am a prophet new inspired," &c.

If Gaunt is one of the most picturesque characters in this play, the Duke of York, his brother, and also uncle of Richard, is the most estimable. He is a perfect exemplar of a loyal man and upright friend—of one who has the honesty to rebuke the faults in his sovereign, and, at the same time, to maintain without compromise the prerogative of his crown, in the teeth of those very faults which have caused it to totter on his brow. He, in his erect and steady attachment to his king, forms a striking contrast to the self-seeking adherence of those sunshine courtiers and flatterers, who shroud themselves from the first flaw of adversity that rocks the structure which their rapacity has endangered.

In the character of the Duke of York is to be noticed the distinction that the poet has preserved between the prevailing qualities of the two brothers—both being bold, open-speaking men. Gaunt's open-speaking betrays the bitterness of a man who has suffered personal wrong: at the same time he is too proud to manifest his sense of the injury offered to his individual self through his son's banishment. With a plausible show of magnanimity, therefore, he makes no allusion to this circumstance, which nevertheless is evidently rankling in his bosom; but, with the licence of a dying man, he vehemently upbraids the king upon the general maladministration of his power:—

> "A thousand flatterers sit within thy crown,
> Whose compass is no bigger than thy head.
> And yet, encagèd in so small a verge,
> The waste is no whit lesser than thy land.
> Why, cousin, wert thou regent of the world,
> It were a shame to let this land by lease:
> But, for thy world, enjoying but this land,
> Is it not more than shame to shame it so?
> Landlord of England art thou, and not king:
> Thy state of law is bond-slave to the law."

York, no less honest, has not the same motive for bitterness in his reproof: he therefore only deprecates his nephew's headlong injustice. How finely has the poet preserved the distinctive shades of demeanour in the two men! Before Richard enters, (who is coming to visit his dying uncle,) York endeavours to mitigate the virulence of his brother Gaunt, and says:—

> "The king is come; deal mildly with his youth;
> For young hot colts being rag'd, do rage the more."

And upon the death of Gaunt, when Richard commands the seizure of all his "plate, coin, revenues, and movables," to the detriment of Bolingbroke, his son and heir, York only appeals to him; he does not denounce; he pleads to Richard for Richard—he protects him against himself. His eloquence is the eloquence of a sincere heart, and no eloquence reaches the heart but that which comes from it. This noble expostulation, commencing, "How long shall I be patient?" is in the 1st scene of the 2d Act. It is the language of a purely loyal and honest man; and when the weakly unjust king will not be counselled to his own honour and interest, but repeats the order for the confiscation of his kindred's wealth, York takes his leave, declaring he "will not be by the while."

True, however, to his character, when Bolingbroke returns from banishment, and commences open rebellion against the crown, the first to denounce the act and attest his allegiance is honest old York. Having been appointed regent during the king's absence on his Irish expedition, he despatches Lord Berkley to know Bolingbroke's intention in coming back with an armed retinue: and, like an impetuous man, before Berkley can have fulfilled his mission, he has himself come up with the invader, and personally puts the question he had despatched. Agreeably do these by-plays of action carry out the summary of the whole character. Excellently, too, his reply to the plausible Bolingbroke fills it up; who kneels to his uncle. Here, again, is one of Shakespeare's hints of character and conduct. Bolingbroke, like a wily fox, is ever fawning and kneeling—kneeling to draymen, kneeling to *any* body that "has aught to give." He kneels to his sovereign when in the very act of dethroning him, and receives that tremendous rebuke:—

"Fair cousin, you debase your princely knee,
To make the base earth proud with kissing it.
Me rather had, my heart might feel your love,
Than my unpleas'd eye see your courtesy.
Up, cousin, up; your heart is up, I know,
Thus high, at least." [*Touching his head.*]

And he takes little more by kneeling to his uncle York;—but that man is a mere apprentice in treason who hath not bronzed both face and heart for his work; and Bolingbroke was a pattern usurper.

The most dramatic point in the conduct of the Duke of York is the scene in which he is taken by surprise with the news of Bolingbroke's invasion; and the most beautiful and pathetic is his description to the Duchess of the famous entry into London of the two monarchs. The former scene is a vivid picture of a flustered man, who has lost his self-possession from consciousness of the responsibility attaching to his office of regent. A noticeable peculiarity, too, in the scene is, that the manner of York reveals the *old* man in a nonplus and perturbation. [*Enter a servant.*]

"My lord, your son was gone before I came.
"*York.* He was?—Why, so! go all which way it will.
The nobles they are fled; the commons they are cold,
And will I fear revolt on Hereford's side.—
Sirrah, get thee to Plashy, to my sister Gloucester;
Bid her send me presently a thousand pound.
Hold, take my ring.
"*Serv.* My lord, I had forgot to tell your lordship:
To-day, as I came by I callèd there;
But I shall grieve you to report the rest.
"*York.* What is it, knave?
"*Serv.* An hour before I came, the duchess died.
"*York.* Heaven for his mercy! what a tide of woes
Comes rushing on this woful land at once!
*I know not what to do.* I would to Heaven
(So my untruth had not provok'd him to it)
The king had cut off my head with my brother's.—
What! are there no posts despatch'd for Ireland?—
How shall we do for money for these wars?—
[*To the queen.*] Come, sister,—cousin, I would say.—Pray pardon me.—
[*To the servant.*] Go, fellow, get thee home; provide some carts,
And bring away the armour that is there.— [*Exit serv.*]
Gentlemen, will you go muster men?—
If I know how, or which way, to order these affairs,
Thus disorderly thrust into my hands,
Never believe me. Both are my kinsmen:
The one is my sov'reign, whom both my oath
And duty bids defend; the other, again,
Is my kinsman, whom the king hath wrong'd,
Whom conscience and my kindred bids to right.
Well, somewhat we must do.—Come, cousin,
I'll dispose of you.—Gentlemen, go muster up your men,

> And meet me presently at Berkley castle.
> I should to Plashy too;
> But time will not permit:—all is uneven,
> And everything is left at six and seven."

The other scene—the pathetic one alluded to—is old York's description to his duchess of the two kings' (Richard and Bolingbroke) procession into London. It is the 2d of the 5th Act, commencing:—

> "My lord, you told me you would tell the rest,
> When weeping made you break the story off,
> Of our two cousins' coming into London."

Unscrupulous loyalty (as a mere principle) forms the paramount quality in the character of the Duke of York; for, when Richard resigns, or rather is deprived of his crown, and Bolingbroke becomes the accepted king, York freely transfers his allegiance; and in his zeal of fidelity he even becomes the accuser of his own son, Aumerle, whom he has detected in a conspiracy against the usurper.

The foresight of Shakespeare in developing his characters is noticeable in the instance of the renowned Harry Percy. He is introduced with his restless, counterplotting father, the Duke of Northumberland, in this play; but, being a mere youth, and only commencing his career of public life, he betrays no token of the "gunpowder Percy," as we afterwards behold him in the play of "Henry IV.," when the sinews of his nature had attained the hardness and vigour of manhood. This is remarkable as indicating the poet's comprehension of the whole champaign, as it were, of a character;—in this play of "Richard II." *preparing* us only for Percy's after-development in "Henry IV.;" for this latter play had, most probably, not been written, and it was not acted for, I believe, two or three years after that of "Richard II." There is one slight indication —and but a slight one—of Percy's after-explosive character, in the 1st scene of the 4th Act, wherein he justifies the conduct of Fitzwater against the impeachment of Aumerle—not, however, worth the quoting.

The character also of Northumberland is consistently maintained throughout this and the two succeeding plays of "Henry IV.,"—proud, fierce, restless, restive, exacting, captious, and unrelenting. What magnificent lessons does the poet read us in the retributions which, soon or late, revealed or suggested, always succeed a career of injustice,—"sowing the wind, and reaping the whirlwind." His moral upon this point is a personation of, and running comment upon the sacred text, that "wrath pursueth the unjust man, and his violent dealings fall upon his own head." The way in which Shakespeare has carried out this principle with all the turbulent characters in his dramas is as satisfactory as it is complete. The after-career of Northumberland is comprised in Richard's short dismissal of him, the last three lines of which are golden truths. In the anguish and bitterness of resentment at his turbulent disloyalty, he exclaims:—

> "Northumberland, thou ladder, wherewithal
> The mounting Bolingbroke ascends my throne,
> The time shall not be many hours of age
> More than it is, ere foul sin gathering head
> Shall break into corruption: thou shalt think,
> Though he divide the realm, and give thee half,
> It is too little, helping him to all:
> He shall think that thou, which know'st the way
> To plant unrightful kings, wilt know again,
> Being ne'er so little urged, another way
> To pluck him headlong from th' usurped throne.
> *The love of wicked friends converts to fear;*
> *That fear to hate;* and hate turns one, or both,
> To worthy danger and deserved death."

There are two short episodes in this play which gently relieve the oppressive routine of mistakes and misdeeds—of violence and injustice—of disaster and sorrow, remorse and despair, that follow us at every step. The first is the scene at Langley, where the gardener is moralising, in the hearing of the queen, upon the reverses that have befallen her lord. The application of his craft to the policy of government is simple and unpretending. He says to his fellow-labourer:—

"Oh what pity is it
That he had not so trimm'd and dress'd his land
As we this garden! We, at time of year,
Do wound the bark, the skin of our fruit-trees,
Lest, being over-proud in sap and blood,
With too much riches it confound itself:
Had he done so to great and growing men,
They might have liv'd to bear, and he to taste,
Their fruits of duty. Superfluous branches
We lop away, that bearing boughs may live.
Had he done so, himself had borne the crown,
Which waste of idle hours hath quite thrown down."

The scene closes with the queen discovering herself to him, and with a characteristic and touching little sentiment from the successor of our old father Adam. When she has gone, he says:—

"Poor queen!
* * * * * *
Here did she fall a tear. Here in this place
I 'll set a bank of rue, sour herb of grace;
Rue, even for ruth, here shortly shall be seen,
In the remembrance of a weeping queen."

The other slight episode, and a more beautiful one, is where the groom comes to visit his royal master in prison. The gentle nature of Shakespeare has here made the humblest dependants on the king the most worthy-hearted and constant. He was deserted by his "velvet friends," and commiserated by the lowly denizens of serge and woollen. "Misery," says Trinculo, "makes a man acquainted with strange bedfellows;" and, indeed, calamity does reduce the high and the low to one common level. Then it is that the real gentility of our nature displays itself; for true gentility, the gentility of the heart, knows no grades in society—clothes do; and hence the confusion which arises in vulgar minds in this thoroughly aristocratic nation of ours as to the distinction between the gentleman and the vulgar man; the covering—the husk, is all in all with them, not the quality of the sweet and oily nut within. In this world of ours, a man to be a conventional gentleman, need have no heart, no oily nut of kindness; better none, perhaps; (for it is vulgar to possess feelings;) but if he have a fashionable husk, good clothes and unexceptionable gloves, he takes precedence of him with the homely exterior: as the qualification for a "respectable man" is, that he should "keep a gig." The poor groom was the only true gentleman at heart of all Richard's retainers, and very natural and pretty is their interview:—

*Pomfret Castle.* [*Enter groom.*]

"Hail, royal prince!
"*K. R.* Thanks, noble peer;
The cheapest of us is ten groats too dear.
What art thou? And how com'st thou hither,
Where no man ever comes, but that sad dog
That brings me food, to make misfortune live.
"*Groom.* I was a poor groom of thy stable, king,
When thou wert king; who, travelling towards York,
With much ado, at length have gotten leave
To look upon my sometime royal master's face.
Oh, how it yearn'd my heart when I beheld,
In London streets, that coronation day,
When Bolingbroke rode on roan Barbary!
That horse that thou so often hast bestrid,
That horse that I so carefully have dress'd!
"*K. R.* Rode he on Barbary? Tell me, gentle friend,
How went he under him?
"*Groom.* So proudly, as if he disdain'd the ground.

"*K. R.* So proud that Bolingbroke was on his back!
That jade hath eat bread from my royal hand;
This hand hath made him proud with clapping him.
Would he not stumble? Would he not fall down,
(Since pride must have a fall,) and break the neck
Of that proud man that did usurp his back?
Forgiveness, horse! why do I rail on thee,
Since thou, created to be aw'd by man,
Wast born to bear? I was not made a horse;
And yet I bear a burden like an ass,
Spur-gall'd and tir'd by jauncing Bolingbroke."

I scarcely know any scene of the like slight pretension that makes a more touching appeal to one's feelings of humanity than this simple recognition of kindness and gratitude between the poor groom and his fallen, unhappy master. Stevens calls this scene "a silly one!" From what has transpired of Stevens's moral and social character, we may accurately conclude that he possessed just so little feeling and good taste as to make such a comment.

This play of "Richard II." has been denominated a "heavy one," which means that it is not distinguished by various and rapid action, or abrupt and startling incident. It opens with misrule and injustice; it continues with intrigue, dissimulation, and treason; and ends in sorrow, remorse, and a dastardly murder. The principal character, it is true, never commands our admiration or esteem; at the same time, he never loses our sympathy, and this undoubtedly rises with his reverse of fortune and his calamity. It is in the last acts of his career that the poet has rescued him from inevitable contempt. The dignity of the tragic drama is vindicated in his person, the moment the tide has turned against him:—in the last three acts, therefore, from his first setting foot in England, after the Irish rebellion, through all his heart-burnings with his stony usurper; the vulgar revilings of the populace,

> "His face still combating with tears and smiles,
> The badges of his grief and patience;"

and the yet more vulgar insolence of Northumberland; up to the climax of his assassination, our sympathies accompany him, and we feel that he was a misdirected and an unhappy man, who, under other circumstances, (had the "good Queen Anne" lived, for instance,) would have been good and estimable: he had a heart, if not in the strict sense a "great man;" for he had strength of purpose upon occasion, and displayed it.

But if Shakespeare had conferred no other benefit upon his species by his amazing genius, the practical lessons he has read to the highest and the lowest in every grade of society in these, his domestic histories, are alone inestimable. And not only are they poems glowing with the sunlight of his imagination, but they are profound essays in moral philosophy, preaching to us all the beauty of rectitude and self-respect under the most trying fortunes; and how dreary a mistake, even in the midst of a dazzling prosperity, is the heart that is not sustained by the consciousness of a worthy purpose. Moreover, he is the most honest of chroniclers; for, with all his reverence for the "divinity," (in the abstract,) "that doth hedge a king," he never for one moment, either expressed or implied, compromises in a king's misdeeds the great principle of truth and justice. Living in an age when the "divine right" was assumed as a state axiom, and when the monarch was pronounced to be literally the vicegerent of God on earth, and, like the head of the Roman Church, "infallible," yet Shakespeare never hesitates to reason with that monarch upon "righteousness, and temperance, and of the judgment to come." No herald more eloquently blazons the kingly attributes and virtues, and no monitor more clearly and openly denounces the royal assumption of irresponsible power to commit injustice. No man was less of a flatterer—less of a sycophant, than Shakespeare. He was a member of a profession, and joint-proprietor of a theatre, that, till of late years, have derived their chief source of emolument from the patronage of royalty and the aristocracy. The taste of the age has undergone a change as regards the classes just named; that is an affair of preference. I confess, however, that I am jealous for the glory of the world's brightest gem; and would not have the most insignificant Briton, still less the most illustrious, lukewarm towards him, when I consider how much he has done for universal humanity, and for women in particular.

Shakespeare lived, too, in an age when adulation formed part and parcel of every writer's stock-in-trade; the poet of the "Faery Queen" was an immense capitalist of the article; and some flattery was especially looked for from an author in our dramatist's peculiar position with regard to his sovereign, as well as the most influential nobles of her court; and yet, throughout his thirty-seven plays, will be found but one direct compliment and one implied one to Elizabeth. The former is in "Henry VIII.," and put into the mouth of Cranmer upon the birth of Anne Boleyn's child; an occasion which, to have avoided, would have been ungracious and churlish, not to say ungrateful: the other is in the "Midsummer Night's Dream;" and there the compliment—a truly fanciful and elegant one—is so veiled, that in all probability, scarcely any one at the time immediately recognised the poet's allusion; the queen would do so, for she had a hawk's eye for that quarry. Oh, those were indeed golden days for poetry and dramatic literature! We, with our steam-presses and millions of books, can have little conception what must have been the excitement when it was announced that the greatest genius of his own age, or of any other, had composed a *new play!* presenting events that the million had learned in parcels only, and by tradition; for the majority, very few, indeed, could read them: histories of their own country and kindred; the characters personated by men of rare talent. Those were, indeed, days for the drama! when the bulk of society did not assemble to carp and to cavil, to question, and object to everything—which in modern idiom is called "criticism"—to sneer and to damn; but with the implicit reverence of childhood, to be instructed as to what had been done in the world before them; and to believe and feel that such language as they heard could have come only from one divinely-instructed in the great lesson of benevolence and loving-kindness towards the whole brotherhood of humanity, and of belief and confidence in goodness working out its own "exceeding great reward;" and this was the lesson that Shakespeare learned; and this was the lesson he taught.

XVI.

# Merchant of Venice.

# XVI.

# MERCHANT OF VENICE.

IF I were required to adduce a signal proof of the question that Shakespeare lived beyond his age as a moral and social philosopher, I should not hesitate to ground my proof upon the way in which he has worked out the story of the "Merchant of Venice," as regards the character, behaviour, and treatment of the most important person in the drama—the Jew.

Shakespeare lived in an age when the general feeling towards the sect in which Shylock was born and educated could scarcely be called a prejudice—'tis too mild a term—it was a rancour, a horror, venting itself in injustice and violence, pillage, expulsion, and, if possible, extermination of the race. I cannot suppose that he was wholly untainted with the antipathy that had been fostered for centuries before him, for he was familiar with the legends of revenge and cruelty that had, at various periods, been perpetrated by Jews, when individual opportunities of gratifying their own natural lust of retaliation had presented themselves. He was familiar with the story of Hugh of Lincoln, and with the murder of the Christian babe in Chaucer's story of the Nun's Tale; and he felt that here was atrocity for atrocity committed,—a course that never yet produced, and never will produce, the redress of an original wrong. He belonged to that faith, and throughout his writings he has urged its grand tenet, which inculcates the wickedness as well as the folly of revenge. But Shakespeare, in becoming the social and moral reformer of his species, possessed that point of wisdom in knowing, as it were by instinct, that he who desires to change a master-section in an age's code, whether it be civil or social, will not accomplish his end half so readily and effectually by an unconditional and wholesale opposition, as by a partial and rational extenuation. They who aim at reforming the masses,—who desire to lead, must at all events make a show of following. Nothing does the common mind resent more vehemently than the presumption of a single individual professing to be wiser than, and to dictate to, his whole race—the experience of all ages and of every day proves this. It was not for Shakespeare, whose profession it was to provide for the intellectual entertainment of his nation, to perk in their faces his individual opinions: it was much that he did not foster their prejudices, that he did not pander to their vices and inflate their self-love,—and he has not done this. He himself has laid down the principle upon which the drama should be constructed and sustained, and upon no other will it survive.

Upon this, his grand principle, therefore, it appears that the poet, in delineating the character and conduct of Shylock, as well as of his Christian opponents, has, with his large wisdom, preached a homily upon injustice to each sect and denomination of religionists, with a force and perspicuity of argument, as well as knowledge of human nature in its melancholy prejudices, that, to me, as I reflect upon his impartiality, his honest dispensation of justice, as displayed in this drama, place him centuries in advance of his age, and the production itself among the greatest efforts of human genius. If any reader have a doubt of the poet's sense of justice towards that most ill-used tribe, let him read the works of other writers of the period where the character of the Jew has been introduced. It is true, Shylock has been punished for his motive of revenge,—and justly; for it was an atrocious refinement of the passion, claimed and substantiated upon the worst of all unjust grounds—the right of legal justice;—no tyranny being equal to the wrenching of law for penal purposes. It is also true that the injuring party, in the first instance—the Christian—is brought off triumphantly; but in that age, or indeed in any age, the multitude could never have sympathised in a rigid fulfilment of such a compact, or of any compact that should sacrifice the one party for the benefit of the other.

But, after all, who does not sympathise with Shylock? Who, with the most ordinary notions of right and wrong, derives any gratification from the merchant Antonio's being brought off by a quirk of law, and that law an unjust one, which decreed the demolition of the Jew's whole wealth and estate? Shakespeare has made out a strong case for Shylock,—startling, indeed, it must have been to the commonalty in his time. Shylock says the finest things in the play, and he has the advantage in the argument throughout. If the motion of revenge *be* justifiable, (and his own moral code, "An eye for an eye, and a tooth for a tooth," bear him out,) he has all the odds against his adversaries:—

"Hath not a Jew eyes? hath not a Jew hands, organs, dimensions, senses, affections, passions? fed with the same food, hurt with the same weapons, subject to the same diseases, healed by the same means, warmed and cooled by the same winter and summer as a Christian is? If you prick us, do we not bleed? if you tickle us, do we not laugh? if you poison us, do we not die? and if you wrong us, shall we not revenge? If we are like you in the rest, we will resemble you in that. If a Jew wrong a Christian, what is his humility?

revenge: if a Christian wrong a Jew, what should his sufferance be *by Christian example?* why, revenge. The villainy you teach me I will execute; and it shall go hard but I will better the instruction."

This is strong "lex talionis," or tooth-for-tooth argument; and strong extenuation for that age; ay, and even for our own very Christian age.

But who shall say that this very play has not been instrumental in breaking down the barriers and mounds of intolerance and persecution for faith's sake? This noble production has, I believe, among other philosophical appeals, tended to assuage the fury of class and party prejudice, and persecution. Its course through those deep and savage ravines, wherein the stream of class-opinion was confined, and amid which it brawled and raved, tearing and wasting all before it, is gradually becoming diverted; and if it still exist, (which, alas! we all can sadly answer,) it has, nevertheless, mainly expended its force, and is slowly spreading in an inert ooze over the social champaign. The age of Diabolism is passing away; and a spirit of bearing and forbearing—the "doing unto others as we would be done by"—is becoming recognised and largely debated; and only let a question be brought to the debating point, its settlement is at no very remote distance. It is now the few only who hold fast by the integrity of the "right of might;" and the "might" is changing with the many into a calm principle of equitable adjustment.

So much is the leading principle of Christianity doing for us; gradually, but as surely as the progress of matter: and so much, in the pure spirit of its principle, did our Shakespeare anticipate and provide nearly three centuries ago.

It gives me pleasure to find that my feeling of the ethical working of this play is confirmed in a pamphlet lately brought out by Victor Hugo. The eloquent French writer has a beautiful passage in illustration; he says:—"Shylock has gained what is better than his cause—he has gained the cause of an entire people. He has caused the unknown rights of his race to be recognised, and enabled them to prevail by the exemplary condemnation of that exterminatory code which hitherto had kept them in abeyance. * * * Shakespeare has been the judge of peace in this great litigation; he has reconciled the parties by a compromise, which imposes on them reciprocal concessions. In exacting that Shylock should be converted to Christianity, he did not intend to violate the principle, unknown in his day, of liberty of conscience, he has solely desired that Jew and Christian should alike practise that ideal religion which preaches forgiveness of injuries."

Having thus briefly introduced the subject of the play, and alluded to its most important character; before turning to those of second and third rank, I would say a few words in behalf of Portia; and because she has been strangely accused of "pedantry," the conceit of learning, the antipodes of modesty; and because I think I can prove that there is hardly one of the poet's female impersonations more richly endowed with the crowning feminine attribute, "modesty," than this very lovely specimen of a womanly woman.

It was Hazlitt, one of the acutest of critics, who passed that sentence upon the heroine of this play. His words are—"Portia is not a very great favourite with us;" and he adds, "She has a certain degree of affectation and pedantry about her." I have always regretted that Hazlitt set down that passage. It has often been quoted; and, as his staid opinion, it has awakened a natural opposition to him on the part of those critics who could better perceive the true beauties of Portia's character, than they knew of, or could discern, the variable moods of Hazlitt's temperament. Every one who knew him would feel convinced that he penned those words under some temporary fit of spleen, some wayward, momentary feeling of petulance against *high-bred* women. Hazlitt was very sensitive—personally sensitive—on the score of women's liking toward himself; and he occasionally made some curious mistakes, such as many men who are at once self-diffident and self-confident, intellectually proud, and constitutionally shy (for all the qualities are perfectly compatible) often do make about women, and women's preferences. Even in his writings these peculiarities are plainly perceptible. Turn to his essay "On Great and Little Things," where he professes his admiration for "humble beauties, servant-maids and shepherd-girls;" his own words, declaring, too, that he "admires the Clementinas and Clarissas at a distance," while the "Pamelas and Fannys of Richardson and Fielding *make the blood tingle*." But at the very time that he tries to exalt the ignorant charmers, he permits the reader to perceive that they provoke him with their inapprehensiveness. And in another essay, entitled, "On the Disadvantages of Intellectual Superiority," he, with much bitterness, takes up the opposite side of the question, saying, where he is speaking of the wooing of men of letters, "Women of education may have a glimpse of their meaning, may get a clue to their characters; but to all others they are thick darkness. If the mistress smile at their *ideal* advances, the maid will laugh outright."

Here we find that the pretty ignorants had lost their fascination for him; that he saw through their insufficiency to form the solid and permanent delight of a man of intelligence; whereas, when he wrote that line, "Portia is not a very great favourite with us," the Fannys and the Pamelas chanced to be in the ascendant. His imagination was beguiling him with some image of captivating *simpletonism;* frequently and oddly confounded with *simplicity*, when he asserted that Portia "has a certain degree of affectation and pedantry about her."

The Rev. Sydney Smith, in his admirable paper on "Female Education," accurately defines pedantry to be "an ostentatious obtrusion of knowledge, in which those who hear us cannot sympathise." Now, the only approach to a display of knowledge which Portia makes, is in the accurate exposition she gives of the Venetian law, when, dressed as a doctor of laws, she sets forth, in open court, the state of the case between Shylock and the merchant Antonio. She is absolutely compelled, by the part she has assumed, to make this exposition; and so far from addressing it to "unsympathising" or incomprehensive hearers, she addresses it to those who are actually awaiting from her lips the clear statement of the pending cause, with its facts, circumstances, and contingencies. That she is competent to fulfil the task she has undertaken, we know; and this is confirmed on the spot by the words which are addressed to her in reply—"You know the law; your exposition hath been most sound."

How the lady of Belmont comes to be thus versed in a subject not usual for women to study, the dramatist has accounted for by her connexion and consociation with her kinsman the "learned Doctor Bellario." Thus, so far from Portia's erudition having bred in her either pedantry or affectation, it has, in fact, produced that which Sydney Smith avers a *rightly*-educated woman's learning must always produce, where he finely says, "The great use of her knowledge will be that it contributes to her *private* happiness." And Portia's knowledge not only makes her own happiness, for she is one of the very happiest, the cheerfullest, the most pleasant-spirited of all Shakespeare's women, but it helps to form the happiness of her friends. By her knowledge of law, by her courage in using that knowledge at the right moment, by her intelligence, by her ready wit and presence of mind, she is enabled to save the life of her husband's dearest friend.

In that same paper of Sydney Smith's, already quoted as bearing so aptly on the present subject, he speaks of these two phrases as being current coin in society. "The true theatre for a woman is the sick-chamber." And, "Nothing so honourable to a woman as not to be spoken of at all." These phrases, he says, are "the delight of Noodledom." What a happy term! Ay, and they are the delight, too, of selfdom; they are the cuckoo-cry of this modern school of ours,—the hard school of mis-styled "social philosophy,"—the school which has no other education for women than a serf-like obedience and saying their prayers; and no higher recognition of their "obedience" than the lordly epithet of "fond creatures,"—a title which the "creatures" enjoy in common with the spaniels,—the word "fond," in old dialect, meaning "foolish;" and fools assuredly such women must be who squander any higher emotion than the merest human sympathy upon the disciples of such a school of selfishness.

Had Portia of Belmont known only how to "shine in a sick-room," and to shrink from being talked of, she would never have been able to preserve a human life by her knowledge and eloquence, or to use these qualifications when the emergency needed their public display. Shakespeare knew that women might be made available for greater ornament and utility than mixing effervescent draughts in a sick-room, and sitting in company as dumb as the candelabra on the sideboard. Behold, in his mind, how modest is Portia's behaviour in her own domestic circle. She is the well-bred lady,—accustomed to command, to rank and station, and to dispose of her household, her wealth, her time, herself, as best seems to her; but she bears her faculties meekly, and is dignified, without pride or haughtiness. Her habit of speech is perceptibly un-vain, even in her casual words of course. She says to one of her suitors, while she states the condition of the casket-test:—

> "To these injunctions every one doth swear
> That comes to hazard for my worthless self."

And afterwards she playfully says, in reply to Lorenzo's exclamation, recognising her tones as she approaches :—

> "He knows me, as the blind man knows the cuckoo,
> By the bad voice."

Her greeting to her husband's friend, Antonio, is instinct with lady-like grace and modesty :—

> "Sir, you are very welcome to our house :
> It must appear in other ways than words ;
> Therefore I scant this breathing courtesy."

How delicate that little touch of generosity and modesty, "welcome to *our* house :" she has just endowed her husband with her property.

For still more pointed examples of the perfectly womanly modesty of Portia, note the speech she makes to Bassanio, when he is about to make the trial of the caskets :—

> "I pray you tarry ; pause a day or two
> Before you hazard ; for, in choosing wrong,
> I lose your company ; therefore forbear a while.
> There 's something tells me—*but it is not love*—
> I would not lose you : and you know yourself,
> Hate counsels not in such a quality.
> But lest you should not understand me well,
> (And yet a maiden hath no tongue but thought,)
> I would detain you here some month or two,
> Before you venture for me. I could teach you
> How to choose right ; but then I am forsworn ;
> So will I never be : so may you miss me ;
> But if you do, you 'll make me wish a sin,
> That I had been forsworn."

This is the bashfulness of a new-born passion, struggling equally to express itself and to restrain the too-bold betrayal of its strength. And the speech she makes to him, when he has rightly chosen the casket, modestly tendering herself to his acceptance, is surely the very poetry of prodigality in diffidence :—

"You see me, Lord Bassanio, where I stand,
Such as I am: though, for myself alone,
I would not be ambitious in my wish,
To wish myself much better; yet, for you
I would be trebled twenty times myself;
A thousand times more fair, ten thousand times more rich;
That only to stand high in your account,
I might in virtues, beauties, livings, friends,
Exceed account; but the full sum of me
Is sum of nothing; which, to term in gross,
Is an unlesson'd girl, unschool'd, unpractis'd;
Happy in this, she is not so old
But she may learn; happier than this,
She is not bred so dull, but she can learn;
Happiest of all is, that her gentle spirit
Commits itself to yours to be directed,
As from her lord, her governor, her king."

Is there either "affectation" or "pedantry" in that speech? Is it not rather the exaggerated timidity and self-doubt that spring from the heart's dread of being less than worthy of its chosen object; and which, in its eagerness to become so, commits itself and its conscious imperfections to the loving guidance of the superiority it sincerely acknowledges? Is it like either a vain or a selfish woman, (and "pedantry" and "affectation" imply both vanity and egoism,) Portia's readiness to part with her husband, and to yield his society—even in their bridal hour—at the demand of friendship? When Antonio's letter is read aloud, announcing his disastrous fortune, and intimating how true a comfort the presence of his friend, Bassanio, would afford, she exclaims warmly, and without a moment's debating, "Oh! love, despatch all business and begone!" When she sees him turn pale, on the first perusal of the letter, her words prove her affectionate observance,—all unlike the self-contemplativeness and perpetual self-absorption which confirm the pedantic or the affected woman; but rather the modesty of wifely affection, which claims to share at least the griefs in the lot of him she loves.

One more noble example must in full justice be quoted. It is where Lorenzo applauds her for bearing the absence of her newly-wedded lord for the sake of the friend to whom he has hastened. She replies:—

"I never did repent for doing good,
Nor shall not now: for in companions
That do converse and waste the time together,
Whose souls do bear an equal yoke of love,
There must be needs a like proportion
Of lineaments, of manners, and of spirit;
Which makes me think that this Antonio,
Being the bosom lover of my lord,
Must needs be like my lord. If it be so,
How little is the cost I have bestow'd,
In purchasing the semblance of my soul
From out the state of hellish cruelty!—
*This comes too near the praising of myself;*
*Therefore no more of it.*"

There is exquisite subtlety and refinement of modesty in this passage. There is the delicacy of a mind that dreads even to disclaim merit lest it seem to imply that there exists merit to be disclaimed; and there is the sensitiveness of a profound love, which feels it a kind of egoism to laud that being who is but another self. The fact that this speech is put into the mouth of a new-married bride, a yet maiden wife, enhances tenfold its loveliness of modesty.

But Hazlitt, as if to award some merit to Portia, magnanimously acknowledges that "the speech about Mercy is very well." Upon my life it is, indeed! "But," he then adds, "there are a thousand finer in Shakespeare." I can only say, I rejoice in *such* a confirmation of our poet's intellectual supremacy from *such* a judge! Only think of there being a "thousand finer speeches" than this from one brain:—

"*Portia.* Then must the Jew be merciful.
"*Shy.* On what compulsion must I? tell me that.
"*Por.* The quality of mercy is not strain'd;
It droppeth as the gentle rain from heav'n
Upon the place beneath: it is twice bless'd;
It blesseth him that gives and him that takes;
'Tis mightiest in the mightiest; it becomes
The throned monarch better than his crown;
His sceptre shows the force of temporal pow'r,
The attribute to awe and majesty,
Wherein doth sit the dread and fear of kings;
But Mercy is above this scepter'd sway;
It is enthroned in the hearts of kings;
It is an attribute to God himself;
And earthly power doth then show likest God's,
When Mercy seasons justice."

Cervantes, Shakespeare's contemporary, and worthy to enter with him (which he did, and on the same day) upon an immortal eternity, has a passage written in the like lofty spirit. It is put into the mouth of the high-souled Don Quixote, when he is delivering those wise injunctions to Sancho as guides for his governorship of the island:—"For the delinquent that is under thy jurisdiction, consider that the miserable man is subject to the temptations of our depraved nature, and as much as thou canst, without grievance to the contrary party, show thyself mild and gentle; for, although God's attributes are equal, yet to our sight His mercy is more precious, more eminent than His justice."

The nearest approach, perhaps, that asceticism might make in charge of pedantry and affectation upon the speech of Portia, is when she returns home to Belmont, after she has conducted the Shylock trial, and moralises upon the several objects that first present themselves to her imagination,—as, for instance, she says:—

"That light we see is burning in my hall.

> How far that little candle throws its beams!
> So shines a good deed in a naughty world."

If here be a tinge of affectation, be it remembered that she has come back with her heart full of pleasant reflections from having done a deed of mercy and kindness, and which will most especially gratify him whom she most wishes to please. So far from being affected, it is rather a stroke of art in the poet to put into her mouth, at such a juncture, those little scraps of sentiment and morality,—allowable fees which well-doing pays to self-love. Who could deny the whole of this scene to be purely exquisite?

There is a class of my own sex who never fail to manifest an uneasiness, if not a jealousy, when they perceive a woman verging towards the manly prerogative; and with such, the part that Shakespeare has assigned to Portia in the trial-scene would induce this prejudice against her. All that we can say is, the poet himself appears not to have apprehended female usurpation where love and esteem constitute the principle of either party; and that he intended these to be the rule of Portia's conduct seems unequivocal. To sum up her mental and moral accomplishments, the scrutiniser into her course of conduct will allow that she is at once grave, sedate, witty, social, humorous, cheerful, (and consequently, of course, amiable in every sense;) that she is modest, mentally and socially, bounteous to prodigality; and, to crown all, that she is a dutiful and ardently affectionate wife. All and every of these qualities adorn the character of Portia, and these go to accomplish a perfect woman; and these qualities being acknowledged, it is hoped that she is absolved from the charge of either "affectation" or "pedantry."

Nerissa is a fitting attendant-gentlewoman to Portia. She is lively, intelligent, and ever prompt to enter into the spirit of a plot, a disguise, or a playful equivoque, with her bride-groom-husband. Her first speech is one of those pleasant jests that nestle a gentle philosophy beneath their light wording. When her mistress (in the pretended pouting of one of prosperity's darlings) exclaims—"By my troth, Nerissa, my little body is a-weary of this great world!" she replies:—

"You would be, sweet madam, if your miseries were in the same abundance as your good fortunes are; and yet, for aught I see, they are as sick that surfeit with too much, as they that starve with nothing. It is no mean happiness, therefore, to be seated in the mean [or, medium]: superfluity comes sooner by white hairs, but competency lives longer."

Of Madam Nerissa, however, be it rather more than surmised from indications given, that she is one of that clan who will keep her husband trotting, partly from legitimate and sex-honoured exaction, and partly, perhaps, from liveliness of disposition; and, also, because that he, being a good-natured fellow, will evidently spoil her: and then let us hope he may not have his head tattooed.

That husband, Gratiano, is a most delightful and most natural character. He is one of those useful men in society who will keep up the ball of mirth and good-humour, simply by his own mercurial temperament and agreeable rattle; for he is like a babbling woodside brook, seen through at once, and presenting every ripple of its surface to the sunbeams of good-fellowship. If a pic-nic were proposed, Gratiano would be the man for the commissariat department: and the wines shall be unimpeachable in quantity as well as quality; the ladies shall lack no squire of dames, and the men no stimulus to keep their gallantry from rusting. And, what is better than all, if a friend be in adversity, Gratiano will champion him with good words and deeds, if not with the most sagacious counsel. He would, no doubt, talk a man off his legs; and, therefore, Shakespeare has brought him as a relief against the two grave men, Antonio and Bassanio, who, being both anxious on account of worldly cares, resent his vivacity, and they are at all events as peevish as he is flippant and inconsiderate. Bassanio says of Gratiano that he "speaks an infinite deal of nothing;" that "his reasons are as two grains of wheat hid in two bushels of chaff; you shall seek all day long ere you shall find them, and when you have them, they are not worth the search." The best of all this is, that Bassanio himself advances no claim to be the censor of his lively companion, for in comparison with him he is dull in capacity, and the very observation just quoted follows one of the most agreeable and sensible speeches in the play—made by "the infinite-deal-of-nothing" Gratiano. Shakespeare has made the best apology for the Merchant and his friend; but his own love of cheerfulness with good temper could not fail to throw liberally into Gratiano's scale, and he has nowhere produced a better defence of natural vivacity. Moreover, he has not made Gratiano selfishly boisterous—indulging his own feelings only: he first manifests a solicitude for Antonio's lowness of spirits, and then he rallies him. These are the small and delicate lights thrown into his characters that render them exhaustless as studies, and give us that indefinable, rather, perhaps, that unrecognised and unconscious interest in all they say and do, and which, to the same extent, appears to be the almost undivided prerogative of Shakespeare alone.

Here is the natural introduction to the conversation alluded to. Gratiano says:—

"You look not well, Signior Antonio;
You have too much respect upon the world:
They lose it that do buy it with much care.
Believe me, you are marvellously chang'd.
"*Ant.* I hold the world but as the world, Gratiano;
A stage, where every man must play a part,
And mine a sad one.

"*Gra.* Let me play the fool:
With mirth and laughter let old wrinkles come;
And let my liver rather heat with wine,
Than my heart cool with mortifying groans.
Why should a man, whose blood is warm within,
Sit like his grandsire cut in alabaster?
Sleep when he wakes, and creep into the jaundice
By being peevish? I tell thee what, Antonio,—
I love thee, and it is my love that speaks,—
There are a sort of men whose visages
Do cream and mantle like a standing pond,
And do a wilful stillness entertain,
With purpose to be dress'd in an opinion
Of wisdom, gravity, profound conceit;
As who should say, 'I am Sir Oracle,
And when I ope my lips, let no dog bark!'
Oh, my Antonio, I do know of these
That therefore only are reputed wise
For saying nothing; when, I am very sure,
If they should speak, would almost damn those ears,
Which, hearing them, would call their brothers fools.
I'll tell thee more of this another time;
But fish not, with this melancholy bait,
For this fool-gudgeon, this opinion."

It is after this friendly rally that the grave Merchant (and when Gratiano has departed) turns to Bassanio, and with a half-wondering disdain says, "Is that anything now?" But if, as has been surmised, Shakespeare entertained a positive antipathy to the quality of melancholy in the mental constitution of man, he has, with his usual instinct of justice, greatly redeemed the character of the Venetian Merchant from objection on that ground. Antonio's gravity is no mere assumption to gain men's suffrages, but one which he would fain remove, while he encourages a motive of cheerfulness in others, as shown in the description of his parting with Bassanio, by a mutual friend—Act II., sc. 8. But his whole bearing is that of a greatly noble, brave, and generous friend.

His final speech, when he is preparing to pay the forfeit of his bond, is a strong attempt to speak and bear himself courageously and consolingly to his friend. It concludes with the sort of grave smile and attempted jest with which, at such a moment, a serious and sincere-hearted man would make an effort to cheer those he loves. When Portia, as the young doctor of laws, says, "Come, merchant, have you anything to say?" Antonio answers:—

> "But little; I am arm'd, and well prepar'd.
> Give me your hand, Bassanio. Fare you well!
> Grieve not that I am fall'n to this for you;
> For herein Fortune shows herself more kind
> Than is her custom. It is still her use
> To let the wretched man outlive his wealth,
> To view with hollow eye, and wrinkled brow,
> An age of poverty; from which ling'ring penance
> Of such misery doth she cut me off.
> Commend me to your honourable wife!
> Tell her the process of Antonio's end;
> Say how I lov'd you: speak me fair in death;
> And when the tale is told, bid her be judge,
> Whether Bassanio had not once a love.
> Repent not you that you shall lose your friend;
> And he repents not that he pays your debt:
> For, if the Jew do cut but deep enough,
> I'll pay it instantly with all my heart."

Upon due occasion, Antonio should always be cited as the foremark and exemplar of a commercial nobleman; and the Venetians were a nobility of merchants. In his conduct, too, Antonio has manifested that the most romantic prodigality of friendship is perfectly compatible with, nay, it imparts a lustre to the caution and gravity of the trading character.

Launcelot, the clown, tells Jessica that she "cannot be the Jew's daughter:" but, I fear me, Jessica has a worse taint in her blood than Launcelot's imputation would infer; for she robbed her own kindred to enrich the stranger; the directly reverse action, and the natural action, too, of all her tribe; and which, I confess, gives the pretty little Jewess no more than a skin-deep interest with me. To her personal liberty Jessica possessed the chartered right of all nature; to the appropriation of her father's wealth—for Christian behoof—she had not even an ancestral excuse, for the Jews "*borrowed*" of the Egyptians. Her conduct and tone of speech, too, at the time she is purloining the jewels—"Here, catch this casket, it is worth the pains," and "I will gild myself with some more ducats, and be with you straight"—all tallies with her general want of sentiment and delicate feeling. Moreover, Shakespeare has not redeemed her character by putting into her mouth even one little word of regret at leaving her old and forlorn parent,—an unusual thing with him,—but which is so pointed as to appear a provision on his part to preserve the consistency of her character. The Christians have stripped him bare to the pitiless world; they have taken from him "the prop that did sustain his house;" and to the bitter trial of his child's desertion, is added the intelligence, that she *gave her mother's ring for a monkey!* He exclaims at the news, "Thou torturest me, Tubal; it was my turquoise; I had it of Leah *when I was a bachelor;*" adding, with a fine Hebraism, "I would not have given it for a wilderness of monkeys!" O consistent Shakespeare! this was not the girl to be touched with remorse at her unfilial conduct. Squanderers and gamblers have no sense of justice; (for she was a gambler, too;) they are always selfish. Truly, the poor Jew's punishment, like Cain's, was "greater than he could bear." I have no desire to hypercriticise, or to see more in our poet than he himself intended; but the very circumstance of Jessica's trifling with the Clown upon her conversion from the faith of her fathers, strikingly harmonises with her general tone of character. She would have turned Mohammedan, or Buddist, or Spinning Dervis, or Spinning

Jenny, or spinning *anything*, and danced a polka at her new faith: flimsy, thoughtless, and unstable. The scene, alluded to with Launcelot is the 5th of the 3d Act. They enter in the midst of their conversation, and he says:—

"Yes, truly; for, look you, the sins of the father are to be laid upon the children; therefore, I promise you, I fear you. I was always plain with you, and so now I speak my agitation of the matter; therefore, be of good cheer, for truly I think you are damned.

"*Jes.* I shall be saved by my husband; he hath made me a Christian.

"*Laun.* Truly, the more to blame he; we were Christians enow before; e'en as many as could well live, one by another. This making of Christians will raise the price of hogs: if we grow all to be pork-eaters, we shall not shortly have a rasher on the coals for money."

It is Jessica who, in that delicious garden-scene with her lover, makes the well-known deep-thoughted remark, "I am never merry when I hear sweet music." And Lorenzo gives the equally fine solution of the sentiment, followed by the most superb eulogy upon the "concord of sweet sounds" that ever mortal penned. He says:—

"The reason is, your spirits are attentive:
For do but note a wild and wanton herd,
Or race of youthful and unhandled colts,
Fetching mad bounds, bellowing, and neighing loud,
Which is the hot condition of their blood:
If they but hear perchance a trumpet sound,
Or any air of music touch their ears,
You shall perceive them make a mutual stand,
Their savage eyes turn'd to a modest gaze,
By the sweet power of music: therefore, the poet
Did feign that Orpheus drew trees, stones, and floods;
Since naught so stockish, hard, and full of rage,
But music for the time doth change his nature.
The man that hath no music in himself,
Nor is not mov'd with concord of sweet sounds,

Is fit for treasons, stratagems, and spoils ;
The motions of his spirit are as dull as night,
And his affections dark as Erebus.
Let no such man be trusted."

The love-scenes in "Romeo and Juliet" are grand, by reason of the tumult and ferment of the affections turning up the heart's root of passion, devotion, and self-prostration to the soul's idol ; but for the calm and full contentment of luxurious ease in the enjoyment of a blissful consummation, there is no scene like this between little Jessica and her Lorenzo. By the way, he is surely quite as amenable to the charge of "pedantry" as the ill-praised Portia ; for he talks sentiment and philosophy to his little wife like a professor in a college ; whereas in the hands of an inferior poet, he would have talked the common platitudes of the love-maker. Lorenzo can, and very gracefully does, dally and sport with her in a contest of similes to their marriage-night, and very classical and pretty they are. Afterwards, turning upon the full glory of the Italian moonlight, he breaks into that angelic rapture :—

"How sweet the moonlight sleeps upon this bank!
Here will we sit, and let the sounds of music
*Creep* in our ears : soft stillness and the night
Become the touches of sweet harmony.
Sit, Jessica : look how the floor of heaven
Is thick inlaid with patines* of bright gold ;
There's not the smallest orb which thou behold'st,
But in his motion like an angel sings,
Still quiring to the young-eyed cherubins :
Such harmony is in immortal souls ;
But whilst this muddy vesture of decay
Doth grossly close it in, we cannot hear it."

Query—somewhat "pedantic" that, for a lover to discuss

* PATINE, from the Latin, *patina ;* the gold plate with which the priest covers the chalice at high mass. Poetically applied to the stars.

the Platonic theory of the spheral motion to his mistress. Lorenzo is a specimen of an elegant-minded, happy young bridegroom; and that is one of the most enviable beings under God's heaven.

The "Merchant of Venice" opens with introducing the two subordinate characters, Solanio and Salarino, in conversation with the Merchant himself, upon the subject of the inconstancy of the sea, and the anxiety of mind incurred by having commercial ventures abroad on that element; thus preparing the mind of the reader for the loss of Antonio's argosies as a natural event. As characters in the drama, they offer little worthy of notice, unless it be of disgust at their ridiculing the Jew in his distress upon losing his daughter and his jewels; and yet it must be confessed that in the 1st scene of the play some beautiful poetical imagery is put into the mouths of these two insignificant persons when conversing with Antonio upon the anxiety attending commercial speculation. One says—

"My wind, cooling my broth,
Would blow me to an ague when I thought
What harm a wind too great might do at sea.
I should not see the sandy hour-glass run,
But I should think of shallows and of flats,
And see my wealthy Andrew dock'd in sand,
Vailing her high-top lower than her ribs,
To kiss her burial. Should I go to church,
And see the holy edifice of stone,
And not bethink me straight of dang'rous rocks,
Which touching but my gentle vessel's side,
Would scatter all her spices on the stream,
Enrobe the roaring waters with my silks,
And, in a word, but even now worth this,
And now worth nothing?"

That portion of the plot in this great drama which turns upon the destiny of the caskets, is like the grafting of an

Arabian tale upon a common stock of civic adventure. It certainly forms a fanciful and interesting contrast to the stern and painful realities that preserve a simultaneous movement with it. The critic, Schlegel, says that "this love-intrigue, as associated with the trial-scene between Shylock and Antonio, being not less extraordinary, becomes natural and probable by means of the other." This is ingeniously said; and the enthusiastic eulogist of our poet has said some delightful things upon this play; but I would submit that he has not precisely hit the mark of Shylock's character, when he says that "his morality is founded on the disbelief in goodness and magnanimity," and that "his hate is naturally directed against those Christians who possess truly Christian sentiments; the example of disinterested love of our neighbour seems to him the most unrelenting persecution of the Jews."

Shylock's "morality" appears to me founded on the great law of wild nature, *ratified by his own national code;* and all his arguments and all his actions are the offspring of the horrible injustice burnt into his own feelings and those of all his tribe: hence his scorpion-like hatred of the Christians; and not merely because one man lent out money without interest, bating the rate of usance in the money-market,—that is an apology, and a natural one for such a man to urge to himself. No; Shakespeare, with his consistent love of justice, has punished him for his cruelty; but, in the persecution exercised towards him by the professors of a sect who are enjoined to "do justice and love mercy," he has read a lesson which ought, if it do not, to last through all time.

And now, for a pleasant wind-up, "talk we of Master Launcelot; or, Master Launcelot Gobbo; or, good Gobbo; or, good Master Launcelot Gobbo;" who is a foster-brother, if not of the same family with Master Launce, in "The Two Gentlemen of Verona." In the old editions, Gobbo is called a clown, and in character he is a sort of mongrel between the thoroughbred jester-clown and the cur errand-boy. The vein of humour that distinguishes this class of persons must have been popular in Shakespeare's time, since he has repeated the character on various occasions; and although it has passed away from us, yet it still possesses more than an obsolete interest by reason of its quaint idiosyncrasy. Launcelot is a sort of "arabesque" character in the order of humanity; exhibiting the prevalent feature of likeness, with a portentous flourish of half-meaning, and which passes for embellishment. He is a fellow who will scramble through the world with a "light heart and a thin pair of inexpressibles." His spare diet at the Jew's does not waste his humour, and conscience will scarcely sit heavily on him in the night-watches, since the gravest misdemeanour that can be laid to his charge is that he runs away from a master in whose service he swears he is "famished:"—his master's character of him being—

"The patch is kind enough, but a *huge feeder*."

Nevertheless he says—"You may tell every finger I have with my ribs." And yet, with all this inducement, he sedately balances the question between his conscience to remain, and the temptation of Old Scratch to run away; and Old Scratch being right—for once—carries the debate:—

"Certainly, my conscience will serve me to run from this Jew, my master. The fiend is at my elbow, and tempts me, saying to me, 'Gobbo, Launcelot Gobbo, good Launcelot, or good Gobbo, or good Launcelot Gobbo, use your legs, take the start, run away.' My conscience says, 'No; take heed, honest Launcelot; take heed, honest Gobbo;' or, as aforesaid, 'honest Launcelot Gobbo; do not run; scorn running with thy heels.' Well, the most courageous fiend bids me pack:—'Via!' says the fiend; 'Away!' says the fiend; 'for the heavens, rouse up a brave mind,' says the fiend, 'and run.' Well, my conscience, hanging about the neck of my heart, says very wisely to me, 'My honest friend, Launcelot, being an honest man's son,'—or rather an honest woman's son; for, indeed, my father did something smack, something grow to, he had a kind of taste;—well, my conscience says, 'Launcelot, budge not.' 'Budge,' says the fiend. 'Budge not,' says my conscience. Conscience, say I, you counsel well; fiend, say I, you counsel well:—to be ruled by my conscience, I should stay with the Jew, my master, who (Heaven bless the mark!) is a kind of devil; and to run away from the Jew, I should be ruled by the fiend, who, saving your reverence, is the devil himself. Certainly the Jew is the very devil incarnation; and, in my conscience, my conscience is but a kind of hard conscience to offer to counsel me to stay with the Jew. The fiend gives the more friendly counsel:—I will run, fiend; my heels are at your commandment. I will run."

XVII.

# Henry the Fourth.

# XVII.

# HENRY IV.

---

THAT astute founder of the dynasty of the house of Lancaster (Henry IV.) is a practical and memorable example of the axiom, that the wrencher of a civil institution to his own individual aggrandisement had need look out for squalls and tempests; for, as he "soweth the wind, so shall he reap the whirlwind." Henry Bolingbroke had doubtless received egregious injustice at the hands of his cousin, the headlong and headwrong Richard II.; but he himself was as clear a pirate of the crown as if no drop of his grandfather's blood had flowed in his veins. He dethroned his relation, and, perhaps, accomplished—at all events, he has the credit of having connived at—his assassination. But from that moment to the day of his death, Henry lived in a perpetual storm with his turbulent barons,—with those who upon principle opposed his usurping the crown, but most especially with the party that helped him to his "bad eminence;" for no sacrifices of grants and endowments that he could have made would have assuaged their craving of reward for the services they had rendered him. At the close of the tragedy of Richard II., Shakespeare prepares us for the coming discontent and insurrection on the part of the powerful Percy family, by putting into the mouth of the unfortunate king that prophetical warning to Bolingbroke of the bitter fruit that would ensue from such an alliance; and the opening of the present drama (for the two parts form one drama) reveals to us the usurper in sharp collision with this same Northumberland and his son.

This division of the play—the heroical—is conceived in the very highest spirit of chivalry and martial daring. The terrible valour of Percy, and the flaunting heroism of Prince Harry, are drawn with a fervour and dramatic fitness and art, and contrasted with wonderful brilliancy of effect. This power that Shakespeare possessed was in itself almost miraculous, carried, as he carried it, to such a point of perfection; but when we come to the *detail* in the characters, to the casual development of remote and subsidiary thoughts, feelings, and actions, it really seems as if he were indued with all the peculiarities of each individual character, or that he had imparted to them all *his* genius, that they might deliver themselves perfectly.

The two most important, if not the *chief* actors in the serious scenes of this drama, are Prince Harry and Harry Percy, of whom a remarkable list of references might be made confirmatory of the "individuality" sustained in the portraiture of the two men, from the outset to the close of their career. The former will hereafter come under examination; here, therefore, it were sufficient simply to remark, that as Hal the roysterer, as Prince Harry, and afterwards, in isolated royalty, as Henry V., he appears accurately and consistently, one and the same man.

The other extraordinary character—the tornado of the north—Harry Percy, most commonly surnamed "Hotspur," is of the same order and genus with the illustrious "representative" character in "King John," the brave, the steadily-loyal, and the grateful Falconbridge. And yet, withal, there is a palpable distinction to be drawn between the two characters; of the same genus, but of distinct individuality. Both are fiery and impetuous men; both perilously brave; both of noble and generous natures; and here, it should seem, the class-likeness ceases. In the midst of his greatest excitations, Falconbridge always displays presence of mind and deliberation. Hotspur evinces no deficiency in the one quality, but he has neither the deliberation nor the judgment of Falconbridge. Indeed, Hotspur has little judgment, and less deliberation. The soliloquies of Falconbridge are pregnant with sound sense and a flaunting sort of mess-room humour. Hotspur has no reflectiveness; he *acts,* he does not *soliloquise.* The only time that he discourses in soliloquy he is commenting upon the letter he has received from the party whom he had endeavoured to enlist in the rebellion; and most characteristic of the man are his ejaculations as he comes upon the writer's phlegmatic doubts of the success of their enterprise. It commences in the 3d scene of the 2d Act. The *manner* as well as the language of Percy are sustained with wonderful consistency of individuality. One of the most prominent features of his personal character is that of *perpetual restlessness,* to which may be added abundant determination, always combined with rashness and indiscretion. There is one peculiarity in the personal individuality of Hotspur which is quite as carefully detailed as that of any character that Shakespeare has drawn. In the identity of Falconbridge we have no other distinction, no other personal association with him than the general one, of his athletic frame. He is a man of thews and sinews. Speaking of his mother's husband, he says—"Sir Robert never holp to make this leg." In Hotspur, on the other hand, we have constant allusion to some *peculiarity* or other, which makes us feel as though we had known him. First, there is the total lack of repose, already alluded to: he is like a wild beast newly confined. Then, his impetuosity of disposition naturally shows itself in perpetual interruptions during consultations, the most celebrated of which occurs in the 3d scene of the 1st Act. It is the one in which the king orders him to send in his prisoners unransomed. The remainder of the scene (when the king has quitted it) is passed in a series of explosions and interruptions, till the patience of his uncle Worcester begins to fail, and he expostulates with him—"Good cousin, *give me audience for a while.*" Hotspur apologises—"I cry you mercy!" and again bursts in upon Worcester's first words. At length the uncle concludes—"Farewell, kinsman! I will talk to you when you are better tempered to attend."

Then his father, Northumberland, irritated with his unreasonable interruptions, takes him to task—

> "Why, what a wasp-tongue and impatient fool
> Art thou to break into this woman's mood,
> Tying thine ear to no tongue but thine own."

They try again, and again Worcester concludes—"We'll stay your leisure."

It is interesting to trace throughout the career of Percy the total absence of all repose in the character. Not only is he never quiet himself, but he resents inaction in others. He resents his father being in ill health. "Zounds! how has he *leisure* to be *sick* in such a justling time?"

Again, in a subsequent scene, a messenger enters—

> "My lord, here are letters for you.
> "*Hot.* I cannot read them now."

Prince Henry bears testimony to his hurry-skurry life where he says:—

"I am not yet of Percy's mind, the Hotspur of the North; he that kills me some six or seven dozen of Scots at a breakfast, washes his hands, and says to his wife—'Fie upon this quiet life! I want work.' 'O my sweet Harry,' says she, 'how many hast thou killed to-day?' 'Give my roan horse a drench,' says he; and answers, 'Some fourteen,' an hour after—'A trifle, a trifle.'"

It is worth observing here, that the poet has made a marked point of this "roan horse" of Percy's. He has used it as a means of drawing attention to a point of individuality in Hotspur, who manifests a true soldierly interest and judgment concerning his horse. He asks his servant whether "those horses have been brought from the sheriff?" The man answers, "One horse, my lord, he brought even now." And Hotspur instantly shows that he has noted its points—

> "What horse? A roan, a crop-ear, is it not?
> "*Serv.* It is, my lord.
> "*Hot.* That roan shall be my throne."

In this same scene (the 3d of the 2d Act) there is ample proof of his restlessness. When the Lady Percy makes him a remonstrance, and with it a vivid picture of his altered manner and perturbed sleep, gently demanding the cause, he does not rest to answer her, but shouts to his servant, asking some questions about the despatch of a packet. And when his wife persists in affectionate expostulation, he breaks from her, bidding her "come and see him ride," knowing that when once on horseback he shall be beyond reach of her catechising.

His soldierly bluffness and restless nature are again confirmed in his indifference to music.

Percy is no man of business—in his own profession. He is for everything being done extempore, and without calculating the supply. At the first council with Glendower, Mortimer, and the others, met to plan the campaign, after summoning them to sit down, he says, "A plague upon't! I have forgot the map,"—the thing of all others upon such an occasion to be remembered. How pleasantly all this dovetails with the impetuous and restless man.

When his uncle, Worcester, and Sir Richard Vernon return from the parley in the royal camp, and Worcester says, "There is no seeming mercy in the king," Hotspur darts out his answer, "Did you beg any? God forbid!" Not only is he perpetual motion personified, and irascible to boot, but he displays every feature of unmisgiving bravery. So sanguine is he, that the word "failure" is not to be found in his nomenclature. He even turns the disappointment of his father Northumberland's not bringing up his forces into a probable *advantage.* Worcester says:—

> "Your father's sickness is a maim to us.
> "*Hot.* A perilous gash, a very limb lopp'd off:—
> And yet, in faith, 'tis not; his present want
> *Seems* more than we shall find it:—were it good
> To set the exact wealth of all our states
> *All at one cast?* to set so rich a main
> On the nice hazard of one doubtful hour?
> *It were not good;* for therein should we read
> The very bottom and the soul of *hope,*
> The very list, the very utmost bound
> Of all our fortunes."

This piece of sophistry is the transcript of a sanguine man. Douglas, who possesses the same proportion of judgment with Percy, and is equally rash and sanguine, coincides at once in this remarkable opinion.

Whether in council, whether in the field, even whether he is in the society of ladies, Percy is the same restless, untiring individual. Another striking personal characteristic in the man (and which is referred to several times) is his thick and inarticulate utterance,—a blemish which Lady Percy says of him was turned into a grace. Glendower fleers at him for this defect, and he himself twice alludes to it in the space of half a page. First:—

"Arm, arm with speed: and fellows, soldiers, friends,
Better consider what you have to do,
Than I, *that have not well the gift of tongue*,
Can lift your blood up with persuasion."

Again:—

[*Enter a Messenger.*

"My lord, prepare, the king comes on apace.
"*Hot.* I thank him that he cuts me from my tale,
For *I profess not talking*."

The last characteristic, and which is ever the concomitant of true greatness in every sphere,—Percy is no flatterer, and he rejects flattery from others. He makes an awkward sort of apology to Douglas for having praised him. In short, he is the perfect exemplar of a man of mere, *forlorn-hope bravery;* and his apotheosis is finely uttered by Prince Hal over his dead body in the battlefield:—"Fare thee well, great heart!" &c.—4th scene of the 5th Act.

The fathers also of the young heroes are portrayed with undiminished fidelity. Henry, the king, advanced in years, is the same man as young Bolingbroke,—cool-headed, prudent, keen, and steadily clutching all he had raped; jealous of his son, whom he drove into riotous and profligate courses.

Northumberland, equally grasping, fails through excess of his own overreaching and dilatory policy. Fierce, and even brutal in party-spirit—demoniacal in revenge. His speech upon hearing the news of his son Hotspur's death assumes even a Satanic dignity from its ferocious spirit of retribution:—

"Let one spirit of the first-born Cain
Reign in all bosoms, that, each heart being set
On bloody courses, the rude scene may end,
And darkness be the burier of the dead!"

Among the second and third rate members of the drama may be instanced, first, that rancorous and uncompromising partisan, the Earl of Worcester, whose hatred of Henry, seated by himself and Northumberland on the throne of Richard, induces him even to betray his trust as messenger between the king and the rebel party on the eve of the Shrewsbury battle. Worcester's object being to keep open the wound of discontent in his party, refuses to report to Hotspur the pacific overtures of the king. It may indeed be urged in his extenuation, that Worcester knew by experience the cold, unrelenting, and grasping disposition of Henry. With some show of prudence, therefore, he will not risk the chance of Percy's demonstrative and generous nature being touched by his sovereign's offer of reconciliation. Consequently, when he and Sir Richard Vernon return from the parley in the royal camp, he at once decides:—

> "Oh, no! my nephew must not know, Sir Richard,
> The liberal, kind offer of the king."

He then details his reasons for this course of procedure; but Vernon, in the true spirit of an honourable man, maintains that Percy ought to be made acquainted with the whole interview. In Worcester's conduct upon this occasion we have an example of the fatal effects of the bitterness of party-spirit. Had he then fulfilled his duty, the rebellion might have been cancelled, and many worthy spirits spared a violent extinction. But Worcester was a coarse-minded and rasping politician,—if the term politician be fitly applied to the mere turbulent deposer of one monarch, and rebel to another, simply for the gratification of his own selfish purposes. But how distinctly manifest, in these great historical dramas, is the fact, that from the era of John downwards, the monarchy in this country has almost always been, more or less, in abeyance to the aristocracy, and has indeed been sustained by the antagonism of parties in their own order; and these instinctively nourished and fostered by royalty itself, to preserve its own individuality, and even its "local habitation and name."

Vernon is by much the noblest of all the "subordinates" in the play. His constancy to the rebel party does not prevent his bearing honourable testimony to the merits of their opponents. His admiration of the gallant bearing of Prince Harry is in the purest spirit of chivalry, and *true* chivalry always carried honour—which is justice—to the verge of romance in generous dealing. It is Vernon who gives that superb description of the prince and his comrades, whom he had seen preparing for the campaign, in the 1st scene of the 4th Act, Part I. Vernon is the moderator in the party: he is the only one impressed with the dignity of impartiality; and therefore he would be the man—for steadiness of principle—to be intrusted beyond a whole council of such men as Worcester. He *was* constant to his cause; and although we regret that such a character should have paid the rebel's penalty with one like Worcester, yet the moral conveyed in the sacrifice to loyalty and quiet government is a valuable one.

In direct contrast to the character of Vernon, may be cited that notable instance of treachery and meanness, Prince John of Lancaster, younger son of the king. Here is the phylactery of his vices—wily, wary, cold, calculating, indirect, faithless. In act, treacherous and cruel. No wonder Falstaff hates him; he hates him personally and socially, and *no* wonder, with his own quicksilver nature; because, as he says, "A man *cannot make him laugh.*" Beyond this playful reason, however, (containing a profound instinct beneath its apparent superficiality and lightness,) the acute perception and shrewd wit of Falstaff discerned the heartless nature of the young fellow, and he loathed him accordingly, with all the genuine disgust of a genial and cordial spirit.

It is worthy of remark (as noting that strict principle of consistency in Shakespeare's mind) that John of Lancaster inherits from his father, Bolingbroke, many of his qualities.

His smooth speech, his politic reserve, his artful manner, his lavish promise, and his breach of pledge, are all to be traced as characteristics by descent. It will be remembered how the father receives Richard II.'s murderer, Exton, when he had done the deed, in pursuance of a *hint* dropped by the usurper, who would so largely benefit by that king's death; not with expected commendation and reward, but with rebuke, opprobrium, and sentence of perpetual banishment. (See the closing sentences of "Richard II.") In the same way does the son deal by the rebel leaders who trust to his princely word. The scene (the 2d of the 4th Act, Part II.) is an edifying example of the cool unblushingness with which princes can (*occasionally*) dispense with that strict adherence to their plighted honour which should of right distinguish them above all men. It is a remarkable and curious combination of hypocrisy, cant, pretence, false-seeming, false-protesting appeal to holiest things, as guarantees to truth in dealing, and used as blinds to the vilest treachery; causing us to marvel that it can be a prince who thus acts and speaks, until we call to mind a parallel instance *much nearer to our own times.*

At the convocation of the Archbishop of York, Mowbray, and Hastings, the prince pledges to them the redress of all those grievances which have rent the kingdom and raised the rebellion. He says to the Archbishop:—

> "My lord, these griefs shall be with speed redress'd;
> *Upon my soul they shall.* If this may please you,
> Discharge your powers unto their sev'ral counties,
> *As we will ours.*"

The rebels (evidently not knowing their man) trust to his honour and his soul, disband their forces, and are immediately sent off to execution. The concluding answer of Prince John to the amazed Archbishop's expostulation, is in true keeping:—

"*Arch.* Will you thus break your faith?
"*P. John.* *I pawn'd thee none.*
I promis'd you redress of these same grievances
Whereof you did complain; *which, by mine honour,*
I will perform with a *most Christian care.*
But for you, rebels,—look to taste the due
Meet for rebellion, and such acts as yours.
Most shallowly did you these arms commence,
Fondly brought here, and *foolishly sent hence.*
Strike up our drums, pursue the scatter'd stray;
*Heaven,* and *not we, hath safely fought to-day.*
Some guard these traitors to the block of death,
Treason's true bed, and yielder up of breath."

This might be deemed an act of TREACHERY, but modern courtesy would style it merely a "COUP D'ETAT!" the one fully worthy of the other.

Among the subordinate characters, not one is drawn with more replete originality than that of Owen Glendower. His whole deportment and manner are not only national, (which was to be expected,) but the tone of conversation in the man is that of a provincial-bred one. He delights in recording the local traditions and manners connected with his own personal identity. His credulity is provincial and active; his temper is that of his nation, sudden, and inflammable as straw, and as quickly extinct. With all his faith in the mysterious and the miraculous, however, Glendower is a grave, precise, and unimaginative character. These peculiarities are amusingly and most naturally illustrated in the scene where Hotspur hoaxes and irritates him. Like a truly matter-of-fact and circumscribed man, too, he does not at once perceive Hotspur's intention, but doggedly and obtusely repeats his own assertion in answer to the other's ridicule. Now, this is the very transcript of a hide-bound imagination. Having once revealed the stupendous fact, that when *he* was born "the frame and huge foundation of the earth shaked like a coward;" and Hotspur provokingly replying, that it would have done the same thing "had his mother's cat kittened, though he himself had never been born;" yet he contents himself with repeating the same words; for many minds—*bores* especially, fancy that *repetition* is *confirmation,* and that it carries with it conviction. "I say, the earth did shake when I was born." "And I say," again retorts Hotspur, "the earth was not of my mind, if you suppose, as fearing you, it shook." Curiously enough, Shakespeare has made him repeat the words even again, that there may be no doubt as to his own intention in developing the manner of the man; and, as contrasted with the fiery nature of Percy, the effect of the scene is very masterly. And not the least remarkable feature in it is the perfect consistency, as well as distinction, that the poet has maintained in the character of the two irascibilities. Both are consistent in themselves, and both are preserved with admirable breadth of colouring. After running on with a tissue of his amazing endowments, challenging the admiration of the company, Hotspur, instead of answering him any more, says, with inimitable raillery, "I think there is no man speaks better Welsh; I'll to dinner." When Glendower leaves the scene, the irritable temper of Hotspur is also excellently displayed in his reply to Mortimer; who has been protesting against his worrying the old man, "Peace, cousin Percy; you will make him mad." And, on Glendower going out, Mortimer again expostulates most naturally; the whole scene is like an actual occurrence. "Fie, cousin Percy! how you cross my father!" Then Hotspur bursts forth:—

"I cannot choose; sometimes he angers me
With telling me of the moldwarp and the ant,
Of the dreamer Merlin and his prophecies,
And of a dragon, and a finless fish,
A clip-wing'd griffin, and a moulten raven,

A couching lion, and a ramping cat,
And such a deal of skimble-skamble stuff
As puts me from my faith. I tell you what,
He held me last night, at least nine hours,
In reckoning up the several devils' names
That were his lackeys. I cried, 'H'm,' and 'Well,' 'Go to,'
But mark'd him not a word. Oh, he's as tedious
As a tirèd horse, a railing wife;
Worse than a smoky house. I had rather live
With cheese and garlic in a windmill, far,
Than feed on cates, and have him talk to me
In any summer-house in Christendom."

The part occupied by Owen Glendower is insignificant as to the quantity of *words* to be spoken, but it is a choicely good one as regards the character to be displayed, and which should be intrusted only to an actor of intelligence and quick feeling. His social and kind nature is inferred from his cavaliering the ladies Percy and Mortimer, and introducing them, before their husbands depart for the war. And in that little scene, which, by the way, is one of the most agreeable in the whole play, by reason of its familiar domestic unpretendingness, the several characteristics of the men are set forth to the very life:—Mortimer, the newly-married one, with his head in his pretty wife's lap, regretting only that she can speak no English and he no Welsh; but then he says, with bridegroom devotion:—

"I understand thy looks: that pretty Welsh
Which thou pour'st down from these swelling heavens
I am too perfect in; and, but for shame,
In such a parley would I answer thee.
I understand thy kisses, and thou mine,
And that's a feeling disputation:
But I will never be a truant, love,
Till I have learn'd thy language; for thy tongue
Makes Welsh as sweet as ditties highly penn'd,
Sung by a fair queen in a summer's bower,
With ravishing division to her lute."

She sings to them a favourite national ballad. Hotspur, who must have everything done extempore, bids Lady Percy sit down, that he may dispose himself in the same manner:—"Come, Kate, quick, quick, quick; that I may lay my head in *thy* lap:" and he instantly begins some impudent tricks; for one moment she requests to be informed if he "wish to have his head broken," and immediately before rates him with "Lie still, ye thief, and hear the lady sing in Welsh." Hotspur is no chamberer; and he has a supreme contempt for music, for he says, (of course for the sake of teasing,) "I had rather hear, lady, my brach [his hound] howl in Irish." A lovely touch of nature, however, here occurs—where the poet pays a compliment to the sweet power of music, even upon the rough nature of Hotspur; at the same time exhibiting him the man of society and gentle breeding. Lady Percy is still talking on to him, when he interrupts her with—"Peace! the lady sings!"

Poor Lady Percy! the sequel of her story is a sad one, and we sympathise with her in its truth. When the honour and fame of her husband are to be chronicled, she speaks greatly, though she is quite subordinate till then; and then the factious rebel her father-in-law stands a cipher before her. Her reproof to him is tremendous, at the same time most womanly; and her tribute to the memory of her lord is the heart-full eloquence of a worthy wife. The scene is the 3d in the 2d Act of Part II., where she is dissuading old Northumberland from engaging in the new insurrection after the fatal event at Shrewsbury. He talks of his "pledged honour" to the enterprise,—an argument which she turns upon him with stinging rebuke, enough to shrivel the man up like scorched parchment:—

"Oh, yet, for God's sake, go not to these wars!
The time was, father, that you *broke your word*
When you were *more endear'd to it than now;*

When your own Percy, when my heart-dear Harry,
Threw many a northward look, to see his father
Bring up his powers; but he did long in vain.
Who then persuaded you to stay at home?
There were two honours lost,—yours and your son's.
For yours,—may heavenly glory brighten it!
For his,—*it stuck upon him, as the sun*
*In the gray vault of heav'n;* and by his light
Did all the chivalry of England move
To do brave acts: he was indeed the glass
Wherein the noble youth did dress themselves.
He had no legs that practis'd not his gait;
And *speaking thick*,* which nature made his blemish,
Became the accents of the valiant;
For those that could speak *low* and *tardily*,
Would turn their own *perfection* to *abuse*,
To seem like him; so that, in speech, in gait,
In diet, in affections of delight,
In military rules, humours of blood,
He was the mark and glass, copy and book,
That fashioned others. And him,—O wondrous him!
O miracle of men!—*him did you leave*
(Second to none, unseconded by you)
To look upon the hideous god of war
In disadvantage; to abide a field
Where nothing but the sound of Hotspur's name
Did seem defensible:—*so you left him.*
Never, oh, never do his ghost the wrong
*To hold your honour more precise and nice*
*With others than with him!* let them alone:
The marshal and the archbishop are strong:
Had my sweet Harry had but half their numbers,
To-day might I, hanging on Hotspur's neck,
Have talk'd of Monmouth's grave."

Sir Walter Blunt is the last of the serious characters, among the subordinate ones, to whom especial notice may be dispensed; and he would have passed with the others but for the

* Rapidly and inarticulately.

purpose of simply referring to his unimpeachable loyalty. At the battle of Shrewsbury, he, with several others, accoutre themselves in the royal insignia, in order that the attention of the enemy may be distracted from the real sovereign. This is said to be an historical fact, and a remarkable one, as connected with such a motive and such an event. The self-devotion and bravery of the man are illustrious;—scarcely so the conduct of the king, who could even listen to, and still more sanction such prodigality of service from personal consideration. There is food for thought in Falstaff's apostrophe upon noticing the dead body of the noble partisan:—" Soft! who art thou? Sir Walter Blunt!—there's '*honour*' for you—here's no vanity!"

In proceeding to notice the comic characters in the two parts of " Henry IV.," can it be conceded that Falstaff was a " subordinate?" A subordinate!—is he not almost the sole preoccupier of the mind whenever it recurs to these plays? Why, Sir John is principal and paramount in all places, and on all occasions. He makes his entry, and the scene is filled; he makes his exit, and our " eyes are *idly* bent on him who enters next." He played second to no one. Prince Hal understood him as well as any of them; but the whole synod could never take the lead when Sir John was present. He was no subsidiary,—no attendant planet of any orb; he was himself a constellation,—a system! His path was eccentric, and comet-like; I will therefore (" by particular desire,"—of myself) depart from the general plan of the work, and devote a few words to this immortal and unequalled character. And first of all, truly speaking, Falstaff *is* a secondary person in these dramas,—he *is* a " subordinate;" the main plot of the play could proceed without him. It was the circumstance of Shakespeare's having introduced upon so many occasions persons unessential to the plot, equal, if not superior, to his chief characters, that suggested the plan of these Essays.

The character of Sir John Falstaff is, I should think, the most witty and humorous combined that ever was portrayed. So palpably is the person presented to the mind's eye, that not only do we give him a veritable location in history; but the others, the real characters in the period, compared with him, appear to be the idealised people, and invented to be his foils and contrasts. As there is no romance like the romance of real life, so no real-life character comes home to our apprehensions and credulities like the romance of Sir John Falstaff. He is one grand identity. His body is fitted for his mind,—bountiful, exuberant, and luxurious; and his mind was well appointed for his body,—being rich, ample, sensual, sensuous, and imaginative. The very fatness of his person is the most felicitous correspondent to the unlimited opulence of his imagination; and but for this conjunction, the character would have been out of keeping and incomplete. Fancy a human thread-paper with Sir John's amount of roguish accomplishment! No power of reasoning could induce a motion of sympathy with such a compound. In most men, wit is the waste-pipe of their spleen in contemplating the happiness of others; in Falstaff it is the main supply of a robust structure, and is the surcharge of fun and good temper. His wit is the offspring and heir to his love of laughter, the overflowing of his satisfaction with himself, and his good terms with all men. He keeps both body and mind in one perpetual gaudy-day; his is the saturnalia, the carnival of the intellect, and his body he rejoices with sack-posset, and his mind with jokes and roars of laughter; and with him each acts upon and with the other,—the true sign of a strong constitution. Falstaff's is not a "clay that gets muddy with drink;" his sensuality does not sodden and brutify his faculties, but it quickens their temper and edge. It gives wings to his imagination, and—to use his own words—fills it with "nimble, fiery, and delectable shapes." He is amenable to the charge of a host of vices, any one of which would strand and shipwreck an ordinary character. He is an indicted coward, a braggadocio, a cheat, a peculator, a swindler, and a liar, &c., &c., and yet, withal, so far are we from voting him to Coventry for all his delinquencies, there are few of us who would refuse to "*march* through Coventry" with him, at the head of his scarecrows; and one reason for this tolerance—not to say this sleeve-laughing encouragement of his villainous courses on the part of all ranks and classes—is, that he himself appears to have adopted and indulged in them from an irrepressible love of humour and mad waggery. He is no hypocrite; and men, from instinct, and especially your men of the world, can extenuate many vices, rather than that of hypocrisy. What bold impudence in that speech! "If my wind were but long enough to say my prayers, I would repent." He also tells the Lord Chief-Justice—who he knows well enough knows *him*—that he "lost his voice with holloing and singing of anthems." His impudence is sublime; and that very impudence forms no insignificant item in his humour: for the grand secret of Falstaff's wit, and humour too, consists in an impenetrable and imperturbable self-possession. He proposes Bardolph—one of his rogues, as known as the church-steeple—to the silk-mercer as security for his payment. He is never thrown off his guard; or, if so, he is never foiled: he recovers himself like a rope-dancer. In the famous eleven buckram-men scene, when the tables are turned upon him, and his scouring-off laid bare, his resource is—"Do you think I did not know ye? By the Lord, I knew ye as well as he that made ye." When his men, Pistol, Nym, and the rest, are accused before Justice Shallow of robbing Master Slender, while he is drunk, Sir John takes upon himself to dismiss the charge against them, with those remarkable words:—"You hear all these matters *denied*, gentlemen:—you hear—the men *deny* it."

His lying, which proceeds quite as much from an impulse of humour as from a desire to deceive, is so florid and romantic that no mortal is taken in by it, except his hostess, Quickly, and she lends him ten pounds after having him arrested for a debt. The broadest and most commonly-known example of his lying is when he pretends he knew the prince all the while that he is relating the encounter with the eleven men in buckram; but the richest specimen of his varied talent at impudent cheating, lying, and roguery, surely is the one just referred to—of the arrest by his landlady. It is in the 1st scene of the 2d Act, in the 2d Part of the play. His explanation to the Chief-Justice of the cause of his hostess's indictment is an epitome of his whole conduct. He says, "My lord, this is a *poor mad soul,* and she says, up and down the town, that *her eldest son is like you.* She hath been in good case, and the truth is, poverty hath distracted her." The judge, not deceived by him for one moment, orders that he shall pay her demand; and while he is conversing with Master Gower about the news of the rebellion, we hear Falstaff saying to his poor gull of a hostess—"As I am a gentleman!" "Ah! 'faith, you said so before." "As I am a gentleman! Come, no more words of it."

"*Hostess.* By this heavenly ground I tread on, I must be fain to pawn both my plate and the tapestry of my dining-chambers."

This move of hers has lost her the game. He takes advantage of her parley, and answers her objection:—

"Glasses, glasses, is the only drinking: and for thy walls, a pretty slight drollery, or the story of the Prodigal, or the German hunting in water-work, is worth a thousand of these bed-hangings and these fly-bitten tapestries. Let it be ten pound if thou canst. Come, an' it were not for thy humours, there is not a better wench in England. Go, wash thy face and draw thy action. [We see that she has been blubbering and fretting.] Come, thou must not be in this humour with ME. Dost not know me? Come, come; I know thou wast set on to this.

"*Host.* Pray thee, Sir John, let it be but twenty nobles; i' faith, I am loath to pawn my plate; in good earnest, la.

"*Fal.* Let it alone. *I'll make other shift; you'll be a fool still.*

"*Host.* Well, you shall have it, though I pawn my gown. I hope you'll come to supper. *You'll pay me altogether?*

"*Fal. Will I live?*"

He has won the day; and then, turning to Bardolph as she is going out, he says, "Go with her, with her; hook on, hook on." Is not this real life?

Falstaff is equal to any exigence; he is never foiled, but usually comes off with flying colours by means of his astounding, and always laughable, effrontery. When this is recognised and resisted, he still saves himself with a flash of humour or a quirk. No one but Shakespeare could have brought such a character in competition with the Lord Chief-Justice of England, and yet have maintained the supremacy of each party. At the close of the scene just quoted, as soon as his hostess is dismissed, he turns with all the coolness of a privy counsellor to the judge and Master Gower, and endeavours to join in their conversation respecting the news of the rebellion. His lordship, however, gives him the cut direct, by steadily addressing himself to Gower, and attending to none of the knight's questions; but Sir John is wide awake to that "dodge," so he drives in between them and plays upon the judge with his own guns. The Chief-Justice says to Gower, "I have heard better news.

"*Fal.* What's the news, my good lord?

"*Ch. J.* Where lay the king last night?

"*Gow.* At Basingstoke, my lord.

"*Fal.* I hope, my lord, all's well; what is the news, my lord?

"*Ch. J.* Come all his forces back?

"*Gow.* No; fifteen hundred foot and five hundred horse are marched up to my lord of Lancaster against Northumberland and the archbishop.

"*Fal.* Comes the king back from Wales, my noble lord?

"*Ch. J.* You shall have letters of me presently; come, go along with me, good Master Gower.

"*Fal.* My lord!

"*Ch. J.* What 's the matter?

"*Fal.* Master Gower, shall I entreat you with me to dinner?

"*Gow.* I must wait upon my good lord here; I thank you, good Sir John.

"*Ch. J.* Sir John, you loiter here too long, being you are to take soldiers up in the counties as you go.

"*Fal.* Will you sup with me, Master Gower?

"*Ch. J.* What foolish master taught you these manners, Sir John?

"*Fal.* Master Gower, if they become me not, he was a fool that taught them me. This is the right fencing grace, my lord, tap for tap, and so part fair.

"*Ch. J.* Now the Lord lighten thee! Thou art a great fool."

The effect of that little scene,—the impassible coolness of effrontery of the one, and the irritation of the other, is managed with pure dramatic art. It is also in accordance with human action and passion, that the person (particularly one in authority) who has been outwitted in a brain encounter should be fidgeting for an occasion to redeem his faded dignity. Old Gascoigne, therefore, watches the knight like a rat-dog. This is the second check he has received at his hands. He perceived him in the street; and knowing he had been concerned in the Gadshill robbery, sends his attendant to summon the knight before him. He, however, is quite alive to the movement, and says to his little page—"Boy, tell him I am deaf:" and with admirable humour he maintains his delusion. The scene, which is long, and ludicrous as long, is the 2d of the 1st Act, Part II.

Hazlitt says the best way to answer the impugners of Milton is to "take down the book and read to them." Of a surety, the best, and infinitely the pleasantest, way of delivering a summary upon the genius of Falstaff, is to select a scene bearing upon each phase of his character, and allow it to pass for both comment and illustration. But, then, may not this be the case with *all* the characters in these plays, and of course most especially with those that exhibit such broad and varied marks of individuality upon them as this, the most extraordinary creation of all his or any other writer's comic personifications?

With the genial spirit in which his sweet nature was conceived, Shakespeare contrives to throw in some dash of feeling—a motion of our common humanity—some extenuation, even in his worst characters; for, whatever they were besides, they were also men, and unmitigated evil belongs only to the origin of all evil—not to human nature. With the accurate perception, however, of true morality, he has not imparted to the character of Falstaff—attractive as it is for its sociality, wit, humour, and imagination—any of those intrinsic qualities which would set him up as an object of imitation,—of course in his convivialities, his roystering, and other laxities; but he has associated them with the meaner vices of profligacy, turning these to the fullest account in completing the character. Gross as the knight is, and wonderfully as the poet has relieved that grossness by the most brilliant flashes of wit and drollery, no mortal, it is to be presumed, ever arose from reading the plays in which he shines with a less firm appreciation of the wealth of virtue in all its senses; still less could any one desire to mimic his propensities. This cannot be said of some modern creations that might be instanced, which, from their sneers at sympathy and mutual confidence—their constant depreciation of the most generous feelings of our nature, inducing suspicion and distrust of all human profession, would go to sap the foundations of what alone can support the social fabric.

It was requisite to our poet that the dissolute young prince should, in his scenes of extravagance, have immediately about his person companions endowed with accomplishments sufficiently eminent to induce him to "daff the world aside, and bid it pass." He has, therefore, enriched Falstaff with infinite wit and humour, combined, moreover, with uncommon sagacity and acuteness in appreciating the characters and dispositions of men; but to these great qualities there is the set-off of degrading and even rascal propensities. With talents less brilliant, Falstaff would not have attracted Henry, who, historically, was himself a man of talent and quick discrimination: with less bloated profligacy he would have attached him too much, and by so doing have compromised the laws of civilised society; which, with well-regulated minds, form also the dramatic law,—to show vice her own scorn, virtue her own feature.

Pages upon pages have been written concerning this remarkable character; and indeed the subject seems all but inexhaustible, notwithstanding what has been said of his being the best commentator on himself. One eminent writer, several years ago, (Mr Barnes, editor of the *Times*,) contributed some ingenious papers which appeared in the *Examiner*, their object being to prove that Falstaff was not a coward. What to say to this, decidedly, is questionable. "*Decidedly*" he ran away at Gadshill; he counterfeited death at the Shrewsbury fight when Douglas attacked him; and he stabbed the *dead* Percy in the thigh, which act, with the lie crowning it, villainous as it was, may rather come under the denomination of knavery than non-bravery, because he turned it to sordid advantage. And, lastly, when the sheriff's officers are proceeding to arrest-him, he bids Bardolph "cut off the villain's head;" he offers no personal resistance himself. Nevertheless, and notwithstanding all these and more "counts" that might be adduced against him, the imputed cowardice of Falstaff does not arise so much from a principle of fear—downright, pallid horror—as from a constitutional love of ease, a sense of enjoyment, and repugnance—from inability—to disagreeable exertion. He does engage, it is true, in the brawl with Pistol at Hostess Quickly's; but even here he first tells Bardolph to "quoit him down;" and knowing the amount of Pistol's mettle, he himself at last drives him out; but, upon his return, he vapours about it sufficiently, as though it had been his maiden fight. He says to Doll—"The rogue fled from me like quicksilver." And she answers—"And thou followed'st him *like a church.*" He also in the last battle took Sir John Coleville prisoner, who offered *no hint of resistance;* for which courtesy he says—"Thou, like a kind fellow, gavest thyself away gratis; and I thank thee for thee:" and, in speaking of his prowess to Prince John, he says—"He *saw me*, and yielded: that I may justly say with the hooknosed fellow of Rome, 'I came, saw, and overcame.'" All this is but the cowardice of ease—and fat. Now, Pistol is a blusterer and an unadulterated coward. Parolles, too, is a fanatic in poltroonery—a devout coward. The sense of fear, and its results, are totally different in the two men, Parolles and Falstaff: how Dr Johnson should have compared them for one moment is wonderful! Parolles is dull, and mean, and bad-natured, as well as a coward. Falstaff cheated at every turn; he kept out of harm's way, and laughed immoderately at his economy of exertion and escape from danger. In the fight, he "leads his ragamuffins where they are peppered." He proves (as if in joke) the estimate he gave of them to the prince, who says—"Tell me, Jack, whose fellows are these that come after?"

"*Fal.* Mine, Hal, mine.

"*P. Hal.* I did never see such pitiful rascals.

"*Fal.* Tut, tut! good enough to toss: food for powder, food for powder: they'll fill a pit as well as better:—tush, man; mortal men, mortal men.

"*Westmoreland.* Ay, but, Sir John, methinks they are exceeding poor and bare,—too beggarly.

"*Fal.* Faith, for their poverty, I know not where they had that; and for their bareness, I am sure they never learned that of me!"

By the way, his description of these scarecrows, and of his manœuvre in impressing them—to the misuse of the king's exchequer—is one of the famous points in the character, and a superb one it is, (Henry IV., Act 4, Scene 2., Part I.) "If I be not ashamed of my soldiers, I'm a soused gurnet," &c. After having read it, the conclusion one must come to is, that it is more the manner of one who has the courage to laugh down strife and running into danger, than it is the conduct of a coward in grain. What can be a finer hoax than his pulling out his bottle of sack during the fight, when the prince desires him to lend him his sword? In short, I think with Mackenzie, in his essay upon the character, that "his cowardice may be placed to his *sagacity*, and that he has a lively sense of danger, but not the want of self-possession which arises from fear." But the finest dissertation upon the character of Falstaff is decidedly the essay by Mr Morgann. As a specimen of neat and elegant writing, with ingenious special-pleading, it stands distinguished in our literature; at the same time it must be acknowledged that the author is so bent upon proving Shakespeare to have intended the fat knight to be considered a man of courage—absolute "courage"—that the essay has more the air of a barrister's defence than a calm dispassionate inquiry after truth.

The finest point in this wonderful character for vivacity and brilliancy, I cannot but think, appears in those displays of fancy that now and then burst from him in a clatter of images and similes, like the sudden explosion of complicated pieces of firework. When he runs upon this vein his imagination seems inexhaustible, and that it could run on, and at that rate, for ever. One of the most ludicrous of these exhibitions of intellectual pyrotechnics occurs in the well-known scene where Bardolph ventures his small talent at ridicule of his master's corpulence, and is received with that tremendous broadside of retaliation upon his own flaming proboscis :—

"Do thou amend thy face, and I will amend my life. Thou art our admiral—thou bearest the lantern in the poop; but 'tis the nose of thee. Thou art the knight of the burning lamp.

"*Bard.* Why, Sir John, my face does you no harm.

"*Fal.* No; I'll be sworn I make as good use of it as many a man doth of a death's head, or a *memento mori.* I never see thy face, but I think upon hell-fire and Dives that lived in purple; for there he is in his robes, burning,—burning. If thou wert any way given to virtue, I would swear by thy face; my oath should be, 'By this fire, that's God's angel!' But thou art altogether given over; and wert indeed, but for the light in thy face, the son of utter darkness. When thou ran'st up Gadshill in the night to catch my horse, if I did not think thou hadst been an *ignis fatuus*, or a ball of wildfire, there's no purchase in money. Oh! thou art a perpetual triumph,—an everlasting bonfire light. Thou hast saved me a thousand marks in links and torches, walking with thee in the night betwixt tavern and tavern; but the sack thou hast drunk me, would have bought me lights as good cheap, at the dearest chandler's in Europe. I have maintained that salamander of yours with fire any time this two-and-thirty years, —Heaven reward me for it!

"*Bard.* S' Blood, I would my face were in your belly.

"*Fal.* Gad a mercy! so should I be sure to be heart-burned."

This is perhaps the finest specimen of his "humour," with imagination; — the finest quotation of his "wit" — pure wit, as regards thought and language—is surely the celebrated eulogy of Sherris sack;—in the 3d scene of the 4th Act;—it follows, in the most natural way, after his parley with that cold-blooded trickster, the young Prince John of Lancaster, who, in taking leave, says, "I shall speak better of you, Falstaff, than you *deserve;*" and the fine old self-appreciater replies after him, "I would you had but the *wit; 'twere better than your dukedom.*—Good faith, this same young sober-blooded boy doth not love me; nor a man cannot make him laugh; but that's no marvel, *he drinks no wine.*"

The last scene that we have with the fat old mountain of flesh and iniquity is a somewhat affecting one; and it should seem, by common consent, that the poet has visited his sins upon him with a degree of harshness. Moreover, it is not unusual with the critics to impute to cold-heartedness Henry V.'s peremptory and sudden dismissal of all his old co-rioters. It may be asked, however, what other course he could pursue, upon taking the reins of government? and, at all events, to Falstaff he promised "competence of life, that lack of means enforce him not to evil;" and he concludes with enjoining the Lord Chief-Justice "*to see performed the tenor of his word.*" That the knight and all his companions are, immediately after the king's exit, packed off to the Fleet prison by the judge's order, looks very like revenge for the old offences that had passed between them. Nathan Drake says (quoting no authority) that the imprisonment of Falstaff was the ultimate cause of his death; and Mrs Quickly, in the subsequent play of "Henry V.," before describing the death-bed scene of the knight, says, "The king has killed his heart." Stowe gives the following record of the circumstance:—"After his coronation, King Henry called unto him all those young lords and gentlemen who were the followers of his young acts, *to every one of whom he gave rich gifts,* and then commanded, that as many as would change their manners, as he intended to do, *should abide with him in his court;* and to all that would persevere in their formerlike conversation, he gave express commandment, upon pain of their heads, never after that day to come into his presence."

Certain it is, that we are accustomed to consider the thieves and outlaws of the early periods in the same light and of the same standing with the common highwaymen of the last century ; and, morally, there was no difference between them; but, as a class, they were as distinct as the ancient minstrel and the modern street ballad-singer. The great marauders of former days were usually men sprung from the *upper* classes in society; "younger sons of younger brothers" of the gentry, who possessing no inheritance, having no useful accomplishment, not being able either to read or write, and being desperate in fortune, when there were no wars toward, and no foreign pillage rife, turned their craft upon their fellow-countrymen. The lively author of "Microcosmography," (Earle, Bishop of Salisbury,) in his "Character," "The Younger Brother," describes him precisely as here mentioned. He says, "When he can get no employment as a soldier, he *takes to the road;*" that is, turns highwayman. Bishop Earle lived during the reign of the revered Charles II. The gentry have contrived matters better for their younger incumbrances within the last one hundred and fifty years, and the profession of thieving gradually declined to the rank of the Du Vals ; (who was a gentleman ;) thence still lower, to the Turpins, and ending with the Jack Shepherds and the Abershaws. Robin Hood, Earl of Huntingdon, was nothing more nor less than a titled thief. In the more civilised era of the nineteenth century we steal the property of foreigners.

Shakespeare, of course, was as intimately acquainted with Stowe's history as we ; we may therefore conclude that he had a motive in deepening the retribution visited upon the profligate old knight, whose accomplishments had made him an object of peculiar attraction and even of sympathy in his reverses.

In the concourse and train of kings and princes, knights and highwaymen, it is pleasant to come upon that little scene in the inn-yard at Rochester, and listen to the natural talk of those carriers, puddering about with their lanterns, telling the hour of the night by the constellation "Charles's wain over the new chimney," and grumbling at the new ostler's corn. "The peas and beans are as dank as a dog," and they "give the poor jades the bots." All things have gone wrong "since Robin ostler died; he never joyed after the price of oats rose." The whole scene, with all its still-life accompaniments, is like a picture by Teniers, or a rival chiaro-scuro by Rembrandt.

The character of Ned Poins requires but slight mention. He, by the way, was a "younger brother;" he says so; he, therefore, is a gentlemanly link between the royal thief-general and his plebeian subalterns. Poins is Prince Hal's shadow, and though not witty himself, is the cause of wit in others; witness Falstaff's banter, "That Poins has no more valour than a wild duck;" and "The prince favours him because their legs are both of a bigness."

After Falstaff, the most perfect characters in the play are Shallow and Silence, the Gloucestershire justices. Here again we have Shakespeare's astonishing power in individuality-portraiture. It is impossible to conceive a stronger contrast, a more direct antipodes in mental structure than he has achieved between Falstaff and Shallow; the one all intellect, all acuteness of perception and fancy, and the other, the justice, a mere compound of fatuity, a *caput mortuum* of understanding. Not only is Shallow distinguished by his eternal babble, talking "infinite nothings," but with the flabby vivacity, the idiotic restlessness that not unfrequently accompany this class of mind; (if such a being may be said to possess mind at all;) he not only tattles on—"whirr, whirr, whirr," like a ventilator, but he fills up the chinks in his sentences with *repetitions,* as blacksmiths continue to tap the anvil in the intervals of turning the iron upon it. But Shakespeare has presented us with a still stronger quality of association in minds of Shallow's calibre, that of asking questions everlastingly, and instantly giving evidence that the replies have not sunk even skin deep with them, rushing on from subject to subject, and returning again to those that have been dismissed. For instance:—

"*Shal.* Oh, the mad days that I have spent! and to see how many of mine old acquaintance are dead!

"*Silence.* We shall all follow, cousin!

"*Shal.* Certain, 'tis certain; very sure, very sure; death, as the Psalmist saith, is certain to all; all shall die. How a good yoke of bullocks at Stamford fair?

"*Sil.* Truly, cousin, I wasn't there.

"*Shal.* Death is certain. Is old Double of your town living yet?

"*Sil.* Dead, sir.

"*Shal.* Dead! see, see! He drew a good bow; and dead! He shot a fine shoot. John of Gaunt loved him well, and betted much money on his head. Dead! He would have clapped i' the clout at twelve score; and carried you a forehand shaft a fourteen, and fourteen and a half, that it would have done a man's heart good to see.—How a score of ewes now?

"*Sil.* Thereafter as they be; a score of good ewes may be worth ten pounds.

"*Shal. And is old Double dead?*"

Again, for his repetitions. When he is preparing to enlist the men for Falstaff:—"Where's the roll? where's the roll? where's the roll? Let me see, let me see, let me see. So, so, so, so; yea, marry, sir. Ralph Mouldy! Let them appear as I call; let them do so, let them do so. Let me see: where's Mouldy?"

His provincial habit of life is also indicated by his constant recurrence to his metropolitan days,—the "mad days that he had spent at Clement's Inn." The idea of Shallow having been a roysterer at *any* period of his life! the very constitution of the man's mind confutes his boast, without the testimony of Falstaff; and that is the finest burlesque portrait that ever was drawn:—

"This same starved justice hath done nothing but prate of the wildness of his youth, and the feats he hath done about Turnbull Street, and every third word a lie, duer paid to the hearer than the Turk's tribute. I do remember him at Clement's Inn, like a man made after supper of a cheese-paring. When he was naked, he was for all the world like a forked radish, with a head fantastically carved upon it with a knife. He was so forlorn that his dimensions to any thick sight were invisible: he was the very genius of famine; you might have thrust him and all his apparel into an eel-skin:—the case of a treble hautboy was a mansion for him—a court!"

There is no point in which Falstaff's wit glows more brilliantly than in that remarkable power of *exaggeration*, and the above (a portion only of the entire portrait) is a confirmatory specimen.

As if it were not sufficient triumph for the poet to have achieved such a contrast as the two intellects of Falstaff and Shallow,—in the consciousness and the opulence of unlimited genius, he stretches the line of his invention, and produces a foil even to Shallow—a climax to nothing—in the person of his cousin, Silence.

Silence is an embryo of a man,—a molecule,—a graduation from nonentity towards intellectual being,—a man dwelling in the suburbs of sense, groping about in the twilight of apprehension and understanding. He is the second stage in the "Vestiges;" he has just emerged from the tadpole state. Here again a distinction is preserved between these two characters. Shallow gabbles on from mere emptiness; while Silence, from the same incompetence, rarely gets beyond the shortest replies. The firmament of his wonder and adoration are the sayings and doings of his cousin and brother-justice at Clement's Inn, and which he has been in the constant habit of hearing, without satiety and nausea, for half-a-century. With one of those side-wind indications for which Shakespeare is remarkable, we are informed through Silence that Shallow has ever been repeating the stories of his London days:—

"Ha! cousin Silence, that thou hadst seen that that this knight and I have seen! Hey, Sir John, said I well?
"*Sil.* That's *fifty-five years ago.*"

* * * * *

At another time he says, as though Silence had been now first introduced to him, "I was once of Clement's Inn, where I think they will talk of 'mad Shallow' yet."

"*Sil. You were called 'lusty Shallow' then, cousin.*"

Like a provincial-bred man, also, Silence thinks no heroes can be so great as those of his own neighbourhood. When, therefore, Pistol, in announcing the death of the old king, says to Falstaff, "Sweet knight, thou art one of the greatest men in the realm," Silence assents from politeness, *but* with a reservation—"By'r Lady, I think he be; but Goodman Puff of Barson ———." Again, when they are all at dinner, and Silence waxes drunk, he suddenly falls to singing, so that Falstaff says, "I didn't think Master Silence had been a man of this mettle."

"*Sil.* Who, I? I have been merry twice and once, ere now."

It is noticeable, too, that even this scene of conviviality does not draw him out to the achievement of an entire song; but he trolls out odds and ends, which he associates with the last words he hears in the conversation. Shallow says, "Be merry, Master Bardolph: [and to Falstaff's page,] my little soldier there, be merry."

"*Sil.* [*Sings.*] Be merry, be merry, my wife has all."

Again, when Davy pledges Bardolph—"A cup of wine, sir!" Silence chimes in with, "A cup of wine that 's brisk and fine." But the capstone to his revelry is when he accepts Falstaff's pledge to a bumper, and the knight, patronising him, says, "Why, now, you have done me right!" Silence's reply is worth a whole mint:—

> "Do me right,
> And dub me knight, Samingo!
> *Is't not so?*
> "*Fal.* 'Tis so.
> "*Sil. Is't so? Why, then, say an old man can do somewhat.*"

So real is this extraordinary scene, that even his scraps become shorter and shorter, at length ending in two or three words; and when the party breaks up, Falstaff says, "Carry Master Silence to bed!"

There is one speech by the "knight of the burning lamp," the immortal Bardolph, which will answer the purpose of comment and illustration of his character. It is when Shallow asks him if his master, Sir John, be married? and he replies, "Your pardon, sir, a soldier is better accommodated than with a wife." Shallow rejoins:—

> "It is well said, in faith, sir; and it *is* well said, indeed, too. 'Better accommodated!' it is good; yea, indeed is it. Good phrases are surely, and ever were, very commendable. 'Accommodated,' it comes of *accommodo;* very good; a good phrase."

Bardolph thinks he is quizzing him for his use of the word, and defends himself:—

> "Pardon me, sir, I have heard the word. *Phrase* call you it? By this good day, I know not the *phrase;* but I will maintain the *word* with my sword to be a *soldier-like word,* and a word of *exceeding good command,* by Heaven! 'Accommodated,' that is, when a man is, as they say, 'accommodated;' or when a man is—being—whereby—he may be thought to be—'accommodated,' which is an *excellent thing!*"

Not content with filling his scene with three such worthies as Falstaff, Shallow, and Silence, the poet stretches on the career of his imagination, and introduces that whiskered cat-a-mountain, Ancient Pistol; a character quite as grotesque and amusing in his walk as the half-witted justices. Pistol, however, is not an original invention of Shakespeare's; but he was intended to be a satire upon some euphuistic and bombastious characters that are to be found in other plays of his time; and Mackenzie says that he has even taken identical passages, in all their "robustious periwig-pated" absurdity, and putting them into Pistol's mouth, they become the natural effusions of a braggart and a poltroon.

If Shakespeare really intended to represent Falstaff as a coward, a white-livered fellow, although very questionable that such was his design, he has produced a complete distinction in the effects of the passion in the two men. In Falstaff it was policy; in Pistol it was negation, an incompetence of the principle of self-respect, as in Parolles.

Pistol is introduced to bring the news of Henry IV.'s death, and he does it like a showman. This scene, with its variety of character and richness of humour, will form a choice voluntary as conclusion to our homily. There is Pistol with his fustian; Falstaff humouring him in his bombast, and spouting blank verse, too; Shallow bewildered and obfuscated, and Master Silence whiffling his scraps of ballads. "What wind blew you hither, Pistol?" says Falstaff:—

"*Pist.* Not the ill wind which blows no man to good. Sweet knight, thou art now one of the greatest men in the realm. * * *

Sir John, I am thy Pistol, and thy friend,
And helter-skelter have I rode to thee;
And tidings do I bring, and lucky joys,
And golden times, and happy news of price.

"*Fal.* I pr'ythee now, *deliver them like a man of this world.*

"*Pist.* A foutra for the world, and worldlings base!
I speak of Africa, and golden joys.

"*Fal. O base Assyrian knight! what is thy news?
Let King Cophetua know the truth thereof.*

"*Sil.* [*Singing.*] 'And Robin Hood, Scarlet, and John.'

"*Pist.* Shall dunghill curs confront the Helicons?
And shall good news be baffled?
Then, Pistol, lay thy head in Furies' lap.

"*Shal.* Honest gentleman, I know not your breeding.

"*Pist.* Why, then, lament therefore.

"*Shal.* Give me pardon, sir. If, sir, you come with news from the court, I take it there is but two ways,—either to utter them, or to conceal them. I am, sir, under the king in some authority.

"*Pist.* Under which king, Bezonian? speak, or die.

"*Shal.* Under King Harry.

"*Pist.* Harry the Fourth, or Fifth?

"*Shal.* Harry the Fourth.

"*Pist.* A foutra for thine office!—
Sir John, thy tender lambkin now is king;
Harry the Fifth's the man. I speak the truth:
When Pistol lies, do this, [*makes a contemptuous gesture,*] and fig me, like
The bragging Spaniard.

"*Fal. What! is the old king dead?*

"*Pist.* As nail in door: the things I speak are just.

"*Fal.* Away, Bardolph! saddle my horse.—Master Robert Shallow, choose what office thou wilt in the land, 'tis thine. —Pistol, I will double-charge thee with dignities. * * * * Carry Master Silence to bed.—Master Shallow, *my Lord Shallow*, be what thou wilt; I am fortune's steward. Get on thy boots; we'll ride all night.—O sweet Pistol!—Away Bardolph! [*Exit Bard.*] Come, Pistol, *utter more to me;* and, withal, devise something to do thyself good. Boot, boot, Master Shallow; I know the young king is sick for me. *Let us take any man's horses;* the laws of England are at my commandment. Happy are they which have been my friends, and *woe unto my Lord Chief-Justice!*"

XVIII.

# Richard the Third.

# XVIII.

# RICHARD III.

---

SHAKESPEARE derived his authority for the dramatic history of Richard III. from the life of that monarch written by Sir Thomas More; a biography well calculated for theatrical purposes; scarcely so for the sacred purposes of truthful history; for that in the person and character of the "crook-backed tyrant," the engine of party misrepresentation was urged to its greatest high-pressure power, few who have looked into the histories of the Tudor succession will be hardy enough to deny. It is neither my cue nor my inclination at this period to enter the dark labyrinth of the controversy respecting that signally bold usurpation, and to debate the plausibility of a single individual's attaining the power within the short lapse of a few months—of a few weeks, indeed, to compass the death of his own brother; of three noblemen, councillors of the successor to the crown; of the successor himself, with his brother; and lastly, of his own wife: but I would simply observe, that to give credence to all that was written to blacken the memory of Richard for the purpose of confirming Richmond in the succession, the reader may afterwards, with like child-like faith, transfer his belief to the veritable history of King Bluebeard, or of any other royal ogre. It is a remarkable fact, as Walpole has asserted in his "Historic Doubts," that there is *no proof at all* of so dire an atrocity having been committed, as the murder of the young king and his brother in the Tower. Not their prison, as is generally supposed, from our associations with that building, from the uses to which it has since his time been appointed: but their residence, as was usual in that period, for the purposes of security as well as state; where they had their guards and their retinue, and where difficulty of accomplishing their assassination, by reason of all these combined circumstances, and without its transpiring by one vent or another, (the more especially as Brackenbury, the Governor of the Tower, and Tyrrel, the reputed murderer, were both living in the time of Henry VII., when confession and proof of the deed would have advanced the interests of all parties—both its perpetrators and the deposer of the York dynasty;) the circumstance, I say, of there being no tangible clue to so extraordinary a series of treasons, treachery, and murder, should lead us to receive all history connected with the biography of its leading characters cautiously and sceptically. I do not mean to convey the idea that Richard III. was an *estimable* character, still less an immaculate one; but that all the accounts that have come down to us concerning him were written by political and temporising adversaries, even descending to the distortion of his body and limbs. Whereas, the celebrated Countess of Desmond, who survived to an extraordinary age, more than a hundred years, stated that she danced with him at the coronation of his brother, Edward IV., and that, with the exception of the king, he was the handsomest man at court, Edward being celebrated for his personal accomplishments. Now, making allowance, under the circumstances, for some partiality on the part of the Countess toward's a man of Richard's rank and station, to say nothing of his acknowledged courtly tongue, we cannot suppose him to have been the monster of deformity that he has been depicted by his enemies. However, as already said, it is not my intention to enter upon that dark problem—the fate of the young princes, and the guilt or innocence of their uncle; much upon this point will be found to interest the reader, after going through Sir Thomas More's beautifully-written, but Lancastrian life of the Protector, and our popular histories, which are grounded upon it, by turning to Walpole's special pleading in his "Historic Doubts," also to that agreeable little piece of antiquarian gossip, William Hutton of Birmingham's "History of the Battle of Bosworth;" and lastly, to the "Life of Richard," by Caroline Halsted, a work distinguished by assiduous and careful research, with impartiality of judgment.

My business is with Shakespeare's Richard, a delineation of wonderful energy, vigour, and intellectual ascendency. But no ordinary reader need be reminded that the "Richard III." of Shakespeare and the "Richard III." of the actors have very little in common,—so little, indeed, that Mrs Inchbald, in her "British Theatre," has computed the number of lines in the *acting* copy that have been retained from the *original* drama, to consist of no more than three hundred and thirty-one entire lines—scarcely one act out of the five; the remainder is a hash of scenes, speeches, scraps, broken lines from other plays; the dying speech of Richard, for instance, being the curse uttered by Northumberland in the 2d Part of "Henry IV.," upon hearing the news of his son, Hotspur's, death; and, to crown all, Cibber, who concocted this prodigy of a medley, with amusing conceit foisted his own bombast into the company of Shakespeare's magniloquence, and "with its darkness dared affront his light." Some worthy atonement, however, has been made in our own time to the poet's insulted memory, by producing, in their original form, plays which, for nearly a century, had kept possession of the stage, bearing his name, (as cheats inscribe great craftsmen's names upon worthless goods,) but so mutilated, deformed,—even totally changed and re-written, as scarcely to be recognised. The reformation alluded to is in the case of the "Tempest," and "King Lear," of which the former acting versions were two signal examples of the disgusting morality and dramatic taste of the Frenchified era of Charles II., and the age succeeding it. The experiment, however, was made some years ago by Mr Macready, of performing this play according to the text of Shakespeare; and the same attempt was made at Sadlers Wells, when under the direction of Mrs Warner and Mr Phelps. In answer to the question I put to the lady as to the spirit in which it was received by their audience, she said, "Certainly with *respect;* and that they were much impressed by those terrible scenes in which Margaret of Anjou appears."

Let not English playgoers profess a veneration for the genius of Shakespeare while they allow Colley Cibber's tiger-cat version of "Richard III." to keep possession of their stage, and to have the poet's name affixed as being the author of it.

THE Richard of our poet is a thorough man of the world,—bold, practical, direct, and prompt. He is gratuitously as well as politically cruel. Expediency with him is law; it were even his religion, if such a word could be combined with such a being. He will pause at no obstacle to achieve a purpose; and at no result, however revolting, does he ever relent. The wonderful elasticity of his genius carries him over all barriers. "At one slight bound, high overleaps all bound" or limit to his desire. The whole of his career, to its close—and most especially at the close—excites our admiration from the wonderful energy and skill with which he uses his resources. In our astonishment, we almost lose sight of the former tyrant; and—so innate is the love and reverence of power, with resolution, in the human mind—we contemplate him solely as a brave man who has been over-mastered and crushed by numbers.

The leading characteristics of Richard's mind are, scorn, sarcasm, and an overweening contempt. It appears as if contempt for his victims—rather than active hatred and cruelty—were the motive for murdering them. Upon our first meeting him, in the play bearing his name, he sounds the keynote to his whole character—that of contempt—in the celebrated apostrophe to his own person :—

> "I, that am curtail'd of this fair proportion,
> Cheated of feature by dissembling nature,
> Deform'd, unfinish'd, sent before my time
> Into this breathing world, scarce half made up,
> And that so lamely and unfashionable,
> That dogs bark at me as I halt by them."

His ambitious nature, his bounding, elastic intellect, but, above all, his want of faith in goodness, conspire to produce this tendency to despise and degrade every surrounding being and object, even (as just quoted) his own person.

He is never sincere and truly in earnest but when he is about to commit a murder.

> "Then, since the heavens have shap'd my body so,
> Let hell make crook'd my mind to answer it."

This is his introduction to the reader ; and in his last scene he indulges the bitterness of his soul in a sneer at those visions which, but a few moments since, have so appalled him ; and he recklessly attacks the very power whose influence he had just before been compelled to acknowledge. He then says :—

> "Let not our babbling dreams affright our souls ;
> Conscience is but a word that cowards use,
> Devis'd at first to keep the strong in awe."

It is to be observed, moreover, that the first feeling every victim excites in him is that of "contempt." The instant they leave him, his first ejaculation—even in the throb of triumph at the success obtained by his own intellect—is always one of contempt for his dupe.

Upon Lady Anne's quitting him after that keen encounter of their wits; when he succeeds in wooing and winning her at the very time that she is attending the funeral of her husband, whom he himself had killed, he breaks forth into that demoniacal sarcasm :—

"Was ever woman in this humour woo'd?
Was ever woman in this humour won?
I'll have her; but I'll not keep her long.
What, I that kill'd her husband, and his father,
To take her in her heart's extremest hate;
With curses in her mouth, tears in her eyes,
The bleeding witness of her hatred by;
Having God, her conscience, and these bars against me;
And I no friends to back my suit withal,
But the plain devil and dissembling looks;
And yet, to win her—all the world to nothing!"

After his scene with the court of Edward, in the 1st Act, he says, in all the boldness of a contemptuous supremacy :—

"I do the wrong; and first begin to brawl.
The secret mischief that I set abroach,
I lay unto the grievous charge of others.
Clarence,—whom I indeed have cast in darkness,—
I do beweep to many simple gulls;
Namely, to Stanley, Hastings, Buckingham;
And tell them 'tis the queen and her allies
That stir the king against the duke my brother."

And the scene itself where Clarence is being conducted by Brackenbury and his guard to the Tower; and his making the "simple Clarence," as he sneeringly calls him, believe that he has been doomed to prison through the machinations of the queen and her family, is another instance of the contempt resulting from his sense of intellectual superiority over all others that come in collision with him. His insolent and vigorous supremacy in the following dialogue displays the master-poet. After feigning his surprise at the act—which he himself had ordained and compassed—he breaks forth in a tone of indignant remonstrance:—

"Why, this it is, when men are rul'd by women:
'Tis not the king that sends you to the Tower;
My Lady Grey, his wife, Clarence; 'tis she
That tempers him to this extremity.
Was it not she, and that good man of worship,
Anthony Woodville, her brother there,
That made him send Lord Hastings to the Tower;
From whence this present day he is deliver'd?—
We are not safe, Clarence; we are not safe.
"*Clar.* By Heav'n, I think there is no man secure,
But the queen's kindred, and night-walking heralds
That trudge betwixt the king and Mistress Shore. * * *
"*Brack.* I beseech your graces both to pardon me;
His majesty hath straitly given in charge,
That no man shall have private conference,
Of what degree soever, with his brother.
"*Glo.* Even so! an please your worship, Brackenbury,
You may partake of anything we say:
We speak no treason, man. We say the king
Is wise and virtuous; and his noble queen
Well-struck in years, fair, and not jealous.
We say that Shore's wife hath a pretty foot,
A cherry lip, a bonny eye, a passing-pleasing tongue;
And the queen's kindred are made gentlefolks.
How say you, sir? Can you deny all this?
"*Brack.* With this, my lord, myself have naught to do.
"*Glo.* Naught to do with Mistress Shore? I tell thee, fellow,
He that doth naught with her,—excepting one,
Were best to do it secretly, alone.
"*Brack.* What one, my lord?
"*Glo. Her husband, knave:—Wouldst thou betray me?*"

This turning of the tables upon the king's officer, and making him the defendant, where he had been the plaintiff, is a specimen of Richard's suddenly available talent. When the party have gone out, he says, with a diabolical jeer:—

> "Go, tread the path that thou shalt ne'er return,
> Simple, plain Clarence!—I do love thee so,
> That I will shortly send thy soul to heaven,
> If heaven *will take the present at our hands.*"

This should be the very triumph of insolence and contempt, with calculating cruelty.

Again, when Queen Elizabeth leaves him, after his arguments have won her sanction to his addressing her daughter, his contempt again breaks forth:—

> "Relenting fool, and shallow, changing woman!"

Even upon slight and casual occasions the same tone occurs, and thus the harmony of the character is maintained. His muttered sneer, upon receiving his mother's benediction:—

> "And make me die a good old man;
> That is the butt-end of a mother's blessing."

Again, his lightly and carelessly sending the Bishop of Ely for strawberries from the prelate's garden in Holborn, in the midst of their conversation. Here we have an act of insolence with contempt.

And, lastly, his cruelty and ingratitude towards his jackal, Buckingham, who wrought hard to help him to his bad eminence; who had performed for him the ninety-nine time-serving villainies, but cannot do the hundredth—that of murdering the children in the Tower. All these examples, I think, warrant our pronouncing the master-key in Richard's mind to be "contempt," and which adds a venom to his cruelty. And thus, again, the position so often maintained in behalf of Shakespeare's genius—that, let us only lay hold of a clue in any one of his characters, and pursue it to the end, we shall find all to be clear, harmonious, and consistent. In the character of Richard, I am not sure that the poet does not mean to convey that his cruelty towards his species, for the purpose of achieving the end of his ambition, is not the result of the great leading characteristic of his mind—that of "contempt."

In all this complication of high intellectual qualities in the character and conduct of Richard, Shakespeare makes manifest his own instinctive and powerful sagacity in selecting, and in his style of fashioning such a being for the hero of a great dramatic poem. A mere human tiger, roused into action only by the smell of blood, would have been but a subject for a third-rate poet, and who would have made a regular Sawney Beane of the character. But Shakespeare has invested his Richard with a halo of accomplishment—he is infinitely superior to the persons by whom he is surrounded. Speaking of his own genius, he says, and with a just appreciation:—

> "Our aiery buildeth in the cedar's top,
> And dallies with the wind, and scorns the sun."

With these qualities he has conjoined a wanton hardness of heart; a politic, and, upon occasion, even a ribald cruelty; and a total defiance and scorn of all faith in a principle of goodness. He is as perfect an incarnation of evil as that Satanic conception of the great epic poet.

Among the subordinate agents in the play appears the little York, a spirited sketch quite in Shakespeare's own manner. Quick, keen, and intelligent, he is precisely the lively, observant child that might be expected as the growth of a court and in troublous times, and yet manifesting all the caution—consistent, nevertheless, with a sprightly nature—which such times inspire. He is first introduced with his mother and grandam. Their anxiety and dread—the sad consequences of experienced age, and such an age of turbulence as they lived in—are beautifully contrasted with his gay young prattle:—

"*Duch.* I long with all my heart to see the prince:
I hope he is much grown since last I saw him.
"*Qu. Eliz.* But I hear no: they say my son of York
Hath almost overta'en him in his growth.
"*York.* Ay, mother, but I would not have it so.
"*Duch.* Why, my good cousin? it is good to grow.
"*York.* Grandam, one night as we did sit at supper,
My uncle Rivers talk'd how I did grow
More than my brother: 'Ay,' quoth my uncle Gloster,
'Small herbs have grace; great weeds do grow apace.'
And since, methinks, I would not grow so fast,
Because sweet flowers are slow, and weeds make haste.
* * * * * *
Now, by my troth, if I had been remember'd,
I could have given my uncle's grace a flout,
To touch his growth nearer than he touch'd mine.
"*Duch.* How, my young York? I prithee let me hear it.
"*York.* Marry, they say my uncle grew so fast,
That he could gnaw a crust at two hours old;
'Twas full two years ere I could get a tooth.
Grandam, this would have been a biting jest.
"*Duch.* I prithee, pretty York, who told thee this?
"*York.* Grandam, his nurse.
"*Duch.* His nurse! why, she was dead ere thou wast born.
"*York.* If 'twere not she, I cannot tell who told me."

He had heard his mother say it. She rebuked him for being "too shrewd," saying to the others, "Pitchers have ears." Here is a touch of caution thrown in, the natural birth of surrounding plots and machinations.

In Shakespeare's abundance of individualising various characters of similar semblance, he has placed in juxtaposition with little York the young son of Clarence, whose innocent simplicity is no less natural than the other's innocent shrewdness. The sweet credulity which can perceive no guile beneath kindly demonstration, and the boyish quickness which instinctively discerns evil, without power to ward off its sinister approach, are equally touching exemplifications of childhood nature. How the pure, bright honesty of childish feeling shows in those few words of Clarence's young son, when, after describing his uncle Gloster's caresses, and his grandam drops a hint of Richard's deceit, the boy exclaims, "Think you my uncle did dissemble, grandam?" she replies, "Ay, boy." And he answers, with the confidence of a clear young spirit, "I cannot think it." This comes with bright effect against the sharpwitted precocity of little York's colloquy above quoted.

The latter's pert and sly taunts to his uncle Gloster, in the presence of the young king, are better known from their introduction on the stage; but they are most naturally managed, and as skilfully contrasted with the sweet, gentle sketch of his brother, the little king, whose premature thought has taken the character of pensive care and unnaturally early wisdom.

Shakespeare not unfrequently makes his children talk beyond their years, and at times almost greatly; nevertheless they still wear the childlike air and manner,—so completely did he invest himself for the time in the spiritual garment of each character as he summoned it to the scene. The questions the little king puts to his uncle Gloster respecting Julius Cæsar, who he had been informed was builder of the Tower, and his precocious reflection upon the character of that great Roman, strictly harmonise with his forced maturity of mind, and yet the manner of his speech is youthful. He says:—

> "That Julius Cæsar was a famous man:
> With what his valour did enrich his wit,
> His wit set down to make his valour live:
> *Death makes no conquest of this conqueror;*
> *For now he lives in fame, though not in life.*"

Although here is sound philosophy, and that it is somewhat precocious in reflection, yet how perfectly is the language in which it is expressed that of a superior-minded child.

The description of these two innocent children,—"Fairest flowers, no sooner blown than blasted,"—as they lay victims about to be sacrificed, forms an exquisite picture, and such a one as Shakespeare, in the opulence of his mind, loved to put into the mouth of a subordinate character. It is uttered by Tyrrel, the agent of Gloster's cruelty:—

"The tyrannous and bloody act is done,—
The most arch deed of piteous massacre
That ever yet this land was guilty of.
Dighton and Forrest, whom I did suborn
To do this piece of ruthless butchery,
Albeit they were flesh'd villains, bloody dogs,
Melting with tenderness and mild compassion,
Wept like to children in their death's sad story.
'Oh, thus,' quoth Dighton, 'lay the gentle babes,'—
"Thus, thus,' quoth Forrest, 'girdling one another
Within their alabaster innocent arms;
Their lips were four red roses on a stalk,
Which in their summer beauty kiss'd each other.
A book of prayers on their pillow lay;
Which once,' quoth Forrest, 'almost chang'd my mind;
But, oh, the devil'—there the villain stopp'd;
When Dighton thus told on:—'We smother'd
The most replenishèd sweet work of nature,
That from the prime creation e'er she fram'd.'"

The two murderers employed by Gloster to despatch Clarence, are drawn with a terribly bold and masterly hand. They are not only designed with a marked difference from any other of Shakespeare's murderers, (such, for instance, as those just quoted, and those in "Macbeth," who are gentlemen of fallen fortunes,) but these have such perfect individuality as to be unlike, and quite distinct from each other. Throughout the scene you recogise the one ruffian from his companion, though no otherwise designated than as, "1st Murderer and 2d Murderer," being third or fourth class characters in the play. From the preliminary short interview with Gloster, where the 1st Murderer alone speaks, and assures the duke,—

"My lord, we will not stand to prate;
Talkers are no good doers:—be assur'd,
We go to use our hands, and not our tongues;"

down to the scene where they perpetrate the deed, the first man displays the bold, ruthless, callous villain, dashed with a spice of ferocious humour; and the other is a vacillating creature, whom circumstances, and not predisposition, have made what he is. Here is a short portion of dialogue—not familiarly known, but full of pithy meaning, illustrative of the poet's discrimination, as well as distinction of character, even in the least important persons on the scene; and who yet are of "similar mark and likelihood." The 2d Murderer says:—

"What, shall we stab him as he sleeps?

"*1st Mur.* No; he'll say 'twas done cowardly when he wakes.

"*2d Mur.* When he wakes! why, fool, he shall never wake until the great judgment-day.

"*1st Mur.* Why, then, he'll say we stabbed him sleeping.

"*2d Mur.* The urging of that word 'judgment' hath bred a kind of remorse in me.

"*1st Mur.* What! art thou afraid?

"*2d Mur.* Not to kill him, *having a warrant* for it; but to be damned for killing him, from the which no warrant can defend me.

"*1st Mur.* I thought thou hadst been resolute.

"*2d Mur.* So I am—to let him live.

"*1st Mur.* I'll back to the Duke of Gloster, and tell him so.

"*2d Mur.* Nay, I prithee, stay a little. I hope my holy humour will change: it was wont to hold me but while one tells twenty.

"*1st Mur.* How dost thou feel thyself now?

"*2d Mur.* 'Faith, some certain dregs of conscience are yet within me.

"*1st Mur.* Remember our reward when the deed's done.

"*2d Mur.* Zounds! he dies; I had forgot the reward.

"*1st Mur.* Where's thy conscience now?

"*2d Mur.* In the Duke of Gloster's purse.

"*1st Mur.* So when he opens his purse to give us our reward, thy conscience flies out.

"*2d Mur.* 'Tis no matter; let it go: there's few or none will entertain it.

"*1st Mur.* What if it come to thee again?

"*2d Mur.* I'll not meddle with it; it is a dangerous thing, *it makes a man a coward;* a man cannot steal, but it accuseth him; a man cannot swear, but it checks him; 'tis a blushing shame-faced spirit, that mutinies in a man's bosom; it fills a man full of obstacles; it made me once restore a purse of gold, that *by chance I found;* it beggars any man that keeps it; it is turned out of all towns and cities for a dangerous thing; and every man that means to live well, endeavours to trust to himself, and live without it.

"*1st Mur.* Zounds! it is even now at my elbow persuading me not to kill the duke.

"*2d Mur.* Take the devil in thy mind, and believe him not; he would insinuate with thee, but to make thee sigh.

"*1st Mur.* I am strong-framed; he cannot prevail with *me.*"

After they have killed Clarence, the 2d Murderer, true to his first infirmity of purpose, says:—

"A bloody deed, and desp'rately despatch'd!
How fain, like Pilate, would I wash my hands
Of this most grievous guilty murder done!"

The women in this play serve as means to exhibit the power of Richard in swaying to his purposes persons the most averse from him and his interests. They cannot withstand his will when once he sets resolutely to work to show them what that will is, and to exercise his force of intellect in influencing and bending their minds to his. Lady Anne is won from the very side of her murdered husband's murdered father's coffin to accept the suit of him who was the murderer of both; and Edward's widowed queen, in the midst of her lament for her two princely boys, is lured into consent that her daughter shall wed with the man who untimely stopped their breath to usurp their crown and birthright, when he deigns to use his subtle tongue in persuasion. And if all this appear dramatic high-colouring, be it borne in mind that there is historic repute in confirmation of it.

The only one who confronts him with dauntless unsubmission equal to his own is Queen Margaret. She has lost all—has nothing more to concede, therefore she is beyond his attempts to subdue. Her sum of wrongs invests her with a martyred majesty which seems to place her above earthly royalty. She steps forward and stands before him like an accusing spirit, to arraign him for the blood he has spilt, for the anguish he has caused. She comes face to face with him, like an impersonation of woe for the murdered husband and son his hand had slain, and seems a living pre-embodiment of those ghastly spectres which subsequently haunt his remorse-broken slumbers. The effect of Queen Margaret's appearance, despair-crowned and breathing curses, in the earlier scenes of the play—is that of a human ghost foreboding the aftercoming of those shadowy apparitions of his victims that surround Richard's tented bed on Bosworth field of battle, which was to be his death-bed.

The character of Buckingham is here drawn with skilful and consistent delineation. He is a weak man, morally and mentally; and, like many weak men, he instinctively clings for support to a powerful intellect like that of Richard, while flattering himself that he assists and guides it by his own aid and counsel. Buckingham is lavish in protestation—always the resource of the weak, conscious of their own lack of strength in earnest meaning. He is duped by Richard's pretence of submitting to his advice and direction,—a certain mark of weakness in one unable to perceive Richard's superior intelligence. He is fluent and sophistical,—a sure token of feeble wisdom and lack of sound argument. He is vain of his powers of oratory, and has immense conceit of his gift at dissimulation,—an infallible proof of wanting sense, both in morals and understanding. He thus vaunts his ability to deceive :—

> "Tut! I can counterfeit the deep tragedian ;
> Speak and look back, and pry on every side,
> Tremble and start at wagging of a straw,
> Intending deep suspicion ; ghastly looks
> Are at my service, like enforcèd smiles ;
> And both are ready in their offices,
> At any time to grace my stratagems."

Such a boast as this made to Richard—that master in the art of dissembling! The effect is almost ludicrous of the man's blindness of self-conceit. Accordingly, Richard, with his humour of shrewd policy, does not fail to take inward-laughing advantage of it, and uses the vaunter as a convenient tool. It is Buckingham who suggests the hypocritical device of Richard's causing himself to be found by the civic train when they come to offer the crown, engaged in pious-seeming occupation :—

> "Look you, get a prayer-book in your hand,
> And stand between two churchmen, good my lord ;
> For on that ground I'll make a holy descant :
> And be not easily won to our requests ;
> Play the maid's part, still answer nay, and take it."

He is evidently vain of his slyness and cleverness in trickery, and he proceeds to play out the got-up scene of farcical "nolo coronari" between Richard and himself before the lord mayor, aldermen, and citizens, with all the relish of a weak-minded and weak-moraled man. Richard makes him his cat's-paw so long as it suits his purpose; but the instant he perceives that the weak-souled creature is even weak enough to have conscience-qualms after so much weakness of paltering with right, he flings him by with the sneer—

> "High-reaching Buckingham grows circumspect."

He does not choose that the blind fool he has hitherto known so subserviently hoodwinked and linked to his purposes, should now presume to scan them, much less to demur and shrink from their fulfilment. From first to last, Buckingham's career with Richard contains an impressive lesson on weakness enmeshed by unscrupulous strength, when involved in the net by its own folly and vanity.

Some of Shakespeare's most insignificant scenes abound with notable axioms and aphoristic wisdom. For example, in that short and apparently unimportant one in this play, where some citizens meet in the street and talk, gossip-wise, about the ill-ordering of government from the factious state of parties, the king's death, and the extreme youth of his successor, the Prince of Wales, one of the citizens says, with the grave prudential tone of mercantile foresight :—

> "When clouds are seen, wise men put on their cloaks;
> When great leaves fall, then winter is at hand;
> When the sun sets, who doth not look for night?
> Untimely storms make men expect a dearth.
> All may be well; but if God sort it so,
> 'Tis more than we deserve, or I expect.
> "*2d Cit.* Truly, the hearts of men are full of fear;
> You cannot reason almost with a man
> That looks not heavily and full of dread.
> "*3d Cit.* Before the days of change, still is it so.
> By a divine instinct men's minds mistrust
> Ensuing danger; as by proof we see

The water swell before a boist'rous storm :—
But leave it all to God."

The serene piety and resignation of this little scene, coming in contrast with the treason and cruelty with which the whole argument of the drama is fraught, is conceived in the full spirit of Shakespeare's prevailing philosophy.

He is also accustomed to introduce a character as a sort of chorus, to detail the progress of events to his audience, as the choruses of the ancient tragedy were appointed to do. So in this ; he has a short scene in the 3d Act, headed

"*A Street—Enter a Scrivener,*"

who says :—

"Here is the indictment of the good Lord Hastings ;
Which in a set hand fairly is engross'd,
That it may be to-day read o'er in Paul's ;
And mark how well the sequel hangs together.
Eleven hours I have spent to write it over,
For yesternight by Catesby was it sent to me.
The precedent was full as long a doing ;
And yet within these five hours Hastings liv'd,
Untainted, unexamined, free, at liberty.
Here 's a good world the while !—Who is so gross
That cannot see this palpable device ?—
Yet who so bold, but says he sees it not ?—
Bad is the world, and all will come to naught,
When such ill dealing must be *seen* in *thought.*"

This slight passing scene appears to me accurately suggestive of the smothered feeling of indignation that boils in men's minds under a tyrannical dynasty ; and, indeed, so well is this under-current of opinion depicted in the subordinate characters in Shakespeare's historical plays, that they ought in nowise to be omitted in the representation, since they form part of the perfect whole designed by the great master. He, no doubt, intended that the minds of the audience, while dazzled by the glare of romance and pre-eminence which surrounded the chief actors in life's drama, should at the same time be presented with the counterbalancing reflection of the ill effects produced upon the mass of the people during the transit of such fiery meteors.

XIX.

# Coriolanus.

# XIX.

# CORIOLANUS.

---

I DO not suppose that there ever was embodied a more perfect representation of the abstract principle of aristocratic assumption than we find delineated in the play of "Coriolanus;" the dramatic moral of which (as Hazlitt has sarcastically summed it up) is, "that those who have little shall have less; and those who have much shall take all that others have left." Certainly there is no tyranny like the tyranny of a class, whether it be patrician, plebeian, or military: and perhaps the most oppressive of all is the government of a soldiery, because its ruling principles are opposed to the dignity of reasoning beings; for it enforces unconditional and implicit submission in the teeth of common sense,—and peremptory obedience even to the violation of the common law of instinct and humanity. As an illustration of this remark, I would require no stronger argument against the principle of the "One Institution," as Thomas Carlyle calls a soldiery, than the simple fact, that there must have been hundreds of men of high honour, and of as high intelligence, in the French army that invaded Rome in 1849, who, from principle, were opposed to the duty that they, by their oath of allegiance, were compelled to fulfil. The machinery of a military despotism are the limbs of sentient mortal beings, and its aggrandisement, consummation, and glory, their sighs, and blood, and tears, and death. That men who are born and educated in that stubborn faith of the Meccan prophet,—that to die in the lap of war is to insure an immortal retribution of elysian glory and sensual enjoyment,—should "go to their graves like beds," is reconcilable with a principle; but that, eighteen hundred years after the command, which we believe to be Divine, was promulgated,—that men should "do justice and love mercy;" should "love their neighbours as themselves;" should "resist not evil," but "turn their cheeks to the smiter;" and the whole Christian-professing world recognising and preaching this command,—they should, nevertheless, train and keep in sleek condition hordes of their fellow-men, like hounds in a kennel, ready to let slip and be laid on any scent, the prey of which is to be hunted down, is a thing which I cannot comprehend, and cannot reconcile with reason; it is, indeed, the greatest moral anomaly of the Christian era. We daily elbow in the street men who, we know, are in constant preparation to stab a fellow-being at a word of command; and we think no more of their vocation than if it were to cut down so many trees. We feel no congeniality with the man who is hired to take the life of an uncomplaining sheep; but we contemplate with complacency him who, for hire also, has maimed and killed his fellow-men.

Is this incongruity to be reconciled by the fact, that mankind have an instinctive reverence for mere power; that they are dazzled by the manifestation of physical force; that they are ever "strong upon the strongest side;" that they sympathise more with the general who has laid waste a town, than with the terrified inhabitants who have fled houseless into the unsheltering fields and roads? A flying community before an invading army; a hunger-starved mob dispersed by fifty dragoons, are not picturesque objects—not objects of respect; we sympathise less with their discomfiture and destitution than with the triumphing power that has effected it. There are few whose breasts do not reverberate the exultation of Volumnia at hearing the trumpets of her victorious home-returning son, Coriolanus. It is a complete abstraction of the aristocracy of war; and terribly grand is that bloody pæan. We lose the idea of a *woman* in the speech, and are absorbed in that pagan personation of contest and carnage. From the Roman matron she rises into an incarnation of the goddess Bellona:—

> "Hark! the trumpets.
> These are the ushers of Marcius: before him
> He carries noise, and behind him he leaves tears:
> Death, that dark spirit, in 's nervy arm doth lie;
> Which, being advanc'd, declines, and then men die."

All readers of "Coriolanus" scoff at and despise the starving citizens for their vacillation and ill-reasoning; and all entertain a tacit respect for the dictating power and measureless contempt that distinguish the hero of the play. Hazlitt goes so far as to assert that Shakespeare entertained the same sentiment; and he has paid the poor compliment to the great soul of the poet by explaining this emotion to have arisen, in all probability, from some feeling of "contempt for his own origin;" but this can scarcely be the case,—for we find that his family was more than "respectable," in the conventional sense,—its heraldry tracing to the reign of Henry IV.; but were this not the case, I believe his soul to have been elevated far above the distinctions of class and rank, although he sued for the privilege of his heraldic coat. His was the aristocracy of mind. Besides, I maintain that, in his finely-balanced mind and constant sense of even-handed justice, he has pleaded *for*, as well as against, the plebeians; and, if they are to be reproached for incontinence and inconsistency, I find no special pleading in behalf of the petulance, the inconsistency, and treason towards his native land, as manifested in the hero of the play. He has made out a case for the hungry citizens, with all their folly and vacillation; and he has read no flattering lesson to the exclusive and insolent patrician, with his vulgar scorn of what he styled "the rank-scented many." This is one chord in the grand harmony of Shakespeare's mind: we never find him making any character or set of principles a stalking-horse behind which to shoot his own prejudices, or even mere opinions, whether civil, political, or religious,—so little, indeed, has he done this, that it were difficult to decide upon the one; and it is still a question for controversy, whether he was of the Reformed or of the old Catholic Church. He was most just, as well as gentle-hearted,—the great master-spirit, as it were, of human thought and human action,—too great to descend from his altitude and identify himself with the party-pudderings and squabbles of political Big-endians and Little-endians. Well for him—and most well for the high cause of human amelioration! Had he given up to *any* party-dogmas "what was meant for mankind," he had not at this moment been the unquestioned authority upon every point in philosophy,—civil, moral, and social;—*the* poet of humanity,—the practical teacher of our best interests in this life, by cherishing good and kind deeds, and sweet, and cheerful, and grateful thoughts, as opposed to selfishness and that deep immorality which Thomas Carlyle boldly terms the "damnable putrescence of modern cant"—the cant of turning this green and shining world, given to us by a boundless Beneficence, into a sterile promontory of bigotry and hopeless ingratitude.

I have fancied that in the three superb Roman dramas of Shakespeare,—"Coriolanus," "Julius Cæsar," and "Antony and Cleopatra,"—we discern in his treatment of his subjects a wonderful harmony of manner and language, according with the several eras in which the scenes are laid. In the early period of the Commonwealth, when Coriolanus flourished, we note a simplicity of manner, conduct, and even language, congenial with the then inornate state of society. A massive and Doric simplicity pervades the whole character of the diction of the "Coriolanus." His celebrated apostrophe to his native city, upon entering the Forum, is a beautiful specimen of the language of the whole drama :—

> "The honour'd gods
> Keep Rome in safety, and the chairs of justice
> Supplied with worthy men! Plant love among us.
> Throng our large temples with the shows of peace,
> And not our streets with war."

When Julius Cæsar flourished, the dialect had become polished; his own "Commentaries" are pure classical language; customs and manners had attained a high tone of civility; the schools of philosophy were instituted; oratory walked in golden sandals; Cicero was in his zenith. That play, therefore, is saturated with forensic wisdom; we have grand set speeches, and references to the Stoic philosophy.

In the play of "Antony and Cleopatra" we have all the lusciousness and languor of the Sybarite existence, with the gorgeous imagination and oriental diction of a luxurious climate. In no one of his plays has he surpassed the "Antony and Cleopatra" in splendour and richness; as Hazlitt has beautifully said, "Shakespeare's genius has spread over the whole play a richness like the overflowing of the Nile." It is not too much to suppose that there was previous intention in all this; but what does it not say for his wonderful comprehension and harmony in design, forethought, arrangement, and development?

Among the secondary characters in this play of "Coriolanus," the most estimable, as well as the most interesting, is old Menenius, the patrician and senator. He forms an amiable link between the two orders; he is precisely the character a nobleman should be; wearing the insignia of his rank with a bland and easy dignity; gracefully condescending, and even familiar with the commonalty, sympathising with their wants, difficulties, and privations; and this gives him the privilege to speak to them with the authority of his longer experience, with better education and knowledge. This same sympathy, too, which they all recognise, gives him the warrant to visit their misconduct and their senseless waverings, their vacillations, irrational turbulence, and revolt, with an asperity which they would ill bear from another who cared less for them and their destitute condition. It is observable, that throughout all his displeasure and petulance against the mob, Menenius never makes use of a cruel or even unkind speech: in his spleen he is sufficiently and humorously contemptuous; but we hear no such expression as the scoundrelly exultation of Coriolanus at the approaching war with the Volscians, when he says—

> "I am glad on 't; then we shall have means to vent
> Our musty superfluity;"

a speech admirably in character with one who considered the masses below him in the commonwealth only as so much material to build up his own pomp and ambition. Menenius has described his own nature and temper in that sparring scene between himself and the tribunes of the people, Brutus and Sicinius. It is a happy display of a testy, wayward, and humorous old man, with a rich vein of kind-heartedness running through his crusty temper. The scene is the opening one of the 2d Act.

The character of Tullus Aufidius is well placed in opposition with that of Coriolanus. It is no vulgar foil, no bald contrast; but it is superficially bright only. Beneath a show of martial eminence, which fits him to be the hero's antagonist, he possesses a low soul, which places him intrinsically beneath the great Roman. Where Coriolanus is proud,

Aufidius is ambitious; where Coriolanus is loftily self-conscious, Aufidius is aspiringly self-seeking. Exteriorly, Tullus forms no unworthy rival in arms with Caius Marcius; but interiorly, morally, he is immeasurably below him. With his usual delicacy, but vigour of delineation, the poet has depicted this from first to last. At the very outset we behold Tullus burning with desire to cope with Marcius, and to win some share of that warlike renown for which he is famous. He has a fever of military jealousy upon him, which has its hot and its cold fits. He is seized with one of the latter on finding that Coriolanus is under his own roof, a poor and banished man; finding his great rival thus within his power, it allays his thirst of competition, and substitutes in its place a complacent feeling of patronage, which takes the appearance of chivalrous sentiment. But this impulse soon passes, and his old professional jealousy is rekindled at the first view of Coriolanus's reinstation in command. His vulgar nature cannot bear the sight of the other's pre-eminence; and this perpetual consciousness of inferiority goads him into ever sharper desire to attain superior rank. It makes him basely rejoice when he beholds Coriolanus give way to the pleading of his mother and his wife; it impels him to the villainy of working his downfall; it urges him to treachery and murder-crime. As an instance of Shakespeare's subtlety in drawing these moral portraitures, it is to be observed that Aufidius, even at the best of his behaviour towards his noble rival, when he receives him with kindliness at his house at Antium, always addresses him as "Caius Marcius;" and the secret rankling which prompted the name is betrayed in open avowal where he subsequently calls him so, and the other exclaiming "Marcius!" he retorts—

> "Ay, Marcius, Caius Marcius; dost thou think
> I 'll grace thee with that robbery, thy stolen name
> Coriolanus in Corioli?"

His jealous sting of enmity is constantly revealed, not only by acknowledged feelings, as where he says—

> "At the last,
> I seem'd his follower, not partner; and
> He *waged me with his countenance*, as if
> I had been *mercenary*;"

but also by side-wind touches of evidence. It is in the moral inferiority of Tullus Aufidius, thus subtly drawn, that Shakespeare has presented him as an effective opposite to the principal character.

The Roman commander, Cominius, and the Roman officer, Titus Lartius, are fine and spirited sketches. Cominius is the patrician in every word and phrase. It is he who utters one of the grandest and most poetical speeches in the play—the panegyric on the deeds of Coriolanus, delivered before the senators in the capitol; it occurs in the 2d scene of the 2d Act. He says:—

> "The deeds of Coriolanus
> Should not be utter'd feebly.—It is held,
> That valour is the chiefest virtue, and
> Most dignifies the haver: if it be,
> The man I speak of cannot in the world
> Be singly counterpois'd. At sixteen years,
> When Tarquin made a head for Rome, he fought
> Beyond the mark of others:—our then dictator,
> Whom with all praise I point at, saw him fight,
> When with his Amazonian chin he drove
> The bristled lips before him: he bestrid
> An o'er-press'd Roman, and i' the consul's view
> Slew three opposers; Tarquin's self he met,
> And struck him on his knee: in that day's feats,
> When he might act the woman in the scene,
> He prov'd best man i' the field; and for his meed
> Was brow-bound with the oak. His pupil age
> Man-enter'd thus, he waxèd like a sea;

And in the brunt of seventeen battles since,
He lurch'd* all swords of the garland. For this last,
Before and in Corioli, let me say
I cannot speak him home: he stopp'd the fliers;
And, by his rare example, made the coward
Turn terror into sport: *as weeds before*
*A vessel under sail, so men obey'd,*
*And fell below his stem:* his sword, death's stamp,
Where it did mark, it took; from face to foot
He was a thing of blood, whose every motion
Was tim'd with dying cries: alone he enter'd
The mortal gate of the city, which he painted
With shunless destiny; aidless came off,
And with a sudden re-enforcement *struck*
*Corioli like a planet:* now all 's his;
When by and by the din of war 'gan pierce
His ready sense; then straight his doubled spirit
Requicken'd what in flesh was fatigate,
And to the battle came he; where he did
Run reeking o'er the lives of men, as if
'Twere a perpetual spoil: and till we call'd
Both field and city ours, he never stood
To ease his breast with panting."

Titus Lartius, the sturdy veteran, proclaims himself in some of the first words he utters:—

"I'll lean upon one crutch, and fight with t' other,
Ere stay behind this business."

And the whole subsequent tone of the character is true to the bold announcing key-note thus struck.

Sicinius and Brutus, the two tribunes of the people, are thorough specimens of a brace of vulgar demagogues. In their very first scene, they manifest the grudging envy, the malignant spirit which actuates them against Marcius; and their vile nature exposes itself in the low motives they attribute to him. They are constantly on the watch for factious

* Won the garland from all swords.

opposition and vexatious objection. They meanly incite the people, and prompt them into animosity against him. They take advantage of his defects of temper—his irascible and tornado disposition—to urge him into self-destruction. They do this with the little cunning of little minds, and the unscrupulousness of base politicians. It is principally their venting their splenetic remarks *behind his back* which gives so hateful an effect to their comments: had they urged their objections to his face, they might, and they ought to have commanded attention, for there is truth in what they adduce of his overweening pride. It is their hole-and-corner plotting and scheming, as well as animadverting surreptitiously, which imparts so dastardly a character to their movements; by not daring to impeach him openly, betraying their sense that they cannot do so with strict justice. The unfairness with which these faction-mongers proceed, is indicated in strong colours where they order the man, who brings the unwelcome news that the Volsces are marching upon Rome, "to be whipped," accusing him of having raised the report for mere party purpose. One exclaims, "Nothing but his report!" and the other, on hearing the addition that Marcius is said to lead the Volscian power, rejoins—

> "Rais'd only that the weaker sort may wish
> God Marcius home again.
> "*Sicin.* The very trick on't!"

Ay, precisely the kind of trick that these gentry were well versed in; the trick of spreading false reports to stir popular excitement. No wonder they suspected it to be a hatched rumour, and ordered the fellow who promulgated it to be forthwith scourged. No one better than they could estimate his desert.

This play is rich in short secondary scenes—of much significance, notwithstanding their brevity and apparent unimportance, and which serve to exemplify Shakespeare's system of art in this respect. Witness all the mob or citizen scenes; the one between a Roman and a Volsce, in the 3d scene of the 4th Act; that between Aufidius and his lieutenant, in the 7th scene of the 4th Act; and the 5th of the 5th Act, where Tullus Aufidius, the three or four conspirators of his faction, and the lords of Antium, meet to confer respecting Coriolanus's having committed the Volscian cause. In this last scene the various interested motives which sway each set of speakers in turn, while all are discussing the same point and affecting to deplore *the others'* loss, are made amusingly, though incidentally apparent. Aufidius betrays his besetting military jealousy; the conspirators betray their disappointment at missing the expected Roman spoil; and the lords of the city show their dissatisfaction that "*the benefit of our levies*" should have been "given away." Shakespeare saw into, and made men reveal, their secret hearts like a recording angel.

There is but one subordinate character among the females in this play, and that is Valeria, the friend of Volumnia and Virgilia. The part is necessarily a very slight one; yet, being a patrician lady, and an intimate of the principals, the poet takes occasion to exalt her qualities with the reader through a third party. Coriolanus describes her as

> "The noble sister of Publicola,
> The moon of Rome; chaste as the icicle
> That's curded by the frost from purest snow,
> And hangs on Dian's temple."

A passage which, for the beauty of the poetry, and as a lustrous image of woman's perfection, I should suppose has never been surpassed. In the 3d scene of the 1st Act, where Valeria comes to pay a morning visit to the two ladies, we again have an example—even upon so minim an occasion—of Shakespeare's perception of all the characteristic points to be produced, and with advantage. One would suppose, from this effective little scene, that he had put himself upon "a course" of etiquette, and had taken honours and degrees in the science of making "morning calls." Ladies, I believe, upon these occasions—those at least who are well-bred and sweet-tempered—always select a subject for conversation which shall be most grateful to the ear of their hostess; so the courtly Valeria knows that nothing can better please the mother and grandmother than to talk about and praise the little Marcius; and an admirable picture she draws of the future warrior. The grandmother, Volumnia, says—"He had rather see the swords and hear a drum, than look upon his schoolmaster." The visitor replies—"On my word, the father's son. I'll swear 'tis a very pretty boy. O' my troth, I looked upon him o' Wednesday half-an-hour together; he has such a *confirmed countenance*." In that comprehensive term of one word Shakespeare has conveyed the perfect ideal of a self-willed character. It has been frequently remarked that we cannot alter a phrase or an epithet of his without injuring it. Let any one try to select a word more apt to the purpose in this instance of conveying the idea of a sturdy child, and his success will be fortunate—not to say, singular. Valeria continues—

"I saw him run after a gilded butterfly; and when he caught it, he let it go again; and after it again; and over and over he comes, and up again; catched it again: or whether his fall enraged him, or how 'twas, he did so set his teeth and tear it; O I warrant, how he mammocked it!"

There's the epitome of the father who "fluttered the Volscians about, like an eagle in a dove-cote." Here's strict harmony of keeping. The grandmother, only too proud of the child, can pay the act no higher compliment in her own mind, than by pronouncing it "one of his father's moods."

She has just before, in the true spirit of a Roman woman, affirmed—

> "The breasts of Hecuba,
> When she did suckle Hector, look'd not lovelier
> Than Hector's forehead, when it spit forth blood
> At Grecian swords contending."

After reading this very unimportant part of Valeria, and which consists of but about half-a-dozen short sentences, no one, I should think, would be so hardy as to maintain (which nevertheless has been asserted in the fanatical spirit of criticism) that Shakespeare slovened his insignificant characters in order to throw his principals into high relief. Even the common soldiers in this play have their full appointment, and an honourable one it is. Heretofore in several instances notice has been taken of the pains he has bestowed in delineating all the component qualities that go to form the legitimate common soldier. In a collective body, the soldier is of "no mark or likelihood;" he is one rand in the great rope of an army, whose aggregate might is to tear down or raise up empires. A body of soldiers looks like one man seen through a multiplying lens; a thousand are marching like one, and one is multiplied into a thousand. Not only do they move simultaneously, but they seem as if one thought actuated the whole mass. Abstractedly and distinctively, however, the common soldier is an object of no common interest; and our poet evidently thought so, from the position he has assigned him in the several plays of "All 's Well that Ends Well," "Henry V.," "Antony and Cleopatra," and in the one now under consideration. The occupation of the soldier is to march, countermarch, fight, storm towns, sever nations, and dislocate empires. He does not appear to be a denizen of the land that gave him birth; he should always be abroad; and when he returns home, he should be sent abroad again; and he himself seems to think so, for he looks upon his own country only as a resting-place till some active foreign duty turns up, and then he undertakes it with the same coolness that a reaper goes to the harvest-field. He is a fine picturesque character, too, the common soldier. He goes through his toiling eventful life under suns that scorch like a blast-furnace, in infectious swamps, or on bleaching plains; and in the twilight of existence he creeps home, mayhap both maimed and rheumatic in all his joints, to die in a hospital. His career, indeed, is jestingly summed up by the Clown in "Pericles."—"What would you have me do? go to the wars, would you? where a man may serve seven years for the loss of a leg, and have not money in the end to buy him a wooden one."

The English common soldier has not a chance of the highest advancement in his profession; and this, if an injustice, at all events renders him an object of additional interest and sympathy; and perhaps it is well for him that it should be so, for he has no inducement to be envious of his comrades in rank. A gap that is made by death in *his* order does not advance him. He is disinterested; and another attractive feature in his character is, that he is devoid of meanness. My heart aches when I contemplate a common soldier, because I feel that there is a fellow-creature, most probably possessing many of my own sympathies for his species, whose eyes would fill with tears at a tale of noble sorrow; and who, nevertheless, commits a whole life of mistake in contributing to the cause of that sorrow. May the fulfilment of that time speedily arrive—and it must arrive, or Christianity is an institution of *this* world—when every brother, of every clime and colour, shall "sit under his own vine and his own fig-tree, and no man shall make him afraid."

The scene alluded to in this play is the vivid conversation of Tullus Aufidius's soldiers when the banished Coriolanus comes to claim the protection of his enemy's hearth. There is not a more characteristic dialogue in the whole drama; or, of its class, in any other of the poet's dramas, while there are several touches of nature and of human action fully worthy of the prominent parts. Here is an abridgment of the whole scene, (the 5th of the 4th Act,) containing that portion only in which the soldiers are engaged:—

"*Scene—A Hall in Tullus Aufidius's House—Music within—Enter a Servant.*

"1*st Serv.* Wine, wine, wine! What service is here! I think our fellows are asleep. [*Exit.*

"*Enter a second Servant.*

"2*d Serv.* Where's Cotus? My master calls for him.—Cotus! [*Exit.*

"*Enter* CORIOLANUS.

"*Cor.* A goodly house. The feast smells well; but I appear not like a guest.

"*Re-enter* 1st SERVANT.

"1*st Serv.* What would you have, friend? Whence are you? Here's no place for you:—pray go to the door.

"*Cor.* [*Aside.*] I have deserved no better entertainment in being Coriolanus.

"*Re-enter* 2d SERVANT.

"2*d Serv.* Whence are you, sir? Has the Porter his eyes in his head that he gives entrance to such companions? Pray, get you out.

"*Cor.* Away!

"1*st Serv.* Away? Get you away.

"*Cor.* Now, thou art troublesome.

"2*d Serv.* Are you so brave? I'll have you talked with anon.

"*Enter* 3d SERVANT. *The first meets him.*

"3*d Serv.* What fellow's this?

"1*st Serv.* A strange one as ever I looked on; I cannot get him out of the house. Prithee, call my master to him.

"3*d Serv.* What have you to do here, fellow? Pray you, avoid the house.

"*Cor.* Let me but stand; I will not hurt your hearth.

"*3d Serv.* What are you?

"*Cor.* A gentleman.

"*3d Serv.* A marvellous poor one.

"*Cor.* True; so I am.

"*3d Serv.* Pray you, 'poor gentleman,' take up some other station; here 's no place for you. Pray you, avoid. Come.

"*Cor.* Follow your function; go, and batten on cold bits. [*Pushes him away.*

"*3d Serv.* What, will you not? Prithee, tell my master what a strange guest he has here.

"*2d Serv.* And I shall. [*Exit.*

"*3d Serv.* Where dwellest thou?

"*Cor.* Under the canopy.

"*3d Serv.* Under the canopy!

"*Cor.* Ay.

"*3d Serv.* Where 's that?

"*Cor.* I' the city of the kites and crows.

"*3d Serv.* I' the city of kites and crows? What an ass it is! Then thou dwellest with daws, too?

"*Cor.* No; I serve not thy master. * * * Thou prat'st, and prat'st. Serve with thy trencher. Hence! [*Beats him away.*

"*Enter* AUFIDIUS *and* 2d SERVANT.

"*Auf.* Where is this fellow?

"*2d Serv.* Here, sir. I'd have beaten him like a dog, but for disturbing the lords within.

"*Auf.* Whence com'st thou? What would'st thou? Thy name? * * * *

"*Cor.* A name unmusical to the Volscians' ears, and harsh in sound to thine.

"*Auf.* Say, what 's thy name?
Thou hast a grim appearance, and thy face
Bears a command in 't; though thy tackle 's torn
Thou show'st a noble vessel. What 's thy name?

* * * * *

"*Cor.* My name is Caius Marcius, who hath done
To thee particularly, and to all the Volsces,

Great hurt and mischief; thereto witness may
My surname, Coriolanus."

He then relates the circumstance of his banishment, and willingness to join issue with his old enemy to lay waste his native country. The two, hand in hand, go in, and the servants advance:—

"*1st Serv.* Here's a strange alteration!

"*2d Serv.* By my hand, I had thought to have strucken him with a cudgel; and yet my mind gave me; his clothes made a false report of him.

"*1st Serv.* What an arm he has! He turned me about with his finger and thumb, as one would set up a top.

"*2d Serv.* Nay, I knew by his face that there was something in him. He had, sir, a kind of face, methought,—I cannot tell how to term it.

"*1st Serv. He had so; looking, as it were,*—would I were hanged, but I thought there was more in him than I could think.

"*2d Serv.* So did I, I'll be sworn. He is simply the rarest man i' the world.

"*1st Serv.* I think he is; but a greater soldier than he, you wot one.

"*2d Serv.* Who? my master?

"*1st Serv.* Nay, it's no matter for that.

"*2d Serv.* Worth six on him.

"*1st Serv.* Nay, not so neither; but I take him to be the greater soldier.

"*2d Serv.* 'Faith, look you, one cannot tell how to say that. For the defence of a town our general is excellent.

"*1st Serv.* Ay, and for an assault too.

"*Re-enter* 3d SERVANT.

"*3d Serv.* Oh, slaves! I can tell you news; news, you rascals!

"*1st Serv.* What—what—what? Let's partake.

"*3d Serv.* I would not be a Roman of all nations: I had as lief be a condemned man.

"*1st and 2d Serv.* Wherefore? Wherefore?

"*3d Serv.* Why, here's he that was wont to thwack our general—Caius Marcius.

"*1st Serv.* Why do you say 'thwack our general?'

"*3d Serv. I do not say thwack our general;* but he was always good enough for him.

"*2d Serv.* Come, we are fellows and friends: he was ever too hard for him; I have heard him say so himself.

"*1st Serv.* He was too hard for him directly, to say the truth on't: before Corioli, he scotched him and notched him like a carbonado.

"*2d Serv.* An he had been cannibally given, he might have broiled and eaten him too.

"*1st Serv.* But, more of thy news.

"*3d Serv.* Why, he's so made on here within, as if he were son and heir to Mars: set at upper end o' the table; no question asked him by any of the senators, but they stand bald before him. Our general himself makes a mistress of him; sanctifies himself with's hand, and turns up the white o' the eye to his discourse. But the bottom o' the news is, our general is cut i' the middle, and but one half of what he was yesterday; for the other has half, by the grant and entreaty of the whole table. He'll go, he says, and sowle the Porter of Rome gates by the ears. He will mow down all before him, and leave his passage polled.

"*2d Serv.* And he's as like to do it as any man I can imagine.

"*3d Serv.* Do't!—he will do't; for, look you, sir, he has as many friends as enemies; which friends, sir, as it were, durst not—look you, sir—show themselves, as we term it,—his friends, whilst he's *in directitude.*

"*1st Serv. 'Directitude!' What's that?*

"*3d Serv.* But when they shall see, sir, his crest up again, and the man in blood, they will out of their burrows, like conies after rain, and revel all with him.

"*1st Serv.* But when goes this forward?

"*3d Serv.* To-morrow; to-day; presently; you shall have the drum strike up this afternoon: 'tis, as it were, a parcel of their feast, and to be executed ere they wipe their lips.

"*2d Serv.* Why, then, we shall have *a stirring world again.*

This peace is nothing but *to rust iron,* increase tailors, and *breed ballad-makers.*

" *1st Serv.* Let me have war, say I: it exceeds peace as far as day does night: it's spritely, waking, audible, and full of vent. Peace is a very apoplexy,—lethargy; mulled, deaf, sleepy, insensible; * * * and *it makes men hate one another.*

" *3d Serv.* Reason; *because they then less need one another.*"

There is a class of men who, from their natural powers, seem born to command; but who, from a restless and jealous spirit, can bear no one near their state; proud, imperious, domineering, insolent, they must be the "be all, and the end all, here,"—ay, and "hereafter" too, if the thing were possible. Men, whose talents all per-force admire; but *with* whom—from their overbearing tempers—no one can act. Such, in a great measure, seems to have signalised the career of Coriolanus. In his triumphs all bore testimony to his merit,—even the commonalty whom he hated, and who knew that he hated them: when, however, the plebeian faction became predominant, the tempestuous disposition of the man spurned all counsel—all entreaties to temporise and manœuvre;—no! they should "unroof the city" before he would abate one jot of his will. He was therefore deserted by his own "order," and "whooped" out of his birthplace by the men he had despised. What a grand moral lesson!

This noble drama is the history of Plutarch vivified and brought home to the bosom-feelings of every man who is wise enough to perceive the stupidity, as well as the injustice, of all faction for class-aggrandisement.

XX.

# Measure for Measure.

# XX.

# MEASURE FOR MEASURE.

FOR the store of golden axioms on moral and social wisdom that it contains, no one of Shakespeare's dramas stands more grandly conspicuous than that of "Measure for Measure." Moreover, it displays a wider range of character, morally contrasted, than almost any other. We have the brutal stupidity of Barnardine, the callous offspring of vicious ignorance, whom the prospect of a shameful death cannot rouse to sensibility; the cruel and practical indifference of Abhorson, the gaoler and hangman; the putrid infamy of the creatures haunting the suburban stews; the vile and cold-blooded hypocrisy of virtue in Angelo—the more heart-sickening from that hypocrisy, as palpable disease is preferable to the scrofulous treachery of roseate health, when the worm of death is at the core; and ascending from that "lowest deep" in morality to the benevolent-hearted Provost, the well-meaning and patriotic, but certainly weak Duke, up to the angelic purity of the sainted Isabella, the heroine of the piece, and foremark of the whole community, and to whom the foremark of comment is consequently due.

Isabella is a curious combination of staid self-possession and the most shrinking modesty. She has a fine and even powerful mind, but it is in conjunction with a retiring nature, rendered even *bashful* by habit and education. She is *very young*. The poet has distinctly marked this in several portions of the play, and she has been brought up for a nun. Most people seem to consider Isabella as a full-grown woman, with a confirmed manner, and a confident, nay, a self-satisfied disposition. To me she is much the reverse of all this. I find her to be, upon close and careful examination of the character, as Shakespeare has drawn it, a girl of naturally fine understanding and admirable judgment, together with an unvain and most unselfish spirit. She is hardly aware of her own mental powers, for there has been hitherto little opportunity for their exercise. Her answers to Lucio, her brother's friend, when he comes to beg her intercession with Claudio's stern judge, are indicative of self-doubt and distrust of her own qualifications for the office of pleader. "Alas! what poor ability's in ME to do him good?" And when Lucio urges her, with, "Assay the power you have," she falteringly replies, "My power! Alas! I doubt," as if but too fearful that *she* can do naught to meet this calamity. Her brother's first description of her fully bears out the view here taken of the character. He speaks of her modest, silent habit, together with her *tender years*, where he says—

"In her youth
There is a prone and *speechless dialect*,
Such as moves men;"

and her power of intellect is denoted in the words—

"She hath prosperous art
When she will play with reason and discourse,
And well she can persuade."

Isabella has been called "cold." But with what generous impulse she speaks, when, hearing of her brother's offence with Juliet, she exclaims, "Oh, let him marry her!" with the genuine trust of youth, believing that *reparation* is the best *expiation.* Note, also, the enthusiastic eagerness with which she is willing to augment austerities in her approaching convent life. She asks, "Have you nuns no farther privileges?" And upon sister Francesca's answer, "Are not these large enough?" Isabella replies—

> "Yes, truly: I speak not as desiring more;
> But rather *wishing a more strict restraint*
> Upon the sisterhood, the votarists of St Clare."

This is precisely the lavish zeal with which a very young person enters upon vowed duties. Her prodigal regardlessness of life, too, is perfectly characteristic of youth. Of her own, of her brother's, of Mariana's, she is, each in turn, equally prodigal when misfortune threatens. Of her own she eagerly speaks:—

> "Oh, were it but my life,
> I 'd throw it down for your deliverance
> As frankly as a pin."

Is that the speech and act of a cold-blooded person? Of her brother's life she is no less profuse when staked against honour:—

> "Better it were a brother died at once,
> Than that a sister, by redeeming him,
> Should die for ever;"

and she is thus profuse because she feels sure that *he, too,* would be so, knowing the alternative; for she says, rather than this—

> "Had he twenty heads to tender down
> On twenty bloody blocks, *he'd yield them up.*"

And of Mariana's life she shows the same disregard when knowing that it is made miserable by Angelo's unkindness; for she exclaims, "What a merit were it in death to take this poor maid from the world!" Such being precisely the way in which young ardent natures feel when *first coming* face to face with the stern griefs of life.

Isabella's warmth of indignation, when she finds her brother less indifferent to death, compared with dishonour, than she had believed, might redeem her from the charge of "coldness;" but even this has been turned against her, one critic going so far as ungenerously and unjustly, and unwarrantably as ungenerously, to sneer at a "virtue" that is (he says) "*sublimely good at another's expense.*" Jenny Deans would, of course, be placed in the same category of this writer's contempt with Isabella. From all that we are shown of her character, Isabella's "virtue" is as noble and unselfish as it is unaffectedly sincere and pure. It has courage for all things but evil-doing in hope of advantage. She herself says, when urged by the Duke to undertake an attempt of a difficult nature—"Let me hear you speak farther; *I have spirit to do anything that appears not foul in the truth of my spirit.*" *This* is not the language of a cold-natured woman.

She has been accused of lukewarmness in her pleading to Angelo; but read the whole of those two fine scenes carefully, and I insure the congruence—that the skill of the dramatist is absolute and consummate mastery, in the way whereby he has contrived to preserve the womanly warmth with womanly delicacy throughout. In the first of these two scenes, Shakespeare has managed to exhibit the *impression* of lukewarmness that has been alluded to, *as produced upon the bystanders,* Lucio and the Provost; both of them being present on this occasion. The coarse man of the world, Lucio, not having an idea of the motive that restrains her and holds her in a measure tongue-tied, urges her, almost reproachfully, saying (aside to her)—

> "Give 't not o'er so: to him again, entreat him;
> Kneel down before him, hang upon his gown:

> You are too cold; if you should need a pin,
> You could not with more tame a tongue desire it:
> To him, I say."

Does not the tone and manner of this expostulation also convey the idea of its being addressed to a very young, and not to an adult woman? But the fact is, Lucio, in his dissolute callousness and vice-hardened perceptions, has not a glimmering of the *real cause* of Isabella's apparent coldness; and many who have judged the character, and pronounced it "cold," seem to have equally missed the true source of Isabella's imputed "tameness" here. I can only feel it to be thoroughly consistent with the most generous ardour of nature, such as she gives evidence of possessing beneath her exterior calm and self-retention, that this modest young girl, this maiden recluse, should find extreme difficulty in speaking at all upon the subject she has to treat of; and, upon studying the scene itself, it will be perceived that Isabella's hesitation only occurs when she has to touch upon the subject in question—her brother's fault. The virgin delicacy with which the poet has made her shrink from its absolute mention, and search for any form of words that shall convey the substance of her plea, without naming it, appears the very triumph of dramatic art, and perfectly serves to vindicate the character from the charge of unwomanly coldness, while exquisitely inferring its womanly modesty and reserve.

On all other points Isabella's conduct is warmth and earnestness to the uttermost. With what fervour and force of solemn argument she presses her appeal for mercy! When Angelo puts her off with—

> "Your brother is a forfeit of the law,
> And you but waste your words,"

she rejoins—

> "Alas! alas!
> Why, all the souls that were, were forfeit once;

And HE that might the 'vantage best have took,
Found out the remedy. How would you be,
If HE, which is the top of judgment, should
But judge you as you are? O! think on that,
And mercy then will breathe within your lips,
Like man new made."

In the second of these two great scenes, (the pleading scenes,)—great in their wonderfully artistic conduct throughout,—Isabella is *alone* with Angelo; and the poet has depicted her difference of bearing with miraculous tact and delicacy. Upon her entrance, the very first words Angelo utters awaken the feminine instinct, the sensitive perception of his altered manner and ominous meaning. She at once shrinks from it, and seeks to ward it off, by endeavouring, as long as possible, to misunderstand and misbelieve it. She will not allow herself to own that it is there, and will not allow him to make it manifest through his indirect speech. The way in which she parries this dreaded meaning is so intensely true to modest womanhood, that no one but Shakespeare, (whom an enthusiastic friend once declared to be half a woman, so tender and delicate was his poet-nature, as well as noble and exalted,) no one but he could have penned the words uttered by Isabella during this scene. They are full of all the innocent-artful turns and defences that women, possessing both moral and mental susceptibility, resort to in a circumstance of such critical difficulty as the one at issue between herself and Angelo. She evades his licentious inferences as long as possibly she can, by ingenious replies framed so as to preserve the ambiguity she would fain have him keep to; then, when forced upon her comprehension, she takes affecting refuge in appeal:—

"I have no tongue but one: gentle, my lord,
Let me entreat you speak the former language."

And when his unrelenting purpose will not withhold its expression, she adopts the course (so perfectly womanly!) of imputing a better motive to him than she is conscious he is actuated by, in a last lingering hope of inducing him to retract, by arousing within him a sense of moral shame:—

> "I know your virtue hath a licence in 't,
> Which seems a little fouler than it is,
> To pluck on others."

And lastly, when she finds nothing will avail to restrain him from open avowal of his foul wish, she bursts forth into indignant eloquent protest against his "most pernicious purpose."

I have ventured the rather to enlarge upon my views of this pure-charactered being, Isabella, because I feel that she has received scant justice hitherto from critics of my own sex—critics, best as well as worst—and because I think it a reproach upon men that they should treat injuriously one of the most beautiful-souled among Shakespeare's beautiful-souled women.

Can anything be more finely contrasted in character, as moral contrasts, than the two portraits of Lucio and the Provost in this play? The one is a young gallant—a roisterer "about town"—a thorough man of the *im*moral world; a socially-esteemed "gentleman." Among the list of persons, he is styled a "fantastic," but also one of the "gentlemen." He dresses well; he frequents what is termed "good society," say, genteel society. Virtuous ladies would not protest against his being admitted to the company they frequent. Well-bred gentlemen would not disdain to associate with him. He is known to be tainted with vices, but they are fashionable vices, in some (so called) gay courts; vices that have a tender, palliating nomenclature affixed to them, and which enables their perpetrator to obtain a passport into decent communities. He would be called (with a half-serious shake of the head) a "gay deceiver," a "wild young fellow," a wicked "Lothario," and so be endured, if not pardoned, for the sake of his station and easy effrontery; which, combined, suffice to make him be thought agreeable; and of a surety his legs would be tolerated under gentle mahogany. Yet this man is a liar, a backbiter, and a profligate. He basely neglects his illegitimate child, and with coward selfishness deserts its miserable mother. He maligns the absent Duke, and not only eats his words when he finds that they are likely to draw him into mischief, but accuses another of their utterance. He is a slanderer and a moral poltroon; yet is he one of that class of gentry who, by dint of position, by birth, an impudent brazen assumption, and unimpeachable costume, passes current as a dashing young fellow; dissipated certainly, but of highly-respectable connexions; and who, by and by, when he has "sown his wild oats," in other words, is battered and precociously "used up," and is all but mentally impotent, will subside into a respectable member of society, and possibly be a justice of quorum, and commit "petty rogues" to prison-labour.

Totally different from this man is the grave, sensible, and really respectable Provost. He is a person in an inferior grade; no higher appointment than that of head-gaoler of the prison. But he is mild, kind, gentle-hearted; full of charity and forbearance towards those original temptations to sin, and circumstances of sin, which form extenuation, though not vindication of sin. In the fault of the youthful Claudio he can perceive temperament, unrestrictive teaching, and a desire to amend; which should all plead against the fault receiving so stringent a punishment as is awarded to it. Even in the hardened Barnardine, the worthy Provost can discern that spark of retrievable matter which should be fostered into hope of reformation, rather than extinguished in impatient haste. He says, with the true spirit of divine hope—that hope which bids us not despair of even the, apparently, most destitute of lost souls:—

> "What if we do omit
> This reprobate, till he were well inclin'd."

The Provost in this play is, as it were, an impersonation of that more merciful spirit of justice which would rather deal correctively than penally with human error. That spirit which, taking into consideration how ill-taught and ill-advised the childhood of most criminals has been, is inclined to treat those criminals with more of leniency than severity. That spirit which, pitying the slender opportunities of knowing better and doing better that fall to the lot of the generality of pauper-infancy, leans toward the tolerant rather than the inexorable in judging their after misdeeds. That spirit which, aware of the inefficient means that have been taken to *prevent* vice, dreads too harshly to *punish* vice. That spirit which, conscious that the education of the destitute child is too often suffered to be but the training to become the self-providing thief, fears to inflict a penalty which should, in strict justice, fall on those who took no pains originally to make him an honest man. But as the great wit-humanist of our own day—Douglas Jerrold—says, with his own fine and peculiar irony, "To *reform* man is a tedious and uncertain labour; *hanging* is the sure work of a minute."

We are made to recognise throughout the delineation of the character of the Provost, (as contrasted with that of Lucio,) how far higher is *moral* elevation than *social* elevation. For the keeper of felons we have esteem and reverence; for the conventional gentleman—the gentleman about town, we come not short of contempt, and even loathing. There is only one redeeming touch in all Lucio's nasty character. It is, that with all his moral degradation he has yet sufficient perception of good left, to be sensible of the purity and holy whiteness of Isabella. He holds her in genuine veneration, and says to her:—

> "I would not—though 'tis my familiar sin

With maids to seem the lapwing, and to jest,
Tongue far from heart,—play with *all* virgins so:
I hold you as a thing ensky'd and sainted;
By your renouncement, an immortal spirit;
And to be talk'd with in sincerity,
As with a saint."

Shakespeare solaces his heavenly spirit with these single redeeming touches in his worst characters; for he knows that human nature, even in its most deplorable deviations from what it should be, and from what it naturally is, has its strange latent points of good, that still hover and linger there to claim affinity with that which might perchance have been cherished into virtue by benign and wholesome influences, instead of being smothered and perverted to evil by sinister ones.

In the very blackest and vilest of the personages in this drama—the bad old woman, who gains a livelihood by trading in vice—the poet has developed just one solitary touch, that rescues her from utter abhorrence and abandonment. She pays for the keep of the wretched offspring of Lucio; rather than suffer the child to starve, which its own parent would have done.—"His child is a year and a quarter old, come Philip and Jacob; *I have kept it myself;* and see how he goes about to abuse me." Shakespeare always courageously shows how nature asserts her unquenchable power over even the most unhappily-corrupted hearts.

In the power of displaying "individuality" of character, we see the poet to no more advantage than in his several grades of official men; from the constable in ordinary up to the justice of the peace; all, whether prominent or subordinate, are finished portraits. Elbow, the constable in this play, and Dogberry in "Much Ado About Nothing," are brothers of the same class; both conceited and ignorant; both perverting and "abusing the king's English;" and both calling themselves "the poor Duke's officers;" a joke that Shakespeare evidently liked, from his repeating it. Elbow is intent upon clearing his wife before Angelo from a scandal of Pompey; a scene abounding in the most ludicrous phraseology and rich caricature of justice-room evidence and examination:—the opening of the second act.

Connected with this same scene, figures a prodigious specimen of a being, in the person of "Master Froth;" styled in the *dramatis personæ,* "Froth, a foolish gentleman."

Master Froth is a sample of the "order in creation, 'idea-less.'" He is one of that class of human beings who, like a certain class of reptiles, appear to exist quite as well without brains as with brains. Some amiable naturalist—Buffon, mayhap—tried the experiment upon a tortoise, of taking out its brains, in order to ascertain whether the animal could dispense with its cerebral accomplishment. The brain of a tortoise being no larger than a pea, he theorised that the difference between a pea and nothing could make no difference to the poor beast. The result (it is said) confirmed the hypothesis; the poor beast blundered on without, as before with, its pea of brain. And thus blunder on some human tortoises—brainless—through life; to all intents and purposes of mere going on, as well as though they had their full pea-complishment of skull furniture. But they may go right, or they may go wrong, as the case may be. If they go right, it is from pure good hap; if they go wrong, it is from utter futility and incapacity to keep out of harm's way. Master Froth strays from the right path from sheer vapidity; he frequents low dissolute haunts from no graver cause than idleness and vacuity of mind. He fools away his time, his money, and his health, only because he is master of his leisure and of "fourscore pound a year," with ne'er a pea-pulp in his cranium to guide him in their due disposal. He just manages to "blunder on," and that is all. He has not so much beneath his "most weak pia mater" as will help him to a single spontaneous notion. He never originates a remark; never offers an opinion. He can only answer; only return syllable-rejoinders to what is demanded of him: "No, indeed;" "Ay, so I did;" "All this is true." These form the "high-level" of his ability. The only time he ventures upon an ascent above this "tableland" of mind, and ventures at a *reason* for what he says, he flounders and pitches headlong. Directly he attempts a "because" he is ruined! The Clown, in the course of the examination before the Provost and Escalus, asks Froth whether he has not a fancy for sitting in a certain room in their tavern; and he avers that he has so, adding, "*because* it 's an *open* room, and *good* for winter." Simple reply is the only safe course for Froth. Let him once open his mouth for anything beyond this, and he proclaims himself a fool—an aboriginal fool. By the way, he is knowing in dates. Your fellows who know nothing else, are apt to be recondite in dates. They are unerring on points of chronology. So, when the Clown, in his zeal for accuracy, appeals to Master Froth for confirmation whether his father did not die at Hallowmas, Froth corrects him, with—"All-hollond-eve." But after this exertion, and his breaking down in his sole "because," he drops into silence until the Lord Escalus summons him to answer his cross-questioning, and to receive a piece of wholesome advice. Upon which, pea-brain Froth once more relapses into his yeas and nays, and his "Yes, an't please you, sirs;" and is again tempted beyond his depth in reply to his lordship's counsel to keep clear of mischief and tavern-haunting, with, "I thank your worship. For mine own part, I never come into any room in a tap-house but I am drawn in." You see he can 't utter six words without betraying what a hopeless gull he is. Well may that brazen fellow, Pompey, bid Escalus look in Froth's face as a guarantee for his harmlessness. He may look into the "'blankness' of that dark ;" he will find nothing there : it is responsible only for *vacancy;* it is fatuity made absolute :—

" *Clown.* I beseech you, sir, look in this gentleman's face. Good Master Froth, look upon his Honour ; 'tis for a good purpose. Doth your Honour mark his face ?

" *Esc.* Ay, sir, very well.

" *Clown.* Nay, I beseech you, mark it well.

" *Esc.* Well, I do so.

" *Clown.* Doth your Honour see any harm in his face ?

" *Esc.* Why, no.

" *Clown.* I 'll be supposed upon a book, his face is the worst thing about him. Good, then ; if his face be the worst thing about him, how could Master Froth do the Constable's wife any harm ? I would know that of your Honour."

The postulate granted, the logic is fair, and the conclusion self-evident. But if there is no " harm" in the poor simpleton, neither is there any good in him. He is too effete, too flabby, to mean, or to be worth anything. As Rochefoucauld truly says, " A fool has not *stuff* enough in him to be good." There can be no virtue in Froth ; and he is Froth no less by nature than by name. No spirit, no essence, no body in him ; nothing, in short, but " Froth."

Pompey, the Clown, is a copy from the life, so far as his original calling goes. One class of the domestic fool-jester in our poet's time was a hireling attendant at the taverns and places of profligate resort in the suburbs of great towns. Here the dramatist, for his purpose, had to introduce such a personage ; and he has drawn him with all the bold strong colours required by the occasion. But he has given him humour, in a degree redeeming the coarseness ; and wit, that points the moral, while it helps to withdraw attention from the grosser details of the picture that he judged it needful to draw.

The philosophy of making the Clown meet in the gaol, imprisoned for debt, so many of the idle young men about town whom he had formerly encountered in haunts of dissipation, is sound doctrine, and sufficiently indicates the motive which induced the treating of so untoward a subject.

There is one speech he makes—a sharp satire upon *respectable* iniquitous trades—which alone lifts him into importance among the *dramatis personæ*:—" 'Twas never merry world since, of two *usuries*, the merriest was put down, and the worser allowed, by *order of law*, a furr'd gown to keep him warm ; and furr'd with fox and lamb skins, too, to signify, that craft being richer than innocency, stands for the *facing*."

If there be one speech more familiar than another in our mouths, when talking of Shakespeare, it is, that take what subject we may for discussion, we shall find that he has been beforehand with us, and (which is more) that he has left little or nothing to be said after him. Who would suppose that he had anticipated the modern boasted discovery of the impolicy, not to say the folly, of sending young delinquents to the common gaol for the purpose of amendment, by correction? Yet, in the slight sketch of the reckless and incorrigible Barnardine, we have a practical treatise upon the immorality, as well as the futility, of visiting crime with the indiscriminate punishment of incarceration. In the case of the character just referred to, the Duke is made to inquire of the Provost, "What is that Barnardine, who is to be executed in the afternoon?" The Provost replies, "A Bohemian born, but here nursed up and bred; one that is a prisoner *nine years old*." With that apparently casual, but premeditated little fact, the poet, like a great moral philosopher, deduces the after life of the man ; and with surpassing vividness, in a short scene, has he given that result in the mature criminal, which must naturally ensue from such a course of correction visited upon a nine years' victim. Barnardine has become, as the Provost describes him, "A man that apprehends death no more dreadfully but as a drunken sleep ; careless, reckless, and fearless of what's past, present, or to come; insensible of mortality, and desperately mortal."

The young delinquent who learns the force of morality, the power of justice, the rights of mankind, the duties of himself to his neighbour, and of his neighbour to him, from prison-walls, having no other instruction for his tender years than the hard truths to be gathered from their stony tutelage, runs no chance of becoming any other than the brutal, insensible Barnardine. For the multitudes of Barnardines, prison-taught and prison-punished in actual existence, who will be responsible at the last great account? Those who adjust matters so, that no other teaching is provided for juvenile thieves than prisons, gaols, houses of correction, and penitentiaries; or the childish malefactors themselves, who know no better than that to pilfer, to cheat, and to lie, are legitimate means of gaining a livelihood, until taught that they are perilous to soul and body by the State education of the "Stone Jug," and bread and water? Shakespeare, in the story of Barnardine, read us a profound lesson in penal legislation *two hundred and sixty-three* years ago. May it be turned to profit now!

In the full spirit of this prologue, the sturdy gaol-bird is introduced to us in person. Pompey, who is both a prisoner and deputy hangman, is sent by Abhorson, the head-executioner, to summon him for death: "Sirrah, bring Barnardine hither."

"*Clo.* Master Barnardine! You must rise and be hanged, Master Barnardine.

"*Abhor.* What, ho, Barnardine!

"*Bar.* [*within.*] A murrain o' your throats! Who makes that noise there? What are you?

"*Clo.* Your friend, sir, the hangman. You must be so good, sir, to rise and be put to death.

"*Bar.* [*within.*] Away, you rogue, away! I'm sleepy.

"*Abhor.* Tell him he must awake, and that quickly, too.

"*Clo.* Pray, Master Barnardine, awake till you are executed, and sleep afterwards.

"*Abhor.* Go in to him, and fetch him out.

"*Clo.* He is coming, sir; he is coming: I hear his straw rustle.

"*Abhor.* Is the axe upon the block, sirrah?

"*Clo.* Very ready, sir. [*Enter Barnardine.*

"*Bar.* How now, Abhorson? What's the news with you?

"*Abhor.* Truly, sir, I would desire you to clap into your prayers; for, look ye, the warrant's come.

"*Bar.* You rogue, I have been drinking all night. I am not fitted for it.

"*Clo.* Oh, the better, sir; for he that drinks all night, and is hanged betimes in the morning, may sleep the sounder all the next day.

"*Abhor.* Look you, sir; here comes your ghostly father. Do we jest now, think you?

[*Enter Duke, disguised as the Friar.*]

"*Duke.* Sir, induced by my charity, and hearing how hastily you are to depart, I am come to advise you, comfort you, and pray with you.

"*Bar.* Friar, not I. I have been drinking hard all night, and I will have more time to prepare me, or they shall beat out my brains with billets. I'll not consent to die this day, that's certain.

"*Duke.* Oh, sir, you must; and therefore I beseech you, look forward on the journey you shall go.

"*Bar.* I swear, I'll not die to-day for any man's persuasion.

"*Duke.* But hear you——

"*Bar.* Not a word; if you have anything to say to me, come to my ward; for thence will not I to-day."

Keeping to his text, that this poor caged wild beast from nine years, has been the victim of a mistaken discipline, Shakespeare, with his large heart, puts the following answer from the Duke to the Provost, who has inquired, "How he found the prisoner?"

"A creature unprepar'd, unmeet for *death*;

And, *to transport him in the mind he is,*
*Were damnable.*"

And in the last scene of the play he reads a lesson to all penal legislators in disposing of untaught ill-used criminals, so nurtured, and from early youth. The Duke in his proper person, as governor, says, "Which is that Barnardine?" "This, my lord," answers the Provost.

> "*Duke.* Sirrah, thou art said to have a stubborn soul,
> That apprehends no farther than this world,
> And squar'st thy life according. Thou'rt condemn'd;
> But, for those *earthly* faults, *I quit them all,*
> *And pray thee, take this mercy to provide*
> *For better times to come.* Friar, advise him;
> I leave him to your hand."

Truly, an hour were well bestowed upon this fine drama, did it contain no other sermon than is set forth in the treatment of Master Barnardine.

And from this episode, turn we to that point in the conduct of the plot referring to the second interview of Isabella with Angelo, while he is expecting her, and is meditating his wicked purpose, for a specimen of self-knowledge, conveyed in language that, for boldness and originality, is exceedingly striking. It is in the poet's finest manner:—

> "When I would pray and think, I think and pray
> To several subjects: Heaven hath my empty words;
> Whilst my invention, hearing not my tongue,
> Anchors on Isabel: Heaven in my mouth,
> As if I did but only *chew* his name,
> And in my heart the strong and swelling evil
> Of my conception. * * * O place! O form!
> How often dost thou with thy case, thy habit,
> Wrench awe from fools, and tie the wiser souls
> To thy false seeming! Blood, thou art blood:
> Let's write 'good angel' on the devil's horn,
> 'Tis not the devil's crest."

And then, as she is coming into his presence, how fine the reflection upon his own agitation :—

> "O heavens!
> Why does my blood thus muster to my heart,
> Making both it unable for itself,
> And dispossessing all my other parts
> Of necessary fitness?
> So play the foolish throngs with one that swoons;
> Come all to help him, and so stop the air
> By which he should revive: and even so
> The general,* subject to a well-wish'd king,
> Quit their own part, and in obsequious fondness
> Crowd to his presence, where their untaught love
> Must needs appear offence."

Scan this writer as we may; come to him as often as we may, the more reason do we find for admiration. Some fresh beauty, some latent sense, some subtle meaning, some pregnant import, still starts to light as we scrutinise the passages. An instance occurs to me upon the present occasion. Hitherto I have not noticed the artful way in which he has made Angelo, at the commencement of Isabella's first interview with him, answer her at length in replying to her timid and hesitating attempts at pleading for her brother; but as she progresses, and gathers confidence and power, *he gradually becomes silent,* and even allows the bystanders' expressions of interest in her suit to be heard; and then, in the intensity of his own absorption in her and her argument, he utters those few strong self-communing words—"She speaks; and it is such sense, that *my sense breeds with it.*"

The grandest writing, however, perhaps in the play, appears in the arguments produced on both sides with reference to the awful question of death. The Duke (as the Friar) characteristically would induce Claudio to look upon it as a gain, by balancing the bearing the evils of life, in opposition to a

* The commonalty.

riddance of their burthen. But Claudio has every inducement to cling to life. He is in love with life; he has strong affections, strong passions, and is condemned to death for yielding to their sway. In his cràving for life, he would retain it even by the loss of his sister's honour. Perfectly are these characteristics sustained in the three persons of Isabella, Claùdio, and the Duke. The speech of the Friar-duke to Claudio is a lofty argument, but it is a subtle Jesuitical composition; for it has all the air of one who is reasoning as a conventional casuist with a man about to die, and whom it is his object to persuade to indifference. In short, it is a philosophical "condemned sermon." He says—"So then, you hope for pardon from Lord Angelo?" Claudio answers—

"The miserable have
No other medicine, but only hope.
I have hope to live, and am prepar'd to die.
"*Duke.* Be absolute for death: either death or life
Shall thereby be the sweeter. Reason thus with life:
If I do lose thee, I do lose a thing
That none but fools would keep. A breath thou art,
Servile to all the skyey influences,
That dost this habitation, where thou keep'st,
Hourly afflict: merely thou art death's fool;
For him thou labour'st by thy flight to shun,
And yet run'st toward him still. Thou art not noble;
For all th' accommodations that thou bear'st
Are nurs'd by baseness. Thou art by no means valiant;
For thou dost fear the soft and tender fork
Of a poor worm. Thy best of rest is sleep,
And that thou oft provok'st; yet grossly fear'st
Thy death, which is no more. Thou art not thyself;
For thou exist'st on many a thousand grains
That issue out of dust. Happy thou art not;
For what thou hast not, still thou striv'st to get,
And what thou hast, forget'st. Thou art not certain;
For thy complexion shifts to strange effects,
After the moon. If thou art rich, thou'rt poor;

For like an ass, whose back with ingots bows,
Thou bear'st thy heavy riches but a journey,
And death unloads thee. Friend hast thou none;
For thine own bowels, which do call thee sire,
The mere effusion of thy proper loins,
Do curse the gout, serpigo, and the rheum,
For ending thee no sooner. Thou hast nor youth nor age;
But, as it were, an after-dinner's sleep,
Dreaming on both; for all thy blessed youth
Becomes as agèd, and doth beg the alms
Of palsied eld: and when thou art old and rich,
Thou hast neither heat, affection, limb, nor beauty,
To make thy riches pleasant. What 's yet in this
That bears the name of life? Yet in this life
Lie hid more thousand deaths: yet death we fear,
That makes these odds all even."

This is the tranquil exposition of one who is upon very good terms with the world; who has the trade-wind of fortune in the "shoulder of his sail;" and who contemplates the storm and shipwreck of life as a contingency; not as the most certain event in this world. People do not talk in that calm manner of the "grim fiend" when he is glaring at them over the shoulder. Two stronger and more characteristic speeches on the opposite sides of a question surely never were penned by the same man. There is the stoical philosophy of the Duke, simply contemplating the event of death; and in the other, the terror and dismay of Claudio, who is trembling on the brink of eternity, and is about to be thrust over the precipice. The one is the philosophy of resignation, where there is no demand for it in the teacher himself; and the other a display of the futility of the argument, where the demand for resignation is absolute; the revolt of nature against the hollow plausibility for a contented endurance. The one a cool, a frigid ratiocination; the other, an awful and terrible reality. *More* powerful lines than these can never have been uttered. They are like a prolonged shriek:—

"Ay, but to die, and go we know not where;
To lie in cold obstruction and to rot;
This sensible warm motion to become
A kneaded clod; and the delighted spirit
To bathe in fiery floods, or to reside
In thrilling region of thick-ribbèd ice;
Or to be imprison'd in the viewless winds,
And blown with restless violence round about
The pendent world; or to be worse than worst
Of those that lawless and incertain thoughts
Imagine howling! 'tis too horrible!
The weariest, and most loathèd worldly life
That age, ache, penury, and imprisonment
Can lay on nature, is a paradise
To what we fear of death."

As regards that portion of the plot of "Measure for Measure" which turns upon the Duke's retiring from his government, and leaving the stringent execution of his neglected laws to a deputy, while he, in his monkish disguise, watched from under his cowl the progress of events, no useful purpose can result from such masquerading, seeing that when the law is about to be enforced, he comes forth in the nick of time and pardons all the delinquents. However, it makes an agreeable *stage*-mystery; and not the less so, from the audience being all the while admitted to the secret. The story itself is a deeply-interesting one, and has been more than once paralleled in history. The last and most signal instance (with an awful tragedy for its consummation) occurred after Monmouth's rebellion, in the person of that fiend in human shape, the atrocious Colonel Kirk; an act so enormously wicked as to exalt common diabolism into virtue by the contrast.

In a brief summary of the right tendency of this play, let it be observed, that the only man who is deservedly punished is the grossly loose character, Lucio; and he is compelled to marry one fully worthy of him. Angelo having a *sense* of goodness, and being moreover a repentant sinner, is united to the virtuous woman whom he had treated with unkindness. Moreover, the Clown is converted into an under-gaoler, and the suburbs of infamy are all broken up.

---

A glorious being, indeed, was this same son of the Stratford woolstapler! Well might Thomas Carlyle exclaim, "The noblest thing we men of England have produced has been this Shakespeare."

I believe that he would have been equal to any age of any period in the world; and this, because he was endowed with real magnanimity of character—magnanimity in its extended, not conventional sense of the term. He was, indeed, a true genius, a true poet, a great-souled man; and, therefore, he would have advanced upon any age in which he might have been thrown. That should seem to be the definition of a true genius; not merely to compass the world of Mind and Matter, but also to throw a halo around it, like the golden ring encircling the orb of Saturn;—to re-fashion, to dilate, to urge on his acquired knowledge for the glorification and well-being of his brother-pilgrims in the walk of humanity. A true poet, as before said, is a "creator." He does not merely record that which he encounters in the external world, he combines, he modifies, he refines; he even suggests to nature. A true poet despises nothing that is contrived and fashioned, and because it is essentially part and parcel of his own faculty; therefore, I would say, that if Shakespeare could come among us again in the flesh,—his spirit I trust to be ever present with us, happy in the happy thoughts that he has left as a legacy to his brethren,—he would be among the first to appreciate the *great* qualities of our age of practical and mechanical science. He would never have thought disdainfully, even slightingly, of our machinery ; because he would have known that the sublimation, the omniscience, the omnipotence of the science pervades the whole universe, from the starry worlds in their convolutions to the mechanical structure of a gnat's wing. He would, therefore, have come among our boilers and our shafts, our wheels and our pinions, our duplex and our eccentric movements, and, ten to one, but he would have put us upon some track to multiply our produce one hundred fold. We should never have heard from him the nonsense about over-production, while there were thousands of even his own countrymen who were without clothes against inclemency, or sufficient food for their bellies. He gave proof enough that he was elevated above the "low ambition" of party-spirit, because he was too great to descend to the sneaking cunning of manœuvre. The most assiduous reader of his works could not decide what were his opinions, religious or political. He contented himself with the simple mission of teaching mankind a cheerful reliance upon the mercy and benevolence of our good God ; to be just and kind to all men ; to seek out the *good* in things *evil,* and not, after the new philosophy, of ferreting out whatever of evil may lurk in things good. He strove to make men wiser and better, and, therefore, happier.

Such was the expansion of his mental faculty, that it should seem nothing would have come amiss to him ; for to whatever study he might have directed his mind, that he would have rendered precious. And what superb things would he not have uttered upon our steam-enginery ! How he would have glorified our locomotive power, surrounding all with the gorgeous hues of his imagination, adding beauty to utility ; for whatever is useful assumes a beauty when touched with the magician-poet's pencil ; as our poet-painter, Turner, converted a common-place steam-boat in the Hebrides—the most mechanical of ocean constructions—the triumph of art and utility amid the grandeur and romance of nature—into a feature of grace and enchantment in his picture. There it was, stemming away against wind and tide, like the war-horse, shouting "Ha, ha!" to the roar of the antagonist wind and waters; asserting its own prerogative of power; disgorging its smoky volumes, touched by the golden beams of the setting sun.

The poet who underrates the inventive mechanical faculty, is no poet, but a fool; and the mechanic who sneers at the imagination of the poet, is nothing but a mechanic—a mechanic "of all work." No one would have helped on the real nobility—the middle class in the community—the key-stones of the social arch, in their struggles and strides towards social perfectibility, like our divine-hearted, our beloved Stratford yeoman; and what he has left to us all—to the whole world, will yet fulfil this, if he be studied with a devout faith and a loving heart.

And let the "outward-sainted," who so blithely catch at and question his coarsenesses, and thence infer his immorality, be reminded that these are two distinct things, and that each can and does exist independently of the other. Indelicacy of speech does not necessarily involve immorality of principle, or immorality comprise coarseness of language. (These platitudes cease to be such with a large bulk of the community.) There are books, not readable aloud in the present conventional state of civilisation, which are, nevertheless, purely moral in principle; and others could be cited (of our own age) containing not one objectionable term, the tendency of which is to sap the dearest institutions of social life. Let it then be borne in mind, that although Shakespeare sometimes transgresses the rules of modern decorum, he has never sought to undermine the foundations of moral rectitude. He does not varnish—he does not even polish vice; and he never gives a questionable complexion to naked, unsophisticated virtue. For a full example of this, refer to the moral of this misunderstood and misrepresented play of "Measure for Measure;"—read that frightful scene in the "Pericles, Prince of Tyre;" and after rising from the perusal of the whole play, say whether he has not made the heroine, Marina, come forth from the horrid ordeal like an angel of light. She has gone through the furnace, and even the smell of the fire has not passed upon her garments.

Again, Shakespeare never sneers at real piety, and he never hints a contempt for the dearest and most sacred privileges of our social union; and therefore he ranks with the greatest of ethical writers, as he is confessedly the greatest of imaginative ones.

I can only say, in conclusion, and it is a triumphant one, that the most crystal-hearted women in my own little circle of acquaintance are the greatest studiers—not merely readers—of his plays.

THE END.

# ERRATA.

Page 54, line 11, for "fa niente," *read* "far niente."
Page 71, line 24, for "abjuration," *read* "adjuration."

CPSIA information can be obtained
at www.ICGtesting.com
Printed in the USA
LVHW110758120522
718525LV00003B/15

9 783375 001872